Duncan watched the cottage across the river for signs of movement, his skin fevered with anticipation.

She was beyond those walls. He was certain of it, for her presence was a throbbing pulse in his veins. Soon, the door would open and she would appear, the Witch of Devil River.

"Witch" was an imprecise term—Cassandra Ferguson McKenna was more sorceress than witch, able to channel the power inherent in earth and stone, in the elements and living things. She was a demonoid, the immortal daughter of a fiend-possessed human, and Duncan was Dalvahni, a warrior sworn to the pursuit of rogue demons, or "djegrali," as they were also known.

And therein lay the problem.

His and Cassandra's very natures set them at odds, but the heart counted not the cost. Thus, he lingered near his sweet torment day after day, hoping for a glimpse of her, a starving man scrabbling for crumbs tossed from her table.

Also by Lexi George

Demon Hunting in Dixie
Demon Hunting in the Deep South
Demon Hunting in a Dive Bar
Demon Hunting with a Dixie Deb
And read more Lexi George in
So I Married a Demon Hunter

Demon Hunting with a Sexy Ex

A Paranormal Romance

Lexi George

LYRICAL PRESS
Kensington Publishing Corp.
www.kensingtonbooks.com

LYRICAL PRESS BOOKS are published by

Kensington Publishing Corp.
119 West 40th Street
New York, NY 10018

All Kensington titles, imprints, and distributed lines are available at special quantity discounts for bulk purchases for sales promotion, premiums, fund-raising, educational, or institutional use.

Special book excerpts or customized printings can also be created to fit specific needs. For details, write or phone the office of the Kensington Sales Manager: Kensington Publishing Corp., 119 West 40th Street, New York, NY 10018. Attn. Sales Department. Phone: 1-800-221-2647.

Lyrical Press and Lyrical Press logo Reg. U.S. Pat. & TM Off.

First Electronic Edition: September 2017
eISBN-13: 978-1-60183-179-8
eISBN-10: 1-60183-179-X

First Print Edition: September 2017
ISBN-13: 978-1-60183-180-4
ISBN-10: 1-60183-180-3

Printed in the United States of America

*Thank you, Alicia Condon, for "getting" me.
Tammy and Lauren—thank you, too. You are
brainstormers supreme.*

Chapter One

It was time.

Duncan watched the cottage across the river for signs of movement, his skin fevered with anticipation. She was beyond those walls. He was certain of it, for her presence was a throbbing pulse in his veins. Soon, the door would open and she would appear, the Witch of Devil River.

"Witch" was an imprecise term—Cassandra Ferguson McKenna was more sorceress than witch, able to channel the power inherent in earth and stone, in the elements and living things. She was a demonoid, the immortal daughter of a fiend-possessed human, and Duncan was Dalvahni, a warrior sworn to the pursuit of rogue demons, or "djegrali," as they were also known.

And therein lay the problem.

His and Cassandra's very natures set them at odds, but the heart counted not the cost. Thus, he lingered near his sweet torment day after day, hoping for a glimpse of her, a starving man scrabbling for crumbs tossed from her table.

Cassandra did not return his regard. She was prickly, his lady, and not one easily to forgive. He had hurt her most cruelly in the past. The knowledge was a wound Duncan had carried lo these many years. It would take time and patience to reclaim her, but he, too, was immortal.

Time, he had aplenty.

He caught a fleeting glimpse of her through the glass panes of the door, and his blood quickened. It was ever thus with Cassandra, this almost painful heightening of the senses, the feeling of being fully *alive*, a heady mixture of excitement, longing, regret, and desire. Her house was fashioned of clapboards and crowned by a pitched metal roof. Behind the cottage, a grove of heavy-limbed oaks stood sentinel. Situated on a bend in the river, the dwelling afforded a pleasing prospect, and Cassandra could often be found on the porch breathing in the damp perfume of early morning or listening to the bugs singing at twilight.

Duncan's heart gave an eager jerk as the door swung open and Cassandra stepped out of the house carrying a wooden bread bowl. The air hissed, unnoticed, from his lungs and he drank in the sight of her, absorbing every detail with his enhanced vision. Gods, she was lovely, a beguiling mixture of feminine beauty and strength. The air was thick with humidity, and she wore her fair locks in a casual knot on top of her head for comfort. Wisps of the blond silk had come undone and curled at the nape of her neck. She was clad in shorts and a thin cotton T-shirt that molded to the plump curves of her breasts. Her feet were bare. She was ever wont to run around without shoes, he recalled, swallowing at the sight of her bare legs. He wanted to drag his tongue from the bottoms of her feet to her earlobes, and everywhere in between. Her skin would be soft and smooth, and she would smell of roses and summer rain.

She strode purposefully across the porch and took a seat in one of the chairs. Determined and resolute in all she did, his Cassandra. Plopping the bowl in her lap, she began to shell the garden peas in the container, a slight crease between her elegant brows. Vexing vegetables, to cause his lady to frown. The young woman he remembered had bubbled with laughter, but this Cassandra rarely smiled. She had, in fact, become something of a recluse. The blame for that lay at his door, Duncan knew. 'Twould be his pleasure—nay, his *duty*—to coax her from the doldrums.

He strode out of the woods to the riverbank.

"I bid you a good e'en, Cassandra." A magical push sent his voice across the broad expanse of water. "And I wish you joy."

At the sound of his voice she jumped from her chair, scattering the pea pods across her feet.

"You again," she said in accents of deepest loathing. Tossing the bowl aside, she stomped off the porch and down the sloped lawn to the water's edge. "I told you to stay off my property. Don't make me get my gun."

Duncan opened his arms wide. "Fire away, milady, an it please you." He pulled off his T-shirt and tossed it aside. "Aim your weapon here," he suggested, patting his chest with one hand, "and put me out of my misery, for I can bear your disfavor no longer."

"I wouldn't waste the ammunition on you." She propped her hands on her hips. "Get out of here, Duncan. How many times do I have to tell you to leave me alone?"

"As many as you like, sweetheart."

"Meaning you have no intention of leaving."

"Meaning I am going for a swim. Care to join me?"

"Not in this lifetime."

"Suit yourself," he said.

Removing the jeans and the undergarment humans called "boxer briefs," he dived into the water. The river was deep and chilly, even after the long Alabama summer, and he swam to the bottom to explore. The floor was sandy and strewn with brown and white rocks. Gardens of green frothy plants waved in the current. A turtle swam past, rolling a yellow eye at him in surprise. An olive-colored fish with a jutting jaw glared at his intrusion and darted away with an indignant swish of its tail.

Surfacing near the bank on Cassandra's side of the river, he found her crouched on her hands and knees, her anxious gaze on the water.

"Worried about me, sweet?" Treading water, he gave her a slow grin. "No need. I can hold my breath a long time."

She scrambled to her feet with an indignant huff. "I don't doubt it, you big blowhard. Go away, Duncan. I mean it."

"Alas, I cannot. I fear I have developed a cramp."

"Bullshit." She made a circular motion with her hand. "Turn around, mister, before I call the sheriff and report you for trespassing."

"You do not own the river."

"No, but you so much as set a toe on my land, and there'll be hell to pay."

Duncan heaved a wounded sigh. "That is no way to treat a neighbor."

Her elegant brows drew together in a scowl. "Neighbor? What are you babbling about?"

"I bought the parcel across the river from you. The owner—er—*former* owner and I signed the papers a sennight ago."

"Liar. Lucinda Hall's tight as tree bark. She wouldn't sell you squat."

"Your attack on my verity pains me. A Dalvahni warrior does not lie. However, I will admit that your assessment of the lady's character is not unjust. Be that as it may, we have reached an agreement."

"Oh, yeah? How much?"

Duncan gave her a look of reproach. "That is a private matter between me and Madam Hall. I am surprised at you, Cassandra. You were not wont to be so mercenary."

"I meant how much land did she sell you, and you damn well know it," Cassandra said, clenching her teeth.

"A goodly portion. The land between Cain Road and the McCant farm."

"*What?* That's fifteen hundred acres."

"Roughly, yes."

A dull flush crept up her neck and spread across her cheeks. "I don't believe you."

Duncan sighed, "That, my love, you have made abundantly clear. Howe'er, 'tis true, I assure you. Would you care to see the deed?"

"Don't call me—oh, forget it. I can guess how you talked the old skinflint around. You put the whammy on her. That's low, Duncan. Even for you."

"Again, you misjudge me. I did not 'put the whammy on her,' as you so crudely suggest. I made her a handsome offer and she accepted." Duncan floated, arms out, in the water, surveying her through drooping lids. "You are canny with spell craft. If you wanted the land so badly, why did you not use magic?"

"Because *I* don't use magic to take advantage of norms," she snapped. "That's cheating." Her eyes narrowed at a faint tapping sound from the woods across the water. "What's that noise?"

"Workers building a house." He gave her a lazy smile. "For me, on my land. Would you care for a tour? I should dearly love to know your thoughts on the location of my new dwelling."

"You can build it on the moon, for all I care. Barring that, stay on your side of the river, if you know what's good for you."

He widened his eyes at her. "How can I do that, my love, when *you* are what is good for me?"

She suggested he do something anatomically impossible to himself and stormed off.

Much better, Duncan decided, watching Cassandra stomp back to the house. He'd far rather see her angry than pensive. Sad Cassandra tore at his heart. Cassandra in an outrage delighted and aroused him.

All in all, it had been a productive afternoon. Executing a smooth tumble turn in the water, Duncan swam back to his side of the river.

Cassie swept into the house and slammed the door so hard the glass panes rattled. Ooh, he made her spitting mad. She paced the wide hall that divided the dogtrot in two. The nerve of Duncan, the unmitigated *gall*. Odious, detestable male. Worlds to choose from and he plunked his preternaturally fine ass across the river from her. Why was he doing this? She'd made it clear they were kaput. He'd shredded her heart into confetti once, and she had no intention of going back for seconds. *Fool me once, shame on you*, she thought. *Fool me twice, shame on me.*

Was he gone? She sprang back to the door to make sure he hadn't followed her—naked, no less. The guy didn't have an appropriate valve, and he seemed to take unholy pleasure in pestering her. To her relief, he was headed back across the river, his big, muscular body cleaving the water. He reached the far bank and climbed out, giving Cassie an eyeful of his strong back and sculpted buttocks. The demon hunter was fine, she'd give him that, with broad, well-muscled shoulders that tapered to a lean waist, and powerful thighs and calves. His shoulder-length brown hair clung to the back of his neck in a sleek, wet pelt. He looked over his shoulder, as though sensing her regard, and Cassie jumped back. God forbid he catch her spying on him. Duncan Dalvahni had an ego the size of Texas.

She resumed her pacing. She and Duncan were over and done with. Ancient history. She'd worked hard and now ran a flourishing business. She wasn't the ignorant country mouse he'd known. She would not allow him to fluster her.

But he will, a sly inner voice whispered. *Be honest. He already has. You haven't relaxed since you found out he was back in Hannah, and now he's practically on your doorstep. You know what he is. Pushy. Dominating. Aggravating in the extreme. He's bound to make a nuisance of himself.*

Drat Lucy Hall, anyway. Cassie could cheerfully throttle her. She'd offered a dozen times over the years to buy the ten acres across the river, but Lucy wouldn't budge. Then Duncan shows up with his smooth talk and laughing eyes, and the treacherous old biddy sells him the whole kit and caboodle. Unbelievable. Unacceptable. *Unbearable.*

She should leave and let him have it, but Hannah was *her* home, dammit. Magic ran deep here, and business was good. Most of her customers were kith, the demonoid term for their kind, although she did a brisk trade selling charms and potions to norms. She liked living on the river. She liked her friends and her house. She liked her herb garden.

No, by golly, Duncan could leave. He didn't have ties here. He wasn't from Earth, much less Behr County. If he insisted on homesteading across the river from her, so be it. She would not tuck tail and run. She'd ignore him. Be polite and keep her distance. He could sashay around naked till the cows came home, as far as she was concerned. She'd thank him sweetly for the peep show and go about her business. That should roast his chestnuts.

The Regulator clock on the wall chimed once, and Cassie eyed it in alarm. That clock hadn't run for years. Trouble was coming . . . maybe even death. She shook off the feeling of doom. Duncan's arrival had unsettled her. The clock had chimed because she'd slammed the door, shaking the wall, not because of some dire portent. Good grief, Duncan's announcement had her turned every which way but Sunday. She should go for a drive to clear her head. Maybe she'd pay Lucy Hall a visit. Ask her up front if she'd sold Duncan her land.

The steady tapping across the river continued, tightening Cassie's nerves until she thought they would snap. Duncan was building a house. Across the river from her. They were going to be neighbors. Even if she never saw him, she'd know he was there, lounging in his new digs, smug in his Duncan-ness.

Arggh.

She had to get out of here. Now, before she spontaneously combusted.

Mind made up, Cassie marched down the hall for the back door. Her favorite cowboy boots were sitting under a cane-bottom chair, and she snatched them up and shoved her feet into the worn leather. Grabbing her purse off the hall tree, she flung open the door and stepped onto the back stoop, swaying as a feeling of dread engulfed her. She wrapped her hand around a porch post for balance and peered into the gloom. Something was off. The stand of oaks that protected her property were whispering in alarm. Everything else was silent. No doves cooing in the underbrush. No bugs cajoling the coming of night in symphony. She stood there for a long moment, trying to pinpoint the danger. The perimeter of her property was set with spell lines to alert her to danger, and an invisible barrier across her driveway screened her visitors. If anyone or anything crossed the magical line, *bing*. Bells rang in the house and garden to let her know she had company. Letting her eyes go slightly unfocused, she checked the wards around her place. The spell lines were intact. Nothing seemed amiss. Lord, she was being fanciful. Silly to let an old clock spook her.

She'd parked her truck near the garden to unload some bags of fertilizer. Draping her purse strap over her shoulder, she left the porch and started down the drive. She'd almost reached the Silverado when the werewolf attacked.

Chapter Two

The beast charged out of the trees on all fours with a heart-stopping growl. It was a young male, no more than nineteen or twenty, from Cassie's best guess, and he'd half-shifted. Moth-eaten patches of reddish-brown hair covered his body, vicious claws tipped his large paws, and his snout bristled with sharp teeth. He was hunched and misshapen, and the skin peeping through the blotches of fur was a sickly gray. A pair of furry wolf ears sat atop his elongated head.

Cassie yanked on the door handle of the truck. Locked. The werewolf pounded down the driveway in a blur of motion, spewing gravel and dirt as he ran. Foam flecked his slathering jaws, and his eyes burned red with madness. How had he gotten past her security system? She *must* remember to run a spell check tomorrow.

If she lived.

She scrabbled in the side pocket of her purse for her keys, her heart doing a rapid tattoo against her ribs. Her fingers brushed a pen, a lipstick, and a wadded receipt. No keys. The werewolf was closer now, so close she could hear his labored breathing. She risked a quick glance at him and shrieked. He was almost on top of her, his black lips peeled back, exposing his deadly fangs. She whirled to run back to the safety of the house. Too far. She'd never make it. Desperate, she swung back around and whacked the werewolf on the nose with her purse, putting all her strength behind the blow. He yelped in pain. Hurling the purse at him, Cassie dived headfirst into the bed of the truck. Murmuring the first protection spell that popped into her mind, she bounded to her feet. Below her, the werewolf was tearing her abandoned handbag to bits. His head jerked up and he spied her standing in the truck. With a howl of rage, he leapt at the vehicle, his head and shoulders punching through Cassie's hastily erected ward.

For a moment, he dangled there, back legs sawing at thin air, his sharp claws gouging the side of the Silverado with a metallic screech, then the shield collapsed and he fell into the bed of the truck. Surging to his feet, paws sliding on the slick liner, the werewolf fixed his eerie red gaze on Cassie.

"N-nice doggie," Cassie stammered as the werewolf raised his hackles and rumbled low in his chest. "There's a good boy."

The beast pounced with a snarl. Cassie screamed and threw her arms in front of her face, bracing for the agony of slathering jaws tearing at her flesh, and heard a dull thud at her feet. Something hot and wet splashed her skin. Lowering her arms, she saw the werewolf's severed head lying on the floor of the truck. Blood spurted from the neck stump and pooled on the polyurethane bed liner. The malformed body twitched once, twice, and went still.

"Cassandra, are you hurt?"

The sound of Duncan's harsh voice jolted Cassie out of her stupor. He stood balanced on the lip of the truck, a bloody sword in one hand. His hair was still damp from his swim, and he was dressed once more in jeans and a T-shirt. Despite his modern clothing, he looked every inch the hard, dangerous warrior. The change in him shocked her. The easygoing, teasing guy who'd mocked her from the river was gone, and his sherry-colored eyes, usually alight with gentle humor, were cold and implacable.

This was the Duncan she remembered. Stern. Fierce. Dangerous. Lord, she'd forgotten what a badass he could be.

Raising a shaking hand, Cassie brushed a stray lock of hair out of her face. "I . . . I'm fine. He came out of the woods . . . so fast. I tried to get in the truck, but I couldn't find my keys."

The sword in Duncan's hand vanished, and he jumped lightly into the bed of the Silverado. He nudged the carcass with his boot. "What ails the demonoid? He has not fully shifted."

"He's not a demonoid," Cassie said, unable to resist the temptation to correct him. "He's a werewolf. There are two packs in Hannah, Pack Lyall and Pack Randall. This one's a Randall." She pointed to the dead wolf. "See those reddish streaks in his fur? Those are Randall markings. The Lyalls are dark-haired with silvery markings."

"Fascinating." Duncan held out his hand. "Allow me to help you alight from the carriage."

"I don't need your help. I can take care of myself."

"Of a certainty. You had things well in hand when I arrived."

She flushed. Okay, so she'd blanked under pressure and cast a simple guardian spell, a respectable bit of magic, if one wanted to protect a home from burglary and theft. Woefully inadequate, however, against a furious werewolf.

"Thank you for . . . for your assistance," Cassie ground out. Good manners dictated that she thank him for saving her, but Duncan had a way of making her forget her upbringing. "There. Happy?"

"I am happy you are unhurt. I am not happy you were in danger."

"I didn't ask to be attacked by a werewolf. And if I had, it's no business of yours."

"My dear girl, if you had asked to be attacked by a werewolf, it would be very much my business. You can't expect me to live across the river from a madwoman."

He was impossible. Cassie drew herself up. "I'm going inside."

"An excellent notion. You are in dire need of a good wash."

She glanced down and gasped. Her hands and arms were splattered with blood, and so were her shorts and shirt. Gore crusted her boots.

The children—images of their broken and mutilated bodies flashed through her mind. There had been blood then, too. The forest floor had been drenched with it. But for Maggie's flowered cotton pinafore and Jimbo's boots, she would not have recognized them.

A white mist flickered at the edge of her vision and spread. The truck pitched beneath her feet, and she fell.

When she came to, she was lying on her back on the couch. Her boots were gone and her legs were elevated on pillows.

"Feeling better?" Duncan laid a cool cloth on her head. "Your color is returning, thank the gods."

Cassie swatted his hand away and sat up. "Don't touch me. And get out of my house."

His tawny brows rose. "What has cast you into the boughs? You fainted. I caught you and brought you inside." He searched her face, his expression of lazy amusement fading. "Ah, I see. This is about the little ones."

"You *left*." Duncan's return had ripped the scab off the wound, and the old rage and grief bubbled to the surface. "*I am Dalvahni. I cannot be with you. Your blood is tainted with evil.* That's what you said, and then you left. You chased that monster into the area and bolted. Less than a week later, Jimbo and Maggie were dead. I promised my brother I'd take care of them. If you had been here—"

"Don't you think I know that?" Duncan was white around the mouth. "If I could turn back the clock and save them, I would and gladly, but even a Dalvahni warrior cannot bend time."

He reached for her, and she jerked away.

He dropped his hands in defeat. "I left, it is true, but it did not take me long to regret my arrogance," he said in a low voice. "I came back, but you were gone and the younglings were dead. That I could not undo, but I never stopped looking for you or the monster that killed them."

Cassie gave him a seething look. "That monster was my mother, remember?"

It certainly wasn't something *she* could forget. Whoever said ignorance is bliss had been right. For years, Cassie had wondered about her birth mother. What she'd been like. Why she'd disappeared without a trace. She couldn't ask her family. Her older brother, Jamie, had refused to talk about their mother. As for Luke McKenna, the only father she'd known, he became stone-faced and mulish when her mother was mentioned, so Cassie had quickly learned to avoid the subject, but that didn't mean she hadn't wondered. Had her mother died, or simply walked away from the grinding exhaustion of life on an isolated farm? People did that back then, walked into the sunset and disappeared.

The not-knowing had nearly driven Cassie crazy.

Be careful what you wish for, because she had the answers now, and she wished to God she'd stayed in the dark. Her mother, Cybil McKenna, had been demon-possessed. Since a human taken by a demon seldom lived long, Cybil should have died within a year— two, at the most. But Cybil had been a conjurer and a healer, not a norm, and she'd used magic to bind the demon to her. If she died, so did the demon.

The spell had worked, and Cybil had lived, but dark magic has a price. She was transformed into the Hag, a monster with an insatiable hunger for human flesh. So monstrous a craving that the Hag had killed her own grandbabies, Jamie's sweet son and daughter, the children entrusted to Cassie's care at Jamie's death.

At the time, neither Cassie nor the Hag had guessed their connection. Jimbo and Maggie had been nothing to the Hag but fresh meat.

Jamie's children weren't the Hag's only victims. The Hag had slashed a bloody swath through Behr County for years. Eventually, the attacks subsided and the Hag had faded into legend. More than a century later, Cybil had moved back to Hannah, assumed the name Ora Mae Luker, and taken up residence on the river. In outward appearance, she was a sweet little old lady with an affinity for growing prize pumpkins and squash. In reality, her penchant for gardening disguised a bustling marijuana business. Drug dealer or granny, the demon inside her would not be controlled for long, and bloodlust soon had the Hag on the prowl again.

Circumstances had thrown Cassie in the Hag's path and, to her horror, she'd discovered the monster's true identity. The Hag, the fiend who'd murdered Jamie's children, was her *mother*. The knowledge made Cassie want to peel out of her own skin.

"You are not your mother, Cassandra," Duncan said, as though reading her thoughts. "The Hag's sins are not your own."

"*I* know that. Still, I'm surprised you stay in the same room with me, seeing how you're a demon hunter and so *perfect*."

Duncan sighed. "You are angry because I rejected you, and rightly so. I was an unmitigated ass. But you have brooded long enough, Cassandra."

Cassie rubbed her temples. She was tired and her head had started to ache. She rose from the couch and gave him a steady look. "I don't want to fight with you, Duncan. I'm going to take a shower. When I come out, be gone."

She strode out of the living room without waiting for an answer and went into her bedroom, closing the door with a sigh. This was her sanctuary. She'd left the aged walls unpainted, grayed and silvered by time. The ceiling was whitewashed to contrast with the exposed beams that supported the roof. The furniture in the room was simple: a large four-poster bed, a bedside table, and a chest of drawers. A chair and a half with squishy cushions sat by the window overlooking the river. The bed linens were white, the pillows fluffy. Scented candles were scattered around the room. The lamps in the room that had once burned oil had been wired for convenience. Cassie had been raised on candlelight, but she gladly embraced modern convenience, including electricity, indoor plumbing, and hot and cold running water.

She took a deep breath and closed her eyes, willing the serenity of her retreat to seep into her pores, calming her shattered nerves. Over the muffled rush of the river and the sound of the wind in the trees came the steady rat-a-tat-tat of hammers in the distant woods.

Her eyes flew open. Damn Duncan and his insomniac construction crew. Was she to be robbed of peace in her own home? It was beyond bearing.

She shoved away from the door and stripped out of her bloody clothes with a shiver of revulsion. The late-afternoon light pouring through her bedroom windows was golden and hazy with dust motes. Hard to believe violence had touched this place not long ago.

Something was up in the werewolf community. This was her third sick were in a month. Several weeks earlier, two members of the Randall pack had come to her complaining of the belly gripe. They'd been nervous and uneasy, starting guiltily at the slightest sound. She'd given them a tisane of cumin and goldenseal and sent them on their way.

If Mac had come to her, perhaps she could have helped him, too.

Her blood ran cold when she recalled the madness in the young were's eyes and his obvious signs of physical distress. Mac Randall had suffered from something a lot more serious than the backdoor trots. Something that went beyond mere illness.

Something that smacked of dark magic.

Her instincts as a conjurer and healer were roused, and her professional ethos was offended. Dark magic was dangerous. It was not something norms or untrained kith should dabble in. Power equaled responsibility, and Cassie despised sloppy magery.

Whoever had done this—kith, norm, or were—had crossed the line and caused grievous harm. They must be stopped before someone else got hurt.

Stepping into the shower, she turned the water on and let it run until it was hot. She soaped her body and washed her hair, then stood under the water a long time, trying to wash away the horror and sadness of the day.

Duncan was back. She could stand in the shower until she pruned, but she couldn't wash away that fact. He was sorry he'd hurt her, and he'd never stopped looking for her. All these years, she'd lived with the painful certainty that she'd been discarded without a qualm, scorned and despised. God, she'd loved him. Losing him and the children within days of one another had nearly killed her, but she'd endured and moved on.

Moved on, huh? Then why are you still angry? The thought made her squirm. Damn Duncan. She'd been fine until he'd shown up, stirring the pot. Moving in on top of her. Skinny-dipping in her river. Whacking werewolves with his sword. Sure, he'd saved her from a horrible death, but did he have to cut the poor kid's head off? What was she supposed to do now, show up at Zeb's place and say oops?

She got out of the shower and towel-dried her wet hair, then slipped into clean clothes. Unearthing a pair of hiking sandals from the bottom of her closet, she shoved her feet into them and padded into the hall, letting out a startled yelp when she spied a familiar figure.

"Dammit, Duncan, I told you to go home."

He pushed away from the wall. "What about the werewolf? Do you plan to return him to his kin?"

Now he was a mind reader. Great.

"Yes, but I don't need you." Cassie realized with a prickle of annoyance that she was beginning to sound like a broken record. "The last thing I need is two alphas dancing around one another."

Duncan's brows rose. "An he threatens you, 'twill be a dance of death. But worry not, sweet. As *I* killed the werewolf, I will be the one to make redress."

"Now, see here, Duncan, you can't waltz in here and—"

The doorbell rang, startling her. She glanced at the bell on the wall in annoyance. Why hadn't it dinged? Damn, damn, damn. There was something seriously wrong with her alarm system.

She started for the door. *Whoosh*, Duncan got in front of her, sword in hand.

"Stay back," he said. "The dead were's kin could wait without, seeking bloody vengeance for his death."

"Cool your jets, Drama Boy," Cassie said. "A ticked-off werewolf wouldn't ring the doorbell. It would come through the window or take the door off the hinges."

Duncan lowered his sword. "Your observation has merit. I admit, mine own experience with werewolves is somewhat limited." The doorbell chimed again. "Whoever he may be, your visitor is most insistent. You may proceed."

"Gee, thanks." Cassie's voice dripped with sarcasm. "I can't tell you how grateful I am to have your permission to answer the door in my own house."

Duncan inclined his head and stepped aside. "Appreciation noted."

Cassie gave him a darkling glare and flung open the door. A blue-jeaned waif hovered on her back stoop, her slim body tensed and poised for flight. She was young, with a cap of strawberry-blond hair, pale, freckled skin, and a pair of large, melting eyes straight out of a Margaret Keane portrait.

The girl looked familiar. Kith, more than likely—purple eyes were common among demonoids. Cassie had seen her before, but where?

The waif's anxious gaze darted past Cassie and found the big warrior standing in the hall.

"There you is, Mr. Duncan," she cried in a throbbing voice. "You got to help me. I'm in a pickle, fer sure."

Chapter Three

"Easy, child. You are safe." Taking the trembling girl by the arm, Duncan ushered her inside. "Whate'er has overset you can soon be remedied, I promise you."

His rich voice washed over the young woman and, like magic, she stopped shaking. Cassie observed this effect with a twinge of resentment. He'd always had a way with wild things, able to coax the shyest creatures from the shelter of the woods to lie at his feet. She gave herself a mental shake for being petty. Good Lord, why should she care if Duncan was kind to the girl? No skin off her teeth.

Because she's a demonoid, like you, and Duncan wasn't kind to you. He rejected you, remember?

Oh, yeah, there was that. But that was old news. Water under the bridge. She and Duncan were over.

Taking the quaking young woman by the shoulders, Duncan said, "Tell me what has happened to distress you?"

The girl shot a frightened look at Cassie.

"You are quite safe, I promise you." Duncan released her and stepped back. "This is Cassandra. Unless I am much mistaken, she will stand your friend." He turned to Cassie. "Will you not?"

"Of course." Cassie gave the big-eyed waif a reassuring smile. "But, please, call me Cassie. And your name is . . . ?"

"Verbena."

The name rang a bell, but Cassie could not place it.

"What is toward, Verbena?" Duncan asked again.

Verbena gave her wet cheeks an angry swipe. "It's them Skinners. They been pecking at me for months to come home, but I don't wanna. They was mean to me. Made me sleep in the yard with the dawgs and fight 'em fer scraps."

"Renounce the scoundrels and be done, then," Duncan said. "The Skinners dare not molest you whilst you are under Conall's protection."

Conall Dalvahni was a cold, ruthless bastard, and Cassie had disliked him on sight. Much to her surprise, however, her friend Rebekah—Beck to those who knew her well—had fallen in love with the guy.

Cassie shot Duncan a glance. Beck was kith, but Captain Hardass had overcome his aversion to Beck's demon blood, and the wedding between a demon hunter and a demonoid had been one for the record books.

"Well?" Duncan said when the girl did not answer.

Verbena scuffed the toe of her shoe on the plank floor. "I left. I ain't working at the restaurant no more."

"I confess I am surprised by this news," Duncan said. "I thought you were happy there."

"I was." She looked flustered. "Mr. Conall and Beck been good to me. Give me a job and new duds, a-and a place to stay."

The light bulb went off, and Cassie snapped her fingers. "I know you. You're Verbena Skinner. You worked at the shifter bar before—"

She faltered, realizing with dismay that she'd just put her foot in her mouth.

"Before that polecat Earl Skinner burnt the place to the ground?" Verbena's eyes flashed. "You can say it."

Cassie's cheeks heated. "Sorry. But I thought—"

"That Earl was my brother and old Charlie Skinner was my dad? Nope, and I'm glad. Charlie tried to have me kilt. Throwed me to the demons for sport, like I was no-count."

"That's terrible." Cassie stared at her in horror. "Why didn't someone stop him?"

"Who's gon' stop Charlie, and him the head of the clan?" Verbena snorted at the suggestion. "Specially since Charlie worked a deal with the demons and them Skinners thought they was gon' get rich. Nope, they didn't give a hoot about me." She pressed her lips together. "Which is Jim Dandy by me, 'cause *I* ain't no Skinner. Happens my mama caught a baby from a traveling man. Van Pelt. Verbena Van Pelt—that's my name now. Took my mama's name, on account I don't know my real daddy's name."

Cassie couldn't blame Verbena for not wanting to be associated with the Skinners. White trash, the lot of them, an inbred clan of moonshiners and thieves with a reputation for skullduggery and violence. Only the year before, Charlie Skinner had been murdered. Drowned in his own 'shine after a bad batch of hooch poisoned some of the kith. No one would buy Skinner whiskey after that. Scuttlebutt had it the Skinners had fallen on hard times. Served them right, Cassie decided, for treating the girl so abominably.

"Old Charlie's dead now," Verbena continued, as though reading Cassie's thoughts, "and nobody's seen hide nor hair of Earl since the day he set fire to the bar. Reckon he lit out afore the sheriff arrested his sorry butt for arson. I hope he stays gone. If I never see him agin, that'll be a day too soon."

"No doubt," Cassie murmured.

She knew what had become of Earl, but she'd keep her mouth shut about it. Earl Skinner had been eaten by a dragon, an honest-to-God, fire-breathing dragon. Hannah was a strange little stewpot of bizarrity, but that was weird, even for around here. Norms didn't believe in dragons. Didn't believe in demons or demon hunters, or demonoids, either, for that matter. And a darn good thing, too. In Cassie's experience, scared norms were dangerous. The dragon and Earl were dead. Best for everyone—particularly the kith—if the norms stayed none the wiser.

"This is all very well," Duncan said, frowning at Verbena, "but you have yet to explain why you left Conall's protection."

Verbena twisted her thin hands. "I seen them Skinners poking around the restaurant. Joby Ray—he's the head of the family now—said he'd come to fetch me home. Said if I didn't do what I was tole, he'd cause trouble, so I skedaddled. Hid in the woods a few days and tried to figure what to do. Don't mind telling you, I was stumped. Got no place to go." She looked up at Duncan with huge, trusting eyes. "Then I thought of you. Recollected you was kind to me and . . ." Verbena swallowed. "Thought maybe you'd help me."

"Of course I shall help you, child," Duncan said at once, "but how did you know where to find me?"

"Oh." Verbena turned red. "Heard you talking at the restaurant a while back. You told Mr. Conall you was staying on the river to be near—" She shot Cassie a quick glance, her blush deepening. "Anyhoo, knowed right off where you was staying, on account of the dawgs."

Duncan's face clouded with puzzlement. "The dogs? I fear I do not follow."

"It was my job to run Old Charlie's hunting dawgs, see?" Verbena explained. "If I didn't run 'em and run 'em good, I'd get walloped. Know these woods like the back of my hand. Knew right off where you was staying when I heered you talking. Found your campsite, but you was gone. Heard a commotion in the woods and came on them fellers what's building you a house. It's gon' be a honey when they's done, Mr. D. They told me where you was, and here I am."

Verbena's matter-of-fact account of her life with the Skinners sickened Cassie. If Charlie were alive, she'd curse him into next week for what he'd done to the poor girl.

"What did the Skinners want with you?" Duncan asked.

"It's on account o' my talent, I reckon." Verbena drew herself up. "They thought I was a dud, but turns out I'm what you call an enhancer."

A "dud" was the derogatory term used by kith to refer to those of their kind without talent, but Cassie had never heard of an enhancer.

She puzzled over the strange term. "When you say 'enhancer,' do you mean you augment the talents of others?"

Verbena wrinkled her nose. "Augment? Whazzat?"

"Increase," Duncan explained.

"Oh. Well, then, yeah. Leastways, that's what Toby and Mr. Conall says."

Tobias Littleton was a cagey old shifter with a nose for magical talent, and Cassie's oldest friend. She and Toby went way back. He'd been the bouncer and co-owner at Beck's Bar, a shifter joint that had catered to kith before Earl burned it down.

"If Toby says you're an enhancer, then you're an enhancer. But Conall?" Cassie rolled her eyes. "Please. Much he knows about the kith."

"He must needs know something," Duncan said. "He is married to one of your kind. From all appearances, he adores his wife."

Cassie's throat tightened. *Your blood is tainted with evil. I cannot be with you.* Those had been Duncan's words to her.

She lifted her chin. "Guess Conall's not a judgmental jerk, like some people."

Verbena's big eyes widened. "Mr. D, you been a-judging on Miz Cassie?"

"Once and long ago, when I first learned she was a demonoid. I had no notion your race existed, and the discovery . . . Well, suffice it to say, I was disconcerted."

"Disconcerted?" Cassie gave a bitter laugh. "You said I was an abomination."

"I was cruel—this I freely admit," Duncan said. "And I soon came to regret it." He held out his hands to Verbena. "I have begged the lady's pardon most humbly. Alas, she cannot forgive me."

Verbena turned her limpid gaze on Cassie. "How long you been a-holding on to your mad?"

"A while."

"How long's a while?"

Mischief danced in Duncan's eyes. "More than one hundred of your earth years."

"A hunnert—" Verbena shook her head. "Jehoshaphat, that's a long time to stay swole up."

"Indeed it is." Duncan countered Cassie's furious glare with a bland look. "A very long time."

"You gotta stick up, Miz Cassie, it's plain to see," Verbena said. "It don't do to sit on things like a broody hen. Sours your stomach and makes you mean."

"It has certainly given her the crotchets," Duncan agreed. "She has been wroth with me lo these many years."

Cassie decided to ignore this, and turned to address Verbena. "So now Joby Ray realizes you're an enhancer, he wants you back?"

"'At's right." A satisfied little smile played around Verbena's lips. "Turns out them Skinners ain't doing so good. Their moonshine b'ness has went bust and most of 'em can't manage a decent shift no more." She pressed her lips together. "But I ain't going back. I *ain't*."

"No, indeed, you shan't," Duncan said in his calm, soothing way.

Verbena's defiance faded. "I'm a big one for talkin', but you don't know 'em like I do. They's mean as a snake-bit dawg, and they got places to hide a body where they won't never be found. They set the hounds on me this morning. Would've caught me, too, but Bo-Bo found me first, and so I knowed they was coming."

"Bo-Bo?" asked Cassie.

"My dawg," Verbena said. "He was a mutt, see, like me. Nobody else wanted him, so I raised him from a pup. Had to leave him behind when Old Charlie tried to have me kilt." Her mouth quivered. "Like to broke my heart to shoo him away, but I knowed if Joby Ray caught me, I'd 'uv been done fer. Them Skinners plan to lock me up and never turn me loose." She turned her pleading gaze on Duncan. "That's why I come to you."

Duncan executed a curt bow. "I am at your service, but what of Hank? I thought the two of you had an understanding."

"Hank's gone." Verbena blinked rapidly and looked away. "Took off a few months back. Said he couldn't be sure about . . ." She blew out a breath. "Anyways, he's gone."

"Hank?" Cassie looked from Duncan to Verbena.

"He was the chef at the restaurant, but he ain't no more." Verbena dashed the back of her hand across her eyes. "He was in the papers, see? That food feller from the *Mobile Press* called Hank a canary artist, or some such mess."

Cassie suppressed a ripple of mirth. "Do you mean a *culinary* artist?"

"That a fancy word for cooking?"

"Yes."

"That'll be it, then." Verbena flushed at her mistake. "Hank got real tetchy after he made the paper. Hightailed it lickety-split a few days later."

"Ah," Duncan said with a wise nod. "Hank feared your talent as an enhancer had something to do with his success. This bruised his manly pride, so he departed."

Verbena heaved a sigh. "That's it, and no bark."

"I confess I am disappointed in Hank." Duncan frowned. "I did not think him such a maw worm. Howe'er, that being the case, you are well rid of the dickhead."

Cassie made a strangled sound. "Duncan Dalvahni, where did you learn such a word?"

"Dickhead? The Dalvahni translator equips us with local vernacular to enable us to assimilate. The term means 'a stupid or ridiculous person,' and is most aptly used to refer to a man. Did I not use it correctly?"

"To a T, but I never thought to hear you say it."

Duncan's eyes twinkled. "Methinks I am unexpected."

"Oh, you're unexpected all right," Cassie muttered. "Unexpected like a freaking natural disaster."

Duncan put a hand to his ear. "What was that, my love?"

Cassie scowled. "How many times do I have to tell you? I am not your—"

The crunch of tires on gravel interrupted her. Someone was here. She glanced at the bell on the wall in annoyance. It hadn't rung. Again. The clapper must be busted.

There was the muffled thud of a vehicle door shutting, followed by the sound of booted feet.

"You in the house," a man shouted. "Send Beenie out, or we're coming in."

Chapter Four

Verbena gave a startled squeak and scooted behind Duncan. "That's Joby Ray. Lord a-mercy, them Skinners done found me."

"Stay inside. I'll deal with this." Cassie gave Duncan an inclusive glare. "Nobody, but *nobody*, bosses me around in my own home."

"You got a gun?" Verbena peeked around Duncan with a doubtful expression. "Onliest way to get rid of a Skinner is to shoot 'em dead." After a moment's reflection, she added, "Knives work, too—and axes and shovels and a whole bunch o' other tools. Pizen will kill 'em—if'n you can get the varmints to drink it. Don't seem likely, so a gun would be better."

"She has no need of weapons." Duncan's sword appeared in his hand. "I will accompany her."

"No, you will not," Cassie said. "This is kith business."

"Fear not. I am the soul of discretion. They will never guess that I am Dalvahni."

Cassie gave him a *duh* look. "Give me a break. You're tall. You're handsome, and you're muscled to the max. And you're waving around a meat cleaver. Trust me, they'll know."

"You think me handsome?" His laughing eyes teased her. "I am gratified."

"Don't let it go to your head," Cassie said. "I don't like you worth a damn, but I'm not blind. For God's sake, do as you're told for once and stay inside with Verbena."

She spun on her heel and strode down the hall. She kept a variety of hiking staffs in a rack by the back door to enhance her magic: poplar wood to aid in banishment spells, apple for harmony and fairy magic, ash and basswood for healing and love spells, cherry for spells of detection, and cedar for invocation, to name a few. Wands were less cumbersome and more portable, but too obvious. Nothing screamed *Look at me, I do magic and shit* like a wand, and she didn't want to draw the attention of the norms. But nobody thought twice about her carrying a staff, not when she lived alone in the woods on the river. And if anyone did give her a funny look, the word "snakes" dispelled suspicion. Alabama was crawling with snakes, some fifty species, and rattlers, cottonmouths, and copperheads were among them. And there were snakes of the two-legged kind, as well, like the Skinners. Cassie held her hand over the bristle of walking sticks. Which staff should she use? She'd had a run-in or two with old Charlie before he'd died, and he'd been a piece of work. Charlie had tried to hire her. Offered her money to hex the Furrs, his competition in the moonshine trade. He hadn't been happy when she'd declined. If this Joby Ray character was anything like his brother, then he was a slimeball maximus. Better take something to counter bad energy, she decided. After a moment's hesitation, she selected an elder staff studded with blue chalcedony. That should combat negativity nicely. If not, she'd bean him over the head with the damn thing.

Flinging open the door, she stepped onto the porch. The air shimmered beside her and a whiff of a woodsy scent told her that Duncan had ignored her admonition not to interfere and had followed her out of the house. Color her not surprised. On the plus side, he'd made himself invisible. She'd forgotten he could do that.

"I know you're there," she said through her teeth. "What part of 'stay inside' did you not understand?"

"Worry not, my sweet. My cognitive abilities remain unimpaired." His disembodied voice spoke out of the ether. "Though I doubt not you will acquit yourself well with these scoundrels, I desire to see them for myself."

He was impossible. She could stand here talking to the ozone, or she could get on with the task of delousing her property.

Pasting a pleasant smile on her face, she strolled down the steps to greet the interlopers, the elder stick clutched in one hand. Six ferrety-faced, shifty-eyed men stood in her driveway. A wormy-looking lot, Cassie concluded, assessing the men with the practiced eye of a healer, as though they suffered from the same wasting disease.

And they *smelled* to high heaven, a sickly-sweet odor that reminded her of rotting fruit.

They appraised the place with calculating eyes. Mentally tallying her belongings and their worth, no doubt. A sticky-fingered lot, the Skinners. So many members of the clan had been arrested for burglary and receiving stolen property, they could have their own recovery group, and bring stolen cookies to the meetings.

A middle-aged man with bandy legs and the slicked-back hair of a televangelist stepped to the front of the mangy cluster of men. His face was gaunt, as though he'd lost weight—a lot of weight, and fast. He was dressed in baggy jeans and a short-sleeve shirt, unbuttoned to display his scrawny physique. A few hairs straggled across his narrow chest and trailed down his sunken belly.

Hitching up his jeans, he swayed closer. "Name's Joby Ray Skinner, and these here are some of my kin. You Cassie Ferguson, the one folks call the witch?"

Cassie planted the elder staff in front of her. "That's the norm term, but I'm kith, same as you."

Not exactly the same, thank God. They were both demonoids, but the Skinner family tree didn't branch.

"That right?" His slimy gaze roved over her, lingering on her breasts in a way that made her skin crawl. "Could be, I reckon. You got the eyes. You a shifter?"

"No. I have other talents."

"I bet you do." He grinned, showing small, pointed teeth, like a possum's. "Right, boys?"

There was a chorus of grunts and whistles from his kinfolk.

"Charming." Cassie pointed her staff at the dusty black Ram 3500 mega cab sitting in her drive. Three nervous hounds paced in the back of the vehicle. "Nice truck."

Fifty grand plus worth of nice, unless Cassie was mistaken.

"Ain't ours," a cadaverous man at the back of the group volunteered. "We brodied it. Stupid norm left the keys in it."

"Shut up about that. That's Skinner b'ness." Joby Ray gave Cassie an oily smile. "Nice place you got here. Kinda remote, though. Ain't safe for a purty thang like you to live alone."

"Oh, I'm not alone." There was an invisible demon hunter hanging around, somewhere. "And I've got a security system."

Her magic was on the fritz and so were her alarms, but the Skinners didn't know that, thank goodness. Later she'd reset her wards, but first to deal with this riffraff.

The easiest thing would be to turn the girl over to them, the voice whispered in her head. *Why get involved? It's not your style.*

No, but Verbena was alone and in trouble, and Cassie knew what that felt like. She couldn't turn the girl over to this white-trash posse and look herself in the mirror.

She gripped the staff. "What can I do for you, Mr. Skinner? I have a variety of spells and potions that might interest you."

"Don't want none of your juju. We come for our kin."

He stepped around Cassie, his acrid scent washing over her.

She hurried to block him, barring his way with the staff. "And who might that be?"

"My niece, Verbena. Worried about the poor little thang. We had a fallin'-out, see? I come to welcome her back into the fold."

"Verbena's staying with me."

"That right?" Joby Ray's sunken eyes narrowed. "Why would a fine lady like you wanna rub elbows with a gal like Beenie?"

"Our friendship is recent." *Like a few minutes old.* "I give her room and board in exchange for her help around the place."

Whoa, where'd that come from? It was one thing to lend a helping hand, another altogether to take someone on to raise. The Skinners were trouble, and she was asking for it.

"That's real kind of you," Joby Ray said, "but it's time Verbena came home."

"And if she doesn't want to?"

"She'll want to. Blood's thicker 'n water. We's kin."

"Some family," Cassie said. "Verbena's told me how you treated her."

"Don't get your ass in a pucker. The gal's a whiner, but we love her jes' the same." Cupping his hands to his mouth, he yelled, "Beenie, get your ass out here."

"No," Verbena hollered back from inside the house. "Ain't gonna."

"Make me come after you, girl, and I'll beat you raw."

The door opened and Verbena stomped out of the house, her face pale and set. "Go 'way, Joby. I ain't coming with you."

"Don't be like 'at, gal," Joby Ray wheedled. "I done brought your sweetheart."

Reaching behind him, Joby Ray jerked a young man forward. This specimen of Skinner pulchritude was clad in filthy jeans and a grimy T-shirt, and he had long, stringy blond hair and a wet mouth like a fish. Like the rest of the clan, he was emaciated and unhealthy looking.

"Wha?" Fish Mouth's lips worked and his pale eyes bulged. "I ain't marrying Beenie. She's a stick and ain't got no tits. 'Sides, I done got a girl."

Joby Ray whacked Fish Mouth upside the head. "Shut up, peckerhead. You'll marry who you're told, and I say you're gon' marry your cousin."

"I ain't marrying him," Verbena shouted. "And we ain't cousins. I ain't no Skinner."

Joby Ray's pointy face darkened. "We give you vittles and a place to stay. You owe us."

"You threw me to them demons like I was a chicken leg. I don't owe you jack diddle."

Cassie gave the staff a threatening flourish. "You heard her. Now leave."

Joby Ray's sallow complexion splotched with rage. "I don't give a good goddamn what she says, she's coming with us."

Grabbing the end of the staff, he shoved Cassie aside and barreled toward the porch with the rest of the Skinners at his heels.

Cassie regained her balance and slammed the elder staff into the ground. "*Stop.*"

To her shock, the earth billowed like a sheet, knocking the Skinners off their feet and sending them tumbling across the yard like chess pieces on an upended board. Cassie stared at the staff in her hand. A dislocation spell of that magnitude took an enormous amount of power, and she'd been off her game for months. What just happened?

Behind her, the dogs in the stolen truck set up a howl. Bewildered, Cassie glanced around. The Skinners were groaning and getting to their feet, but the dogs weren't looking at them. They were looking at her truck, parked by the garden at the side of the house.

"Eek," she yelped when she saw the cause of the disturbance.

The slain werewolf had risen from the dead—or part of him had. Dripping blood and gore, the severed head drifted across the yard like a hideous paper lantern blown by the wind.

"That there's Mac Randall." Joby Ray's voice was a high-pitched squeak. "You done cut off his damn head. I thought you and Zeb was keeping company. The alpha ain't gon' like it when he finds out you done kilt his nephew."

"I did not—" Cassie protested, but she was drowned out by a roar from the dead werewolf.

The fanged, hideous mouth parted. "Depart, miscreants, and return upon penalty of death."

Fish Mouth shrieked and bolted for the purloined truck. Flinging the driver's door open, he threw himself inside. The remaining Skinners hotfooted it after him, knocking one another down in their haste to escape. Scrambling inside the Ram, they slammed the doors.

"Come back here, you chickenshits," Joby Ray shouted as the big vehicle rumbled to life. "We ain't leaving. Not without Verbena."

If the Skinners heard, they gave no sign. They were staring at Cassie's truck, their faces white behind the windshield. The decapitated corpse had risen to its feet. Turning blindly toward Joby Ray, the headless body swung its legs over the side of the Silverado and slid to the ground. The corpse lumbered across the yard, a disjointed Frankenstein with arms outstretched for Joby Ray.

There was a chorus of muffled shrieks from the interior of the black truck.

"Christ on a tricycle," a Skinner yelled. "Whatchoo waiting for? Let's get out of here."

Fish Mouth wheeled the truck around and spun off in a cloud of dust.

"Shit," Joby Ray said, backing away from the advancing ghoul. "Shit, shit, shit."

Grabbing his sagging jeans in both hands, he tore after the truck, cursing a blue streak as he went.

"So much for chivalry," Cassie said, watching Joby Ray rabbit it down the driveway. "Nice work, Duncan. You scared them off."

The bloody corpse wobbled and folded to the ground in a heap of limbs. A moment later, Duncan appeared, the severed werewolf head dangling from one hand.

"What is Zeb Randall to you," he asked in thunderous accents, "and what is the meaning of 'keeping company'?"

Verbena rose, ghostlike, from behind one of the huge ferns Cassandra kept by the back door.

"It means Miz Cassie and Zeb been having a thang," she said.

"That's right, ain't it, Miz Cassie? The Randall big dawg been sparkin' you?"

"Zeb and I have had dinner a few times," Cassie said, avoiding Duncan's gaze. "But that was a year ago."

Her words sent a shaft of pain through Duncan's heart, and he let the werewolf head drop to the ground and roll away unheeded. The Provider, the translator that allowed the Dalvahni to travel from sphere to sphere, conversant with the language and customs of the various places they went in pursuit of the djegrali, had properly deciphered Joby Ray's words.

Cassandra had been with another.

The world went red.

"Did you lie with him?" Duncan demanded.

"Don't take that tone with me. I don't answer to you."

He roared and brought his hands down in a slashing gesture. Clumps of dirt and rock spewed into the air, and deep trenches opened on either side of his feet. Verbena squeaked and ducked inside, slamming the door behind her.

"Answer me." Duncan drew in a ragged breath. *"Did you lie with him?"*

"None of your damn business."

"I disagree. For years, I have searched for you, knowing that one day we would be reunited."

"Well, give you a big old prize." Cassandra planted her feet and glared back at him, uncowed. "But here's the disconnect. *I* didn't know you were looking for me. You said a Dalvahni warrior couldn't be with demon spawn, and you took off, and you made it clear you weren't coming back."

"Yes, by the gods, I spurned you, and I was a fool." Duncan was shouting, but he didn't care. "I knew my mistake within the fortnight and returned to beg your pardon. To tell you that I love you. That I was wrong to leave. That I am nothing without you, but you were gone. I kept looking, and I *never* gave up." His lips twisted. "Alas, I have been casting my net at the moon."

Cassandra's lovely face was pale and set. "Don't you dare make this about me." Her knuckles were white around the staff. "I was broken when you left. Couldn't eat or sleep. I wanted to *die*."

Duncan reached for her. "Cassandra, listen. I—"

"No, you listen." She jerked away from him, her violet eyes

bright with unshed tears. "Then Baby Rose came down with a fever. Scarlet fever, probably, but there wasn't a doctor around, so who knows." Her mouth trembled and her gaze grew far off. "I shooed Jimbo and Maggie out of the house to keep them from catching it and then I did everything I could think of to save her, but the fever took her anyway. I wrapped her in a blanket and went to tell Jimbo and Maggie their baby sister was gone, but they'd slipped into the woods. I found them near the creek. The Hag had torn them to pieces. Part of me *did* die then. I buried what was left of them underneath the oak tree the next morning and left."

Sorrow washed over Duncan, and bitter regret. He should have been here. She should never have suffered such horror alone.

Anger forgotten in the face of her grief, he closed the space between them.

"Cassandra . . ." His throat tightened with remorse and longing. "If I could but go back . . . spare you this pain and anguish, I would, and gladly."

She gazed up at him, a storm of emotions flitting across her expressive face. She was so near, a heartbeat away. He inhaled, breathing in her light, crisp scent. A single crystal tear hung, suspended, on her lashes. He reached out and caught the droplet on his fingers. She held still, her eyes wide, like a startled doe's. Unable to resist, he let his trembling fingers drift across her cheek.

Her skin was soft and warm. The single, slight caress sent an electric shock of awareness through him that made his knees buckle. He gazed helplessly down at her, his foolish heart pounding at her nearness, at the sheer heart-stopping wonder of her.

Gods, it had been too long. He wanted to taste her, to drink her in. The empty, meaningless years without her had been a desert, and he was dying of thirst.

He bent closer. "Cassandra, my sweetest love . . ."

She gasped and stepped back. "Don't you 'Cassandra' me, Duncan Dalvahni. I'm not a girl anymore. I'm a grown woman with responsibilities and a life."

"A life that has included other men?" He did not conceal his bitterness.

"Yes," she said. "You rejected me, Duncan. Emphatically and completely, and more than a century and a half ago. I like men, and I like sex, and I'm not going to apologize for it, especially to you."

"But we—"

"Were in love?" She looked him squarely in the eye. "Yes, and it was wonderful—while it lasted. Then you left, and it was terrible. No one—*no one*, especially you—will ever hurt me like that again. Whatever we had, Duncan, it's over."

"Do not say that," Duncan begged. "Cassandra, my love—"

She clapped her hands over her ears with a shriek of rage. "Stop calling me that. I am *not* your love. You don't know me, and you sure as hell don't love me. So, for the last time, leave me alone."

She dropped the staff and walked into the house, closing the door behind her with the finality of a death knell.

Chapter Five

Cassie leaned against the door, her insides churning. Duncan had seemed so . . . shattered, and she'd done that to him. She straightened, shaking off her remorse. Duncan had no claim on her. There was nothing between them but memories.

Then why did she feel like a jerk?

A noise outside drew her to the window. With a negligent flick of one hand, Duncan erased the deep ruts he'd made in her driveway. He gestured again, and the dead werewolf floated over and settled into the back of the truck, head and all. Duncan's movements were mechanical, his sculpted features frozen in a hard, unyielding mask. He motioned a third time, and Cassie's truck cover soared out of the shed and across the yard. Before she had time to wonder how he knew where she stored it, the cover settled onto the bed of the truck and closed tight, protecting the carcass from scavengers.

Task accomplished, Duncan turned toward the house. He stood there for a long moment, gazing at the cottage with a hard, empty expression, and then he was gone.

Cassie stared at the spot where he'd been standing. He had that disappearing act down pat. He'd done the same thing, years ago— dissolved into the ether—leaving her to pick up the pieces of her broken heart.

"Good riddance," she muttered, but the words rang hollow.

Her eyes burned. *Enough*, she thought. *You don't get any more of me, Duncan Dalvahni. Not another drop. Not another wasted thought or emotion.*

She spun away from the window and smacked into Verbena.

"Umph," Verbena grunted, stumbling slightly. "Sorry about that. Where's Mr. Duncan?"

"Gone."

"Gone?" Verbena's eyes widened in alarm. "Back across the river? I need to catch him."

She turned and darted away.

Cassie caught her before she reached the door. "Wait, Verbena. I don't think he's across the river. He's a demon hunter. There's no telling where he's gone or if he'll be back. In the meantime, you're welcome to stay with me."

Good Lord, why was she offering this strange girl a place to stay? She didn't know Verbena, and the girl wasn't her problem.

"Beggin' your pardon, miss, but I don't know you," Verbena said, echoing Cassie's thoughts. "And I done caused you enough trouble fer one day. 'Sides, I—"

She paused, her face reddening.

"Feel safer with Duncan because he's a demon hunter? You needn't be afraid. I can protect you."

If her magic cooperated, Cassie silently amended. If she could get her shields up and running again.

If she could figure out why her powers had fizzled in the first place.

"Besides," Cassie continued, squashing her reluctance and doubts, "Duncan doesn't have a place to stay."

"Yes, he do. Got hisself a tent across the river, and he's building himself a house."

"A tent?" Cassie gave a mock shudder. "That settles it. Why rough it when you can stay under a roof?"

Verbena's lip curled. "A tent ain't *roughin'* it. It's a whole heap better 'n sleeping with the dawgs, I can tell you like a friend. 'Sides, Mr. Duncan needs me."

"Duncan is Dalvahni. Demon hunters don't 'need' anybody."

"You wrong. He ain't like that." Verbena's eyes sparkled with indignation. "I heard what you said to him. Heard it plum inside the house. Talking to him like . . . like I don't know what. He *loves* you. Something terrible. And you throwed it in his face like yesterday's scraps 'cause he done hurt your feelings when Jesus was in short pants. Something he's begged your pardon for more 'n once. Heard that, too."

She turned away, shoulders heaving.

Cassie stared at the girl's rigid form in astonishment. This child, this backwoods *ragamuffin*, dared to reprimand her?

"That's between me and Duncan," Cassie said, holding on to her temper by a thread. "You don't know anything about it."

Verbena spun around. "I knowed I seen his face when you tole him to scat. He was broke up."

"He'll live. The Dalvahni are indestructible."

"Not Mr. Duncan. He's different."

"Different how?" Cassie heard herself ask.

"W-e-l-l," Verbena said, her face creased in thought. "He ain't stony-faced, for one thing, like Mr. Conall."

Cassie remembered the ever-present laughter that lurked in Duncan's warm eyes, and had to admit this was true.

Verbena worried her bottom lip. "I shouldn't 'uv said that. About Mr. Conall, I mean. He ain't never been nothing but nice to me, but he . . ." She flushed. "He makes a body nervesome, if you knows what I mean."

Cassie had to admit that she did. The captain of the Dalvahni was intense and intimidating as hell. He gave everyone but his wife, Beck, the cold treatment.

"Mr. Duncan ain't like that," Verbena said, rushing on. "He's *comfortable*. Treats me like a person, and his eyes smile at you when he talks. He's good with animals, too." She stuck out her chin. "Animals can tell about a person. And he's easy on the eyeballs, same as all them Dalvahni fellers."

"A regular paragon." Despite her annoyance, Cassie was amused by the girl's fierce defense of Duncan. Rather like a field mouse championing a lion. "I do believe you're in love with him."

Verbena gave her a look of purest astonishment. "Me, in love with Mr. Duncan? Might as well fall in love with that river out there. It's powerful and strong, and purty to look at, but it don't stop fer no one. Roll right over you and keep on going."

Cassie laughed. "Verbena, I do believe you are a philosopher."

Verbena turned red. "You funning me. I know I ain't book smart." She ducked her head. "Charlie wouldn't let me go to school, but I can read. My mama learned me 'fore she died."

"I promise you, I'm not making fun of you. There are plenty of book-smart people in the world without walking-around sense."

"Charlie didn't hold with books. Said they make folks uppity. Give 'em ideas."

"I have shelves of books, and you are welcome to read them all." Cassie gave her a coaxing smile. "Don't be angry with me. I think Duncan is very lucky to have a friend like you."

Verbena's eyes widened. "Lord, miss. The likes of me can't be friends with the likes of Mr. D. Demon hunters is outta my league. Couldn't stand by and let you say them things about him when they ain't true, that's all."

"Stay with me," Cassie coaxed. "I promise not to say anything rude about Duncan, if it *kills* me."

"W-e-l-l," Verbena said again, wavering. "I reckon I could stay one night."

"Good. You shower while I scrape up something for us to eat. In the morning, we'll put our heads together and decide what to do. Things always seem better in the daylight."

Verbena brushed at her grimy jeans. "I'd love a wash. Ain't had a bath in days, but what am I gon' wear? Left the restaurant in such a hurry I didn't have time to git my duds."

"You can borrow something of mine to sleep in," Cassie said. "I'll throw your things in the washer, and they'll be clean when you get up."

Verbena gave her a piercing look. "Why are you doing this? I ain't nothing to you."

Excellent question, and one Cassie couldn't answer herself.

"Joby Ray," Cassie confided. "I don't like him worth a damn."

"Well, all righty then." Verbena gave her a shy grin. "Reckon we got us something in common, 'cause I don't like him worth a damn neither."

An hour later, they were seated in the kitchen at Cassie's worn farmhouse table having supper. Verbena had bathed and donned one of Cassie's old nightgowns. The sun had gone down and darkness pressed around the house like a woolen blanket. Outside, the bugs and the frogs were having a hoedown throw down, their buzzy noise-making audible through the closed windows. The temperature had dropped, but it was muggy and hot. Cassie had been the first in Behr County to install air-conditioning in her home, and that had been back in the 1940s. Lord, how people had talked, not that she'd given a fig. Air-conditioning was one of the marvels of the modern world and a flat-out necessity in Alabama, as far as she was concerned, unless you enjoyed waking up in a pool of your own sweat.

Verbena pushed back her plate with a little moan of satisfaction. "That was fine, miss, mighty fine."

"I'm glad you liked it."

"Liked" was an understatement. Verbena had downed an astonishing amount of food for one so slender and ethereal looking. Did she have a hollow leg?

"Been living on apples and blackberries the past week," Verbena said, as though guessing her thoughts. "Whadda you call them little brown cakes again?"

"Salmon croquettes." Cassie wiped her mouth with her napkin and set her fork down. The food on her plate was largely untouched. "You've never had them?"

Verbena shook her head. "Fancy fish out of a can? No, ma'am."

Cassie smiled at this description of her simple supper. "Canned salmon is hardly fancy."

"Reckon that depends," Verbena said, considering this. "Skinners grow what they eat, and trap and shoot the rest. Charlie didn't hold with store-bought food, 'cepting for dry goods—meal, sugar, salt, and flour. Them kinda things. Wouldn't a' wasted good vittles on me, anyway. On account of me being a dud, you know."

"They were wrong about that, now weren't they?" Cassie kept her tone light, but the picture Verbena painted of her life made her angry. The Skinners should be whipped like rented mules. "I'm glad you enjoyed your supper. It's not much fun cooking for one."

Verbena gave her a curious look. "You ain't never been married, miss?"

Cassie paused in the act of raising her glass. "No."

"A fine beautiful lady like you? How come?" Verbena reddened when she saw Cassie's expression. "'Scuse me. None o' my business."

Cassie unbent at the girl's obvious chagrin. Taking a sip of tea, she considered Verbena. "How old are you, child?"

Verbena bolted upright in her chair. "Ain't a child. Be twenty years old in a few months."

"Twenty." Cassie bit her lip to keep from smiling. "Practically a relic."

She'd been twenty when she and Duncan had met and fallen in love, a lifetime ago. Several lifetimes ago. In the various incarnations she'd adopted to disguise the fact that she didn't age, she'd been Cassie, Sibley, Chloe, Emma, and Maura, coming full circle to Cassie again.

"My mama was fifteen when she married Old Charlie," Verbena said. "And you can't be much older 'n me." She appraised Cassie. "What are you, twenty-three? Twenty-four?"

"A few years older than that." Almost two centuries older. Lord, this child made her feel ancient. Rising, Cassie gathered the dishes. "Would you care for dessert? There are cookies in the pantry, and ice cream in the freezer."

Verbena stretched and yawned. Her blond hair was damp from her shower, and she looked very young in Cassie's borrowed nightclothes.

"Naw," she said. "I eat another bite, I'll pop."

"You're worn out," Cassie said. "Go to bed. I'll clean up the kitchen."

"And leave you to do the washing up when you done stood on yo' feet, and cooked and fed me?" Verbena jumped to her feet. "I don't think so. My mama would climb outta her grave and kick me to death if'n I was to be so sorry."

Cassie chuckled. "Guess you'd better help, then."

Between the two of them, the kitchen was soon spick-and-span. The odor of fried fish lingered, but a simple air cleansing spell performed by Cassie—to Verbena's delight and wonder—soon remedied that.

Simple I can still manage, Cassie thought, with a wry smile.

There were two bedrooms and a bath upstairs. Cassie showed Verbena to the room farthest from the stairs, made sure she had everything she needed, and went back downstairs to make a phone call. Lordy, she dreaded this.

Hurrying to the landline in the hall—cell phones were useless in Hannah; the crater interfered with reception—she dialed Zeb's number from memory. To her dismay, she got a recording: *Number no longer in service.* She stood there in the hall, receiver in hand, and thought hard. After a moment's reflection, she dialed another number. This time, to her relief, she got an answer.

"Yo," a gruff voice said at the other end of the line.

"Toby? Cassie. Listen, I need your help. Can you get a message to Zeb Randall through the kith wire?"

"Werewolves ain't kith."

"I know, but I can't call him. Zeb's phone is out of order."

"Ain't out of order. Zeb yanked the damn thing out of the wall. Paranoid. Thought the Lyalls were listening in. Won't let anyone else in the pack have a phone, either. Zeb's gone plumb loco."

Cassie gripped the receiver. "Oh, dear. I had no idea."

"Don't see how you could, seeing as how you stay cooped up on the river. You need to get out more, baby doll."

Cassie grinned into the phone. She and Toby went way back. They'd first met in France during World War I, when Cassie had been a volunteer with the Red Cross—wrapping bandages and emptying bed pans, mostly, because she wasn't a trained nurse. Toby, fighting alongside other Alabamians in the 167th Regiment, had been wounded at the Battle of Croix Rouge. He'd been brought to a field hospital, and that's where they'd met.

Gazing into Toby's mismatched eyes—one was purple, the other a glowing topaz—Cassie had known at once that he was like her.

"You're from Behr County," she'd said, without thinking.

Toby had regarded her with familiar kith wariness. *Trust no norm*, their code cautioned, and with good reason. If the norms knew of their existence, they'd be hounded and persecuted. Their safety, their very lives, depended on secrecy.

"What of it?" he'd said. "Lot of Bama boys here."

"I'm from Behr County, too," Cassie had said, raising her voice for the benefit of anyone listening. "Thought you might have news from home."

Glancing around the ward to make sure no one was watching, she'd drawn a shining symbol in the air with the end of her finger. The swirling design glowed bright for a moment, then faded.

"You can trust me," she'd whispered. "I'm like you."

Toby leaned closer and inhaled, then sat back, his expression satisfied. "You're kith, all right." He'd tapped the end of his nose. "This old snoot can smell power, and you know the mark. Who are your folks?"

"Don't have any," Cassie had said, her mind shying away from the image of the graves beneath the tree.

"That right?" Toby had drawled. "Me, neither. Reckon that means we'll have to look out for one another."

They'd been friends ever since.

"Tell you what," Toby said into the phone, recalling Cassie's thoughts to the present. "Deliver the message myself. Whadda I tell him?"

What, indeed?

"Tell him . . ." Cassie took a deep breath and exhaled. "Tell him his nephew Mac has met with an accident."

There was silence on the line, and then, "What kind of accident?"

"It's bad, Toby. Mac is dead. Zeb needs to come to my place."

"You in trouble? Need me to ride out?"

Tears filled Cassie's eyes at the concern in the shifter's voice. "Thanks." To her annoyance, her voice shook, and she cleared her throat. "I'll be okay. Get word to Zeb for me, okay? And try to keep this quiet. This needs to be between me and the alpha."

"You got it."

The phone went dead and Cassie wandered out onto the porch, too restless to sleep. It was dark as the devil's armpit, but lights twinkled in the trees across the river, and the sound of hammering and the rasp of handsaws continued. At least they didn't use power tools, but what kind of construction workers stayed on the job into the wee hours?

The kind that were being paid exorbitant wages, Cassie thought darkly. No telling what Duncan was paying them.

Taking a seat in her favorite rocker, Cassie ignored the sounds across the river, determined to soak in the night air. Silvery streaks of moonlight glinted on the dark water that rolled past, slow and quiet, and sloshed against the banks. The river's lazy demeanor was deceptive. Downstream, Cassie knew, the Devil River grew dangerous and unpredictable.

Like Duncan, she thought, remembering that Verbena had compared him to a river. *Clearly, he expected me to remain faithful to his memory*, Cassie thought. *He's got a nerve. Dollars to doughnuts he's been with other women since we parted ways.*

Not *women*, exactly, she amended mentally. According to Duncan, the Dalvahni were bound by a code of conduct, and one of their rules required them to undergo frequent "sessions" at some place

Duncan had called the House of Pleasure. Thralls, Cassie had learned upon asking, were concubines. Supernaturally *gorgeous* concubines, who subsisted on regular and vigorous intercourse with the Dalvahni.

"They are succubi who require emotion as sustenance," Duncan had explained. "According to the Directive, an unemotional warrior is an efficient warrior. Through sexual congress, there is an . . . er . . . exchange. We empty ourselves of emotion, and the thralls receive necessary sustenance. The relationship is mutually beneficial, as you can see."

"Clear as day," Cassie had said, incensed. "You Dalvahni boys got yourselves a bunch of sex slaves. Shame on you."

"Not slaves." Duncan looked affronted. "Thralls are willing— nay, delighted to accommodate us, for without emotion, they die. They are happy with their lot, I assure you."

"Accommodate—what a lovely way to put it," Cassie said in a dangerous tone. "Are they allowed to leave?"

"They do not wish to leave. The House of Pleasure is their home."

"So, no." Cassie pressed her lips together. "They're sex slaves. You can dress a pig up in Sunday clothes all day long, but it's still a pig."

"What, pray, have swine to do with it?"

"You're a clever fellow. You figure it out."

That had ended the discussion, but Cassie had no doubt the thralls were a service Duncan had continued to employ. A dirty job, but then, someone had to do it. It was his *duty*, after all.

"So, while he's off in some intergalactic whorehouse having himself a good old time, I'm supposed to batten down the hatches?" Cassie thrust the question into the darkness. "I don't think so. How medieval."

But that was Duncan, medieval down to his leather hauberk. She'd been right to be blunt with him. Anything less than the truth would've bounced off his thick skull.

You weren't entirely truthful, a small voice reproved. *You didn't tell him why you broke it off with Zeb. You were attracted to the Randall alpha. You liked him. You liked him a lot. You had every intention of bedding him . . . until Duncan showed up.*

"Duncan, Duncan, Duncan," Cassie cried. "Forget about Duncan. I've got other things to worry about. Like the dead werewolf that's

Saran-wrapped in the back of my truck. Oh, yeah, and my talent's on the blink."

I noticed. The inner voice was smug. *If memory serves, your talent became unreliable around the same time you-know-who showed up.*

"The trouble with my talent has nothing to do with Duncan. I'm going through a bad patch. That's all."

If you say so. What are you going to do about Verbena? A gift like hers is beyond price. People will kill for it, and not just the Skinners. That child is in a world of hurt.

"I'm going to do my best to talk her into staying here," Cassie said. "She can't sleep in a tent with Duncan, for goodness' sake."

Certainly not. It would never do to have a pretty girl like Verbena camping in the woods with Duncan.

"Oh, shut up."

Admit it. You're jealous.

"Am not."

You've always been good at denial, sweetie. Take what happened to Jimbo and Maggie, and little Rose. You blame Duncan, but that one's on you. The children were your responsibility. Jamie was your brother.

Cassie jumped up so hard the rocking chair bammed against the wall.

"I said *shut up*," she yelled, startling the frogs into silence.

I've had my say, the voice replied, unruffled. *But be warned. I'm here and fully loaded with twinges of remorse. It's high time you grew up and stopped being such a crybaby. Oh, yeah—and apologize to Duncan.*

"Apologize to—I wouldn't hold your breath, if I were you."

Helloo. Superego here. I AM you. Apologize, and don't be disingenuous. Squeams hate that.

"Squeams?"

Try not to be dense. I'm the voice of your conscience, of course. What, did you think I was your fairy godmother? Please.

Oh, God, it was official. She was losing it. Abandoning the porch, Cassie fled to her room.

Chapter Six

Duncan reached blindly through the red mist obscuring his vision. Cassandra had sought solace and carnal pleasure in the arms of another while he had lived in a constant, churning state of agony, worry, heartache, and terror that he would never find her again.

She'd been with several others, in fact, according to her own account.

He wanted to tear the world from its frame and bury himself in the smoking ruins.

He materialized in the middle of Main Street, heard a loud blare, like a trumpet sounding, and felt a stunning blow. Sailing through the air, he landed hard on his back on an unyielding surface and stared up at the darkening sky.

There was a metallic thunk, and a human male exclaimed in agitation, "I didn't see him, I swear. He come out of nowhere."

A crowd gathered around Duncan, and a man with a stout, florid face bent over him. "Don't move, buddy. Your legs are busted to hell and back. We'll get an ambulance."

Through a haze of pain, Duncan accessed the Dalvahni Provider. *Ambulance*, the colorless voice of the directory intoned, *a vehicle specially designed by humans to transport sick or injured persons to an institution of healing.*

"No need," Duncan said.

Ignoring the horrified gasps from the onlookers, he sat up and straightened his twisted limbs. His broken bones healed in an instant.

"See?" He got to his feet. "I am perfectly fine."

Turning his back on the stunned humans, he strode to the sidewalk.

"Nice," a silky voice drawled. "Does Captain Hemorrhoid know you're dicking with the norms?"

Evan Beck, Conall's miscreant brother by marriage, leaned against a lamp post, surveying him from beneath drooping lids. The demonoid's purple eyes gleamed with mischief and sharp intelligence.

"Not now, Beck." Duncan gave him a cold look. "I am in no mood to spar with you." Honesty compelled him to add, "Or anyone else, for that matter. Strewth, I am in an evil mood, unfit for man or beast."

Dearly would he love to vent his spleen on some rampaging demon. Alas, things had been woefully quiet in Hannah of late. 'Twas a sorry state of affairs, Duncan reflected gloomily, when one could not count on the djegrali for distraction.

"Wuz up, man?" Evan's gaze was mocking. "I mean, besides being runned over by a car."

In truth, the blow from the car had been nothing compared to the kick in the teeth Cassandra had dealt him. She had been with another. The knowledge was a heavy stone weighing him down, a constant, buzzing drone in his head.

"Do not trouble yourself about me," Duncan managed to say. "'Twas the merest trifle. The Dalvahni are nothing if not resilient."

Evan looked unconvinced. "If you say so, but that shit's gotta hurt, and it makes the norms nervous." He jerked his thumb at the street where a group of humans stood frozen, gawking at Duncan. "Look at the poor sonsabitches. They don't know whether to shit or go blind."

Duncan had made frequent sojourns to Earth in search of Cassandra. As a result, he was more conversant with the local jargon than his brothers. Even so, this odd statement gave him pause.

He blinked at Evan. "Though I feel certain you have a point, I cannot for the life of me fathom what it might be."

"Lemme spell it out for you, slowpoke." Evan straightened and sauntered over. "You did magic in front of a bunch of norms. Unless I'm mistaken, there are rules against that sort of thing."

"The Directive Against Conspicuousness." Duncan was stricken with remorse. "You are right. Alas, I have transgressed."

"Easy, Dunky. Don't go emo on me. I'll handle it."

"My name is not Dunky. My name is—"

"He's healed, praise Jesus," Evan said, cutting off Duncan's protest. Lifting his hands to the heavens, he gave the spectators a radiant smile. "It's a miracle. Now, move along. Show's over."

One by one, the humans dispersed.

"See?" Evan brushed his hands together. "Easy peasy."

"You have my thanks," Duncan said. "I could have altered their memories, but mass adjustments are sometimes tricky."

"Humans are slippery," Evan agreed. "Always the chance you'll miss one, no matter how careful you are."

"Exactly so." Duncan eyed him uncertainly. "You have the gift of memory modification?"

"Nah, I'm messing with you. What happened, you got a broken fluzzit in your whatsperator?"

"I do not understand."

Evan made an impatient gesture. "You beamed yourself into oncoming traffic, my man. Shit-for-brains thing to do. Figured your teleportation device must be busted."

Duncan's face grew hot. "The Dalvahni ability to move from place to place is innate, not based on a mechanical device. Something . . . er . . . distracted me." He gave the demonoid a jerky nod. "I thank you for your assistance, and I bid you good day."

Turning, he stalked away, though, in truth, he knew not his destination.

To his annoyance, Evan caught up with him.

"Headed for the Sweet Shop?" The demonoid fell in beside Duncan. "I'm hungry. Think I'll tag along. What's got you down in the dumps?"

"'Tis not a what, but a who," Duncan said, processing Evan's words. "I had hoped . . ." He shook his head. "Alas, 'twas not to be."

"I know that look." Evan gave him a knowing smirk. "You've got woman trouble. Shorty breaking your balls?"

Duncan stared at him in confusion. "I do not know this Shorty."

"The chick." Evan made an impatient gesture. "The one giving you a hard time. Who is she?"

Duncan gave him a frigid look. "She is not a common doxy to have her name bandied on the street."

"Whew, touchy." Evan clapped him on the shoulder. "Let's grab a bite to eat, and you can tell me all about it."

Duncan shook his head. "I have no appetite."

"Dessert, then. My treat."

Without quite knowing why, Duncan followed Evan down the street and into the eatery known as the Sweet Shop. The interior of this establishment was furnished with scarred tables and booths and decorated with a hodgepodge of signs bearing words of wisdom like *A blind mule ain't afraid of the dark* and *A man's older than his tongue and younger than his teeth.*

They were greeted at the front desk by Viola Williams, the toothsome proprietress of the establishment.

"Evening," she said. "Special tonight's shrimp and grits. 'Course, we got fried chicken and ribs on the menu, same as always." She gave Evan a gimlet eye. "But I don't gotta tell you that. You in here every time the lights are on."

"What can I say?" Evan gave her a smoldering look. "I like the cook."

"You a bad boy, that's what you is." Viola gave him a playful slap on the arm. "Knew it the first time I seen you, with them come-hither eyes and that sexy mouth. You was skin and bones back then, but you picking up. My cooking obviously agrees with you. Got some meat on you now." She gave Duncan the once-over. "Ain't seen you in a while, Duncan. Heard you been busy." Her brown eyes sparkling with mischief, she added in a conspiratorial tone, "Heard you bought some land from Lucy Hall."

"Lucy?" Evan perked up at this. "Is she pretty?"

"Pretty old," Viola said. "Lucy Hall's looking back at eighty and she's tight as Dick's hatband. How'd you get that old sourpuss to sell?"

"I promised to take care of something for her."

Evan smirked. "I'll bet."

Duncan regarded him through narrowed eyes. "I beg your pardon?"

"Aw, don't poker up, Dunky." Evan gave him an engaging grin. "I'm a shit, and I know it."

"Reprobate," Duncan said, unbending. "And the name is Duncan."

"Lawd, listen to you two. Squabbling like brothers." Chuckling, Viola led them over to a booth and motioned to a skinny waitress. "Pauline will take good care of you. Y'all enjoy your dinner."

Pauline glumped up to them. She wore her graying hair in a bun so tight her eyes were slits, and her thin, painted lips were compressed in a rigid line.

"Drinks?" she asked, and clomped off without waiting for an answer.

She returned a moment later with two large glasses of sweet tea, the ubiquitous beverage favored by the locals, and plunked them down.

"Right," she said, whipping a notepad from her apron pocket. "Whatchoo want?"

"Shrimp and grits," Evan said. "The dinner portion, not the lunch portion. And I'll have greens, fried okra, and rutabagas."

"Cornbread or rolls?" Pauline asked, taking notes.

"Both," said Evan, "and bring me an order of fried chicken and a bowl of chicken and dumplings. A bowl, not a cup."

Pauline looked up from her notepad and eyed Evan. "There ain't but the one of you. Where in tarnation you gon' put all that?"

Evan patted his stomach. "Right here. I'm a growing boy."

"Huh." The rawboned waitress's head snapped around at a loud noise. "Lands, Jim Bob's done tumped over his tea again. Man's like a bull in a china shop. Hold on. I'll be back."

Stuffing her order pad back into her apron pocket, she hurried off.

"Didn't want to say this in front of the norm," Evan said, "but I had a little episode a few days back. Monstered out. That shit always makes me hungry."

"You summoned the creature?" Duncan stared at him in consternation. "Has not Conall cautioned you against it?"

"Let you in on a secret, bub. *I* ain't Dalvahni, which means I don't have to do what Conall says."

"Perhaps you do not, but the question remains. Is it wise? The ogre is unpredictable at best."

Evan gave Duncan a surly glare. "I didn't summon anything. Sometimes it happens, okay? Damn witch did a number on me."

Duncan regarded the demonoid with sympathy. A few months earlier, Evan had run afoul of Cassandra's mother, Ora Mae, the witch known as the Howling Hag, with disastrous results.

"A most evil ronyon," Duncan agreed, "but hark and rejoice. The witch is dead."

"Ding dong." Evan's mouth twisted. "Too bad her spells didn't die with her."

"I am told her magic faded with her demise. Her once-lush gardens lie moldering and in ruins."

"That so? Guess I was born under a lucky star." Evan lapsed into gloomy contemplation of his woes. "Whatever she did to me seems to be permanent."

"How long were you her prisoner?"

"Two months." Evan's scowl deepened at the memory. "Two months of hell locked in a dark shed crawling with spiders and centipedes, and shitting in a bucket."

Duncan considered Evan's well-muscled frame. "And yet you seem the picture of health. In fighting form, as it were."

Evan gave a bitter laugh. "I was half-starved when the Hag caught me. She put something in my food to fatten me up, something *magical*." He shook his head. "The old bag planned to eat me. Can you believe that shit? Like those brats in the fairy tale that got lost in the woods."

"Easily, given the creature's foul nature." Whatever humanity Ora Mae had once possessed had been destroyed by the demon inside her. "Fortunately, 'twas a fate you were spared."

"Yeah, but I ain't the same." Evan hunched his shoulders. "You've seen . . . you know."

"Aye," Duncan admitted.

Evan referred to his other self, a dangerous, ogre-like creature with enormous strength, limited intelligence, and a volatile temper.

"Thanks to the witch and her damn meddling, I've got this . . . this *thing* inside me," Evan said, his expression brooding, "and there's not a damn thing I can do about it."

"'Twould behoove you, methinks, to learn to control your temper," Duncan said. "It seems to me the monster is roused by your ire."

"Gee, thanks. You're a big help."

"I do what I can."

Pauline spun back up, notepad in hand. "Now," she said, fixing her beady gaze on Duncan. "What can I get you?"

"No dinner for him. He's going straight for dessert," Evan cut in. "What are his choices?"

Pauline gave him a withering look. "Same as they ever was—dessert menu ain't changed. We got lemon pie, buttermilk pie, coconut pie, chocolate pie, strawberry cake, fudge cake, and 'nanner puddin'."

"What's it gonna be, Dunk? The buttermilk pie's mighty tasty."

Evan's gaze was taunting. "Or are you man enough to handle a little chocolate?"

It was a challenge. The Dalvahni, strong in might and magic, were impervious to drugs and alcohol, but became pixilated on chocolate. Or so Duncan had been told. He'd never been pixilated, nor had the idea appealed. But today . . . the prospect was pleasing.

He brought his hand down on the table. "An excellent notion. Bring me the chocolate pie, a whole one, if you please. Nay, make it two."

"Two chocolate pies, coming up," Pauline said, and stomped off to place their orders.

"Dude, I was kidding." Evan looked alarmed. "You'll get crunk, and it ain't gonna be pretty. Demon hunters and chocolate don't mix."

"So it is rumored, but I have yet to see the evidence."

"Yeah? Well, I have. You remember Grim, right? Brother of yours?" Evan motioned. "Big guy with rusty hair and a temper like a constipated grizzly? He got tanked and ended up parking a car on top of a house."

"I am not Grim. Mayhap chocolate will not affect me."

"What if it does? Then what? Do you want to get caught with your pants down?"

The demonoid, Duncan realized, referred to chocolate's intoxicative properties and its effect on the Dalvahni. The sensible warrior in him cautioned that Evan was right. Vulnerable equaled weak—a warrior could not fight the djegrali if his wits had gone begging. But Duncan did not feel like being sensible. Cassandra had been with someone else. The knowledge made him desperate, half-mad with jealousy.

Perhaps chocolate would help him forget his troubles, if only for a little while. Erase the tormenting thoughts of Cassandra, her sweet body shuddering with pleasure in the arms of another.

"And just so you know," Evan said, interrupting his black thoughts, "cars don't go on top of houses."

"As I do not possess a motor vehicle, that need not concern you."

"Have it your way." Evan sat back in the booth. "But take it from me, no chick's worth the heartburn."

"She is."

Evan shook his head. "That's your dick talking. Never listen to your dick, man. Dicks are selfish and stupid. No brains in the little head. Nearsighted, too. Only got the one eye, see? Take my advice and shove 'at bad boy back in your pants, and find another babe. They're all the same in the dark."

"For me, there is no other."

"For reals?"

"Of a certainty. A Dalvahni warrior does not love easily, but when he does, it is forever."

"Twu wuv." Evan made a face. "Who is she?" He held up his hand at Duncan's black look. "Don't bite my head off. We're not on the street anymore."

"Cassandra." Duncan stared down at his clenched fists. "Her name is Cassandra. You know her?"

"You mean Cassie Ferguson? I know *of* her. Make it my business to know most of the kith and their talents. Safer that way."

"You do not trust your own kind?"

"I don't trust anybody. Period. That's why I'm still alive."

"Focus on the snake and miss the scorpion," Duncan murmured.

Evan shook his finger at him. "Pot and kettle, Dunk. If ever there was a suspicious bunch of mofos, it's you demon hunters."

"An inaccurate term," Duncan said. "The Dal do not have mothers. We were created by the god Kehvahn."

"My point is, you can't be too careful."

The bell on the door tinkled, and a curvaceous young woman with dark hair and creamy caramel skin glided in. The damsel approached Viola, who handed her a white box. Money was exchanged, and the young woman sauntered back toward the exit.

"There. That's a perfect example of what I'm talking about." Evan watched the woman, his gaze on her swaying hips as she left the eatery. "Name's Latrisse Jackson."

"What of her?"

"Can't figure her out." Evan's expression was abstracted. "Know she's not a norm, but she ain't kith, either. Don't know *what* she is, exactly, and that's what bugs me." He tapped his temple. "Knowledge is power, my man."

Pauline sailed up with a tray of food and set a laden plate in front of Evan, then added a basket of bread and a large bowl of savory dumplings.

"Chocolate pie." She placed the quivering, froth-covered confections in front of Duncan with a flourish. "Enjoy."

"For the love of God, don't do it, man," Evan begged. "You'll wind up chasing the moon through a soybean field."

The seductive scent of the pie wafted up Duncan's nose and made his mouth water. Eschewing the plate Pauline had left him, he picked up a spoon.

"To the moon," Duncan said, taking a large bite.

"Demon hunters." Evan shook his head in disgust. "Like talking to a fence post."

Chapter Seven

The pie was smooth as slow-churned butter, almost liquid, and the taste . . . ah, gods, 'twas unlike anything of Duncan's experience. Dark and sweet, with a hint of bitterness, the complexity of the dessert set his brain abuzz with delight and heated his blood with delicious languor. With each bite, the rage and grief tying his guts in knots lessened, and by the time he'd worked his way through the first pie, Duncan was in charity with the world.

Carried away on a tide of goodwill, he studied the demonoid sitting across from him. Conall disliked Evan, but then Conall had never given him a chance. This was unfortunate, Duncan decided. Evan had a way of growing on a person, rather like a corn. Rough. Hard. Painful when pinched or confined, and the devil to be rid of.

Pleased at his own cleverness, Duncan waved his spoon at his companion. "I like chocolate. Know what, Evan? Like you, too. Been watching you."

Evan finished off his shrimp and grits. Picking up a bottle labeled *Pepper Sauce*, he dumped some of the contents on his greens. "Do me a favor and never say that again. It's creepy."

"Been watching you," Duncan repeated, ignoring this admonition. "Know what?"

"What, Duncan?"

"Not a bad sort." Duncan smiled and had the oddest sensation that his lips were sliding off his face. "Not like that Earl Skinner."

"Gee, thanks. Earl was a total skeeze."

"Insulted you. Not my intent. Like you better than Earl. Thought you ought to know." Duncan frowned. "Another reason I like you. Cannot remember why."

Evan took a bite of his greens, and chewed. "Well, I'm alive, for starters—"

"Alive," Duncan repeated.

"And Earl's deader 'n hell. Trust me. I know dead people. I'm a whole lot more fun to talk to."

"That is it. Smart fellow. Like you, Evan. Like you better than Joby Ray. Better than—"

"Got it," Evan said, bringing this litany to a halt. "You like me better than the Skinners. Heard you the first time."

As he floated on an ocean of feel-good, it gradually percolated through Duncan's euphoria that Evan seemed less than pleased by his approbation.

"Like you better than Zeb Randall," Duncan offered. "You know Zeb?"

"Werewolf?" Evan forked some of the yellow vegetable on his plate into his mouth. "Don't know much about him. Don't want to. Don't get the whole pack mentality." He shrugged. "Been on my own since I was a little squirt."

"Know. Raised by demons. Beck told me."

"Did she, now?" Evan's satyr mouth hardened. "Baby sister talks too much."

Evan and Beck were twins. After he was left for dead as a babe by his demon-possessed mother, Evan's life had been a special kind of hell until Beck and Conall had slain the demons who'd enslaved him. Knowing this, Duncan made allowances for the demonoid.

"Horrible," Duncan said. "Tortured you. Sorry for you."

A dull flush crept up Evan's cheeks. "Don't be."

"Like you." Duncan scowled. "Not like Zeb." He slammed his hand down on the table, rattling the dishes and utensils. "Not. Like. *Zeb.*"

"Jesus, take it easy. I heard you. I'm pretty sure people in the next county heard you. What's eating you, man?"

Duncan picked up the sugar dispenser and crumpled it like paper, spraying white granules across the table. "Zeb had a . . . a *thang* with Cassandra."

Evan pried the crushed canister out of Duncan's hand. "No kidding? You like me better than some douche who's been playing patty-cakes with your girlfriend? Well, I'm moist."

Confused by this statement, Duncan consulted the Provider.

Douche, the information source informed him, *is a liquid concoction used to cleanse the female nether regions. Also an insult used to denote a person who is boorish and/or foolish or ignorant. The term "girlfriend" commonly refers to a female companion with whom one has a regular romantic or sexual relationship. Similar in meaning to the term "lover."*

The Provider was silent a moment, processing. *The term "moist" is an informal expression that means sexually aroused.*

Duncan shook his head. "Like you, Evan. No desire to couple with you, though."

"Wha? Who said anything about—" Evan looked up in mid-chew, his eyes widening in comprehension. "Lord, I didn't mean—hey, I don't want to boink you, either."

"Boink?"

"Sex, dude. It means sex."

"Boink." Duncan rolled the word around in his mouth. "Like it. Like to boink Cassandra. Like it very much. Wroth with me."

"From what I hear, Cassie Ferguson's a class act."

"Verily."

"Then word of advice, my man. Don't ask her to 'boink.' Crude. Classy chicks hate that."

"See? That is why I like you." Duncan slapped his knee. "Best of good fellows. Like you better than the douche. Better than Earl. Better than Joby Ray. Better than—"

"Good God, don't start that again."

"Conall does not like you," Duncan felt compelled to point out. "Conall says . . . you a rogue. Not to be trusted."

Evan's lip curled. "Boo-hoo."

"Not a good thing." Duncan was determined to make him understand. "Captain . . . makes a bad enemy."

"Yeah. I cry myself to sleep about it every night."

"Conall wrong about you." Picking up his spoon, Duncan dug into the remaining pie. "Tell him so."

"Don't bother. I don't care what Conall thinks."

"Wrong about you," Duncan insisted. "Should know." He finished the second pie and pushed the empty plate away. "Speak to Grim, too. Grim angry about Dell."

"Grim can bite me." Evan tore into a piece of chicken. "Dell was his bestie until he went googly shit over Sassy, and then Grim ignored him. And *I'm* a villain for showing the poor sap a good time?"

"Mish—" Duncan hiccupped. "Mishuse of i-infor-m-mation. Dalvahni resource."

"Dell is *not* a resource. Not anymore. He's a person, and Grim damn well should know it. He brought him to life."

"Grim lonely." Loyalty compelled Duncan to defend his brother. "Alone . . . long time. Blamed himself . . . Gryff's death."

Evan finished off the piece of chicken and started on another. "Gryff and Grim are twinsies, right?"

Duncan nodded, swaying. "Gryff . . . dead. Djegrali." He made a slashing motion with his hand and nearly fell out of the booth. "Beheaded."

"Huh." There was a speculative gleam in Evan's eyes. "So Gryff loses his head, and Grim slinks off, feeling sorry for himself. He mopes around for a while, gets bored, and makes the Provider—er—Dell . . ." He paused. "What's the word I'm looking for? Sentient—that's it. Grim made the Provider sentient to keep him company."

"Sentient."

"Aren't there rules about that kind of thing? I mean, what's next, a talking toaster?"

Duncan labored over this. "No," he said at last. "Grim did nothing for-for"—he hiccupped—"bidden by the Directive."

"Well, it ought to be. That shit is wrong."

"Not your affair." Duncan's tongue felt thick and sluggish, making conversation a chore. "Between Grim and Kehvahn. Dalvahni god, you know."

"Whatevs."

"Grim is mad because you used Dell to win a fortune. Cheated."

"I did not cheat." Evan took a breath and blew it out. "Not technically. Dell could read the machines. I put money in, and *ka-ching.* Jackpot. Like shooting fish in a barrel."

"Cheated," Duncan insisted.

"Have it your way. I cheated. So what? Dell had fun, and I walked away with a cool three mil." Evan's sulky mouth twisted. "Vegas was next. Dell and I were gonna *own* that town. Then Dell had to go and make himself a real boy, the numb nuts."

This was true. Dell, not content with being sentient, had taken on fleshly form, the body of a stripling, to be exact, and now resided with Grim and his wife, Sassy. Quite unprecedented.

"Got money." Duncan closed his eyes and leaned his head against the back of the booth. "Not . . . need Dell."

"You can never have too much money. Got to think of the future. Take me, for instance. I've started a landscape business. Going like gangbusters." Evan clapped his hands. "Yo, Duncan? How many fingers am I holding up?"

Duncan peeled his eyelids back and peered at Evan. "Eight fingers. Two Evans."

"I knew it. You're sloshed."

"Sloshed." Duncan chuckled. "Funny." He went to prop his elbow on the table and missed. "Play now."

"Play what?"

Duncan's gittern appeared in his lap. He plucked the strings, then launched into song.

"Lord help us," said Evan. "Here we go."

Duncan was tossed upon a stormy sea, the contents of his belly sloshing with each pitch and swell of the waves. A merciless fiend hammered at his head with a mallet and tongs, his mouth and throat were parched, as though he'd gargled with sand, and something extremely foul had crawled into his mouth and died.

The heated pillow beneath his head rose and fell in rhythm with the steady beat of a galley drum, and an errant breeze teased his locks. The wind's gentle play was torment. Gods, his hair hurt. How was such a thing possible? Had pixies woven his tresses in some goodwife's loom whilst he slept?

He cracked his swollen lids and beheld, to his surprise, not the briny deep, but a lacy canopy of green. Patches of blue shone through the leafy netting. The light was blinding, and he squeezed his eyes shut, his temples thudding. For a moment, he feared his stomach would revolt. If this was what humans called bottle ache, or a close approximation thereof, then he found the human fondness for intoxicants incomprehensible.

He lifted his lids again and saw that he was in a forest, though he had no notion of how he'd gotten here. The bolster beneath his cheek was decidedly hairy. Gradually, it dawned upon Duncan that the steady thumping in his ear emanated from an enormous heart, not a drum. The owner of the booming heartbeat was asleep. The huge chest, pale as a snowbank, rose and fell, the beast's black lips fluttering with each exhalation.

Briefly, Duncan struggled to free himself, but the slightest movement set bells a-ringing in his head and made the snakes in his belly writhe.

"Sugar," he said, collapsing back with a groan. "Unhand me, you big ape."

At the sound of his voice, the shaggy mattress beneath him started violently, and Duncan went rolling. A furry white hand shot out, retrieving him.

"Sweet blessed Kehv," Duncan swore, clutching his clanging head in both hands.

Sugar grunted in sympathy and gave him an awkward pat. Tucking Duncan in the crook of one large, hairy arm, he settled against the bole of a tree.

Gradually, Duncan's stomach stopped heaving, and the throbbing in his head subsided to a dull roar. Dropping his hands, he found the pale brute gazing at him, his vivid blue eyes startling in his white, furry face.

"Dunk." Sugar grinned, displaying large, square teeth.

Duncan stared at him. "How did you—"

He paused, straining to remember the details of the evening. It was no use. His mind was an empty well, and everything after the pie was a blank. He concentrated, though the exercise made his head throb terribly, and from the depths of the swampy morass of his brain, a fragment of memory floated to the surface.

You'll get crunk. Demon hunters and chocolate don't mix.

Evan had tried to warn him, but he wouldn't listen.

Duncan met Sugar's guileless gaze. "Did Evan teach you to call me that?"

Sugar chortled in delight. "Ebb." He poked Duncan painfully in the chest with one large, padded finger. "Dunk."

"Ow. Yes. Good boy. Now put Dunk down."

A mellifluous feminine voice interrupted them. "'Tis passing curious, is it not, sister? What is the Dal about, do you think?"

"One can never be certain with a Dal," a second female answered, "but 'twould appear the warrior needs burping."

"By the vessel, methinks you have the right of it. The creature is his mother, then?"

"It seems likely. Regard the tender care she gives her offspring."

With a whistle of alarm, Sugar sprang to his feet. The violent movement catapulted Duncan high into an elm tree. Clinging to a bough, he watched the sasquatch melt into the forest.

"Traitor," he muttered.

After a short, fierce battle with his protesting stomach, Duncan looked down. Two Kirvahni huntresses surveyed him with disdain, a tall, haughty female with flawless brown skin and elegant features, and a petite, curvaceous brunette with eyes the color of cornflowers.

He groaned. The Dalvahni and the Kirvahni had been created by the same god and to the same purpose—to hunt the djegrali—but there, any familial ties ended. The Dal were ferocious warriors, single-minded and unflagging in their zeal to find and extinguish the enemy. The Kir were deadly assassins: pitiless and swift, skilled with the knife and short sword. They were also exacting and cold. Carping. Arrogant. Infuriating. Ill-tempered vipers disguised in comely feminine form.

The tall Kir tapped her chin in thought. "Not his mother, I think. She is too great a beauty to have whelped such a cub."

"He *is* prodigious ugly," her companion agreed. "If not his mother, then mayhap his bride?"

"Perhaps. Rumor has it, the captain of the Dalvahni has taken a demon to wife." The Kir's lip curled. "In truth, the Dal will breed with anything."

Duncan was sorely tempted to belly-spew on the hateful wenches. "Plague take you both," he said, goaded beyond endurance. "Sugar is not my mother or my wife, and you know it. He is a boggy boon."

"Hark, the lummox speaks." The dark-eyed Kir shook her head. "Alas, 'tis but nonsense."

"Boggy boon, sasquatch, bigfoot," Duncan ground out. "These are myriad terms for Sugar's kind, as you would know had you stopped tormenting me long enough to consult the Provider."

The petite brunette drew herself up. "Have a care, sirrah. My sister and I have spent the better part of the night setting things a-right whilst you snored in the woods with your pet ape."

Duncan opened his mouth to retort and shut it again, unease slithering down his spine. The Kirvahni were deft facilitators, dispatched throughout the various dimensions to unravel the worst of magical mishaps associated with the djegrali. By the gods, what had he done?

A third Kirvahni materialized at the bottom of the tree, and this one Duncan recognized. Tall and lean and fiercely lovely, the huntress was clad in soft brown doeskin. Her ruby red hair swung about her slim hips in a long plait. A bow and quiver were slung over one shoulder, and she held a short sword. Her leggings, boots, and vest fairly bristled with knives and other weaponry.

"Greetings, sisters." Taryn's voice was cool as frost. "What is toward?"

Chapter Eight

The dark-eyed Kir leveled an accusatory finger at Duncan. "This Dal is in gross violation of the Directive Against Conspicuousness. He went on a rampage last night in a neighboring hamlet, and 'twas very nearly a disaster."

Taryn arched her brows. "Nearly a disaster, Illaria? I collect matters have been rectified?"

"Certainly."

"Then you have done your duty and can be on your way." When they did not budge, Taryn gave them an enquiring look. "Was there aught else?"

"'Tis the Dalvahni." The face of the one called Illaria was tight with fury. "We would have you know what he has done."

"If the situation has been dealt with, I do not see that it matters."

"It matters to us." The brunette with the blue eyes fairly trembled with rage.

"Very well." Taryn folded her arms. "I am listening."

"There were satyrs," the brunette said. "And centaurs."

"And a great snowy beast the Dal claims is a boggy bane," Illaria added.

"Boggy *boon*," Duncan muttered, though they paid no heed.

"And hundreds upon hundreds of forest creatures," Illaria rushed on. "Fox and fowl, deer and rabbits. A bear and a catamount. Dogs and cats by the dozen and . . . oh . . . too many others to name."

"A veritable menagerie," Taryn said, looking bored. "I confess I do not perceive the difficulty."

"That was but the beginning." The brunette added in the tone of one much afflicted, "There was a nibilanth, a vile little imp who sang songs 'twould put a dock whore to the blush."

"Indeed?" Taryn said. "Did he, by chance, favor you with a ditty about his bollocks?"

The brunette's eyes widened. "Aye. You know him?"

Taryn nodded. "A foul little scamp. His name is Irilmoskamoseril."

"Please, sister," the brunette pleaded, looking around. "Speak not his name, lest you summon him."

"As you wish. Did Sildhjort accompany the nibilanth?"

"Yes. The forest god was in human form," Illaria said. "Silver-skinned, horned, and quite naked. A sylph was with him, and a bevy of human females. They *cavorted*. 'Twas most shocking."

"'Twould be more shocking had they not," Taryn said. "Was Iril—?" A strangled sound from the brunette stopped her. "Oh, bother. Was the imp drinking?"

"To excess," said Illaria. "He turned the fountain in the middle of town into wine. The bear got drunk, and the spirits attracted a large crowd of humans."

"And fairies," the brunette added. "Do not forget the fairies."

Taryn held up her hand. "Let me hazard a guess. The fairies got tipsy and kicked up a rumpus. Tiresome, to be sure, but not unduly troublesome."

Illaria bristled. "The fairies were not the problem. We had things well in hand until the clurichaun showed up."

"A clurichaun?" Taryn clucked in sympathy. "That *is* unfortunate. Noisome, bitter little beasts, in my experience."

"Surly in the extreme," Illaria said. "This one was riding a dog. The poor benighted creature was fagged unto death, to which the nibilanth took exception. The clurichaun took umbrage at the imp's remonstrance and—"

"There was a brawl, I surmise," Taryn said. "'Tis ever thus with the clurichaun."

"'Twas more than a brawl, sister. 'Twas a melee," the brunette protested. "Windows were broken. Carriages overturned. Streetlamps smashed. Pavers pulled up and tossed about. Buildings defaced."

"Disagreeable, to be sure," Taryn said, "but none of this explains why you are so out-of-reason cross with the Dalvahni."

The three females turned as one to stare at Duncan in the tree. He glared back at them, uncomfortably aware that he cut a ridiculous figure but unable to summon the energy to care. His head was a cloth sack filled with burrs, and his stomach was a volcano of acid threatening to erupt.

"'Twas pandemonium," Illaria declared. "There were the fae to be dealt with, and Sildhjort had to be persuaded to leave—and you know how gods can be."

"And that is not the worst of it," the brunette said, her color rising. "Scores of humans required adjustment, including a local constable and his men, and there was massive property damage to set aright. In short, it was a debacle."

"Was it indeed?" Taryn looked unimpressed. "I feel certain you will eventually reach the point of this tale of woe?"

Illaria drew herself up. "The point is, sister, while we struggled to remedy matters, that one"—she shot Duncan a withering glare—"sat atop a statue, much as you see him now perched in yon tree, and played a gittern."

"The Dalvahni lacks musical facility?"

"To the contrary, his music is intoxicating," Illaria said. "The faster he played, the wilder the revelers became, fae, beast, and human alike."

"He drove them into a *frenzy*, sister." The brunette's bosom heaved. "But I do not think you fully comprehend the measure of his transgression."

"Then, pray, enlighten me," Taryn said with a weary sigh. "I am about Arta's business, and time flies."

"There was an ogre," said Illaria. "A great brute with skin like iron and fists like battering rams. Illaria and I scarce escaped with our lives."

Taryn stilled. "At last, you interest me. Did you slay this ogre?"

"Nay." The brunette pointed to a limp figure on the ground some thirty yards distant. "He lies there."

Duncan forced his bleary eyes to focus and saw Evan asleep among the leaves. The demonoid was covered from head to toe with scratches and ugly bruises, and he was naked.

Taryn laughed. "For shame, sisters. I see no ogre. I see naught but a skinned rabbit. Pray, what has any of this to do with the Dalvahni?"

"Everything," Illaria said. "He summoned them."

"Summoned whom?"

"All of them. The centaurs and satyrs. Sildhjort and the imp. The clurichaun. Those insolent fairies and the humans. He summoned them with his infernal strumming. The ogre as well."

"Small wonder you are vexed, then," said Taryn, blinking. "The Dal has certainly been remiss."

"Remiss?" Illaria clenched her elegant jaw. "He is a menace. He should be punished."

Taryn clasped her on the shoulder. "You are sore and weary, sister, and with good reason. Take Jakka and depart."

"But, sister," Illaria protested. "The Dal—"

"The Dal is for Conall and Arta to deal with," Taryn said. "Make your report to the High Huntress. Trust in her wisdom. Then seek your rest. You have earned it."

"But—"

"Now," Taryn said in a firm voice. "I fear I must insist."

With an irritated pop, the Kir dematerialized. Sunk in a misery of self-reproach, Duncan hardly noticed. He had not merely violated the Directive Against Conspicuousness. He'd sundered it.

Pressing his forehead against the tree trunk, he contemplated diving headfirst out of the elm, and rejected the notion. Melodramatic, to be sure, but futile; his broken neck would but heal in an instant.

Glumly, he wondered what his punishment would be. A few thousand years on the far side of the Veil to contemplate his failings? It would be lonely there in the silent darkness. Vast, empty space unbreached by hint of starlight. Forced to contemplate his shortcomings. Forbidden the hunt and the company of his brothers.

Harsh, but bearable. But to be separated from Cassandra for an eternity . . .

His chest tightened until he could not breathe. To lose all hope of winning her back, that he could not bear. He would run mad.

"Well, sir, you have caused a stir." Taryn gazed up at him, hands on hips. "I have a brace of partridges and two fat hares in my pouch. Come down, and we shall break our fast."

Duncan groaned. "Speak to me not of food, I beg you. I am unwell."

"What is this flummery? The Dal and the Kir are impervious to illness." She regarded him narrowly. "Have you, perchance, ingested chocolate?"

"Aye. You have heard of it?"

"The High Huntress warned us to avoid the substance. Supposedly, it affects the Kir and the Dal much the same way that intoxicants affect humans." She shrugged. "I confess I find it hard to believe."

"Alas, it is all too true."

"I see." Taryn studied him. "Conall did not warn the Dal?"

"He did."

"Then why did you not heed him?"

Why, indeed? Duncan wondered.

Because I was jealous and in pain, filled with such fury and longing that I thought I should burn to cinders. Because I wanted to find every male Cassandra has been with and rend them limb from limb.

He kept his thoughts to himself. The Kirvahni would not understand. She could not. She had never been in love, nor would she be. Taryn was too cold and controlled, too aloof and reserved for the all-consuming conflagration that was love.

Before meeting Cassandra, he had been the same, emotionless and detached. Dead inside.

Love had cracked him open and left him vulnerable. Because of Cassandra, he knew yearning and grief, terror and worry, but also laughter, tenderness, and joy.

Laughter, Duncan had found during the long years of separation from Cassandra, kept the darkness and despair at bay, but his newly acquired feelings had set him apart from his brothers, who found his propensity for levity perplexing. Duncan did not care. Cassandra had brought him to life. He would not return to his former self, even if he could.

He noticed the Kir's quizzing gaze, and shrugged. "It seemed a good idea at the time."

"My sisters are seriously displeased. I fear they will denounce you to Arta. Perhaps even take their complaints to Kehvahn."

"In truth, they have reason."

He was too woozy to dematerialize, so he climbed down to join her, moving slowly from branch to branch. Gods, he was weak and dizzy. No more chocolate, he vowed. He was halfway to the ground when a bough snapped, and he fell. He landed on a protruding root. Staring at the sky peeking through the branches, he wondered if he'd broken his back.

Taryn bent over him. "Tell me, was it your aim to fly? If so, you failed. Try flapping next time. In my observation, that is how the birds do it."

Duncan opened his mouth to retort and stopped. Something was dreadfully wrong with his belly. He staggered to his feet and pushed past the startled Kir. Stumbling behind the elm, he expelled the contents of his stomach. He straightened, wiping his streaming eyes, and found the Kir watching him.

"You vomited," she said with detached calm.

"Your perspicacity is a marvel."

"You are a redoubtable warrior, dedicated to duty and the hunt. Your behavior is aberrant." She frowned. "I would have the truth. Did that devil Evan trick you into ingesting chocolate?"

"Oddly enough, the . . . er . . . devil did his best to dissuade me. I would not listen."

"You astonish me. What is it like?"

"To be drunk? Not unpleasant. A sort of untethered euphoria."

Taryn's gaze widened. "Untethered? I confess, the notion holds no appeal. To lose control seems to me of all things most disagreeable."

"The consequences are certainly not enjoyable."

"In truth? You did not enjoy hacking up your entrails?"

What was this? Did the Kir have a sense of humor? Perhaps not so cold, after all.

"Definitely not," he said. "What brings you to Hannah, huntress?"

"The rogue. I have tracked him across the mountains of Ardoth and through the Durngarian mire. The trail led me here."

At her words, Duncan's malaise was forgotten in an instant. "The rogue is here?"

Taryn nodded.

A few moons past, the Dal had received the shocking tidings that a Dalvahni warrior had betrayed his vows, forsaking his brothers and his duty to consort with the enemy. Taryn—not one of the Dal—had been ordered to bring the traitor in. The knowledge galled, though Duncan did not doubt that Taryn was up to the task. She was an excellent tracker, tireless and determined, lethal with all manner of weapons. She would find the traitor and dispatch him with ruthless economy.

Still, it rankled. Sacred vows had been broken, the brotherhood betrayed. The *brotherhood*, not the sisterhood. A Dalvahni warrior should have been named the rogue's executioner, not a Kirvahni huntress.

"Conall deemed it for the best," Taryn said, guessing his thoughts. "'Tis no easy thing to kill a friend."

"You will do it."

She shrugged. "I am Kirvahni. The rogue is not my friend. Come. Let us wake our sleeping ogre."

Striding over to Evan, Taryn nudged him with her foot. "Arise, slug-a-bed. The night has run its course, and morning wanes."

Evan grunted and turned over.

"Observe, he does not heed," Taryn mused aloud. "What is to be done, I wonder? Ah, I have it."

Removing the water pouch from her belt, she dashed the contents in Evan's face. He leapt to his feet, cursing and thrashing.

Wiping the water from his eyes, he scowled at her. "Red? What the hell?"

"Cover yourself, sirrah," she said, giving him a cool look. "Your shortcomings are exposed."

"Cover myself with what, Tundra Twat?" Evan spread his arms wide. "Look around. I ain't got no clothes."

"Hmm," Taryn said. "I perceive your difficulty. Allow me to be of assistance."

Such was the melting sweetness of Taryn's tone that the hair stood up on the nape of Duncan's neck, and he took a hasty step back.

She gestured, and—*ping*—Evan was dressed, though not in the modern mode. He wore a motley velvet coat with fringed tails and breeches. One leg of his breeches was black, the other red. Velvet slippers with curling toes and a multitude of tiny bells adorned his feet, and a large pair of donkey ears sprouted from the floppy felt hat on his head.

Evan looked down at his ridiculous garb. "Not funny, Red. So. Not. Funny."

"You think not?" Taryn tilted her head, considering him. "I, for one, find it highly diverting."

Ping. The donkey hat was replaced by an enormous flowered

bonnet. *Ping, ping.* The bonnet became a wide-brimmed shepherdess hat festooned with high plumes and virulent pink ribbons.

"Stop it," Evan said, glowering at her. "That shit is *rude.*"

"Indeed? I find your vulgar language excessively rude, and I tell you to your face that I will not tolerate—"

She broke off and stilled, listening. Sensing her disquiet, Duncan opened his mind and was flooded by a sense of evil . . . and something else, a jarring impression of bleak emptiness. Something stirred within the void, something grotesque and unrecognizable, something better left to slumber.

"It is the rogue," Taryn said. "He is on the move, and he brings the djegrali with him."

Duncan stared at her in shock. The sick and mindless creature he'd sensed was the betrayer? What perversion of body and spirit could have twisted a Dalvahni warrior in such a manner? The thought was unsettling. The Dalvahni were unassailable . . . were they not?

"You are certain?" Duncan asked.

"Aye. I have tracked him for months and recognize his aura."

Duncan could well believe it. Having encountered that warped presence but once, he would not forget it.

The rogue did not live among them, as Conall feared, playing a double role as spy and traitor. Of this, Duncan was certain. The rogue's very wrongness would betray him.

"What is he about?" Duncan asked.

"One can but guess."

A sudden and chilling premonition gripped Duncan. Cassandra was in peril. He felt it in his bones.

Terror cleared the worst of the chocolate haze from his mind. He should not have left her defenseless, hieing himself off to bury his sorrows in demon chocolate. Despicable.

It was irrational, he told himself, this unreasoning fear for Cassandra's safety. Still, he could not shake the notion that she was in trouble.

"I must away," Duncan said, chilled to the bone.

He reached for the cottage on the river and dematerialized without waiting to see if the huntress followed.

Chapter Nine

Cassie awoke the next morning, sandy-eyed and exhausted. Her churning thoughts and the unceasing tapping from Duncan's property had kept her awake long past her usual bedtime. When she'd finally fallen to sleep, her slumber had been fitful and filled with tremulous visions.

She'd dreamed of the dead werewolf. He'd been standing at the foot of her bed, his severed head in one paw, dripping blood on her floor and white quilt. "Burns," he'd whined as he was swallowed in a white-hot glow.

The dream had shifted, and the werewolf was Zeb, chasing Cassie across a nightmare landscape. "Your fault, healer. Your fault," Zeb growled at her heels. "Mac is dead . . . your fault."

His hot breath scorched the back of her calves, and she ran faster. Clawed hands reached for her . . . and she jerked awake, panting and sweating.

Shaken, she'd risen to check the doors and windows. All was as it should be. Grabbing an ash staff from the rack in the hall for protection, she'd returned to bed, but it was a long time before she'd fallen asleep again.

When she finally did drift off again, the dreams had returned, but this time it was Duncan who'd disturbed her repose. The harsh, beautiful planes and angles of his face tormented her. Firm mouth with a sensuous bottom lip. Chiseled jaw. High, broad cheekbones. Eyes the color of sunlight through scotch that were set beneath slashing tawny brows. Eyes that warmed when he was amused and darkened when he was angry . . . or aroused.

She should not remember that. She did not *want* to remember that.

Tossing and turning, she'd entangled herself in the sheets in her effort to escape him, but it was no use. His sexy, rumbling voice pursued her, his reproachful words echoing through her fevered thoughts.

Alas, I have been casting my net at the moon . . .

Duncan was gone, and judging from the look on his face when he'd left, he wouldn't be back. Probably headed for a galaxy far, far away, never to return. Off saving princesses from dragons and slaying giants.

Or in the House of Pleasure working off his "frustration." She sat up in bed and rubbed her chest to banish the hollow ache. Good riddance, right? The thralls could have his sexy ass. She didn't give a flying hoot in Hades what he did. She'd been fine before His Hotness showed back up, and she'd be fine now he was gone again.

Liar. The knowing whisper was back. *You're consumed with jealousy.*

"Oh, be quiet. Nobody asked you."

She glanced at the clock on the nightstand and gasped. Merciful heavens, it was past six. Toby had said he'd deliver her message, and deliver it he would. Toby was reliable as daybreak. The Randalls could arrive at any moment.

She jumped out of bed and hurried into the bathroom, her mind wrestling with the Randall boy's death.

Could a demon be responsible for the young werewolf's strange behavior? The kith couldn't be possessed, but Cassie had no idea if the same held true for werewolves. She rolled the idea around in her mind. If a demon *had* possessed Mac, that would explain a lot. Demons went through bodies like a hot knife through butter, and they controlled their hosts. Possession would account for the young were's maniacal behavior and his diseased, half-formed appearance. Demons consumed their hosts from within, sapping them of vitality. Weakened by possession, Mac might not have had the strength to fully shift.

The boy had certainly *acted* possessed. His eyes had been crazy and she recalled his labored breathing and the hot huff of his breath on her skin as he'd closed in for the kill . . .

If Duncan hadn't been there . . .

Nope. Not going to think about that. Or Duncan. Most of all, Duncan.

Atta girl, the squeam said with a bored yawn. *You keep telling yourself that.*

Cassie took a quick shower and padded into the kitchen to make a cup of tea. While the tea steeped, she took Verbena's clothes out of the dryer and folded them. Carrying the neat pile upstairs, she placed it outside Verbena's door. Tiptoeing back into the kitchen, she stirred a generous dollop of honey into her tea and carried the steaming mug down the hall. She slid the lock on the door and stepped out onto the porch, bracing herself for the ceaseless knocking of hammers. To her delight, the early-morning peace and tranquility of the river was undisturbed. Duncan's construction workers had finally taken a break. Glory be, and hallelujah.

Silver mist kissed the mirrored surface of the water, and the trees on the far bank were blue-green in the pearly light. Birds rustled and sang among the greenery, and the herb garden on the side of the house perfumed the air with rosemary and thyme. It was a lovely morning, but Cassie hardly noticed. The mug in her hand dropped to the floor, unheeded, and rolled away, leaving a sticky puddle in its wake.

Slack-jawed, Cassie stared at the statue of Jebediah Hannah sitting on her lawn.

Jeb, a hero of the Spanish-American War, had saved Behr County farmers from ruination during the disastrous cotton blight of 1915. *Grow goobers* had been his battle cry, and his leguminous wisdom had won the day. Behr County farmers had survived the blight and prospered. In grateful recognition, the community had commissioned a statue in his honor, and Jeb's likeness stood in the town square, a four-ton marvel of bronze brandishing a two-foot peanut like the sword of retribution.

Cassie closed her mouth and swallowed. Apparently, Jeb had wearied of town life and decided to ruralize. He faced the river, giant peanut raised in challenge to any would-be interloper.

As Cassie considered the ginormous lawn ornament, a thousand disjointed thoughts flitted through her head. Should she call the sheriff? And tell him *what*? What possible explanation could she give him that wouldn't get her locked up? The sheriff would think she'd stolen it.

Reason reasserted itself. No, he wouldn't. Sheriff Whitsun was no dummy. It would take some heavy-duty equipment to move a statue that size, equipment she didn't have access to.

Which begged the question, who had planted Jeb in her yard?

Someone powerful, for sure.

Someone possessed of extraordinary strength *and* magic. Not a werewolf or a shifter. Whoever had done this was practically a demigod or—

The answer to her conundrum dawned, and she stiffened. Oh, no, he didn't.

She marched across the porch to the top of the steps. "Okay, Duncan, you've had your little joke." She glared at the woods on the far side of the river. "Now put it back where it belongs."

Her challenge was met with silence.

"I mean it, Duncan. This isn't funny."

A robin called *hip hip hip*, but there was no other answer.

Seething, she started down the stairs, coming to an abrupt halt as a warrior materialized at Jeb's sculpted feet. Tall, broad-shouldered, and powerfully muscled, the warrior had raggedly shorn golden hair and the face of an Adonis. Dalvahni, without a doubt—that much she knew at a glance—but he wasn't Duncan. Or any other demon hunter of her acquaintance, for that matter.

The stranger's appearance shocked her to the core. There was something different about him, something horribly *wrong*. The Dalvahni were impassive—stoic and unemotional to a fault—but this guy was an automaton. His face was slack, his eyes blank and dull. Shoulders hunched, head down, he moved without the athletic grace of his kind. He was dressed in rags, shirtless and barefoot, the remnants of a pair of leather breeches clinging to his muscular thighs. Intricate black tattoos wound from the bottom of his left foot up his ankle and strong calf, disappeared beneath the tattered cloth that fluttered around his knees, and reappeared at his waist. The ink sleeved his left arm and torso, climbed up his neck and face like strangling vines, and vanished into his hairline.

And the swirling designs *moved*, writhing across his flesh like worms, but if the warrior noticed, he gave no sign.

The door opened, and Verbena stepped onto the porch, looking frail and willowy in Cassie's nightgown, and impossibly young.

She *was* young, Cassie thought, remembering her younger self at twenty. Gracious, she had underwear older than Verbena Van Pelt—

much older—two vintage chiffon teddies, a silk bra, and tap pants were sacheted, tissue-papered, and safely tucked away in her closet for safekeeping. She had *roared* during the twenties—bobbed hair, hot jazz, fast cars, and illegal hooch. It had been the cat's meow.

The Great Depression that followed? Eh, not so much.

Rubbing her eyes, Verbena joined Cassie on the steps. "Rabbit runned over my grave and woke me up."

The warrior's head snapped up at Verbena's sleepy murmur, and he stared at her, his eyes suddenly ablaze in his lean face.

"Lord a-mercy, whozzat?" Verbena said with a hiss of surprise.

"Dalvahni, but there's something off about him," Cassie said in a low voice. "*Very* off."

"Why's he a-staring at me like 'at? I ain't done nothing to him."

"No idea. What *I'd* like to know is what he's—"

Cassie's voice trailed off as a cold wave of dread washed over her, a feeling of hopelessness and absolute evil.

A pulsing black streak appeared over the sandy beach on the far side of the river and widened, and an oily, revolting smell poured out of the gaping hole.

Like microwaved death, Cassie thought, gagging at the noxious stench.

"We got trouble," she told Verbena, backing slowly up the steps. "Demons."

"D-demons? What we gon' do?"

"They're like bees. Don't move, and try not to irritate them. If that doesn't work, we go to Plan B."

"What's Plan B?"

"Run like hell."

Scores of undulating black forms boiled out of the portal. Screeching and gibbering, the demons flew across the river and circled the immobile warrior like a merle of frenzied blackbirds. One of the foul creatures noticed Cassie and Verbena, and shrieked the alarm. The flume of demons froze in midflight, then swept toward the porch.

The warrior jerked, as though waking from a trance, and uttered a harsh caw. Answering in their loathsome tongue, the demons turned aside. Without a backward glance, the warrior lurched across the lawn in the direction of Cassie's truck, and the demons fluttered after him.

"They left." Cassie heaved a sigh of relief. "Thank God. That was close."

Verbena shook her head. "Didn't leave. He called 'em off. Why'd he do that, you reckon?"

"Don't know and don't care. C'mon. Let's get inside."

Cassie's brain whirled furiously. She'd go to Conall at once and tell him what she'd seen. The demons. The portal. The warrior with the blank expression and the writhing tattoos.

A Dalvahni warrior was running with demons. No way to spin that and make it look good. Conall was going to blow a gasket.

Yay. Another fun conversation to look forward to. The good times never ended.

Verbena turned and scurried for the door. Cassie started after her, looking back at the sound of a deep, guttural grunt. Her heart did a slow somersault as a demon stepped out of the yawning opening and onto the sandy bank of the river.

Unlike the others, this demon was solid, a huge thing of twisted limbs, scales and claws, with a misshapen head that ended in a cruel, narrow snout. Half wyvern, half crocodile, the demon stood upright on armored legs the size of tree trunks, a pair of bony wings sprouting from its spiked back.

A second wave of wraiths flowed out of the hole behind him.

"You coming?" Verbena asked, looking back with her hand on the doorknob.

She saw the monster and screamed, and the draco-croc whipped around. The demon had a multitude of wet, gelatinous eyes. The wobbly eyes focused on them and the demon roared. Lashing its tail, the draco-croc spread its wings and launched its heavy body at the house. The wraiths followed, flitting through the air like dirty rags.

Time seemed to slow. In the space of a frozen moment, Cassie was bombarded with a strange overload of sensory information. She heard the languid music of the river and the rustle of a bird in the gardenia bushes on the side of her house, smelled earth and grass and water, and was intensely aware of the delicate brush of the morning breeze against her skin.

An orange and black butterfly flitted past, oblivious to the approaching nightmare. The striations on the insect's checkered wings were a rich, golden-brown color, the same shimmering copper as

Duncan's eyes. His laughing face rose before her, and she tasted the bitterness of regret.

Her conscience was right. She owed Duncan an apology. Too bad she wouldn't live long enough to deliver it.

True dat, if you keep standing here like a knot on a log, the inner voice whispered. *Move it. Now. That thing's coming for you. It's pissed and it has minions.*

Coming to her senses, Cassie grabbed the oaken staff she kept by the back rail. "Get," she barked, stepping in front of Verbena. "Go out the back and hide in the woods. I'll hold them off."

It was an out-and-out lie. Cassie's hands were shaking, and she wanted to throw up. A few wraiths she could handle—maybe—but there must be a hundred of the damn things. And then there was the nightmare. What was she supposed to do about *that*?

"Can't." Panting with fright, Verbena clutched the back of Cassie's shirt. "Mr. Duncan 'ud have my hide if'n I was to leave you."

Duncan. God, she wished Duncan were here. That was one BFD—big fugly demon—coming for them. He'd know what to do. All in a day's work for a Dalvahni demon hunter.

But Duncan was gone, and it was up to her to get them out of this.

Alive, preferably.

Cassie hefted the staff. "He would, huh? Then I guess this is where we find out whether you really are the enhancer."

She studied the metal figure on her lawn. A knight in shining armor, that's what they needed, an old-fashioned champion.

"*Vivere*," she murmured, pointing her staff at Jeb Hannah.

A bolt of lightning shot from the cloudless sky and struck the bronze figure on the lawn.

The statue moved.

Chapter Ten

Due to the lingering aftereffects of the chocolate pie, Duncan miscalculated and materialized on Cassandra's gravel drive, rather than in front of the house. 'Twas shortly past dawn, and light trickled through the thick trees in shimmering strands of green, gold, and silver.

A few strides brought him into view of the cottage. Cassandra's home made a pretty picture nestled on the lip of the river, a welcoming oasis in the woods bursting with cheerful patches of sunflowers, splashes of pink and white crocuses, and banks of purple sage. A slight breeze ruffled the leaves and shivered the blooms in the flower beds. Duncan opened his senses and caught the scents of the rosemary, lavender, and parsley growing in the herb garden, but no sign of danger.

The knot of disquiet in his belly eased. All was well. Cassandra was safe. She was slumbering, no doubt. He'd overreacted. 'Twas oft the case when it came to her. He was a fearless warrior, able to face a legion of demons unperturbed, ride into battle with a smile upon his lips, and endure the wrath of gods and nature alike with a defiant laugh, but the slightest threat to this one woman unmanned him.

It was unnerving and maddening, his peculiar weakness. A Dalvahni warrior did not fret like a wet nurse over a mewling babe. A Dalvahni warrior knew not fear or panic. A Dalvahni warrior was calm. Steady. Unflappable. Cool under pressure and unremittingly logical.

He was all these things . . . except when it came to *her*. She had ravaged his poor, defenseless heart and laid him bare. She was his bane, his passion and obsession.

Taryn appeared, interrupting his musings, with Evan on her back.

The demonoid clung to her like a monkey, an expression of acute misery on his face. The Hag's elixir had added several inches and at least two stone to Evan's formerly scarecrow frame, yet Taryn showed no sign of strain. Like the Dal, the Kirvahni were blessed with enormous strength.

"Any sign of the rogue or the djegrali?" she asked.

Duncan shook his head, heat crawling up his neck. "Nay. I fear I was mistaken."

"Hey, it happens." Evan slid to the ground. "Don't beat yourself up."

The demonoid's face was a delicate shade of green. He still wore the jester's costume and the ridiculous beribboned hat. He glared at Taryn. "Remind me to walk next time. I hate that time-warp shit."

"Ever with the bellyaching," Taryn said. "What a fuss you make about nothing."

"Nothing? I'm sick as a horse. Serve you right if I liquid screamed all over your precious fairy boots."

"Liquid scream?" Taryn's eyes widened at this incomprehensible piffle. "I am unfamiliar with this term."

"It means vomit, Red." Evan stuck out his tongue and made a retching noise. "Gack, yak, hurl."

"Ah, you refer to the process of regurgitation." Taryn gave a wise nod. "Duncan liquid screamed earlier. Verily, 'twas a cascade."

"Big whoop. I'll alert the media 'cause everybody gives a giant shit about that."

"Indeed, 'twas most unusual. The Dalvahni do not vomit, nor do the Kir."

"Let you in on a secret, Red. Nobody gives a flying fart about the demon hunter digestive system. Especially me."

"Well, you should. Knowledge is never wasted, even on one such as you." Taryn tilted one foot to admire her boots. "I am glad you did not liquid scream. I should dislike it excessively had you ruined my boots. They were a present. Except for a lamentable tendency to sparkle, they are nice, are they not?"

"Orgasmic, Red. I'm hard just looking at them."

Taryn wrinkled her nose. "You are a pig. I had as well converse with a chamber pot."

"Hey, I said I liked them."

"You did not say you liked them. You said—" Taryn caught herself. "I refuse to let you bait me. My boots are most excellent. They match whatever I wear, and they are charmed for speed." She paused, her expression thoughtful. "Not that I have need for speed. I am fleet of foot without them."

"And modest," Evan said. "Don't forget modest."

Taryn gave him a scowl. "The point is, but for having to lug your sorry carcass, I should have been here in a trice. There is a good deal more of you than there used to be."

"Are you calling me fat?"

"Do not let it trouble you," Taryn said in a kindly tone. "Those breeches are quite slimming, I assure you. No doubt many females find corpulent men attractive."

"Corpulent? What the hell—now, see here, Red—"

Duncan listened to their raillery with half an ear. His earlier unease had returned. Something stirred in the ether, a sickening disturbance in the atmosphere that made his skin tingle with alarm.

The wind shifted. Taryn stopped bickering with Evan and lifted her head. "Demons," she announced. "A veritable horde of them, judging from the stench."

Duncan caught a whiff of something foul, and his heart lurched. Cassandra was alone but for Verbena, and at the mercy of an army of the djegrali? Sweet blessed Kehv.

Drawing his sword, he sprinted down the drive. Merciful gods, do not let him be too late. If Cassandra were harmed or—

No; his mind veered away from the terrifying half-formed thought. He moved faster, his heart hammering against his ribs. His brain was on fire, and lightning flickered at the edges of his vision, bright flashes the color of blood.

Blood. Cassandra's blood, pouring unchecked from her body and soaking into the ground.

His mind went black. No. *No.*

He streaked out of the woods and down the drive. He looked around, but there was no sign of demons. A loud thump came from the direction of the river. With an agonized shriek, a wraith sailed over the cottage and shattered in midair, the ragged pieces fluttering to the ground like crumbling parchment.

The demons had attacked from the river, and Cassandra was making a stand on the front porch, he realized, though he could not see her from the back of the house. She was fierce, his sweet sorceress, he thought with a swell of pride, and she was holding her own.

For now, at any rate.

Turning, he started around the dwelling to go to her aid and came face-to-face with the rogue on the side lawn. Shock stopped him in his tracks, and he stared at the tattooed golem in disbelief.

"*You*," Duncan said. "You are dead."

This brutish thing had once been his brother? Impossible. This was no Dalvahni. This was naught but an empty shell, the essence of the warrior stripped away.

The rogue returned Duncan's regard without recognition, his expression glazed, his gaze fixed and lifeless.

Ignoring the leaden weight of pity and revulsion, Duncan drew his sword. "Hold, Gryffin."

The rogue's indifferent gaze flickered, and for a moment, Duncan fancied he saw a glimmer of recollection in the rogue's empty eyes. Then a vast host of djegrali swarmed onto the side lawn, a toxic funnel of smoke that wafted and weaved in dizzying patterns like a murmuration of starlings, and the faint spark of something in the betrayer's eyes died.

The demons fluttered around the traitor, covering him in an ashy cloak that smelled of foulness and decay. The swarm parted, and the rogue was gone. Swirling and shifting, the dark, pulsing band swept over Duncan, enveloping him in darkness and a suffocating fetor. Shouting his defiance, he swung his sword this way and that, and was rewarded by howls of anguish and the powdery stench of dead demon. But for every devil he slew, two more appeared, and the stench of the demons befouled his lungs with the odors of smoke, rot, and despair, robbing him of strength.

The hilt of his sword grew slick with blood. Vaguely, he realized he was bleeding from dozens of wounds. As fast as one gash healed, the snarling, biting demons inflicted a dozen more. Duncan sliced a demon in two with his sword; the fiend dissolved in a puff of oily smoke. A dozen more wraiths attacked, slashing him with their talons and rending his flesh to the bone. The pain was incredible. His lungs screamed for relief, his muscles and limbs were heavy with exhaustion. He was diminished, he realized with a vague sense of astonishment. He, a mighty Dalvahni warrior, weakened by the demon chocolate.

Outside the smothering billow of djegrali where light and air and hope existed, something bellowed. Something big. Another demon, no doubt, and Cassandra fought alone.

The knowledge renewed Duncan's strength, and he slashed at the demons, but they were too many. Two of the fiends latched on to his sword arm, gnawing at his flesh, their teeth searing him like hot coals. More demons flowed around his legs, savaging the backs of his thighs. Hamstrung, Duncan crashed to the ground.

Shrieking in triumph, the djegrali blanketed him, clawing and tearing at him like feasting crows. Duncan was a bleeding hunk of pain. His throat and lungs were clogged with demon stench, and blood from the bite marks on his forehead and scalp ran into his eyes, blinding him.

Chewed to death by demons—the thought wafted to the surface of his mind from some dark place of amusement. Not exactly the glorious fate he'd imagined.

Nay, he would not die, not when Cassandra needed him. Roaring, he thrashed and flailed against the smothering carpet, but the demons stuck to him like hot tar, pinning him to the ground and settling on top of him, crushing him with hopelessness and despair.

He gave a soundless howl of pain as a demon savaged the side of his head. Then he heard a second thunderous shout and the djegrali were gone, swept aside like so much chaff.

Duncan sat up. Wiping the blood from his eyes, he beheld an ogre with granite skin, tree-trunk limbs, and eyes like hot currant jelly. An ogre dressed in a jester's costume and velvet slippers and sporting a wide-brimmed hat with plumes and feathers atop his enormous head.

Snatching up a cluster of demons, the ogre rolled them in a ball and squished them. Black sludge ran between his thick fingers and dripped to the ground.

A demon landed on the ogre's face, clawing at his gray skin. *Smack.* The ogre slapped the demon like a mosquito and flicked it away. Bawling like an enraged bull, he batted the djegrali out of the air and crushed them in his great hands, then slung aside the black muck and reached for more.

Shrieking in impotent fury, the group of djegrali that had attacked Duncan fled.

Duncan staggered to his feet. He was covered in blood, one of his ears dangled by a thread of skin, and his shirt and jeans were in tatters. "You have my thanks."

The ogre grinned down at him. "Ebban squash demons." He clapped his huge hands together, sending droplets of pulverized demon into the air. "Squash good."

They turned at a musical cry of challenge. Taryn had arrived and was battling a clutch of djegrali. The huntress's hair had come unbraided, and it shimmered in deep, red waves around her hips like a battle flag. The sight of it seemed to enrage the demons, and they threw themselves at her. *Snick. Snack.* Her sword flashed, precise as it was deadly, dispatching a clutter of demons.

Her lovely face was alight with battle fever. The Kir might be a plague and a nuisance, but, by the gods, she could fight.

The ogre squinted at the huntress. "Red?"

Swatting demons aside, he waded up to Taryn. When a group of demons tried to stop him, the ogre seized them in his great hands and shredded them like rotten rags. They dissolved into malodorous silt and blew away.

The Kir froze, her sword upraised, staring in astonishment at the behemoth. "*Evan?* By the vessel, is that you?"

The ogre pointed to a cut on the Kir's cheek. "Red hurt."

"What?" Taryn touched her face. "That? It is nothing. The merest scratch. But I—"

The ogre plucked her up and dropped her in his pocket. He patted his coat. "Red safe. Demons no hurt."

Taryn popped out of the fabric pouch like a jack-in-the-box. "I am Kirvahni, you overgrown lump, not some missish damsel in need of coddling. Fighting demons is what I do."

"Ebban squash demons."

"I do not—" She shoved a hank of hair out of her face and blew out a breath. "Why do I bother? Talking to you is useless."

She scrambled out of the ogre's pocket, up his thick arm, and onto his broad shoulder. Demons buzzed around them in a stinging cloud. *Snick, snack,* Taryn set upon them once more with her sword. The blade pierced the dark, flitting shapes, and the demons shrieked and wafted to the ground in black tatters.

The ogre groped for the Kir with thick fingers, but she jumped lightly aside, avoiding his grasp.

"Have a care, clod pate," she sang between flicks of her sword. "They are going for your legs."

Dissuaded by Taryn's flashing blade, the djegrali attacked the ogre's lower body, slashing at his massive thighs and calves. The ogre roared and stamped his feet. The bells on his shoes pealed, loud and clear, and with a wail of anguish, the demons disappeared.

Taryn slid down the ogre's back and jumped to the ground, her eyes alight. "By the gods, that was something like," she said. "Did you see them run? Methinks the clangor of the bells is painful to them."

A roar split the air. The sound had come from the front of the house.

"Cassandra," Duncan said, taking off at a run.

He careened around the cottage and onto the sward that sloped down to the water and beheld an astonishing sight. Charred patches scarred the once-green turf, and Cassandra stood on the porch, a wooden staff in her hands. Her blond hair was loose and tempest-tossed. It swirled around her shoulders in pale ribbons of silk, though no wind stirred. She was barefoot and in shorts, her sleek legs braced for combat and her cool, lovely features composed in a determined mask.

The air around her was thick and crackled with power, and a dark funnel cloud whirled above her head. Flashes of lightning streaked out of the purple-black mist, dancing in short bursts around her. Cassandra stood in the midst of the storm like a vengeful Fury, her pale lips moving soundlessly as she summoned the elements to her aid. They answered with a vengeance. The sizzling halo around her formed a shining wall between her and her attacker, a scaly, two-legged lizard with a profusion of oozing red eyes. The monster had jaws large enough to crush an ox, and claws like swords. Flames spewed from the worm's maw, hit the shield, and bounced off.

Cassandra was magnificent, but her weariness was evident. Sweat beaded her brow and ran down her flushed cheeks.

Fear licked a path the length of Duncan's spine. No matter her ability, Cassandra had unleashed more magic than three wizards could safely handle, and the thunderstorm of vast energy she had summoned was volatile and unpredictable. One distraction, one mis-spoken word in the incantation, and she would be burned to ash.

With a shout, Duncan rushed to her defense, a gallant charge that was short lived. Something huge brushed past him, knocking him to the ground.

Furious, Duncan got to his feet and whirled to face his assailant. Creaking and clanging, an animated statue clomped across the back lawn, a huge club in one burnished hand. Slack-jawed, Duncan took a closer look. Not a club—the statue carried a seed pod the locals called a "peanut."

A host of djegrali swarmed around the metal sculpture like dark, angry bees. The giant's armored form was dented and scratched in a hundred places, and covered in scorch marks, but the bronze valiant seemed undismayed. Cheerful, even.

Swinging the peanut, the statue sang in a booming voice,

> *My baby, when you hear them bells go ding-a-ling,*
> *All turn around and sweetly you must sing.*
> *When the birds dance, too, and the poets will all join in,*
> *There'll be a hot time in the old town tonight.*

The gleaming peanut sliced through the air, smacked into a clump of demons, and sent them sailing over the rooftop.

> *. . . a hot time in the old town tonight.*

The metallic knight swung the peanut again, pulverizing another cluster of demons.

Duncan spun at a bellow from the demon lizard. The fiend's spiked tail lashed out, shattering the porch railing and steps in a shower of splintered wood. The shield protecting Cassandra wavered. Duncan gave a battle cry and leapt onto the demon's back. The demon snarled in outrage and bucked, but Duncan tightened his thighs around the demon's shoulders and held on. Sharp scales sliced into his legs like knives.

As he brought his sword up to finish the thing, the world tilted and the demon rolled, crushing Duncan underneath. Stunned and bruised, he lay on his back.

He'd been doing a lot of that lately, he reflected, viewing the world from this position. Humiliating, really, and not in the least dignified. Was he a Dalvahni warrior or a turtle?

The demon sprang up. Lifting Duncan in a taloned paw the size of a cart, the demon gave him a lingering sniff.

"A Dalvahni warrior." The fiend gave an evil chuckle. "My favorite snack."

"By the gods, but you are ugly," Duncan wheezed, looked up into the nightmarish face. "And you reek."

The demon's claws tightened until Duncan felt his ribs crack. Black dots danced at the edge of his vision, and the blood thundered in his ears.

"Too raw for my taste," the demon purred, as though Duncan had not spoken. "But no matter. That can soon be remedied."

The demon opened its mouth, and Duncan found himself looking down a long, dark tunnel. Deep in the fiend's belly, a fire glowed. The demon growled, and the forge flared to life.

In the distance, someone screamed, a long, terrified wail.

Orange-red flames rolled up the demon's gullet. As Duncan braced for the searing heat, an enormous pair of hands closed around the demon's throat and squeezed. The hands closed inexorably, pinching and twisting the worm's sinewy neck like the end of a sausage.

There was an angry, low rumble from the demon's gut, and an expression of ludicrous surprise creased the thing's hideous face. The gooey, red eyes bulged and widened, the hulking body swelled and ballooned, and the demon exploded in a ball of flame.

Chapter Eleven

The blast threw Cassie across the porch like a rag doll. Bruised and shaken, she climbed to her feet. The oaken staff lay at her feet in pieces. She was covered in soot and powdery grit, her nose filled with a god-awful stench—the sickly-sweet smell of rotting flesh combined with smoke and ash—and her ears rang from the explosion.

She felt wrung out and punch drunk from channeling so much power.

Greasy black smoke rolled over the house in thick, choking puffs. Cassie coughed and looked around. Strips of sizzling demon flesh hung in meaty icicles from the porch eaves. Gore splattered the plank floor, windows, plantation shutters, and railings, and pieces of bone were scattered around like shards of broken china. Fat pooled in rancid puddles on the floorboards and congealed in globs on the lawn.

It looked for all the world like someone had blown up a whale.

Not a whale—a demon. Cold terror washed over Cassie as the memories flooded back: Duncan riding the demon like a bucking bronco, his sword upraised; the demon rolling, crushing Duncan underneath before lifting him in a scaly claw; the hideous mouth opening in a bristling yawn.

Flames had belched forth to engulf Duncan, and Cassandra realized that she had wailed, an animal sound of terror that went on and on. Then the ogre had clomped up, ludicrous in a harlequin coat, red and black knee breeches, velvet slippers, and a plumed hat, and had grabbed the demon by the throat. The demon made an almost comical sound of distress and—

Dear God. The damn thing had detonated, and Duncan had been at ground zero.

Cassie staggered across the porch. The rails on either side of the steps sagged drunkenly. "Duncan?" she screamed, frantic. *"Duncan?"*

There was no sign of him, but the ogre stood in a circle of blackened lawn, a vacant look on his doltish face. Fires dotted the grass around him and tendrils of oily smoke smudged the air. The ogre's coat of many colors was a smoking ruin, and he was missing a belled shoe. The creature's feet were huge, the size of a compact car. The gray skin of his bare foot was blackened, curling like crepe paper. Burnt ogre smelled a lot like Boston butt.

So much for eating barbecue any time soon. Maybe ever.

His beribboned hat was gone. Tossed aside by the blast, it sat at the bottom of the slope, a festive straw yurt adorned with ribbons. The jaunty feather was wilted and smoldering.

Cassie eyed the mammoth askance. This was not her first encounter with Monster Evan. She'd met him once before, the day her mother had tried to kill her—*there* was a reunion she'd never forget. Monster Evan had come to the rescue. He'd been big and ugly then, too, but he'd been naked, not dressed like a mummer.

With the help of a troop of vengeful fairies, he'd chased the Hag into the river, and that's where Cassie's mother had died. There was a certain serendipity in that. Mommy Dearest had been eaten by the giant catfish she'd raised from a guppy. Karma was a bitch with razor-sharp teeth, and she was eternally hungry.

Cassie hurried down the steps, giving the ogre wide berth. "Duncan? Where are you? Answer me, dammit."

"I have him," a melodious voice answered. "The explosion sent him into the river. And a good thing, too, for he was a-fire."

The wind shifted, blowing smoke into Cassie's face. She rubbed her stinging eyes and saw a tall, lovely woman dressed in suede leggings and boots wade out of the river. Her long, thick hair flowed around her hips, and she fireman-carried a large bundle of singed rags over her shoulders.

A thrall? Something hot and uncomfortable unfurled inside Cassie, but she shoved the ugly sensation away. She and Duncan were over years ago, and last night, she'd burned that bridge to the ground. She had no right to be jealous. Besides, this gal's air of confidence and the predatory grace with which she moved screamed warrior, not succubus.

Cassie ran across the lawn to meet her. "Is he—oh my God, is he—"

"Dead?" The redhead lowered Duncan to the ground beside Jeb's empty granite plinth. "Nay. A bit singed around the edges, but he will soon recover." Her gray eyes glinted with cool amusement. "Methinks his pride will smart longer."

Cassie scarcely heard her. She fell to her knees beside him, her heart chugging like a piston engine. Duncan was unconscious. His clothes were in shreds, and he was covered in blood and demon gunk. One ear was missing, and half his face was badly burned, as though he'd turned his head at the last second to avoid the blast. The skin of his seared cheek was white and waxy, the edges charred and dark, and leathery in texture. Dear God, was that *cheekbone* peeking through the burnt skin? She shuddered and turned her attention to his other hurts. His jeans and boots had protected his legs, but his torso and arms were a mass of oozing bite marks. Ugly red and purple streaks ran from the ragged wounds.

She pointed to a particularly nasty gash. "What are those?"

"Demon bites," the redhead said. "Djegrali attack. There were a multitude." She spun about, knife drawn, at a sudden clatter from the far side of the river. "By the vessel, what is that clamor?"

"The carpenters must be back," Cassie said, distracted with worry. She pressed her ear to Duncan's broad chest and heard a fluttering thump. "Duncan's building a house."

"Verily? 'Tis his intent to abide here, then?"

"I guess. Ask him." Cassie sat back on her heels. "Right now, the important thing is that he's alive."

"I told you so, did I not?" The redhead arched a superior brow. "I am Taryn, a Kirvahni huntress. And you must be Cassandra."

"Yeah. Listen . . . er . . . Taryn. The Dalvahni are badass and bulletproof, so why isn't Duncan healing?"

Taryn frowned. "I do not know. Demon fire is exceedingly hot. Regardless, he should have recovered in a trice. Death comes to our kind but rarely, and when we are harmed, we quickly mend." She pursed her lips in thought. "Perhaps the chocolate he imbibed last e'en has somehow slowed the healing process?"

"What?" Cassie gave her an incredulous stare. "What's chocolate got to do with it?"

Faint color climbed up Taryn's cheekbones. "Though it pains me to admit it, 'twould seem our races are susceptible to the substance. Duncan was warned of its possible effects. He ignored that admonition and became inebriated on chocolate last e'en." Pausing, she added with scrupulous punctiliousness, "Or so I have been told. I was not there."

"Duncan drunk. On chocolate. Why on earth would he do something so asinine?"

"I do not know." Taryn's steady, gray gaze was disconcerting. "I thought perchance you could tell me."

"Me? Why would I—" She recalled her angry words to Duncan the night before and his bleak expression when he'd left. Her cheeks flamed. "We had a fight, okay?"

"I confess my astonishment. In physical appearance, you seem singularly ill-matched."

"Don't be ridiculous. We had an argument, not a fistfight."

"You quarreled? *That* I can readily believe. The Dalvahni are irascible. What was the source of your dissension?"

"It doesn't matter now. Help me get him to my truck. We have to get him to a hospital."

"No. He is Dalvahni."

"But he—"

"Think of the uproar should a human physick examine him."

Mentally, Cassie kicked herself. "You're right. Of course you're right. I'm not thinking straight."

Duncan wasn't human. The kith avoided human doctors and hospitals for the same reason. Their demon blood set off the machines and raised too many questions. *Unanswerable* questions. The norms would have a field day if they got their hands on a demon hunter.

What should she do? She had to help him. Anxiety and dread beat at her. *Think, Cassie. Think.* She was a mage—when things were working right, that is—able to wield the power that flowed through earth and stone, wind and water, and growing things. She ran a bustling trade in homeopathic herbs and medicines with the norms, but she didn't know a thing about Dalvahni physiology. She couldn't heal Duncan.

The hell she couldn't. She had the enhancer.

Cassie surged to her feet. "Where's Verbena?"

Taryn gave her an odd look. "Who?"

"Young woman with blond hair. She was standing behind me when the demon erupted. I have to find her. Verbena's talent makes others—" Cassie shook her head. "There's no time to explain. Let's carry Duncan up to the house. You grab his shoulders, and I'll take his feet."

"To what purpose?"

Cassie gritted her teeth. "I told you. We need to get him inside."

"You wish to convey him into yon abode?" Taryn shrugged. "'Tis a small matter."

Taryn waved a slim, long-fingered hand, and Cassie caught the familiar, sharp scent of magic. Duncan's body rose from the ground and wafted slowly toward the house.

Show-off, Cassie thought, watching Taryn stride away. Swallowing her spleen, she hurried after her. The demon blast must have knocked her stupid. The Kirvahni were like the Dal—super strong and magically gifted.

Or Taryn could have told you. But that would've been too easy.

"Absolutely," Cassie muttered, hurrying up the hill.

Hands on hips, the Kir stood at the top of the slope in the stupefied ogre's shadow. A few feet away, Duncan's limp form bobbed in the air. "What ho," Taryn said, gazing up at the behemoth. "Here is a beef-witted lunk."

"His name is Evan Beck," said Cassie. "When he's not an ogre, I mean."

"We are acquainted." Taryn's voice was dry as unbuttered toast. "His twin sister is Rebekah Dalvahni. She goes by the sobriquet 'Beck.'"

"That's right," Cassie said, regarding her in mild surprise.

"You know her, then? Perhaps she has mentioned that Evan took her diminutive as his surname in homage to their familial connection."

"Nope. Beck doesn't talk about Evan. They had some kind of falling-out, I think. I take it you and Evan are friends?"

"Are we?" The Kir seemed to consider this. "He is a scamp and a wag. Rude, crude, and selfish. Abominable, unpredictable, and invariably annoying. The varlet even threatened to vomit on my boots. And yet, I have not killed him." Craning her neck, she regarded the ogre. "What say you, Sir Lunk? Are we friends?"

He answered with a wrenching groan. Swaying, he toppled to the ground with a dull boom that shook the house. The massive form shimmered, and Evan lay on the lawn. His clothes shifted with him, conforming to his diminished size.

Or what was left of them. The jacket was pretty much a goner, and the breeches were crusted an inch thick in demon slime. The smell of cooked fat and demon made Cassie's stomach churn.

"At least he's wearing clothes," Cassie said, hurrying over to him. "The last time I saw him in Hulk mode, he was running around naked."

"The ogre is quite large. His raiment, I suspect, cannot withstand the sudden and violent change."

Cassie indicated Evan's old-fashioned garb. "Yeah? So what's up with the ridiculous costume?"

Taryn shifted in sudden discomfort. "When I happened upon Evan this morn, he was bare as a newborn babe." Her mouth tightened. "As he takes great delight in playing the trickster and fool, I decided his manner of dress should fit his behavior." She made a rueful face. "I regret that I lost my temper, but Evan has a rare talent for raising my ire."

"Yeah, Beck says he's a pain in the ass. Wait. You *made* these clothes? Like . . . with magic?"

Taryn inclined her head. "It was nothing. The Kirvahni are adjusters. We make many things."

"Magical clothes. Good grief," Cassie said. "That's why they shrink and stretch." She knelt to examine Evan. "He's burned."

"Of a certainty, he is burned, the care-for-nothing cheese wit." Taryn's tone was savage. "Killing demons is what I do, what I was *made* for. He should have left the matter to me."

Evan's eyelids fluttered at the sound of her raised voice. "Red?"

"Be quiet." Striding over, Taryn scowled down at him. "I am exceedingly wroth with you."

"Exceedingly wroth." A strange smile played about his sensual mouth. "I love it when you talk dirty."

His eyes drifted shut again, and his face went slack.

"Out cold." Cassie got to her feet. "Can you float two at a time?"

"What?" Taryn was staring at Evan.

"Duncan and Evan," Cassie repeated with thinning patience. "Can you float both of them?"

"Yes, of course." Taryn waved a hand, and Evan's body rose from the ground.

"Okay," Cassie said. "Let's get them in the house."

She led the way, stepping over debris and chunks of smoldering demon. The scorched grass crunched beneath her feet, and the smell of blasted decay was cloying. Climbing to the porch, she waited as Taryn guided the injured men up the steps.

Cassie held the door wide. "My room. Down the hall and to the right. I'll be there as soon as I get some supplies."

"Supplies? To what purpose?"

"A party," Cassie snapped, stepping aside to allow Taryn to enter with the patients. "What else?"

Taryn gave her a hard stare, then shrugged and steered the two bodies down the hall.

Cassie started after her, halting when she heard someone call her name. She stepped back onto the porch and saw Verbena lope around the house like a startled gazelle.

"He's gone, Miz Cassie." Verbena's violet eyes were wide. "Done lit out. I hollered at him, but he kept a-going."

"Who kept going?"

"That feller with the big peanut."

"Oh, Lord."

"Knowed it weren't good," Verbena said, taking this as affirmation. "Followed him a ways into the wood. Saw he weren't gon' stop and hightailed it on back."

Cassie gazed at Verbena in horror. If the norms laid their peepers on Jeb, there'd be forty kinds of trouble. She had a sudden vision of Jeb in a standoff with the National Guard, a metallic Godzilla surrounded by a sea of reporters and television crews, fending off helicopters with his giant peanut.

This was not good. This was *definitely* not good. Kith mandate number one: Draw no attention to their kind.

Draw attention, *hell*. She'd taken out an ad and put it in lights.

Cassie shook her head. "I can't worry about that now. Duncan's hurt."

"He is?" Verbena cried. "Oh, no."

"Evan, too."

Verbena's brow wrinkled. "When in tarnation did Miz Rebekah's brother get here?"

"He was the ogre."

"Oh." Verbena's eyes widened in comprehension. "*Oh*. If that don't take the rag off the bush."

Mentally, Cassie was cataloguing the items in her storeroom. "I'm glad you're here. I'm going to need your help."

"Me?" Verbena shrank. "I don't know nothin' about sick folks."

"I'm no great shakes at it either, but we're all they've got."

"But I—"

"You're the enhancer." Cassie fixed her with a challenging glare. "So enhance."

She left Verbena standing open-mouthed at the foot of the steps and strode into the house. Entering her workroom, she paused, her mind spinning with the tasks ahead. First, the men would have to be stripped and bathed, then their burns treated. The shelves in her storeroom were laden with the dried plants and herbs she used in her various spells and homeopathic remedies. After some hesitation, she selected aloe, lavender oil, and calendula and put them in a basket, throwing in a jar of manuka honey for good measure.

Dear Lord, she couldn't do this. She was a wizard, not a doctor, and Duncan's injuries were beyond her meager skills. She knew some folk medicine—that was all they'd had, back in the day—but she'd never had any formal training, unless you counted herb books and the Internet. She knew a few basic healing spells, but she'd *never* treated anyone with injuries as serious as Duncan and Evan's.

Panic gripped her, making it hard to think. What would a norm doctor do? That was as good a place as any to start.

Smoke inhalation, she told herself, straining to remember her days in the field hospital. *Must check their airways and breathing sounds*. Hydration was important, too. She'd have to figure out a way to get fluids down them.

Pain—they'd need something for pain. Duncan's face . . . his poor, beautiful face, and those vicious bites, as if one of Torquemada's inquisitors had gone to town on him with red-hot pincers. Evan's hands and foot were in bad shape, too.

Swallowing a sob, she grabbed a bag of dried poppies to make tea and threw it in the basket.

She stared blindly at the shelves, her mind on the injuries peppering Duncan's torso. The wounds had festered and already leaked a foul-smelling green ichor. Were demon bites poisonous? Though she was half demon, she was working in the dark. No kith school existed where demonoids learned their history and the secrets of their race, but there should be one.

Filing the thought away for future consideration, she decided to make a poultice of marshmallow root to draw out the demon toxins and promote healing. Quickly, she added the necessary ingredients to her basket.

Going to the farm sink, she scrubbed her hands and arms. As she soaped up, she thought back to her initial inspection of the two patients. Of the two, Evan's condition seemed better. The ogre had a hide like a rhino, and consequently, his burns were superficial and largely confined to his hands, upper chest, and left foot. And he hadn't been a demon hors d'oeuvre.

The demons had shredded Duncan.

The breath caught in her throat. Duncan was going to be fine. He had to be.

Why the sudden drama? the knowing voice asked. *You wanted to be rid of him.*

"Not like this," Cassie said out loud. "Never like this."

The workroom door opened, and Verbena slipped inside. She gave Cassie an odd look, as though she'd heard her talking to herself, then silently took her place at the sink.

When the girl had washed, Cassie picked up the basket of herbs and bandages. "Ready?" she asked, swallowing her anxiety.

Verbena nodded, though she looked ready to bolt. "I'll do what I can to help Mr. Duncan."

"We both will." Cassie straightened her shoulders. "Okay. Let's go."

Leaving the workroom, the two of them hurried down the hall.

Chapter Twelve

Evan awoke to searing, unholy pain. He hadn't experienced pain this bad since the 'rents had died. Elgdrek and Hagilth, his demonic "family," had delighted in torturing him. Been good at it, too, the sickos.

Opening his eyes, he looked around. He was in a sunny room, reclining on a bank of pillows on a big bed. Long windows offered a view of the river and a lush flower garden. He frowned, trying to get his bearings. Gradually, the memories trickled back, dim and sluggish. He was at Cassie Ferguson's place, the one they called the witch, and there'd been a demon attack. The nasty buggers had gone after Duncan and Red, and the ogre had busted loose. No wonder he felt three kinds of awful—monstering out drained him and gave him a mother of a shifter hangover, but that wasn't the worst of it. One of the damn demons had exploded.

He caught a faint whiff of violets and wood smoke.

Taryn bent over him. "Ah, you are awake."

Her liquid voice washed over him, easing his pain and making his Johnson sit up and wag. Damn her. She could read the back of a can of motor oil and make him hard. Jesus, he needed to get a grip.

Nah, he needed to get laid, and not by this tight-ass ice goddess, either.

He sat up in the bed and kicked the covers aside. "Can't put anything over on you, Red. You're too smart."

He looked down. Yep, still wearing the awk-tastic trousers, but the multicolor coat and the stupid belled shoes were gone. The source of his agony was obvious. His left foot, chest, and hands were cooked, injured when the demon went kablooey. The skin around the burns was cracked and oozing, and his fingers were covered in blisters the size of silver dollars.

The damn knee breeches were spotless, though, and so was the rest of him. Not a speck of dirt anywhere. He sensed a certain Kirvahni huntress with OCD tendencies at work. Turning his head, he saw Duncan lying beside him. The poor son of a bitch looked bad. Half his face was melted, and the rest of him was a mangled mess. But he was clean, by God, free of demon funk and soot. Taryn was a regular grime-fighting, dust-busting superhero.

She was thorough, you could say that about her. Meticulous, methodical, and painstaking. Focused in the extreme.

He'd love to loosen her up. Rock her universe and make her scream.

But that would be nuts, a total freaking disaster. Taryn Kirvahni was not for him.

"Good job cleaning us up." Holding his hands in front of him, Evan watched Taryn from beneath lowered brows. "Thanks."

"I am, of course, gratified by your approval, but thanks are unnecessary," Taryn said. "I could scarce put you abed as you were. 'Twould spoil Cassandra's lovely linens."

So Nature Gal liked nice things. He made a mental note to purchase a set of Egyptian cotton sheets for the house, then gave himself a swift kick. He was *not* getting Red in the sack. For all kinds of reasons, the most important being survival. She'd probably kill him. For reals. The chick was lethal.

He yelped as the subject of his musings lifted his injured foot and slid a pillow under it. "Ow, watch it."

Taryn bent over him again, her brow creased with concern. "Does it pain you?"

"Like a sumbitch."

"Good. 'Tis what you deserve." She straightened, her full mouth pressed in what he privately called the Schoolmarm Line. "That demon you attacked was one of the morkyn."

"So?"

"So, witless one, a morkyn is the most powerful caste of demon, not a chicken to have its neck wrung. Look at what you have done to your poor hands. What were you thinking?"

"Not much." Evan tossed his hair out of his eyes. "Thinking's not exactly his strong suit."

"Indeed? Then in that respect, you and the ogre are much alike."

"Aw, Red, stop busting my balls. I'm hurt, and I've monstered out twice in twenty-four hours. That shit's hard on a guy."

"Hmm," Taryn said, tapping one foot. "I suppose there is nothing for it but to heal you, though it goes against my better judgment and the Great Directive. *Leave all as you find it, lest, by injudicious interference, you alter the course of events.*"

"And break the rules? You'd implode, Little Miss Stick-in-the-Mud."

"You think me hide-bound?"

"If that's a fancy word for pain-in-the-ass control freak, then yeah."

He was being mean, but he couldn't help it. She drove him crazy.

"The Great Directive is a lodestar, not an imperative," she replied calmly, not rising to the bait. "Others before me have used their talents to aid worthy mortals wounded in combat with the enemy."

She was actually thinking of breaking the rules? For *him*? The knowledge made his chest tighten.

"Yeah, but I'm demon scum," he said. "The good news is I don't need your help." Leaning his head against the pillows, he gave her a sickly smile. "Demon blood, baby. The kith heal fast. I'll be fine in a few days."

"Unfortunately, I cannot tarry. I must be about my business and would see you mended ere I go."

"I'm touched, Red. Really, but no thanks. If you're so all-fired set on healing somebody, take a crack at Duncan. He looks like shit."

"Such is mine intent. I could hardly, in good conscience, heal a demonoid care-for-nobody and refuse mine aid to a brother hunter."

Before he could retort, the bedroom door slammed open, and Cassie stalked into the room. "*What?* I've been worried out of my mind. Terrified that Duncan might . . . that he could . . . that I might not be able to . . ." She shook her head. "And all the while, you could heal him? Why didn't you tell me?"

Taryn arched a brow. "You did not ask."

Cassie was trembling with fury. Of all the imperious, hoity-toity females, Taryn was the worst. Beck had mentioned once that the Dal and the Kir got along like a terrier and a rat in a croker sack. Less than an hour in Taryn's company, and she could sympathize. Taryn could make a preacher cuss.

Still, she had to admit that Taryn had mad skills. In the space of a few moments and without help, the Kir had put both injured males to bed, removing every trace of grime and demon sludge from their bodies in the process.

A nice bit of magic in anyone's book.

Duncan had not regained consciousness. Taryn had stripped him out of his torn shirt and boots and covered him in a white sheet. His head rested against a pillow, his honey-streaked hair swept back from his burned face. From Cassie's angle, his profile was smooth and unmarred, that of a sleeping prince.

"Didn't ask?" Cassie said to Taryn, her voice rising. "I told you I was going to fetch medicines and bandages."

The Kir held up a slim forefinger. "That is incorrect. You said, to be exact, that you were getting supplies for a party."

"That was sarcasm. Nobody in their right mind would have a party at a time like this."

"I thought a party exceedingly ill-timed, but I am unfamiliar with kith customs," Taryn said with a shrug. "In the Blasted Regions of Gorth, members of the Plaveeki tribe bang drums and play pipes around the tents of ailing loved ones to frighten death away. And in the jungles of Yarthac, the tree people eat their dead to discourage predators."

"This is Hannah," Cassie said, striving not to lose her temper. "We don't have a hoedown when somebody's sick, and we don't eat our dead."

"Skinners do." Verbena eased into the room. "Skinners is like rats. They eats anything."

Taryn gave the girl a cool glance. "Thank you. I shall endeavor to remember that. You are?"

Verbena nodded, her eyes wide. "Name's Verbena."

"Greetings, Verbena. I am Taryn." She returned her attention to Evan. "Now, then, sirrah. Shall we proceed?"

"Get the wax out of your ears, Red," Evan said. "The answer hasn't changed. I get the shakes when I monster out. They'll pass."

"There is no need to be afraid." Taryn spoke in a soothing murmur. " 'Twill not hurt. Much, at any rate."

He stiffened. "Who said anything about being afraid? The Hag did a number on me, that's all, and I'm not anxious for more."

"I thank you for the flattering comparison, but the Kir do not practice dark magic."

"Don't poker up, Red. This isn't about you, this is about self-preservation. No telling what your Dalvahni hoodoo will do."

"'Tis bound to be an improvement."

"Typical woman, always trying to change a guy."

"I do not wish to change you, jack-at-warts. I wish to help you. Have you e'er been burned by demon fire?"

"No."

"Then you cannot know how long 'twill take you to heal, e'en given your demon blood. And you have been weakened by the change. Is it your desire to be confined in bed for days, perhaps weeks, an invalid at my tender mercy?"

Evan looked genuinely horrified at the prospect. "Good God, no."

"Then let me help you."

Evan glanced around as though seeking a means of escape. "Aintchu got a rogue to catch, or something?"

"In truth, I do. E'en so, I will abide here, though—"

"Aw, Red. You so schweet."

"Chafing at the delay. You will not enjoy my company, I assure you. I shall make you utterly and completely wretched."

"Shit," Evan said. "This is blackmail."

Taryn folded her arms across her chest. "'Tis a promise."

Evan muttered something extremely foul, then held out his hands. "I can't believe I'm doing this. I must be out of my mind."

"Oh, for God's sake," Cassie said, losing patience. "Stop being a jackass and let her help you. Or not. Duncan's hurt, too."

"So heal him already," Evan said, looking stubborn. "I'm down with that."

"I shall heal you both," said Taryn. "Now silence, little goat, so that I may concentrate."

Taryn placed her hands a few inches above Evan's body and closed her eyes. Green light pulsed from her in soothing waves, washing over him.

Evan stiffened. "Hey, that—" He arched his back. "Stop it, Red. That . . . *yeoowww*."

The burns on Evan's hands, chest, and foot faded and were replaced by healthy tissue. Color tinged his pallid cheeks and pale lips, signaling the return of wellness and vitality.

Chest heaving, Evan collapsed against the pillows. Cassie could have wept with relief. If Taryn could do that for Evan, she could do the same for Duncan. He was going to be all right. They both were. She wouldn't have to try to heal him with spells and guesswork and unguents that might or might not work. Taryn knew what she was doing.

It was going to be all right.

As Cassie watched, Taryn lifted her hands, and the waves spread, suffusing Duncan in shimmering opalescence. At once, the waxy burns on his face softened and grew pink, and the charred edges blurred and disappeared. New flesh budded, knit, and healed. Within moments, Duncan's face was returned to its former glory.

Anxiously, Cassie scanned his features. One cheek might be a tad shinier than the other, but otherwise he seemed fine. Even his torn ear had regenerated.

Something rigid and tight unfolded inside Cassie. Her legs buckled, and she fell to her knees. "Thank God," she said, clapping her hands over her face. "Oh, thank God."

"What ho. This is passing strange."

Cassie stilled, her heartbeat ratcheting into overdrive. Lowering her hands, she saw Taryn gazing down at Duncan, her brow furrowed. "What is it?" Cassie asked, jumping to her feet.

"The demon marks." Raising her arm, Taryn pointed. "They are unchanged."

Cassie rushed to the bed. Taryn was right. Deep scores marred the smoothly muscled skin of Duncan's shoulders and upper chest. Ichor seeped from the raw gashes, crusted over and cracked, oozing anew, leaving damp patches on the white cotton. Slowly, Cassie peeled back the sheet, revealing the hard planes of Duncan's chest. His jeans rode low on his hips, exposing his taut, ridged abdomen. He was built like a god, perfection in masculine form.

Perfection that had been obscenely marred, a Greek statue pockmarked and wasted by time and the elements.

Gazing at Duncan's ravaged body, Cassie felt the last of her anger and bitterness melt away. She hated seeing him like this. The Duncan she knew was strong and dynamic, an indomitable warrior abrim with vitality and purpose, a maddening tease with his laughing eyes and smiling mouth, not this broken wreck. She wanted him hale and hearty, taunting her into a hissy fit from across the river.

Or closer, the inner voice said. *Admit it. You enjoy sparring with him. He makes you feel alive.*

A shiver racked Duncan's big body. Cassie laid a hand on his forehead, then snatched it away. His skin was dry and hot to the touch.

"He's burning up." Hurrying to the chest at the foot of the bed, she grabbed a blanket and spread it over Duncan. "I don't understand. Your magic worked on Evan. Why isn't Duncan better?"

Taryn bit her lip. "In truth, I cannot say. The gods have blessed our kind with unsurpassed recuperative powers. We know not sickness or lasting hurt." She indicated one of the pustulent bites on Duncan's neck. "Observe how the wound scabs and bursts open again? Duncan's body wars with the demon venom for mastery. Alas, I fear the toxin is too strong."

"Meaning?"

"Something has weakened him, something that has made his magic and mine ineffectual."

"Like what?"

"I can only surmise the chocolate is to blame."

Cassie stared at her in bewilderment. "You think Duncan's half-dead because he's got a chocolate hangover? That's crazy."

Evan rose from the bed and stretched like a cat after a long nap, seemingly none the worse for his ogreish adventures. He was a handsome thing, with his dark, sultry good looks and pantherlike grace. He reminded Cassie a lot of his sister.

"You're wrong, Red," Evan said. "Grim got drunk as a road lizard on chocolate a few months back. Other than a bad head the next morning and a shitty attitude, he was okay."

"Grim?" Cassie gave him a blank look.

"Demon hunter. Married Sarah Elizabeth Peterson."

"Oh, yes," Cassie said, remembering. "I know Sassy and I've seen Grim."

Sassy Peterson was perky to the max. Though she and Cassie were very different, they had one thing in common, one very *important* thing. The Hag had done her best to kill them both. She'd taken Sassy and Cassie captive, hog-tied them, and held them prisoner in the old farmhouse on Cassie's property. The Hag had planned to kill

Cassie outright, but her plans for Sassy had been more diabolical. She had planned to *eat* Sassy, consuming her in bits and pieces for her fairy essence. Cassie shuddered at the memory. But there was more to Sassy Peterson than a bubbly personality. Sassy had summoned an army of vengeful fairies, freeing herself and Cassie, and vanquishing the Hag in style. Grim had been there that day—Cassie had caught a glimpse of the big warrior when she'd stumbled out of the cabin, shell-shocked and hysterical. Duncan had been there, too, and they'd had a humdinger of an argument.

"Yeah?" Evan was saying, looking lost in thought. "Now that I think about it, Grim had a shitty attitude *before* he got drunk. Attitude's standard equipment with the Dalvahni." He shot Taryn a sly glance. "The Kir, too. Not a sense of humor in the bunch. Except for Duncan. Duncan's all right."

"Evan, my brother suffers, and my patience dwindles," Taryn said. "If there is a point to your discourse, reach it."

"All right, here it is. It's not the chocolate, so one of two things has happened. Either the Dalvahni have changed. Grown weaker, somehow—"

Taryn made a noise of disapproval. "They have not."

"Or the djegrali have mutated."

"Absurd," Taryn said. "The djegrali are older than the stars. For eons, they have remained unaltered."

"Yeah? Welcome to Hannah, Red. Weird central."

Chapter Thirteen

"Meaning?" Taryn asked, arching a brow.

Evan opened his mouth and shut it again. "Nope. Not going there. Said too much already. You wanna know more, ask Conall."

"An excellent suggestion." Taryn drew herself up. "I shall do that, and now."

"You can't leave," said Cassie. "What about Duncan?"

"I shall seek Conall's counsel on that as well." Favoring Evan with a look that would freeze-dry stone, Taryn vanished.

"Brr," said Evan. "I'm on her list. I *hate* that list."

Duncan moaned and thrashed his head on the pillow. The sound tore through Cassie like a knife. Crossing the room in two strides, she shoved Evan against the wall, her demon blood up and howling for release. She was about to have a meltdown, and it was not going to be pretty.

"It's not Taryn you should be worried about, or Conall," she snarled. "Tell me what you know—*right damn now*—or so help me God, I'll put a whammy on you that'll make the Hag's tinkering seem like child's play."

"Easy." Evan's eyes widened. "No need to get testy."

"This isn't me being testy. This is me being *nice*." Cassie jabbed him in the chest with the end of her finger for emphasis. "But my nice is wearing thin. You think you've been unlucky so far?" *Jab.* "Everything you try, every venture, no matter how small, will go straight in the crapper. You'll lose your shirt, your home, your money. Relationships?" *Jab.* "Nada. You'll be a pariah. Hounded and run out of town on a rail. Your health?" *Jab.* "I'll curse you with a case of the backdoor trots so bad the CDC will declare you a one-man outbreak and quarantine you to protect the public."

Evan stared at her. "Jesus. And I thought your mama was scary."

"Oh, I'm just getting started. That thing between your legs? When I'm done, you won't be able to find it with tweezers and an electron microscope."

"It's a hunch, okay? Conall will have my head if I yap."

"And I'll have your head if you don't. Rock, meet hard place."

The temperature in the room plummeted, and frost coated the walls and floor.

"What the—" Cassie released Evan and looked around.

"Captain Ice Dick, unless I'm mistook." Eyeing her like a snake, Evan eased out of reach. "The artic-waste routine is Conall's calling card, the big show-off. Why don't you ask *him* why your boyfriend's not healing?"

"I intend to. And Duncan's not my boyfriend."

"Never try to bullshit a bullshitter, lady. You just threatened to micro-dick me. Trust me, you're emotionally involved."

Cassie flushed. "It's not like that. We're just—"

"Friends? Keep telling yourself that. Bee-tee-dubs, Duncan hasn't got friendship in mind. He's in *lurv*." Evan made a face. "Told him women are more trouble than they're worth, but he wouldn't listen. You can't tell a demon hunter dick."

Conall materialized with Taryn before Cassie could think of a snappy comeback. It wasn't like that. Really. She and Duncan had history. They were ... frenemies? Exes with baggage? Former flames?

Shrugging off her discomfiture, she turned to address her guests. The captain of the Dalvahni was dark-haired with cold, black eyes. Powerfully built, he radiated a ruthless, implacable energy that screamed authority. Unlike Duncan, he wore his hair short. Jeans and a black shirt that said *Chez Beck's* on the front were molded to his hard, muscular frame.

A huge warrior accompanied Conall and Taryn. Grim Dalvahni was a giant of a man, with long, reddish-brown hair the color of autumn leaves and eyes like beaten gold. Like Conall, he was dressed in jeans. A gray T-shirt stretched across his massive chest.

"Big 'Un. Long time no see." Evan jerked his chin at the huge warrior. "Cassie, this is Grim, the one I was telling you about. Grim, meet Cassandra Ferguson."

"Milady." The warrior had a voice like distant thunder. He eyed Cassie curiously. "I have heard much of you from Duncan."

Cassie didn't have to look at Evan. She could *feel* him smirking.

"You have?" She colored. "I mean . . . how do you do?"

"How do I do what?"

"Oh, for the Lord's—" Evan rolled his eyes. "Sometimes, Big 'Un, you are such a putz."

"I thank you for the compliment." Grim inclined his head. "In Yarthac, the word 'strikynpussle' means 'shining one.'"

"No shit? It means something entirely different here."

"Enough." Conall's hard gaze was on Duncan's battered, unconscious form. "What mischief is this?"

"Demons," Evan said. "Whole passel of them. Our boy looks rough, doesn't he?"

In a blur of movement too fast to follow, Conall grabbed Evan by the neck and shook him. "He is not your 'boy.' He is a Dalvahni warrior, ancient and powerful, defender of the light and shield of the weak. You think this amusing? By the sword, if you had any part in this, you will be wearing your guts for garters."

"Love you, too, bro," Evan wheezed, plucking at Conall's hands. "Nice . . . to know . . . the fam jam . . . has my back."

Conall's white teeth flashed in a snarl. "We are not family, varlet." He gave Evan another shake. "Why does my brother not heal? Answer me."

"Enough, Conall. You misjudge him. 'Tis not his doing."

Everyone turned to stare at the bed. Duncan was awake, his golden-brown eyes dulled by pain and fever. "Evan saved my life today." He tried to push himself to a sitting position and failed. "Twice, in point of fact. I am in his debt."

Conall flung Evan aside. "Is this true?"

"Yeah. I'm a bona fide hero." Sneering, Evan got to his feet. "Chaps your ass, don't it, bro? Duncan got attacked by demons, and I monstered out—"

"You released the ogre?" Grim scowled in disapproval. "That was unwise."

"I've already had this discussion with Duncan. It happens, Big 'Un, okay?"

Conall noticed Verbena and strode up to her. "Verbena, where have you been? Rebekah has been frantic with worry."

Verbena blushed. "I'm terrible sorry to have worried her, Mr. Conall, but I had to leave. Them Skinners is after me."

"Rebekah and I can protect you."

She shook her head. "I caused you enough trouble. You got your hands full, what with the new baby a-comin', and the restaurant, and Hank lightin' out."

"You will come home with me," Conall said in a take-no-prisoners tone. "We will discuss it."

Verbena blanched but held firm. "You know I thinks the world of you and Beck, Mr. Conall, and I'm more grateful 'n I can say for all you done, but my mind's made up." She gave Cassie a sidelong glance. "'Sides, Miz Cassie needs me. Ain't that right, miss?"

"What?" Cassie had been listening with half an ear, her worried gaze on Duncan. "Yes, of course." She jerked her attention to Conall. "I'd like Verbena to stay with me, if that's all right with you and Beck."

Conall bowed. "Verbena is a free agent. We will miss her sunny presence, but the decision is hers. I will inform Rebekah."

Duncan groaned, ending the discussion. He made another valiant effort to sit up in bed and collapsed against the bank of pillows. "Captain, I have grievous news," he said, his breathing labored. "I have seen the rogue, and he is—" He gasped and arched his back in pain. Bloody streaks of infection snaked across his arms and chest. "Rogue . . ." His face was blotched and gray. He groaned and twisted in agony. "Know him . . . Must—"

With a strangled gasp, Duncan slumped against the pillows and was still.

Heedless of his leaking wounds, Cassie threw herself on top of him. "Duncan?" She grabbed him by the shoulders and shook him. "Open your eyes, Duncan. Wake up, damn you."

Grim lifted her from the bed and set her aside as easily as if she were a child. "Fear not for my brother. No demon mischief can withstand the combined magic of the Dal and the Kir."

Cassie nodded and stumbled out of the way, giving the demon hunters access to Duncan. Evan moved to stand beside her at the end of the bed. Numbly, Cassie joined him. She felt a tentative touch on her arm and turned.

Verbena stood at her side, her violet eyes swimming with tears. "He looks bad, miss." The girl's mouth trembled. "Is he gon' die?"

A tear trickled down Cassie's face. Angrily, she wiped it away. "I'll kick him into next week if he does."

As they watched, the trio of demon hunters gathered around Duncan and held out their hands. Green light emanated from them, enveloping Duncan. As the light eddied and pulsed around him, the sores began to heal, the hideous red lines fading to pink and slowly receding.

Verbena clutched Cassie's arm. "Look, Miz Cassie. It's working."

"Yes, I do believe you're right." Slowly, Cassie released the breath she'd been holding. "His wounds do seem to be—"

The streaks pulsed in a sickening fashion and turned black, slithering across Duncan's limp form like hideous worms. His eyes flew open, starting in their sockets. With a horrible gurgle, he convulsed, his big body bouncing on the bed in wrenching spasms. White foam flecked his lips.

The vise around Cassie's heart and lungs tightened. They were losing him. On impulse, she grabbed Verbena's hand and opened her mind, reaching for the magic.

It was a simple ritual, one she'd done countless times by rote. Of late, though, she'd found it increasingly hard to concentrate, and the magic had been elusive. There was no time to fetch a staff to channel the magic, and that worried her. She fully expected the exercise to be a struggle, but today, it was like old times. The power flooded through her in an unbroken rush—her blood sang with it—and the energy flowing from her merged with that of the Dalvahni.

"By the sword," Grim swore as the light they projected deepened from a pale green to deep jade.

The loathsome threads of sickness infecting Duncan's body disintegrated and his unsightly sores healed and disappeared. He sat up with a shuddering gasp, his broad chest heaving, and looked around, his gaze lucid and fever-free. "Sweet Kehv, but you are a gloomy lot," he said. "Why the long faces?"

"My brother." Conall's implacable gaze softened. "It is good to see you recovered. You had us worried."

Cassie regarded Duncan anxiously. Conall was right. Duncan seemed in fine fettle, his once-ravaged skin smooth, sun-kissed, and gleaming with health. A force field of strength and well-being surrounded him, and he vibrated with energy. The combination of Dalvahni woo-woo, her magic, and a dash of the enhancer had restored him, and then some.

Duncan grinned and stretched. "Strewth, but I am famished. What is there to eat?"

His announcement swept away the last of Cassie's doubts. "He's hungry," she said, her lips stretching in a grin so broad it threatened to swallow her ears. "Praise the Lord, I think he'll live."

A wave of sudden dizziness swept over her. Wobbling to the big chair by the window, she sat down.

"Miz Cassie," Verbena cried, fluttering around Cassie's chair. "Help me, somebody. She's done fell out."

Whoosh. Duncan crossed the room, knocking Evan aside. Cassie felt rather than saw him move. There was a slight, almost imperceptible displacement of air, and Duncan was at her side, hunkered at her knees, more than six feet of bare-chested, iron-hard, half-naked male.

"Hey," Evan protested. "Run me over, why don't you?"

Duncan grunted something that might have been an apology and gazed at Cassie, his golden-brown eyes filled with concern. "Cassandra, you are well?"

Cassie raised a trembling hand to her forehead. "Fine. Too much excitement and no breakfast, I think."

"Coming to my aid on the heels of battling a demon has depleted your strength." Duncan's deep voice held censure. "'Twas foolish of you in the extreme."

"Well, excuse me." Cassie's bosom swelled. "Verbena and I saved your *life*, ingrate."

"Termagant," Duncan said without heat. Turning to Verbena, he said, "Repair to the kitchen at once and fetch me a glass of fruit extract from the cold box."

Verbena gaped at him. "Huh?"

"He means orange juice," Cassie said. "There's a container in the fridge."

"Oh." Verbena blinked. "Sure nuff."

She loped out of the room and quickly returned with a jelly jar full of OJ. "Brung you the one with Bugs on it," she told Cassie shyly. "He's m' fave."

"Mine, too," Cassie said. "Bugs is the man."

Frowning, Duncan took the glass from Verbena. "Who is this Bugs?"

Good Lord, he was jealous of Bugs Bunny.

"A cartoon rabbit with attitude and a smarmy mouth," Cassie said, her lips quivering.

His eyes went unfocused momentarily, then cleared. He examined the figure on the glass. "You refer to an anthropomorphic character drawn in a humorously exaggerated way, known for his flippant repartee and insouciant mien. He appeals to your sense of the ridiculous?"

"Big-time."

"I should like very much to meet him."

"Duncan, he's a *cartoon*. He's not real." She blinked at a sudden thought. "Is he?"

"Nay. I dicketh with you, as Evan would say."

"Wrong," Evan said. "That is so *not* how Evan would say it."

"No?" Duncan's gaze did not waver from Cassie. "The Provider is sometimes inaccurate." He held the glass to her lips. "No more talk. Drink."

He was using the Voice, the stern don't-mess-with-me tone he used when in warrior mode, but his eyes were alight with something—was it tenderness? Warmth?—that made her heart give a funny little jerk.

Waves of panic lapped at her belly. Yesterday, she and Duncan had been at odds, separated by their painful past. Today, they were . . .

Well, she wasn't sure *what* they were, and it terrified her. She wanted to go back to the way they'd been before. Wary. Distant.

Sorry, toots. That hat won't go back in the box.

Scowling to cover her discomposure, she snatched the glass from him and drained it. "There. Satisfied?"

"Not even a little, but I doubt we mean the same thing."

Evan sniggered. "Hello. We're still here."

Cassie barely heard him. Duncan's gaze had heated from warm to scorching hot. She looked away, her pulse doing the jitterbug. Duncan wanted her. It was there, in his eyes. She wanted him, too, and she wasn't going to beat herself up about it. She was only human.

No, she was *half* human, and therein lay the rub. Her other half was demon, a hedonistic voluptuary intent on gratification and feel-good, and Duncan was a Dalvahni candy store stuffed to the brim with promised delights. Her human half screamed that candy was bad for her. Her demon half pressed its nose to the window and salivated at the scrumptious display.

Cassie couldn't blame her demon. The guy was temptation walking.

Duncan seemed to guess her tumbled thoughts. He smoothed the crease between her brows with the tip of one finger. "Do not distress yourself. I have waited long for you. I will abide, my love."

Panic welled, swallowing her. "How many times do I have to tell you? I'm not your love."

Conall interrupted them. "I must away, Duncan. In your extremis, you mentioned the rogue. What news have you?"

The warm twinkle in Duncan's eyes died, replaced by something more like sorrow or dread. Turning, he strode across the room to answer Conall's summons. Evan had retreated to the door of the bedroom. One shoulder propped against the frame, he watched Taryn like he was diabetic and she was a particularly tasty, sugary snack he longed to eat, even though he knew it would be bad for him, maybe even fatal.

Cassie could sympathize. Totally.

"—meet with you anon," Duncan was saying to Conall. "'Tis a matter best discussed elsewhere."

Evan pushed away from the door frame, lines of bitterness creasing his mouth. "Meaning without me. God forbid you let the low-life demonoid into your precious little club."

"For once, we are in complete agreement," Conall said. "Of a certainty, you are not to be trusted." His black gaze remained on Duncan, unyielding, ruthless. "Your discretion does you credit, brother, but you need not scruple. Evan knows of the traitor."

"Even so, Captain, I would speak of this another time." Duncan's voice was low, urgent. "My reluctance springs from another concern."

"Set it aside, warrior. I would hear what you have to say, and now."

"I would hear your tidings, as well," Taryn said. "The rogue has led me a merry chase."

"Captain," Duncan said, glancing at Grim, "I beg you would—"

"Speak, warrior," snapped Conall. "That is an order."

"As you command," Duncan said in a toneless voice. "I saw the rogue today in the company of demons. 'Twas clear he is their ally . . . nay, their leader. When I challenged him, the foul things came to his aid and abetted his escape."

Grim clenched his huge fists, his expression hungry. "Name him. I would know this betrayer."

"The traitor is Gryffin." Duncan's jaw tightened. "He lives."

"Curse you, Duncan, you dare jest about *this*?" Grim said. "You go too far. Gryffin is dead. I buried him myself . . . or what was left of him. I buried his *head*."

"Curse me until the stars fade from the sky. It changes nothing. I know not how we have been deceived, but Gryffin lives."

Grim threw back his head and roared, the veins bulging on his neck. Without warning, he disappeared.

"Gryffin was our best and our brightest," Conall said. "You are quite certain of this, Duncan?"

"Aye. We stood face-to-face, I and the betrayer. There can be no doubt."

Conall's harsh features hardened. "Then Gryffin has deceived us, and most foully. I will see him dead for his treachery."

"Not if Grim gets to him first," Evan said. "Did you see his face? He was steamed. Lay you odds he goes after the rogue himself."

"I think not," Taryn said, unruffled. "The rogue is mine, and I will brook no interference."

"But surely you see that this changes everything?" said Conall. "The betrayer has been revealed. Grim cannot be allowed the pursuit, this I grant you—the rogue is his twin." His expression hardened. "As captain of the Dalvahni, the task falls to me."

"You took an oath before Kehvahn and signed the Great Book," Taryn pointed out. "Would you be foresworn, same as the betrayer?"

Conall gave the huntress a withering look and departed in a howling flurry of wind and snow.

Chapter Fourteen

Evan shook the snow from his silky black hair. "Always with the special effects, that guy. Way to piss him off, Red."

"'Twas not mine intent to anger him," Taryn said. "'Twas mine intent to clarify the situation."

"Oh, you clarified it." Evan rubbed his hands together in unholy glee. "You clarified the shit out of it. Pulled the honor card and kicked him in the balls. That burned his onions."

Taryn frowned. "I got nowhere near the captain's bollocks. Nor do I see what onions, burnt or otherwise, have to do with it."

"It's like this, see. Conall's itching to go after the rogue, but his hands are tied, and he's mad as fire about it."

"He may be chafed at present, but the captain is a wise leader. He will realize that mine is the better course, and soon. 'Tis no easy thing to slay a brother."

Evan's smiled faded. "Yeah? Guess this is it, and you'll be taking off."

Cassie got to her feet. The orange juice had kicked in, and the worst of the dizziness had subsided. "I wouldn't be in a hurry to go anywhere, if I were you," she said to the huntress. "If Evan's right and Hannah *is* some kind of supernatural magnet, the rogue will be back."

"Cassandra makes a salient point," Duncan said. "Whate'er has drawn the rogue here will prompt his return. If he has left at all."

"That was my thought as well," Taryn said, a tad too quickly. "I must ascertain he no longer frequents this locale, else I am inefficient."

Evan leaned against the wall, regarding her with hooded eyes. "So now you're staying?"

"For a time," Taryn said, looking away. "Logic dictates I seek the rogue here ere I seek him elsewhere. 'Tis my duty to be thorough."

He yawned. "Sure. Whatev."

"I thought you would be pleased, not out of sorts."

"Who, me? I'm not ticked. Demon hunter's gotta do what a demon hunter's gotta do." He lifted his shoulders in an indifferent shrug. "Go. Stay. It's all the same."

Something flickered across Taryn's lovely face but was quickly masked. "Dissembler," she said, and stalked from the room.

Evan stood motionless for a moment, then cursed and went after her. "Hey, Red, wait up." He broke into a run. "Godammit, Red. *Red.*"

"Wow," Cassie said when they'd gone. "Hard to tell if those two want to fight or hit the sack."

Duncan's lips twitched. "The two things are not necessarily mutually exclusive."

She met his gaze. Suddenly, the room became hot and airless, and the floor tilted beneath her feet.

Breakfast, Cassie thought. *I should have eaten breakfast.*

Two magical outbursts in less than an hour had sapped her strength. That explained her sudden wooziness. It had *nothing* to do with the sensual promise in Duncan's eyes, or the fact that his gaze was setting her skin on fire and heating her blood to a slow simmer.

The demon in her liked the way he looked at her. The demon liked his hella hard body and his oh-so-kissable mouth. The demon wanted to take him up on his unspoken invitation and screw him stupid. Then again, the demon didn't have a heart to be broken. Sure, Duncan was mouthwateringly delicious, and she wanted him so bad her bones ached, but she had a choice. She could stick her head in that buzz saw—again—or she could walk away.

Being of sound mind and body and possessing a healthy sense of self-preservation, she would walk away.

Cassie considered herself a work in progress. No day was wasted, in her estimation, if she learned something. Today, she'd learned several things. One: Verbena was the genuine article. She really was the enhancer.

Two: when casting an animation spell, it behooved a mage to install a timer . . . unless one enjoyed chasing after a runaway bronze statue.

Three: Duncan was her Achilles' heel. She could huff and puff and pretend indifference until the cows came home, but she still cared about him.

He'd nearly died, dammit, and that had scared her shitless. Which proved she was right to shy away from him. Only a fool would open herself up to that kind of hurt a second time, and Cassandra Ferguson McKenna was nobody's fool.

Walk away, she told herself. *Wish him well and walk away. Keep body and soul intact.*

"Tell you what I think," Verbena said, glancing between them. "I think if the ferret-mones got any thicker in here, you could cut 'em with a knife and serve 'em like cheese."

Cassie dragged her gaze from Duncan's. "What?"

"Plain as the nose on my face you two is sweet on one another." Verbena sidled like a startled crab for the door. "Think I'll take a shower, Miz Cassie, if'n it's all right. I smell like stewed polecat."

Cassie closed her sagging mouth. "You know where everything is. Make yourself at home. And for God's sake, call me Cassie."

"Sure thang, Miz . . . er . . . I mean, Cassie." Verbena nodded and darted out, leaving Cassie and Duncan alone.

"Sometimes, Verbena says the darndest things," Cassie mumbled.

Duncan didn't answer. Stood there looking at her, letting her twist in the wind, damn him. He knew she was flustered.

Gloss over it. Yep, that was the best thing. Glide past the elephant in the room like it wasn't wearing a sequined thong and stripper heels.

"If you'll excuse me, I'm going to follow Verbena's example and shower." She backed toward the bathroom. "Exploded demon smells like rancid bacon and charred brussels sprouts. Who knew?"

The fact that she hadn't noticed the stench until now said a hell of a lot about her day. And it was barely past eight-thirty.

Duncan remained silent. If she was smart, she'd keep going. Curiosity, however, got the better of her, and she darted a glance at him. Big mistake. His gaze was a simmering mixture of amusement, tenderness, and undisguised longing.

It wasn't fair, Cassie thought with a flash of indignation. One look from Duncan Dalvahni, and she was down for the count.

No. She would *not* let him do this to her. She was not a schoolgirl to be toyed with. She was a woman grown, seasoned by time and tempests. She'd lived through wars and famines and droughts, hurricanes and cyclones.

Hell with that. She'd learned how to operate the remote control. She would look him in the eye and stand firm.

Or . . . maybe not.

Casting pride to the wind, she turned to flee, but Duncan's words stopped her.

"I want you, Cassandra." His voice was liquid silk. "I burn for you. 'Tis a wonder my bones did not turn to ash years ago from longing. But I meant what I said. I will abide, howe'er long it takes. A year. A century. Ten. It matters not. I will wait."

Cassie was trembling. Taking a deep breath, she turned to face him. "Let me get this straight. If I don't take you back, you'll build a willow cabin at my gate and weave my name in song until I go mad or relent?"

"Strictly speaking, I would be across the river, not at your gate. And while I suppose a willow cabin would do, I had something more substantial in mind. Something with a roof and running water."

"I noticed." Cassie pressed her lips together. "Your construction crew's been at it pretty much nonstop. It must be costing you a fortune."

"Money is of no moment to the Dal, but my apologies if the noise has disturbed you," Duncan said. "The work shall be done, and soon." He paused, his expression thoughtful. "I confess, weaving your name in song had not occurred to me. Should you like it?"

"*No.*" Good Lord, she was shouting. Cassie closed her eyes and opened them again. "I'd *like* you to see reason and go away. We're no good for each other."

"I could go away, I suppose, but I would only return." His mouth twisted in an expression of self-mockery. "I fear I am a pathetic creature where you are concerned."

Cassie gazed at him in mingled panic and exasperation. There was nothing pathetic about him. He was wily and clever, and tenacious in the extreme. He would never give up, stubborn Dalvahni that he was. The harder she resisted, the more he would take it as a challenge.

He was confusing love with lust. He didn't know her, and he sure as hell didn't love her. He was living in a dream world of yesterday that could never be recreated.

Lust she could relate to; she wanted him, too, something fierce. Oh, she had put up a good fight, but the morning's unnerving events had laid bare the truth. So, where did that leave them? An affair—an affair was the logical solution to their problem, in a hair-of-the-dog-that-bit-you kind of way. They would get this *thing*, whatever it was, out of their systems, once and for all. Scratch that maddening itch and move on.

"Attraction has never been the problem," she said, taking the plunge. "I find you irresistible, too, so why fight it? Let's have sex."

He blinked, and Cassie felt a ping of satisfaction. She'd thrown him. Good.

"Friends with benefits, you know?" She gave him a bright smile. "Want to go for a roll in the hay? After I defunk, of course."

"A roll in the hay?" His gaze grew unfocused, then cleared. "You wish to engage in coitus with me?"

Duncan looked poleaxed, like he couldn't believe his ears. Served him right. He'd been driving her out of her mind for months. Sitting across the river, taunting her, teasing her with his gorgeous body and his laughing eyes.

"Plain, uncomplicated sex," she said. "Two consenting adults enjoying one another's bodies. No mushy stuff. No jealousy or insecurity. Sex, and no strings."

"In short, you would be my thrall?"

His *thrall*? Noooo, that wasn't what she'd had in mind, but . . .

Cassie had a sudden vision of herself naked and at Duncan's mercy, his big body moving over her, in her. Something hot and achy unfurled inside her.

His gaze was on her throat, on her rapidly beating pulse. He *knew* his effect on her, damn him.

"Cassandra? You wish to be my thrall?"

"Yeah. Sure." Her voice was husky, and she cleared her throat. "And you'll be mine."

"For how long?"

Cassie shrugged. "As long as it takes. Then we move on."

"Agreed, but with one condition." His eyes, usually filled with so much warmth and laughter, were flinty. "I do not share. I have exclusive use of your body while the agreement holds."

"Of course," she said, striving to sound nonchalant, though her stomach was doing a roller-coaster free fall. "On the condition that I have exclusive use of yours. Deal?"

He gazed at her, his expression stoic. "Very well, fornication it shall be. No emotion. No promises."

It was Cassie's turn to blink. She hadn't expected him to agree. He'd called her bluff, damn him, and she wasn't sure how she felt about that.

"But I give you fair warning," he said. "I mean to ride you hard and often." He looked her up and down, stripping her. "Until I get bored and move on."

He turned and strode away.

"Wait," Cassie said. "Where are you going?"

He stopped in the doorway and looked back. "To the kitchen to prepare a repast."

"Don't you want to talk? About . . . you know . . ." Cassie gazed at him in frustration. "Our agreement?"

"Talking is overrated, and I would have you rebuild your strength. It has been a long time since I slaked my lust in the House of Pleasure. A *very* long time. I mean to make the most of our bargain."

He walked out, leaving Cassie rooted to the spot.

She started at an alarming thought. "Hey," she shouted after him, "the stove is electric. Don't even *think* about building a fire in my kitchen. I mean it."

There was no answer. She should probably go after him, make sure he didn't burn the house down, but she needed to cool off.

I give you fair warning. I mean to ride you hard and often . . .

Sweet Blessed Holy Mother of God, what had she done? Had she lost her mind? She'd agreed to a fling with Duncan. On what planet had she thought that was a good idea?

Planet I-Wanna-Tap-That? the squeam said. *You've been drooling over the guy for months. Screw him stupid and move on. Think of it as a purge.*

"Yeah." Cassie took a deep breath. "I'm doing it for my health."

Exactly.

Having momentarily set at least part of her mind at ease, Cassie's thoughts circled back to the waiting shower. As she turned to head for the bathroom, a short, blond woman materialized on a blast of lemony perfume. She was Safari Jane on the prowl in a khaki mini-dress with a plunging neckline, gold cord lacing, and short, cuffed sleeves. A chin-length bob swung beneath the brim of her straw safari hat, and its leopard-print band matched the wide belt at her hips. Short leopard-print boots with five-inch heels adorned her tiny feet.

The woman looked solid enough, but upon closer inspection, a faint, glowing outline betrayed her true nature. With a ripple of shock, Cassie realized she was looking at a ghost—a bitchy one, if appearances did not deceive. The ghost had the spare, stretched look of an exercise fanatic and perpetual dieter, and there was a nasty sparkle in her blue eyes.

The ghost's belligerent gaze roved over Cassie, taking in her unkempt condition. "Who are you, and why are you covered in pot roast?"

"It's not pot roast," Cassie said. "It's demon goo, and you don't want to know."

"You got that right," the ghost said. "I don't give a shit about your sorry excuse for a life. What I *am* interested in is answers. Like, who are you?" She glanced at the white gold Cartier watch on her wrist. "Make it snappy, sister. I'm on the clock, and time is money."

Cassie stared at the waspish specter. She was no expert on ghosts, but this one clearly had issues. Unresolved issues that made her cranky and unpredictable. The monstrous, egg-laying queen of the parasitoids in *Alien* had a sunnier disposition than this chick.

"I'm Cassandra Ferguson, and this is my house." Cassie was tired, and she *really* wanted a shower—or three. "Who are you, and what do you want?"

"Meredith Starr Peterson. Of *the* Petersons." The ghost whipped out a business card that briefly read *Bitchin' Banshee Services: We're Scary Good* in glowing letters before it disappeared. "The Randall alpha has lost something."

"Zeb hired you to find Mac? Oh, dear. I tried to call him last night, but I couldn't get through. I asked Toby to let Zeb know that Mac . . ." She swallowed, belatedly remembering the beheaded carcass marinating in her truck. "That Mac is . . . um . . . here."

"Mac?" Meredith made a noise like a leaky radiator. "Who the hell's Mac?"

"Zeb's nephew."

"A twat goblin?" The ghost sneered. "Are you freaking kidding me? I'm not here to find some stupid brat."

"Mac isn't a child." Thinking of Mac made Cassie sad. He'd had a lot of years ahead of him, and possibilities, and now he was dead. "He is—was—a young man."

"Was?" Meredith's eyes narrowed to slits. "What do you mean, *was?*"

Cassie drew herself up. "That's between me and Zeb. If you're not here about Mac, why did Zeb hire you?"

"I never said he hired me. I said he was looking for something. Something very special. Heard about it on the network, and I mean to find it."

"You mean like the Internet?"

Meredith rolled her eyes. "No, dimwad. The Ghost Network. I find the alpha's missing article, and my rep as a Finder is made." She dug her manicured nails into the palms of her hands. "I *need* this case."

Cassie eyed the ghost curiously. "Why? You're a ghost."

"You breathers are all alike. You think because we're dead, we don't have needs. You try staring eternity in the face with nothing to do. See how you like it."

"Go haunt something," Cassie suggested. "That's what ghosts do, right? That should keep you busy for a few centuries."

Meredith's face stretched in a ghoulish mask. "I've been banished from my haunt, Slop Bucket. Bitchin' Banshee's all I've got." Her neck stretched like taffy, and she shoved her hideous face closer to Cassie. "Enough talk. Where is it? I know it was here. The damn thing leaves a trail a blind beagle with a head cold could follow."

"Sorry. No idea what you're talking about."

"Gonna play dumb, huh?" The ghost's neck retracted with the metallic snap of an industrial measuring tape. "Don't think you've seen the last of me. I'll be back."

"This is my house," Cassie objected. "You can't come and go as you please."

"Oh, yeah? Try and stop me." Meredith's eyes glittered with malice. "Mer-Mer is on the job. I'll be watching you."

The ghost dissolved with an audible pop, leaving a citrus cloud in her wake.

Chapter Fifteen

Evan flung open the back door and stepped onto the battle-damaged porch. From the distance came a muffled scrape and the steady beat of hammers. Someone was building something, and not too far away. Across the river, maybe?

Didn't matter. Evan shrugged off the noise and looked around for Taryn. Gone, dammit to hell. Good riddance, right? Red was a prickly, pain-in-the-ass, stuck-up, holier-than-thou do-gooder. And those were her good points.

So why the hell did he like her so much?

Whoa. He didn't like Red. She drove him nuts. They were too different. He was earth, and she was fire.

Oh, she tried to hide it, the heat, but it was there, buried beneath the thick layers of ice like some damn dormant polar volcano. He was something of a hand at hiding things himself, so he'd seen through her act almost at once. She was a challenge, Miss Sober Sides, and he enjoyed ruffling her feathers.

Harmless, right? He'd thought so, but somehow, she'd wormed past his defenses and gotten under his skin while he wasn't looking.

Aw, hell. He'd broken his number-one rule and gotten attached. To a demon hunter, no less. Of all the self-destructive dumbassery, that took the prize. Evan Beck, poster child for idiots. He might as well take a nap on a railroad track or sleep in the rain with his mouth open.

But it wasn't too late. He didn't *have* to be a schmuck. He'd never let a woman turn him inside out, and he wasn't about to start now, even if the woman in question had eyes the color of a summer storm.

She had *really* nice eyes. Too tall and skinny, though. He'd never gone for the model type. Nice legs, he had to admit—long and lean and strong, and a mouth that made a man think dirty thoughts. Her mouth was a work of art, full and tender. Made for kissing—a real honeypot when she wasn't riled about something. When she was ticked, which was most of the time, she pulled her lips so tight you couldn't pry them apart with a crowbar.

Evan grinned. Man, he loved to get her goat. It gave him a real kick, the way her eyes flashed and her expression would get all stiff and disapproving. He was going to miss their little spats when she finished the rogue job and left Hannah for good.

He was going to miss *her*.

His smile faded. He didn't want Red to leave. He wanted—

His mind shied away from the half-formed thought. Resolutely, he focused on the real issue. Red had called him a liar and given him the brush-off. No way he was letting her have the last word. She couldn't have gone far, not with the rogue still out there. He'd find her, read her beads for whale shit, then wish her good hunting and walk away, a man in control.

He rolled his neck and shoulders. Yeah. See how she liked them apples.

Lifting his head, he took a lingering sniff and caught Red's unmistakable scent on the breeze. She was in the woods. She hadn't warped off to Middle Earth or disappeared into the never-never in pursuit of the rogue. She was still here.

Something that had been stretched tight to the breaking point inside him relaxed. Not that he cared what she did. Hell, no. He was determined to set her straight, that was all.

He shifted into his go-to animal, a rangy bluetick coonhound, and set off into the forest. The hound's sense of smell was incredible, and the woods were a sensory buffet. His nose caught the scents of pine needles, dust, damp earth, wild mushrooms, and rotting leaves, logs, and bracken. Pale, stubby flowers with three petals and a lemony scent grew beneath the towering trees. The hound nuzzled them without interest. He was on the hunt for something else, something sweeter and more elusive.

He trotted deeper into the woods, moving his head this way and that. His sensitive nose twitched—there, the faint hint of violets mingled with frost and warm female. He had her now.

He took off with a drawling bay, his paws kicking up leaves as he bounded through the woods and tracked her to a tiny glade carpeted in ferns, wood sorrel, bead lilies, and deer's tongue. Sunlight speared the woodland floor in splintered beams. At the edge of the little clearing, dogwoods grew in the shadows of oak and elm, like timid children clinging to their mother's legs, and blue mistflowers displayed downy blooms.

He crept closer and saw Taryn. She knelt in a shaft of light in the center of the glade, her lean form graceful and proud. She was praying, her slender arms raised in silent supplication. Her back was to him, and her legs and feet were blanketed in white clover, her face raised to the forest's green roof. Her eyes were closed, and she'd unbound her hair. The deep red locks brushed her trim hips. Seeing her hair loose gave Evan a strange, hollow feeling, like a starving man looking at a rich man's feast he was forbidden to touch.

He hunkered down in a thick bank of ferns to wait, taking care to make no sound. But to his annoyance, she lowered her arms almost at once and turned her head slightly, as though sensing his presence. His rankling suspicion was confirmed when she turned and looked directly at his hiding place.

"You can stop lurking," she said, rising in a lithe movement. "I know you are there."

Busted, he thought, *but we'll see who has the last laugh.* He would string her along. Play the friendly pooch. Then, when he had her wrapped around his paw, he'd shift. Man, oh, man, he couldn't wait to see her face when he shed his doggy disguise.

He sprang up and trotted into the clearing, head high and muzzle parted in a toothy grin. He circled her, tail wagging, and waited for a welcoming pat or a scruff of the ears. This shit worked every time—chicks loved dogs.

To his surprise, she folded her arms and gazed down at him without interest. His tail drooped, and he eyed her uneasily. Holy shit, was Red one of *those*, a person who didn't like dogs?

And then she spoke, knocking him for a loop. "Evan," she said in a cold, flat tone. "Why do you follow me when you have made your disdain abundantly clear?"

She knew who he was? Holy freaking shit.

He was so startled that he shifted involuntarily. The damn clown pants reappeared as soon as he returned to human form. At least the dog got to have some dignity.

"You knew?" he said, staring at her in dismay. "What gave me away?"

Was he losing his touch? This was bad. This was *real* bad.

"No need to look so perturbed. Your transmutation was complete."

He scowled. "Then how?"

She regarded him for a moment, as though turning something over in her mind, before she spoke. "It is true, is it not, that the kith possess varying talents?"

"Yeah. So?"

"The Kir and the Dal are likewise endowed with different abilities."

"And you pulled some kind of X-ray vision out of the goody bag that lets you see past a shifter's form?" The thought made him feel exposed, naked in a way that being without clothes didn't.

"'Tis a bit more complicated than that." She regarded him steadily. "I see a person's true self. I was chosen to apprehend the rogue because of my particular gift. I can look into the heart of the betrayer, see the essence of the warrior, and judge him accordingly."

"Jury, judge, and executioner, huh? Nice."

"'Nice' is not an apt descriptor." She tilted her head, regarding him. "Would you like to know what I see when I look at you?"

His lip curled. "Don't bother. I can guess."

He knew what he was. It was there every time he looked in a mirror. Liar, thief, panderer, murderer. And his personal fave, the guy who'd tried to kill his own sister. He didn't blame Beck for hating him. He hated himself.

"Your vulgarity and biting wit are bravado you use to keep others at bay," Taryn said, as though he hadn't spoken. "But beneath your shield lurk anger and hate. Vulnerability, also." Her voice softened. "And pain. So much pain."

Evan tensed. "What a load of craptastic psychobabble, Red. You don't know shit."

She regarded him in her grave way. "You are wrong, Evan. I see you. I see the good and the bad. I see your loneliness and need."

"You got it all wrong. I don't need anybody. And that goes double for you."

He turned to stalk off, but her voice stopped him. "The ogre is your rage. If ever you hope to control him, you must first conquer yourself."

He whirled and strode back to her. He was angry, so angry. Light zigzagged at the edges of his vision, red as blood. "Yeah? Well, maybe I don't want to control him. Maybe I *like* the ogre." He was trembling with fury. "Nobody pushes the ogre around. Nobody beats him, or starves him, or buggers him. Nobody can make him do shitty things. And let me tell you, Miss Pure-and-Perfect, after a lifetime of having that shit sandwich shoved down my throat, that's a good thing." He grabbed her by the shoulders and gave her a little shake. "Now leave. Get out of here. Go find your goddamn rogue, and leave me the hell alone."

He tried to let her go. He really did. Everything in him screamed to push her away and run like hell. It was a matter of survival. Instead, he jerked her close and kissed her.

And the world dissolved like crumbling sand around him, and he was falling, falling into her volcano and heat. She tasted like rain. She tasted clean. She tasted like every good and perfect thing that had ever existed.

That mouth, that goddamn honeysuckle mouth was beyond anything he'd imagined. She was redemption, and he couldn't stop kissing her, not if his life had depended on it.

And maybe it did. Kissing Red was stupid. In a lifetime of screwups, hands down, the stupidest thing he'd ever done. He'd survived abandonment, enslavement, rejection, and torture, but he wouldn't survive this. Red was going to hurt him, bust him wide open and end him, but he didn't care. Even knowing she'd destroy him, he couldn't end that kiss. He would have stayed there forever, drinking her in like a man dying of thirst, fool that he was.

She was the one with the strength to end it, not he. She shoved him away and stepped back, her cheeks flushed and her gray eyes, usually knife-sharp and keen with intelligence, dazed. Poor Red. She'd been knocked ass over teakettle. Evan had a sneaking suspicion he looked the same way. He'd kissed Red—*Red*—and he'd liked it.

Liked it? He'd fucking *loved* it. He wanted to do it again. And again.

"I must away." Her fingers went to her lips, as though she could still feel him there. "I have my duty, and you would distract me."

Evan reached for her. "Wait, Red. I—"

She was gone. *Pfft*, into the ether, without warning or sound, without leaving so much as a sparkle in her wake.

Gone, without so much as a goddamn good-bye. Gone, and he had no idea where to find her, where to look, or even if he'd see her again.

Gone. She'd ripped the heart out of him and left him bleeding.

Evan threw his head back and howled.

Cassie blinked at the spot where the ghost had been a moment before. "Slop Bucket, am I?" she said, fuming at the acerbic ghost's insult. "We'll see about that."

She made a beeline for the master bath, vowing to add a ghost repellent spell to the wards around her house. Anxious to remove all traces of Mr. Lizard, she stripped out of her reeking clothes and deposited them in the trash can. The nauseating smell of roasted demon poured out of the receptacle, a stink so strong it was almost a solid. Cassie flung open the bathroom window, tossed the can outside, and headed for the shower.

Demon funk, it turned out, was pernicious. It took her two showers, a bar of orange soap, a box of baking soda, and a soak in the tub to get rid of it. By the time she'd washed and conditioned her hair the third time, she was ravenous and trembling with exhaustion.

She towel-dried her hair, balled it up in a knot with a clip, and smeared lotion on her body. Wrapping a dry towel around her like a sarong, she padded into the bedroom in search of clean clothes and skidded to a halt.

Duncan stood in the doorway, arms crossed, one broad shoulder against the frame. He was fully dressed in a white T-shirt, clean jeans, and boots. The T-shirt was form-fitting and left absolutely nothing to the imagination. Not that flight of fancy was needed. Cassie had seen Duncan in the altogether. The image of his hard, muscled body was permanently burned onto her retinas and imprinted on her mind.

"You changed clothes," she said, and immediately felt like an idiot.

"'Tis a small matter to replicate clothing, once the proper garb is identified so as not to attract undue attention."

"Replicate? You used magic?"

He shrugged. "Of course. It was nothing."

Cassie nodded. It didn't matter what he wore, he was glorious, and they were going to have sex. The thought sent a thousand butterflies dancing against her rib cage. She'd had other lovers over the years, but none of them compared to Duncan.

He straightened. "I would see what I have bargained for."

Expectancy tightened her nerves as he crossed the room. Stopping a few feet from her, he looked her up and down, slowly, starting at her feet, an agonizing perusal that left her breathless. His gaze moved up her bare legs to the curves of her bosom concealed beneath the towel and finally came to rest upon her face.

"The towel, thrall," he said. "Take it off."

"Now? But I—"

"A thrall does not argue. Take it off."

Cassie felt a flutter of uncertainty. She didn't know this pitiless, predatory stranger.

His lips curved in a humorless smile. "Changed your mind?"

She lifted her chin and reached for the towel tucked between her breasts, her heart kicking like a rabbit. "Not at all."

She unwound the towel and let it drop. He looked his fill, his gaze brushing her body like fingers. His unwavering scrutiny lingered on her breasts until her nipples tightened in response and gooseflesh rose on her skin, then moved with agonizing slowness to the blond hair at the juncture of her thighs. He walked around her, taking his time, assessing her without comment, his body so close to hers that she could feel the heat pouring off him, but he did not touch her.

By the time he'd finished his perusal, Cassie's pulse was pounding and her skin tingled with longing. *Touch me*, she wanted to beg. *Put your hands on me. Please.*

He did not. He made a full circle and came to stand in front of her. "Your breasts are fuller and your rump more luscious," he said in the dispassionate tone of someone discussing the weather. "Otherwise, your beauty remains unchanged and as remarkable as I remember. You will do."

"I'm delighted you approve," she snapped.

He reached up without warning and took the clip out of her hair. Her damp locks tumbled around her shoulders. "I like your hair down," he said. "In future, you will wear it that way."

Cassie glared at him, her temper rising. "This is Alabama, and it's hot. I'll wear it down in the bedroom. Agreed?"

"A thrall does not wrangle. A thrall seeks to please. And you mistakenly assume our coitus will be confined to the bedroom." His face was impassive. "Perhaps, if you please me, I will allow you this one concession."

"You're too good," Cassie said in a honeyed voice. "Where do you want me? The bed? The chair? The floor?"

He arched that infernal brow again. "The kitchen—the repast I prepared grows cold."

Turning on his heel, he strode from the room.

Chapter Sixteen

Cassie stared at the empty doorway, her cheeks burning with humiliation. What the hell did Duncan want? He blew hot and then cold. There was no pleasing him.

She spat out a command and motioned sharply with the heel of her hand. The bedroom door slammed with a satisfying thunk. In the nine months since he'd blown back into her life with hurricane force, disturbing her equanimity and cutting up her peace, Duncan had been a constant, nagging presence, like a floater at the periphery of her vision. She never knew when or where she might see him next—a startling appearance in the Sweet Shop where she happened to be enjoying a meat and three, or a casual meeting on the street or in a store—a seesaw of uncertainty that drove her crazy. Then he would disappear, drop off the face of the earth for weeks at a time, leaving her to wonder when he would come back.

If he would come back.

And that drove her crazy, too. Sooner or later, Duncan would reappear, and the cycle started all over again.

I love you, Cassandra. I burn for you, Cassandra. I will wait for you, Cassandra.

He wanted her. He'd made his desire plain countless times with tender words, heated glances, and teasing endearments. And when she'd finally thrown in the towel and admitted that she wanted him, too, he turned into a polar ice cap.

Why? Was he no longer interested, now that the chase was done? Some men—and women—were like that. They wanted what they wanted—until they got it, and then they didn't want it anymore.

Cassie considered the possibility and rejected it. Duncan wasn't human, and he sure as hell wasn't uninterested. He was no longer in control, and that made him furious.

Well, he could get over it, the big, medieval jerk. It was her way or the highway, and so she would tell him, right now. Yes, she cared about him. After today, she could no longer deny that reality, but caring about someone—not wanting them hurt or, God forbid, dead—was a far cry from being in love with them. The ardor she and Duncan had shared back in the day had been supernova hot, but it had burned itself out, leaving nothing but a smoking ruin.

Romance was out of the question, but sex? Sex was clean and uncomplicated. Sex was *fun*. A sexual relationship was what she wanted. What she had to offer. Take it or leave it. Final decision. No negotiations. No compromise. Sex—mind-blowing, *great* sex—but nothing more.

If his ego couldn't handle it, so be it.

Cassie marched to her dresser, retrieved clean panties and a bra, and put them on. Stomping into her walk-in closet, she jerked a clean T-shirt off a felt hanger with so much force the hanger snapped in two. Ignoring the dangling pieces, she snatched a laundered pair of shorts off the closet shelf and stepped into them.

Slipping on a pair of hiking sandals, she tramped out of the bedroom and into the hall, striding purposefully toward the kitchen. Her outrage lasted a few steps and faltered, her senses assaulted by the delightful fatty smell of frying bacon and the tantalizing aroma of freshly made pancakes. She inhaled. Dear God, did she smell maple syrup?

Her hunger, forgotten in the adrenaline rush of desire and outrage, returned with the bruising force of an offensive lineman. Her head roared, and the floorboards warped and pitched beneath her feet. Cassie swayed, and somehow Duncan was there, lifting her in his arms. He was very strong, she noticed absently, resting her head on his shoulder. He'd tied his hair back with a piece of leather, probably to keep it out of the way while he cooked. He had gorgeous hair, light brown shot through with tawny streaks, the color of honey or sunlight on autumn leaves.

She liked the way he smelled, too, woodsy and clean. If she turned her head a little, she could nuzzle his muscled neck. Would he taste as good as he smelled?

There was no time to find out. Duncan carried her into the kitchen and plunked her down at the farm table. With perfunctory efficiency, he set a plate, a knife and fork, and a glass of cold milk in front of her. The plate was laden with pancakes, golden-brown disks of yummy drizzled with syrup. Melted butter ran down the stack in rivulets, pooling on the plate in a maple buttery swirl. The bacon was nicely crisped, the way she liked it.

"Eat." Duncan's tone was cold as the wind off the North Sea. "You have depleted your strength, and your humors are out of balance."

That was a fancy way of saying her blood sugar was low. No surprise there. This wasn't her first magical rodeo. Magic sucked it out of you, and she'd had two big episodes in one day. She'd be fine once she ate.

She opened her mouth to tell him as much, and shut it again. He was wearing his granite face. Mr. Dalvahni was still ticked.

She picked up her fork. "This looks wonderful. Listen, about our . . . er . . . arrangement. We need to talk."

"A thrall does not talk. A thrall uses her mouth for other things." He turned and went back to the stove.

O-k-a-a-y. Fine. She had never been one to beat her head against a brick wall. She didn't feel like talking anyway. She was ravenous and the food smelled divine.

Steam wafted in feathery swirls from the stack of hotcakes. She sliced through the tender mound and brought the first forkful to her lips. The pancakes melted in her mouth, and the combination of butter and maple syrup sent a little zing of pleasure from her brain to the soles of her feet. She swallowed and took a bite of bacon. Some of the syrup had found its way across the plate and onto the brown strip. The combination of salty and sweet was heaven on the tongue.

Cassie made a noise of contentment and tucked in. She was on her second stack of pancakes when Verbena darted into the kitchen. The girl reminded Cassie of a yearling, all legs and knobby-limbed grace. Verbena didn't walk. She scurried, she dashed, she scooted, and she scampered, like some wild woodland creature.

Verbena had showered and donned her freshly laundered clothes. Her damp hair clung in wisps about her cheeks, and her feet were bare. Cassie suspected the girl wasn't in the habit of wearing shoes, whether from preference or neglect. Her huge, violet eyes scanned the kitchen in quick, nervous movements, like a deer wary of predators.

"Hoo-wee, something smells good," Verbena said. "They learn you how to cook in demon hunter school, Mr. D?"

"I am not entirely without ability." He motioned Verbena to the table and placed a loaded plate in front of her, then heaped two more plates for himself and sat down between Cassie and Verbena.

Cassie watched him through her lashes as he poured syrup over a mound of pancakes and started to eat. Although the scarred farm table seated eight, Duncan seemed to take up space for three men. He was a big guy, a warrior built for battle and mayhem, but it was more than that. He exuded a raw, primal energy and the gravitational effect of a planet.

If he was aware of her observance, he gave no sign, methodically working his way through a pile of pancakes big enough to choke a horse, along with a dozen pieces of bacon. He moved on to the second plate. Though he ate quickly and with unnerving focus, not so much as a droplet strayed from his fork or marred the pristine whiteness of his shirt. The guy had excellent table manners, Cassie had to give him that.

She returned her attention to her own food. By the time she'd finished eating, she felt much better. Her head still felt a little achy and she was tired, but the collywobbles were gone.

Verbena pushed her plate away with a satisfied sigh. "That was mighty good, Mr. Duncan." She jumped up and began busing the table with her characteristic quickness. "I'll do the dishes."

"Thank you, Verbena," Cassie said, getting to her feet. "You can throw everything in the dishwasher."

"No, ma'am." Verbena turned the faucet, and water hissed into the sink. "Not if you plan on using it again. Me and machines don't gee haw. Old Charlie used to say I could bust a wheel."

"Old Charlie was full of beans." Cassie grabbed a clean dish towel and grinned at the girl. "Still . . . to be on the safe side, you wash, and I'll dry."

Duncan put down his fork. "Hold. I hear something."

"Probably them fellers working on your house," Verbena said. "Busy as beavers, ain't they? Tap, tap, tap, like a hunnert little hammers agoing at oncet."

"No, 'tis not that." Duncan's expression was intense. "Hark."

Cassie listened and heard a faint, insistent scratching at the back door, like a dog begging to be let in. She threw down the towel and hurried into the hall, but Duncan blurred past her and reached the door first. He threw it open, and a glossy-coated blue dog with tan and black markings bounded inside. The dog whined and rose on its hind legs. Its form shifted and Evan stood in the hallway, still dressed in the knee-length trousers. They clung to his powerful legs and exposed his strong calves.

A shuddering howl came from the woods behind Cassie's house.

"Werewolves," Evan said, his chest heaving. "Bunch of them, headed this way."

Evan's expression was strained, his eyes wild, but she had a hunch it wasn't the werewolves that had upset him. He'd gone into the woods after Taryn. Had they had a fight?

"Where's Taryn?" she asked, watching him closely. "Did you find her?"

His lean, handsome face twisted. "Yeah, I found her," he said with a hoarse laugh. "She's gone. Listen, about the werewolves. There's something off about 'em. They don't smell right, know what I mean?"

"Don't have a dog nose," Cassie said, "but I'll take your word for it. Black and rust markings?"

"Yeah. What do you think they want?"

"My guess is Zeb's come for Mac, and about time. I don't mean to be insensitive, but the poor kid's been dead for hours in the back of my truck."

Evan's eyes widened. "You got a *dead* guy in your truck? What the hell?"

"The alpha's nephew. And technically, he's not a guy. He'd shifted when he—" Cassie made a face. "It's complicated. Did Taryn say when she'll be back?"

"Nope." Evan clenched his jaw and tightened his hands into fists. "Forget about Red—I intend to—and tell me more about this dead werewolf."

"There is not much to tell," said Duncan. "A wolf attacked Cassandra, and I cut off his head. End of story."

"*End of story*? You can't go around whacking off people's heads because you feel like it."

"Duncan didn't have a choice," Cassie said. "Mac was sick or crazed, or on drugs. If Duncan hadn't been there . . ." She shook her head, unable to finish.

"The werewolf tried to kill Cassandra, and I slew him," Duncan said. "And so I shall tell this Zeb, should he ask."

Duncan flung Zeb's name out of his mouth like it was something foul.

A ululating cry shivered the air, this time closer to the house.

"Looks like you'll get the chance," Evan said. "That's the alpha, unless I'm mistaken, and he doesn't sound happy."

"His happiness or unhappiness is not my concern," Duncan replied. "Should he, however, trespass without Cassandra's permission, I shall take the necessary measures."

"Ooh, you'll take *measures*." Evan gave him the squint eye. "We're outnumbered, tough guy. The Skinners are running with the wolf pack."

"The river lies yon." Duncan indicated the door at the opposite end of the hall with a jerk of his head. "Hie thee across, an you are daunted."

"Stop being a dick," Evan said, scowling. "I'm trying to help you. Don't want you to go off half-cocked and get your ass handed to you." He tapped his temple. "Like I keep telling you, knowledge is power, my man."

"Your caution is noted, but I remain undismayed."

A series of sharp yips came from the woods. There was a crash of breaking glass from the kitchen, and Verbena sprang into the hall like a jackrabbit on steroids. "Joby Ray," she squeaked. "He's back. Don't let him get me."

"Hush, child," Duncan said. "You are safe."

His tone of voice was soothing, Cassie noticed with a twinge of envy. But then, he wasn't angry with Verbena. Verbena hadn't insulted his irresistibility with a straight-up offer of sex. Most men got sore when you turned them down. Not Duncan. The booty call next door had offended him.

She would never understand demon hunters, not if she lived a thousand years.

Cassie stepped around Evan and peered through the glass insert in the back door. Her heart gave a sickening little kick. Dark, hulking forms moved beneath the oaks at the edge of her property. The Randalls had wolfed out. Cassie was baffled and more than a little freaked. Toby was supposed to smooth things over, explain that Mac's death had been an accident, a horrible, horrible accident. Tragic, yes, but not worth starting a war. She'd hoped to parley with the alpha, make him see reason. Instead, Zeb had gone on the offensive. This was not good. This was *definitely* not good.

An attack on her would be tantamount to an attack on the kith. Worse, it could draw the attention of the norms, and that would be disastrous. Reprisal from the Council would be swift and absolute. Surely Zeb knew that.

The wild hydrangea bushes parted, and a scrawny coyote slunk out of the trees to sniff at one of the scorch marks on the back lawn. The animal gave a sharp bark, and three rangy coyotes and a slew of sickly weasels, possums, skunks, and rats answered the call, boiling out of the underbrush. The Skinners were here, and in force.

The werewolves crept from the shadows, and any hope Cassie had of settling the business of Mac's death without bloodshed died. Evan's nose had not deceived him. Down to the last wolf, the pack showed signs of a virulent illness, a malignancy that had left them wasted and deformed. Like Mac, they had half shifted, and their pelts were covered in oozing scabs. Fluid leaked from their maddened eyes, matting the fur on their muzzles, and they moved with a shambling gait on their twisted hind legs.

Cassie swallowed. "Oh, my God, what's happened to them? This time last year, the Randall pack was perfectly healthy."

"This time last year, huh?" Evan said. "Is that when you took a walk on the wild side?"

Cassie stiffened. "Zeb and I had dinner a couple of times. What of it?"

"You know what they say. Once you go pack, you never go back."

A muscle twitched in Duncan's cheek. "Enough, Evan. You go too far."

"Aw, Dunky. You know I'm dicking with—" Evan broke off, his eyes widening. "Jesus Horatio Christ, what the hell is that?"

A huge thing had stepped out of the woods. Ten feet tall, the monstrosity had the head, back legs, and tail of a wolf and the belly and torso of a man. Three powerfully muscled human arms sprang from either side of the thing's upper body, and a series of bristling spikes ran down its back. Filthy fur covered the creature's head and lower body in patches, fur with the distinctive Randall black and red mottling.

Cassie swallowed the throbbing lump of fear in her throat. "I'm not sure, but I think that's Zeb."

"That's the alpha? Man, that's messed up." Evan rolled his neck and shoulders and flashed Duncan a reckless grin. "How 'bout it? You ready to kick some werewolf ass?"

"I thank you for the offer, my friend," Duncan said, "but your assistance is not required." With that, he disappeared.

"Duncan?" Cassie spun around. "Where'd he go?"

"To deal with the alpha." Evan made a sound of disgust. "By himself, the cowboy."

"What?" Cassie threw the back door open and saw Duncan materialize on the lawn. "Is he crazy? He'll get himself killed."

Evan grabbed a handful of her T-shirt and yanked her around. "Hit me."

"What?" Cassie stared at him.

There was a strange gleam in his eyes, a sort of rebellious, unheeding madness that made her almost as uneasy as the monsters on her lawn. Evan looked hopped up on something, juiced to the max. Or maybe he had something to prove.

He shook her arm. "There are too many of them. We need the ogre. Hit me. Hard."

"No. There's no time for that."

Cassie pulled away and rushed onto the porch. She heard Evan curse and follow her out the door, but she hardly noticed. Her attention was on Duncan. He stood, unmoving, in the path of destruction, a lone champion in a white T-shirt and jeans.

"Idiot," she breathed, starting down the steps. Belatedly, she realized that she'd forgotten to grab a staff. "*Move*, Duncan. Get out of the way."

It was over before it began. Later, Cassie would recall the almost-battle in brief snatches: the alpha bellowing and charging Duncan, slavering jaws open and sharp claws whistling through the air, claws that could cleave a man in two with a single blow; the howling pack throwing itself after the leader; the Skinner clan skulking at the periphery, nervous, half-starved hyenas waiting to savage a downed antelope.

Time seemed to slow and stretch like refrigerated molasses as the tidal wave of teeth and claws rolled toward Duncan. Then, as the onslaught threatened to engulf him, he raised his hands and gestured, and something astounding happened.

Plop, plop, plop, the pack of werewolves reverted to human form in a repulsive symphony of wet sounds. Howling, the weres rolled on the ground, muscles seizing and contracting at the rapid transformation. *Plop, squelch*, the hideous alpha degenerated with a sickening crunch of bone and sinew. *Thbbtp*, the Skinners shifted, bodies jerking and spasming in pain.

Cassie gaped at the bizarre scene. No more shifters or werewolves, only naked people on her lawn, piles and piles of them. Ugly, naked people, an orgy of them puking and writhing, like a horror art depiction of Dante's *Inferno*.

Duncan waded through the wriggling mass of bodies and bent over Joby Ray. The head of the Skinner clan was on his knees, vomiting in long, racking shudders.

"Gerroff me," Joby Ray snarled. Swatting a hand at Duncan, he scrambled to his feet.

Joby Ray was filthy, covered in dirt, grass, and his own puke. His pocked skin had an unhealthy cast, and his arms and legs were shrunken and bony. His thing and his ball sack were on display, limp and dispirited. He was either oblivious to his nudity or he didn't care.

Cassie cared. She cared a lot. Some shifters—Toby, for instance—retained their clothes when they shifted. Joby Ray obviously lacked that gene, but, oh, how Cassie wished he didn't. Joby Ray wasn't easy on the eyes dressed. Naked, he was the stuff of nightmares. He wasn't beefcake. He was beef stew with lots of gristle and dead, hairy things floating on top.

"Thieving bitch." Joby Ray pointed a grimy finger at Cassie. "It weren't enough you stole Beenie. You went and stole from the pack, too. I hope Zeb rips your tits off and feeds them to the cubs."

Cassie regarded him in astonishment. "Steal from the Randalls? What on earth are you talking about?"

"Like you don't know." Joby Ray spat and wiped his mouth on the back of his dirty hand. "Tell Beenie we'll be back. Skinners keep what's our'n."

Lifting his head, he gave a short, mournful yowl and shambled for the tree line. Groaning, the ailing Skinner clan climbed to their feet and staggered after him.

Chapter Seventeen

"What the hell?" Evan said, watching the Skinners limp into the woods.

"No idea. Unless..." Cassie hesitated. "You don't suppose they mean Mac? But I didn't steal him."

"Perhaps this one can clarify matters." Striding over, Duncan prodded Zeb with his boot. "You. What mean you by this attack?"

The alpha was curled in a fetal knot, shivering and shaking like a man with an ague. At Duncan's nudge, he snarled and sprang to his feet. His appearance shocked Cassie to the core. Zeb Randall wasn't classically handsome like a certain Dalvahni whose initials began with D.U.N.C.A.N., but he'd been far from ugly when he and Cassie had dated. Not so anymore. Zeb's rough-hewn good looks were gone, and he'd aged decades in less than a year. He looked every day of seventy-five years old when, in reality, Zeb had yet to see forty. His big body, naked and on display, was gaunt to the point of emaciation, and his eyes were sunken pools in his heavily lined face. His reddish-brown hair was matted and unwashed, and he smelled of vomit, sweat, and worse.

Zeb was either terminally ill or on drugs. Maybe both.

He barked out a command. Clutching their heads and bellies, the men and women squirming on the ground—some two dozen of them—groaned and obediently struggled to their feet to shuffle around him. The rest of the pack looked no better than the alpha, haggard scarecrows with waxen complexions, open sores on their naked bodies, swollen bellies, and molting hair.

"Zeb, you need help," Cassie said, filled with pity. "You're ill. So is the pack."

Duncan moved to Cassie's side. "Cassandra has the right of it. I am an animedens, a healer of animals. I will help you and gladly, an you allow it."

A woman skulked out of the pack, head lowered. She was gaunt and obviously suffering from some sort of wasting sickness. The letter *R* was tattooed on her thin upper right arm. "Zeb? Please," the woman said, not meeting the alpha's eyes. "My boy's dead, and my girl's dying. Blaze is only eight. Maybe he can help her."

"Shut your yap," Zeb snarled and swung his fist at the woman, splitting her lip. "You got some nerve, coming to me after what your boy did." He glared at the rest of the pack. "Get her out of my sight. She's shunned."

The pack closed in on the woman, snarling. She slunk back, her teeth bared, then broke and ran into the woods.

Zeb rounded on Cassie, a feral gleam in his dark eyes. "Give us the orb. We know you have it."

"I don't know what you mean."

"Liar. Mac stole the orb, and you have Mac. Your dog told us."

"My dog?" Cassie felt a spasm of unease. "You mean Toby? Where is he?"

"Somewhere you won't find him."

"You're making a mistake, Zeb. Toby had nothing to do with Mac's death. That was an accident."

Zeb threw back his head and laughed. Spittle flecked his cracked lips. "You think I give a shit about Mac? I'd have killed him myself if I could have gotten my hands on him, the traitor."

He's bug-shit crazy, Cassie thought.

"Tell you what," she said, striving for a reasonable tone. "If Mac took something that belongs to you, he still has it." She pointed to her truck. "His body's over there. See for yourself."

Zeb gave her a suspicious scowl, then jerked his head at a man and woman. They trotted over to the Silverado in a jiggle of naked flesh, removed the cover, and climbed into the back.

"It's Mac, all right," the woman yelled. "He's dead. Somebody done cut off his head."

"My, she's a smart one," Evan drawled. "Can't slip anything past her. Be sure and mate with that one, Zeb. The pups are bound to be dandies."

"Not helping," Cassie said in a singsong voice.

Evan showed his white teeth. "Don't care."

He vibrated with raw energy. Evan was itching for a fight. Next thing you knew, he'd ogre out. That's the last thing they needed.

If Zeb heard Evan, he gave no sign. The alpha's attention was focused on the truck with scary intensity. "Forget that piece of shit," he shouted. "Find the orb."

The weres bent over the body once more. The woman straightened. "Ain't here, Zeb. It's gone."

Zeb let out a stream of profanity that would peel paint and turned to Cassie. "You'll regret this, bitch. Your dog will die screaming." Raising an emaciated arm, he pointed at her. "And that shit's on your head."

"*No.*" Cassie lunged at Zeb, but Duncan caught her by the arm and pulled her back. She jerked free and glared at the alpha. "You listen to me, Zeb Randall, and listen good. You so much as part Toby Littleton's hair the wrong way, and I'll curse you into next week."

"Your threats don't frighten us. Give us the orb, and we'll let the dog go."

"Are you deaf?" Cassie's voice rose. "How many times do I have to tell you? I don't have the stupid thing."

"Enough." Duncan's sword appeared in his hand. "You have your answer. Cassandra does not have what you seek. Take your kinsman and go."

Evan cracked his knuckles. "Yeah, beat it, Randall. You're starting to piss me off."

Zeb growled and took a step closer, pausing at a shout of alarm.

"Law coming," the man in the back of the Silverado yelled as a Jeep Cherokee came out of the woods and eased to a stop.

Zeb shot Cassie a look of pure, burning hate. "This ain't over. Not by a long shot." He gave a low, yodeling howl, and the pack wheeled and trotted for the woods. The man and woman in the truck jumped down and streaked after them.

"Wait," Cassie yelled after them. "What about Mac?"

Zeb loped away, unheeding.

The driver's side door of the Jeep opened, and the sheriff got out, the badge on his shirt twinkling in the morning sun. He was dressed in jeans and a khaki shirt, and his eyes were concealed behind a pair of sunglasses. He was a tall, broad-shouldered man with short, dark hair, a strong jaw, and a firm, unsmiling mouth. Privately, Cassie had always thought there was something distinctly Dalvahni-ish about

Dev Whitsun, a certain sternness and unyielding strength that bespoke the warrior.

He wasn't Dalvahni—Cassie had checked, and Beck had confirmed it with Conall—but Cassie didn't think he was kith, either. Didn't have the purple eyes, for one thing. Whatever he was, the sheriff was no norm. He screamed super, though Cassie didn't know what kind. There was a certain wolfish quality about him, a razor-sharp intelligence, power, and athletic grace. Cassie wondered if he might be a werewolf but discarded the idea. Sheriff Whitsun was a loner, not a pack animal.

The sheriff crossed the lawn, his long legs making short work of the distance. He paused to watch the Randalls hotfoot it, bare-assed, for the woods, his face without expression, then strode up to them. "Morning," he said in his chocolatey drawl. "Must've been one heck of a party. Seems to have knocked those folks nekked."

"Costume party," Evan said with a straight face. "They came as nudists. The tits and balls were extra."

The sunglasses turned in Evan's direction. "Costume party, huh?" Whitsun said, taking in Evan's bare chest and knee breeches. "Who are you supposed to be?"

"George Washington. Had to lose the velvet jacket—too hot for September—and the wig itched."

Cold sweat trickled down Cassie's back. A few yards away, there was a dead man in her truck. Not a man. A dead *werewolf*, which was worse. Even if she was right and the sheriff *was* some kind of super, that didn't mean he knew about werewolves. Regardless, he'd want to know how the werewolf lost his head. Officers of the law were persnickety like that. People got their heads cut off in their county, they wanted to know why. She tried to think of a reasonable answer and came up blank.

A wave of panic rolled over her. What if Whitsun arrested her? She didn't have time to sit in jail. The Randalls could be torturing Toby this very minute. She needed to find him, and double-quick.

Duncan laid a hand on her shoulder and squeezed. "Be at ease." His breath puffed against her ear, soothing her. "Evan and I will find your friend. All will be well."

Tears welled in Cassie's eyes, but she blinked them away. "Thanks."

Evan was talking rapidly to the sheriff, spinning tall tales of the

epic party they'd had the night before. "The outfit came with a miniature apple tree and hatchet," he was saying. "You know, because old
George never told a lie."

"Cherry tree," said Whitsun.

"Huh?"

"George Washington supposedly cut down his father's favorite
cherry tree, but that myth's been debunked."

Evan tugged on his earring. "You sure about that?"

"Yeah. Look it up. Got a thing about lies. Comes with the job, I
reckon."

Evan turned to Cassie. He still had a brittle, jittery quality about
him, and his eyes were too bright. "You hear that? Damn costume
shop jacked me around. Gave me the wrong frigging tree. I'd give
'em a piece of my mind, if I didn't need it."

"Hate it when that happens," Cassie murmured, keeping her eyes
on the sheriff.

Easier said than done. Her eyes kept rolling toward the truck of
their own accord, like marbles on a slanted board. *Dead guy in the
truck. Dead guy in the truck,* her brain screamed.

Shit. Shitohshitohshitohshit.

Whitsun was looking at her funny, like he suspected something
was off. He didn't know the half of it. This whole freaking day had
been off.

"What brings you here, Sheriff?" she asked, forcing her stiff lips
into a semblance of a smile. "Know it can't be a noise complaint. My
nearest neighbor's more than a mile away." She cleared her throat.
"On account of the party, I mean."

Whitsun studied her from behind the dark lenses. She had the dis-
tinct and disconcerting impression that he was weighing her, sifting
her words for the truth of them.

Got a thing about lies. Comes with the job, I reckon.

For God's sake, she was jumpy as a cricket on a hot sidewalk.
Like the sheriff could read her mind. Please. She was letting his cop
persona rattle her. Cool, calm, and collected, that was how she'd play
this. Cool, calm, and collected. R-i-g-h-t.

Dead guy in the truck. Dead guy in the—

"Got a phone call from Chief Davis at dawn's butt crack," Whitsun said, breaking in on her mental hemorrhaging. "Seems somebody's lifted Jeb Hannah's statue from the town square. Must've

used a forklift. Statue weighs every ounce of four tons. Told the chief as much, but he says it's not the first time old Jeb's gone missing."

Jeb? Cassie breathed a sigh of relief. Was that all? There was no way he could tie her to Jeb's disappearance. The knot of tension in her belly relaxed.

"That so?" Cassie smiled, and this time it was genuine. "What a shame. Some people will steal the nickels off a dead man's eyes."

"You can't tell about folks," Whitsun agreed. "Just when I think I can't be surprised, something comes along, knocks me for a loop."

Cassie seriously doubted that. She had a feeling very little got past Sheriff Whitsun, and even less surprised him. Whitsun was still water, and still water ran deep. He might seem calm as an eggplant on the surface, but underneath things were churning.

"Don't have a forklift, Sheriff, and I didn't steal Jeb," she said.

Whitsun removed his sunglasses and slid them inside his shirt pocket. His eyes were the color of polished steel. Definitely not a demonoid. It annoyed Cassie that she couldn't peg him. Toby would know. Toby could smell a super a hundred yards off.

Toby. Oh, God, *Toby*. A wave of fresh panic washed over her.

"Got a tip from a local fisherman," the sheriff said. "Seems the base of the statue was spotted on your riverfront."

Cassie's stomach dropped. The plinth—she'd forgotten about the plinth. It was sitting in her yard for all to see.

"Ms. Ferguson?" The sheriff looked at her expectantly. "You mind if I look around?"

Yes, her brain screamed. *Yes, I mind.*

But her lips and tongue didn't receive the message. Too much had happened in too short a time, and the old brain matter couldn't cope. A hundred fleeting thoughts flitted through her mind and fluttered away like moths. He was going to find the plinth, and then he'd find the werewolf. She was going to jail, and Toby would die.

Dear God, Toby.

She gathered her scattered thoughts. She was no good to Toby if she panicked. Get rid of the sheriff and find her friend. All she had to do was come up with an explanation that Whitsun would buy. Like . . . um . . .

The plinth? That little old thing? Oh, that's easy to explain. You see, I—

Dead werewolf in my truck? Really? No idea how it got there.

Maybe it crawled in there to die. Lost its head, you say? Whadda you know.

"Uh . . ." she said, floundering and gasping like a beached fish. "Well, you see, I . . ."

The back door banged open, and Verbena dashed down the steps. "Joby Ray and the rest of 'em done skedaddled?" she asked, running up to them, her eyes wide.

"Uh . . . yeah," Cassie said. "Verbena, this is Sheriff Whitsun. He's looking for a missing statue. Seems to think the plinth is on my property."

"Plimp?" Verbena pursed her lips. "That one of them balloon thangs with the writin' on the side?"

"No, that's a blimp," Sheriff Whitsun said. "A plinth is a base a statue sits on. I got a report one was spotted here."

"Oh," said Verbena, nodding in seeming understanding. "You looking for that peanut feller."

"That I am." Whitsun produced a small notepad and a pen from his pocket and started to make notes. "What can you tell me?"

"Why ask me? Ask him yourself, if'n you can get him to quit caterwaulin' long enough to answer you, that is."

The sheriff stopped scribbling. "Excuse me?"

Verbena pointed. "There he is, a-yonder."

Jeb Hannah clomped out of the trees downriver and across Cassie's lawn. His metal body was dinged and scorched in a dozen places, and his wide-brimmed slouch hat was askew. He carried his giant peanut tucked under one arm, and he sang in his hollow voice as he thumped along.

> *After the ball is over,*
> *After the break of morn—*
> *After the dancers' leaving;*
> *After the stars are gone*

"Told yah," Verbena said in a cheerful voice. "He don't never shut up. Never seed such a feller for sangin'."

The sheriff's mouth opened, but no sound came out. The pen and notepad in his hand dropped, unheeded, to the ground. Keeping his gaze pinned on Jeb, Whitsun fumbled for the police radio at his hip.

"Willa Dean?" he said into the box. "Call Chief Davis and the mayor and let them know I've got a lead on that missing statue. What? No, it's on the move. I'll get back with you."

Jeb stomped past them and turned down the gravel lane that wound into the woods, away from Cassie's house.

Many a heart is aching, Jeb belted merrily.

> *If you could read them all;*
> *Many the hopes that have vanished*
> *After the ball.*

The statue disappeared into the trees.

"Excuse me," Whitsun said, taking off at a run for his Jeep. The sheriff climbed in, cranked the engine, and roared down the driveway after Jeb.

"Whatchoo reckon he's gon' do when he catches him?" asked Verbena. "That peanut feller don't mind worth a darn. Does what he pleases, and who's to stop him?"

"That's the sheriff's problem. Boy, am I glad he's gone." Cassie heaved a sigh of relief. "Thanks, Verbena."

"Sure thang," said Verbena, and flitted back to the house.

Evan watched her go, his expression thoughtful. "She's right, you know. Sooner or later, you're going to have to do something about that statue, before some norm sees it and all hell breaks loose."

"I know, I know, but I can't worry about that right now," Cassie said, her brain spinning. "I've got to find Toby. Listen, can you track the Randalls? Or rather, can your dog?"

"Please." Evan sniffed. "My hound could smell an ant fart in a flower shop, and those werewolves *stink*." He wrinkled his nose. "Haven't smelled anything that god-awful since the 'rents died. My demon mammy and pappy smelled like a garbage dump."

Cassie regarded him with sympathy. "That must have been a special kind of hell for you, with your sensitive nose."

Evan shrugged and looked away. "Life sucks, and then you die."

"I will accompany you," Duncan said to Evan. "If they give us any trouble, or if Toby has been in any way harmed, the werewolves will pay. First, though, we needs must bury the dead."

"Yes," Cassie said. "Oh, God, *yes*. Whitsun will be back. Playing dumb about the plinth is one thing, but Mac's body would be hard to explain. I can't believe the Randalls left him for me to bury."

"Shunned," Evan said. "Booted out of the pack. As far as they're concerned, you can dump this Mac fellow on the side of the road."

"For some norm to find?" Cassie shook her head. "That's crazy."

"News flash. So is Zeb."

"We are *not* dumping Mac on the road," Cassie said. "And that's final."

"Suit yourself," said Evan. "But you'd better hope that nosy sheriff doesn't find the grave."

"Nay," Duncan said. "I will—"

A lissome female in black leathers and knee-high boots materialized, interrupting him. Her long, dark hair was twisted into intricate plaits and pulled away from her lovely face, and her large, fine eyes were dark brown. "Greetings, clod pate," she said, looking down her proud nose at Duncan. "We meet again."

"Illaria," said Duncan in the tone of one acknowledging an abscessed tooth. "What do you want?"

"The pleasure of your company, what else?"

"State your purpose. There are things I would be about."

"Fascinating, to be sure, but do you not think it wise to address the matter at hand ere you embark on fresh mischief?"

Duncan gave her a stony look. "I do not take your meaning."

"You decapitated a werewolf and have neglected to dispose of the body—yet another violation of the Directive Against Conspicuousness. The corpse was very nearly discovered by the local shire reeve. I have been sent to remedy the situation."

"Really?" Cassie said, much relieved. "We were trying to decide what to do with Mac's body when you arrived."

"'Tis a simple enough matter." Illaria cut Duncan a scathing glance. "Unless one is an utter dolt. I will remove the body and bury it where it will not be discovered."

"Thank you," said Cassie. "I'd really appreciate it. Don't suppose you could deanimate a statue while you're at it?"

"We monitor the Kir and the Dal. You are neither." Illaria's tone was heavy with disdain. "Your magical blunderings are between you and your council."

Ouch. Well, it was worth a try.

"Did Taryn send you?" Evan said. "Where is she? Did she—" He flushed. "Do you have a message for me?"

"The High Huntress sent me." Illaria looked him up and down, her full mouth curling in contempt. "As for my sister, I bring you no tidings. A Kirvahni huntress does not consort with the likes of you."

Evan's flush deepened, and he started to say something.

"Taryn and Evan are friends," Cassie said, laying a hand on his arm. "He's worried about her. But then, you wouldn't know anything about that."

Illaria stiffened. "Meaning?"

"Meaning you don't have friends."

"That is rank untruth. I have friends. Many friends."

"Really? Because family doesn't count."

Illaria pressed her lips together. "The body," she said in a voice of barely suppressed ire. "Where lies it?"

"His *name* is Mac Randall, and he's over there." Cassie indicated her truck. "In the back. You can't miss him."

That was an understatement. Cassie suppressed a shudder. Poor Mac had been dead more than sixteen hours. He was bound to be ripe.

Twitching like an angry cat, the Kir spun on her heel and marched toward the Silverado.

"Not so fast," Evan said. "I've got a few questions for Mr. Were-wolf before you beam him up."

Illaria halted. "You can speak to the dead?"

"The High Hoo-ha didn't tell you? I see dead people, and they see me. And they do whatever I say."

"Absurd," said Illaria. "I do not believe you."

"Believe it, sister." Evan's expression was bitter. "I'm the frigging Zombie Master, so booyah."

Chapter Eighteen

Duncan felt a stab of excitement. *Of course*. Evan could raise the dead. They would go straight to the source. Ask the dead werewolf about the orb the alpha was seeking. With any luck, discover Toby's location.

How could he have forgotten Evan's peculiar talent? He glanced at Cassandra. The answer was *quite easily*. He'd had other things on his mind. Delicious things.

Infuriating things.

Cassandra's proposition had thrown him into an agony of awareness. She would be his thrall. He was swive-drunk at the thought of being with her . . . and in a black rage.

For nigh unto two centuries, he'd grieved for her, feared for her, dreamed of her, craved her with a longing that was close to madness. At last she would be his once more, but in half measure. She offered her sweet, delectable body for the taking, but her heart, her trust, her *love*? These precious things she withheld.

It was better than nothing, but not nearly enough. He wanted all of her, not just her body.

He strode after Evan and Illaria.

Cassandra hurried after him. "Zombie master?" she said, matching his pace. "Is he serious?"

The lines of tension around her violet eyes made Duncan's heart clench. By the sword, she was his strength and his weakness.

"Yes," he said. "Rebekah did not tell you?"

She shook her head. "Beck doesn't talk about Evan. Not that something like that would come up in conversation anyway. *Nice weather, and, oh, hey, did I mention my brother can raise the dead?*"

"Yes, I can see how that would be troublesome."

They walked up to the truck and watched Evan climb into the back. Illaria stood nearby, hands on hips, surveying the demonoid with a frown. Unsurprising. The Kir were distrustful and scornful of any but their own.

Evan waved his hands, and the dead werewolf rose to its feet in a broken dance of stiff limbs. The neck stump had turned greenish-blue in color, and the half-mutated corpse smelled strongly of rotting meat.

Illaria hissed in surprise. "By the vessel, you did not dissemble. You can raise the dead."

"Yeah." Evan's tone was dry. "I'm on everyone's guest list."

The wind shifted, carrying the stench their way.

Cassandra gasped. "Oh, my God, I think I'm going to be sick."

"Go into the house," Duncan said. "You do not have to see this."

She shook her head. "I'm staying. For Toby."

"As you wish."

Duncan returned his attention to the truck. Evan was regarding his handiwork with a resigned, sickly expression, and Duncan felt a surge of sympathy for his friend. Evan found the zombie as repulsive as Cassandra—mayhap more so, given his sensitive nose.

"Head," Evan said, addressing the corpse in a choked voice.

The body bent with difficulty and a great creaking and popping of joints, and promptly expelled gas.

Evan was directly in the line of fire. "Fuck me," he said, clapping his hand over his nose. The corpse straightened at once, and Evan scrambled back. "Not literally, meat sack. It's an expression. I meant, find your head." The dead were bent once more, groping in the bottom of the truck. "That's right. You're warm . . . warmer. A little more . . . yep. That's it."

The corpse stood, a wolfish head dangling from one clawed hand. The features were mushy and unrecognizable.

"Don't stand there holding it like a goddamn fuzzy purse," Evan said. "Put it on."

The zombie obeyed, plopping the decaying head with its horrible jowls and doggy ears onto his neck.

Evan jumped to the ground. "I swear. You have to tell them every little thing, especially when they're not fresh. Brain rot, yah know?" He snapped his fingers, then whistled when the corpse did not respond. "Hey, dog face. Yeah, I'm talking to you. See the big guy?"

He jerked his thumb at Duncan. "Answer his questions." He stalked away from the truck, his face pale and set. "Fire away, Dunk. He's all yours."

Cassandra touched Duncan lightly on the arm. "Ask him about Toby. Maybe he knows where Zeb's taken him."

Duncan nodded and addressed the zombie. "The alpha Zeb is holding a man prisoner. We need to find him. What can you tell us?"

To Duncan's shock, the voice that emanated from the decomposed head, though male, was hesitant and far younger than he'd expected.

"Not much," the youngling said. "Zeb don't pay any mind to the younger members of the pack."

Duncan regarded the were with a feeling of dread. "How old are you, Mac?"

"Eighteen, sir. Turn nineteen in December." He halted, looking at Evan in confusion. "I-I mean . . . I guess I would have. I'm dead, ain't I?"

"Yeah." Evan's voice was gruff. "You're dead." Turning, he told Duncan in a low voice, "Jesus, Dunk. He's just a kid."

"He would have killed Cassandra." Duncan felt sick. "There was no time to ascertain his age. Certainly, had I known . . . had I guessed his youth . . ."

Cassandra laid her hand on his arm. The skin of her palm was soft and warm. "You didn't know. You couldn't. It was him or me."

She was right. The werewolf had been crazed. Another instant, and he would have torn out her throat. Duncan hated what he'd done, but he would do it again.

And again. Given the choice, he would always choose Cassandra.

He nodded and cleared his throat. "The place where the alpha may be hiding this prisoner, can you hazard a guess where it might be?"

"Don't rightly know, but there's a cave where he likes to stash things."

"Not a big help," Evan said. "Try to be more specific."

"I ain't been there but once," Mac said. "It's near the natural bridge, the one with the arch. There's a big elm on the hill got struck by lightning."

"I know the place," Duncan said. "I came upon it whilst searching for cramp bark and valerian some moons back. I took shelter there in a thunderstorm. The cave lies less than a league from here, near a meandering stream."

"Cramp bark and valerian?" Cassandra murmured, sliding a curious glance at him.

"Lucy Hall besought my help in treating an ailing mare," Duncan explained. He turned back to the zombie. "The orb. Tell me of it."

"Zeb brought it home this past Christmas. Said he was out hunting and saw a falling star. He followed it and found the orb. Zeb was real proud of it. Said it was our totem, that it would bring us luck. Help us whup the Lyalls once and for all. Wipe 'em off the face of the earth."

"Why would Zeb want to do that?" Cassandra sounded shocked. "I know there's no love lost between the packs, but that seems extreme."

"Zeb hates the Lyalls. His pa, Frank—he was the alpha before Zeb—and Jerry Lyall got into a fight, years back. It happened before I was born, but everybody says that fight was something to see. Anyways, Jerry killed Frank, and Zeb ain't never forgot it. He says Jerry cheated, and maybe he's right. Dunno." Mac shrugged. "Zeb was wrong about the orb, though. Brought nothing but misery to the pack. Made folks sick."

"Then why'd you steal it?" asked Cassandra.

"Had to. Zeb tried to blame the sickness on Jerry. Claimed the Lyalls had poisoned us, but I knew better. Everybody did, but they was too scared of Zeb to do anything."

Cassandra exclaimed softly, "You took the orb to save the pack, didn't you, Mac?"

"Yeah. If it was up to me, I'd have left and never come back, but I promised my dad before he died that I'd take care of my mom and Blaze. Couldn't let my baby sister die." Mac's voice grew anguished. "I had to do it, don't you see? I'm the man now. It was my responsibility."

"Oh, Mac," Cassandra whispered. "You poor thing."

Mac didn't seem to hear her. "So I grabbed the orb and lit out. Didn't have a plan, really. Thought maybe if I got the orb away from Blaze, she'd get better. I ran. Didn't know where I was going, just ran." Mac's crusty white eyes turned in Cassandra's direction. "Then

I remembered you, Miss Cassie. Remembered folks say you can do magic. Thought . . . maybe you'd know what to do with the orb." He swayed. "That's the last thing I remember before things went red."

"What does this orb thingy look like?" Cassandra asked.

"That's the weird thing," Mac said. "It's not much to look at. Round as a snow globe and muddy brown. Got a yellow streak down the middle, like a cat's eye. Nothing to get excited about, if you ask me, but Zeb thought it was beautiful. Couldn't stop looking at it." He shuddered. "It . . . changed him."

A memory wriggled to the surface of Duncan's mind, a dim, un-shapen recollection of a striped globe the size of a child's heart, puls-ing with dull, sullen light. "This orb, would you say it has power?"

"Oh, yeah. Zeb would watch it for hours. Stare at it like a televi-sion set. Don't know how he stood it. Hurts to look at the thing. Like looking into the sun, you know?" The youngling shivered, and his head wobbled on his neck at the slight movement. "And when you touch it, it burns."

He held out his clawed hands, now bloated and purple, displaying badly burned palms. The pain, Duncan knew, must have been incred-ible.

His chest tightened. "'Twas brave of you, Mac, to take the orb. Your father would be proud."

"How you figure? Been banished. Betrayed the alpha. Shamed my family."

"Nay, you brought honor to your name. You sacrificed your well-being for others," Duncan said. "'Twas a great gift."

"Think so?" Mac's bloated lips trembled. "Maybe the pack will stop hating me one day."

"I will make certain of it. Where is the orb now?"

"Huh?"

"The orb," Duncan said. "Where is it?"

"Why ask me? You ought to know."

Duncan stared at him in confusion. "I do not understand."

"You showed up here late last night with your posse. Drunk as a skunk, partying hard, and singing to beat the band. There was a naked dude with you. He was silver all over, and so bright it hurt to look at him. You took the cover off the truck, and the shiny dude took the orb."

"This . . . um . . . shiny dude. Did he perchance have antlers?"

"Yup, that's the one."

"Sildhjort," Duncan murmured.

"That his name?" asked Mac. "What is he, exactly? He's not a were."

"Sildhjort is a god, a forest deity, to be precise."

"That explains it," said Mac. "Knew he was something special. The orb didn't burn him, see? Course, he didn't keep it long." He gave a rheumy chuckle. "Handed it quick-like to the swamp booger."

"Swamp booger?" Evan said. "You mean a sasquatch?"

Mac nodded, nearly dislodging his head. "Yep. Band of bigfoot lives around here. Must be thirty or forty of 'em. Zeb thought they were running off the deer, so he killed a sasquatch last year and kept the pelt. Boogers hated us ever since."

"I don't believe it," said Evan.

"Doubtless you do not remember," Duncan told him. "I fear you were not yourself at the time."

"You mean I monstered out. Still, you'd think I'd remember meeting Bigfoot."

Duncan avoided Illaria's gaze. "Not necessarily. 'Twould seem I . . . er . . . enchanted you and the other revelers with song."

"Say what?"

The back of Duncan's neck grew hot. "I am told that I played a gittern and my music summoned a host of magical creatures, including the ogre."

"Wow." Cassandra stared at him in astonishment. "You sing? I had no idea."

Illaria folded her arms across her breasts. "His warbling caused no end of trouble. It took my sister and me the better part of a night to set things aright."

Evan began to laugh. "Dunk, you're the freaking Pied Piper."

"Nay," Duncan objected, affronted. "A Dalvahni warrior does not hire himself out for coin, nor does he prey upon children. The Pied Piper was one of the djegrali. I slew him and returned the children to their families." He scowled at the memory. "A salient detail that fellow Grimm omitted from the tale. I told him as much, but he ignored me. Creative license? Bah."

"You slew the—" Evan shook his head. "I'm going to let that one go. Bottom line, you were plowed on chocolate pie. That's why you don't remember this Yogurt fellow taking the globe thingy."

"Sildhjort. His name is Sildhjort."

"So it's true," Cassandra said, eyeing Duncan. "Chocolate makes you drunk?"

"Aye." He rubbed the back of his neck, eager to change the subject. "To return to the matter at hand, this bigfoot, was he perchance white?"

"Yup," Mac said. "Blazing white—never seen a squatch that color. And that wasn't the only strange thing about him. The orb didn't seem to bother him none. Tossed that thang around like a ball."

"By the sword," Duncan said. "Sugar has the orb. Let us hope he has not mislaid it."

"Sugar?" asked Cassandra. "Who's Sugar?"

"The boggy boo—er—sasquatch."

"The sasquatch." Her eyes held laughter. "You named a sasquatch Sugar?"

"Not I," said Duncan. "His adopted mother, though she insists she bestowed the appellation on him because of his sweet temperament and not due to his unusual coloring."

"Some norm adopted a bigfoot?" Evan shook his head. "This town . . . I swear."

"The lady never married and had no children of her own," Duncan said. "The band rejected Sugar due to his coloring when he was born. They left him in the woods to die."

"They banished him, same as the pack did me," Mac said. "That sucks."

"Indeed, Sugar was most fortunate. The lady found him and raised him as her cub."

Cassandra's eyes narrowed, then widened in sudden comprehension. "Lucy Hall. She's Sugar's adopted mother, isn't she?"

"Yes," Duncan said, "but I beg you will keep it secret. Lucy's greatest fear is that Sugar will be captured by norms or avaricious kith seeking a windfall. Poked and prodded and deprived of his freedom . . . or worse. His happiness and welfare are her chief concern. She lives in terror and dread lest he fall into the wrong hands."

"That's why she sold you the land," Cassandra exclaimed. "You promised the old bat you'd take care of Sugar when she's gone."

She was clever, his Cassandra. He should have known she would guess.

"Yes," he admitted, "but I cannot agree with your assessment of her character. Lucy is a lonely old woman, but kind."

"*Kind?* She's mean as a snake. Maybe if she were nicer to folks, she'd have more friends."

"She keeps to herself and discourages visitors to protect Sugar," Duncan said. "She loves him like a child and would do anything for him."

Cassandra digested this. "I had no idea. Now I feel terrible. All this time, I thought she was a hateful old biddy."

"Love blooms in strange places."

"Love?" Illaria laughed. "By the vessel, warrior, you have gone soft." She turned to Evan. "Release the creature. Other affairs require my attention." She shot Duncan a sardonic look. "The Dal seldom rest, and trouble follows in their wake."

"The Kir require adjustment, too," Duncan said, irritated.

"Aye, but seldom. My sisters have not the Dalvahni propensity for chaos."

"A moment, huntress," Duncan said as Evan raised his arm.

Illaria looked annoyed. "What now?"

"I would say something to Mac." Ignoring the putrid smell that poured off the dead werewolf, Duncan strode closer to the truck. "I am responsible for your death."

"You are?" There was a startled expression on Mac's sagging features.

"Aye. It could not be helped. Still, I regret it. Know this. I will do what I can for your sister. You have my word."

"Mom, too?"

"Your mother as well."

Mac stared down at him, his oozing eyes unblinking. "Thanks, man. You're all right."

Evan made a sharp gesture with his hand. Mac's body collapsed, and the head thudded against the side of the truck.

"Stand aside," Illaria said.

The Kir lifted her arms, and the dead werewolf and its decapitated head floated up and over the ground. A long strip of linen appeared beside the body. The Kir made a twirling motion with her forefinger, and the linen wound itself around the body, starting with Mac's feet.

Duncan bided his time, waiting until the shrouding process was complete. "Nicely done," he said to the huntress. "You may depart. I would see Mac receive a proper burial, and I do not trust you to do the thing right. He was a brave lad, and his family will wish to visit his grave."

"Growing sentimental about your kills?" Illaria's lip curled in contempt. "Perhaps you would care to have his ears as a trophy?" Duncan flinched, and Illaria laughed, pleased to have goaded him. "Bury your kill as you wish, but bury him deep. I have no wish to tidy up after you." She gave their assembled group a contemptuous glance. "I bid you good day. I will not say well met, for a Kirvahni huntress does not lie."

She disappeared.

"Damn," Evan said. "What a bee-yotch."

"My thought exactly." Cassandra turned to Duncan. "Let me grab a staff. I'm going with you to find Toby."

"No," Duncan said. "Evan and I can do the thing faster alone."

"But I—"

"I will set wards about your place to protect you and Verbena in our absence, and Conall will send a warrior to protect you, at my request."

"I have wards, and we don't need a guard. Verbena and I can take care of ourselves."

"Your wards are not working at present."

Cassandra made a face. "Thanks for the reminder. I really need to do something about that."

"Yes," Duncan said. "In the meantime, I will reinforce the protective spells around your property—with your permission, of course."

"Uh-huh. And if I say no?"

"I will do it anyway. I will be more efficient on the hunt an I am not distracted by worry."

She frowned. "This feels wrong. I should be the one going after Toby. He's my friend."

"Beck speaks of Tobias Littleton with great fondness, as well. He has been good to you?"

"Very. Toby and I go back a long way. He's like family." She blinked rapidly, her eyes moist with tears. "I-I'm very fond of him."

"Then I will find him and bring him back to you. You have my word."

She hesitated. "Okay, dammit," she said with obvious reluctance. "Have it your way."

"I intend to." Duncan lowered his voice for her ears alone. "Soon and more than once. Or have you forgotten our bargain?"

She met his gaze, his sweet temptress, and what he saw there made his heart thud. "Not a chance," she said. "I've got a few intentions of my own."

She turned to Evan. "You missed breakfast. Come inside and have something to eat. You can't hunt on an empty stomach." She frowned at his knee breeches. "And you cannot keep running around in that ridiculous outfit. George Washington, really? Of all the ridiculous stories . . ." She shook her head. "I hope you know the sheriff knew you were lying."

"Sure." Evan grinned. "That was half the fun."

Chapter Nineteen

Duncan buried Mac across the river on his property beneath a stately oak and marked the grave with a heavy stone. "Sleep well, youngling," he said, and stepped into the void.

He materialized on Cassandra's lawn. Entering the house, he found Evan sitting at the kitchen table enjoying a hearty breakfast.

"Everything go okay?" Cassandra asked, turning from the stove where she was cooking.

Duncan nodded. "Aye. Mac is at rest."

"You could have waited, you know," Evan said, slathering jam on a piece of toast. "I told you I'd help."

"And I thank you," Duncan said, "but 'twas something I needed to do myself."

"I get it. It's in the handbook." Evan made a zigzag in the air with his fork. "You whack 'em, you bury 'em."

"Something of the sort."

"More eggs and bacon, General Washington?" Cassandra asked, setting a platter in front of Evan.

"Twist my arm." Evan grinned and shoveled more food onto his plate.

After making sure Evan had everything he needed, Cassandra pulled Duncan into the hall.

"There's something you should know," she told him in a low voice. "Blueticks are cold nose hounds. If Toby's in those woods, Evan will find him, but here's the thing. Blueticks have a big bawl mouth—meaning when they bay, you can hear them a mile off." There was a faint worry line between her brows. "If Evan catches the scent and gets excited, there's a good chance he'll make a lot of noise, and Zeb will know you're coming."

Duncan reached out, brushing the furrow between her eyes with the pad of his thumb. "Worry not. We will be fine. Come here, I would have a kiss before I go."

Her eyelids fluttered in surprise. "You want to kiss me?"

"To the contrary, thrall, you will kiss me. Think of it as a gesture of good faith to seal our bargain."

"Very well." Rising on tiptoe, she planted a swift peck on his cheek. "Consider the bargain sealed."

"Not so fast," he said as she whirled to walk away. "That is not the sort of kiss I had in mind."

She stopped and turned to face him. Her eyes were downcast, her expression demure, but her mouth—her sweet, delectable mouth—trembled with mischief. "No?" she murmured. "A thrall is not to blame. A thrall cannot read your mind."

"Ah, remiss of me," he said. "Allow me to allay your confusion." Striding to a long, oak plank bench against one wall, he sat down and patted his leg. "Come, thrall. Sit on my lap."

"A thrall is uncertain. A thrall would not crush you."

"A thrall is foolish." Reaching out, he pulled her close and settled her onto his thighs. "A thrall's weight is slight, and a warrior is Dalvahni and exceptionally strong."

Her bottom pressed against him in a most interesting way. Desire, heady and strong, flooded through him. His flesh quickened, and it was all he could do not to groan and rock his hips in response.

"A thrall will kiss me on the mouth." His voice was husky as he lowered his mouth to hers. "A thrall will kiss a warrior and not stop until bidden."

Cassandra gazed up at him, her face mere inches away. Her eyes were extraordinary, indigo-blue irises with violet centers. He'd never seen their like, not in a thousand different worlds. They reflected her every mood: tenderness, amusement, fury, trepidation.

Desire.

Her eyes were warm now, and sparkled with laughter. "A thrall confesses her worry." She made a show of lowering her lashes. "A thrall greatly fears she may not please a warrior."

"A thrall shall kiss me and find out." His throat closed around the words, his heart thundering like a drum. "A thrall shall do so, and now."

"If a warrior is certain . . ."

Wrapping her slender arms about his neck, Cassandra kissed him, and Duncan forgot to breathe. He forgot the long, lonely years without her. He forgot the bitterness and regret, the searing grief and pain of their separation, the heartsick yearning, the soul-stealing terror that she was dead, that he would never find her, that she was lost to him forever. He forgot his jealousy and anger. He forgot the hurt and rejection of her proposal.

He forgot everything but Cassandra. She was in his arms, where she belonged, and the world was right. She was alive and well. She was his heart and soul. She was woman, goddess, siren, angel, and she-devil in one stunning, irresistible package. She was his everything. He'd been lost without her, breathing in and out. Existing. Surviving, but taking no joy in it. A hollowed-out husk, going through the motions; alive by all appearances, but dead inside.

Like the rogue. The thought drifted through his mind and melted away again, dissolved by the heat of Cassandra's kiss. Her mouth was warm and sweet as ambrosia, and the taste of it was a magical elixir that brought him back to life. Ah, gods, it had been too long. A moment away from her was too long, and he had been without her an eternity of moments. Her tongue brushed his, and he began to shake. Heat ran down his spine and settled in his groin. He was need, raw, aching need, and he could never get enough.

Just when he was certain he would shatter, Evan stepped into the hall, ending the kiss.

"Jesus, you two," he said. "Go make your little porno someplace else. I'm too young for this shit."

Cassandra pulled away, her cheeks aflame, leaving Duncan feeling bereft. Ruefully, he acknowledged that Evan's interruption had been fortuitous. Another instant, and he would have confessed his love for Cassandra right then and there.

That would have been a mistake. Cassandra did not want his love. She wanted his body and nothing more. A passionate avowal would send her running.

She jumped up, obviously flustered. "Evan, did you . . . that is, can I get you anything else to eat?"

"Nah, I'm good," Evan drawled. "Full as a tick. You ready to hit the woods, Dunk?"

Duncan rose. "Of a certainty."

"You'll be careful, won't you?" Cassandra asked with an anxious expression.

She was worried about him, and for the first time, Duncan felt a glimmer of hope. Perhaps she cared for him, a little.

"Aye." Unable to resist, he pulled her close for another kiss. "An it pleases you, milady."

"Do you mind?" Evan said. "I just ate."

Reluctantly, Duncan released Cassandra. "Cease your carping," he said to Evan. "Whither do we go?"

"My place, so I can change clothes."

"Very well," Duncan said, and grabbed Evan by the arm.

"Hey." Evan's voice rose in alarm. "Wait a minute. I didn't mean—"

Duncan stepped once more into the void, materializing in front of Evan's single-story house. The lots on the street were small, the houses uniform in shape and appearance. Having sojourned in Hannah for some time, Duncan was familiar with the area and knew where Evan lived, though he had never been inside the demonoid's dwelling. He looked around with interest. This part of town was called Meadowbrook, an inapposite designation as the area boasted neither, but humans were illogical creatures and much given to fancy. He'd been here before with Conall—Jason Damian, Conall's father-in-law, lived nearby with his wife and younger children.

Evan groaned and slid off Duncan's back. "God, I'm sick as a horse. Why the hell didn't we take Cassie's truck?"

"Because Cassie cannot travel in the way of the Dalvahni, and I would not leave her stranded."

"You are such a worrywart when it comes to that dame," Evan said. "Well, don't just stand there. Let's get out of the street before Old Lady Copeland sees us. She's not a bad old fart, but she'll talk your ears off, and I'm in no mood to explain the clown pants."

Duncan followed Evan up the tiered, winding walk.

"Limestone," Evan said, indicating the pavers at their feet. "And see, I used rough stone to border the beds. The front lawn was flat as a pancake. Brought in fill dirt and topsoil. Landscaped it myself—I'm good with dirt. Added these levels and the shrubs and flowers on each side. I was going for a cottage feel." He climbed two steps on a slope, and stopped. "The house was a complete yawn. Cheap siding and no personality. Real cookie-cutter drudge. I replaced the siding with gray cedar shingle cladding, moved the front door to the left—see the dark wood and the glass cut-outs? Pretty, and it lets in light—and had an A-frame porch with square columns built over the entrance." He propped his hands on his hips, regarding the house with obvious satisfaction. "And wait until you see what I've done inside."

"It is a most handsome abode," Duncan said, amused and surprised by Evan's sudden domestic turn. "You have reason to be proud."

Evan hunched his shoulders. "It's mine, and I like it. Never had a home. The 'rents moved from place to place. We lived out of cars, back rooms, dive motels, and the occasional crappy camper. I promised myself if I ever got free of them, I'd have a real home."

"I grieve for your pain, Evan Beck."

"Whatev. You deal or you die. Come on in."

They went inside, and Evan gave Duncan a tour of the house, pointing out the various changes he'd made. "The old ceilings were low. I had Murphy raise them to nine feet. After being cooped up in the witch's shed for two months, I can't abide cramped spaces."

"This Murphy is a carpenter elf?"

"Is that a thing?"

"Of a certainty."

"Huh. No, Murphy's a norm, but he knows his shit when it comes to building," Evan said. "I had new windows with transoms put in for light, and Murphy knocked down the wall that divided the living room from the kitchen. Made it more open. For entertaining, you know. Saw it on television." He flushed slightly. "I watch a lot of home shows."

"Do you have many guests?" asked Duncan.

"Nah. You're the first, but you never know." Evan's expression darkened. "Thought I might have Red over for dinner one night, but then—" He halted and shrugged. "Dipshit idea, huh?"

"Not necessarily. Can you cook?"

Evan gave him a look. "Can't boil water. Why do you think I haunt the Sweet Shop? But I got a first-rate kitchen. Center island, farm sink, marble countertops, and everything Viking." He shoved his thumbs in the waistband of the breeches. "Guess I could serve her PB&J on my new dishes, huh? Like I said, dipshit idea."

"Evan, you are restive. Did something happen between you and Taryn in the woods?"

Evan's face closed. "Hell, no. Nothing happened. I set her straight and sent her on her way. Make yourself at home while I change."

He stomped out of the room, leaving Duncan alone. Duncan wandered into the kitchen. He'd known a few Norsemen in his time—had been with Beowulf when the warrior slew the djegrali Grendel—and he was curious about the Vikings Evan had mentioned. Alas, there was no sign of them. Bored, he strolled back into the chamber Evan had called the living room and sat down on a leather sofa to wait. 'Twas a pleasant space wherein to linger. A stone fireplace flanked by floor-to-ceiling windows overlooked the back of the property, an empty square of lawn enclosed by a wooden fence. Evan, Duncan surmised, had yet to turn his gardening skills to the backyard.

Duncan was counting the squares in the coffered ceiling when Evan stalked back into the room. He wore jeans, a deep blue shirt with a man on a pony embossed on the front, hiking boots, and an extremely surly glower.

"I kissed her, all right?" Evan said, shoving his hands into the pockets of his jeans.

"Whom did you kiss?" asked Duncan, blinking.

"Red. *Huge* mistake and I know it, so stop ragging my ass."

"I did not—"

"Yeah, but I know what you're thinking. She's Kirvahni, and I'm demon scum. She's a rule follower, and I'm a rule breaker. She's spent her life on the side of Right and Might, and I've spent mine doing shit I don't even want to think about."

"But you—"

Evan held up his hand. "You don't have to say it. I get it. It'll never work. Don't matter anyway, right? She's gone and she probably won't be back, so no point in talking about it." He turned and clomped for the door. "You gon' sit there all day, or we going after Toby?"

Duncan meekly rose and followed Evan outside to a black truck.

Evan stroked the metal side of the conveyance. "This is my baby. Bought her with my casino winnings. F-450, fully loaded. Ain't she a beaut?"

"Vroom," said Duncan, gazing at the gleaming carriage in wistful admiration.

"Damn straight." Evan gave the shining metal carriage another fond pat. "Four hundred and forty horsepower under the hood. Leather seats and heated steering wheel." He opened the passenger side door. "Climb in."

"'Twould be faster to do it my way."

"Not on your life. That shit makes me nauseous. Besides, a grown-ass man riding piggyback isn't dignified."

"It is not as though anyone will see you. We will be in the woods."

"Yeah? Say we find Toby and he's in bad shape? You can't carry both of us." Evan jabbed Duncan's chest. "And I'm not walking my ass out of the woods."

"You cannot drive this conveyance to the mouth of the cave," he protested. "You do realize there will be hiking involved?"

"Yeah, but we can get damn close. And when we're done, I'll need my wheels. Got a business to run." Evan smirked. "After what I saw this morning, I doubt you want me hanging around Cassie's, anyway." He pressed the back of his hand against his mouth and made loud kissy noises. "Unless you're kinky and like folks to watch?"

"I do not take your meaning."

"Some people like an audience when they boink."

"No, by Kehv. I am most definitely *not* interested in that."

"Didn't think so, but you never know."

"You should know. We are friends, are we not?"

"Sure. Whatev."

"Do not 'whatev' me," Duncan said. "It is dismissive and rude. Are we friends, or are we not?"

Evan's brows lowered. "I'm here, ain't I? I'm going into the woods to get tick-bit looking for some dude don't mean diddly to me. And I'm letting you ride in my new truck. What more do you want, a promise ring?"

Duncan clapped him on the shoulder. "I like you, too, Evan Beck. You are my comrade and ally. From this day forth, my sword is yours, an you need it."

"Gah," said Evan. Color high, he stomped around the truck and got behind the wheel. Duncan climbed in beside him. The interior was plush, the dashboard a confusion of buttons, dials, and whirli-gigs. Evan pushed a red circle, and the engine turned over with a sat-isfying rumble.

"Sweet ride, huh?" Evan backed out of the drive and motored down the street. "You need to get you one of these, Dunk. You know how to drive?"

"I am a warrior. I am as much at home on horseback as on foot."

"Translation—no. No worries. The Evster will teach you."

"I thank you."

He could operate any vehicle he desired with magic if need be, but Evan's offer had been sincere, and Duncan would not cheapen it for the world. Perhaps he would purchase a truck of his own and allow Evan to instruct him in driving in the manner of norms. He could become the first Dalvahni to obtain a governmental permit to legally operate a motorized carriage.

He imagined flashing the waterproof card at Conall and his broth-ers, and a slow grin spread across his face.

"Booyah," he said aloud.

"What?"

They had reached Main Street, and Duncan watched the shops slide past the passenger window. "Boo-yah," he said again. "I thought of something amusing and remembered the idiom you used."

"No. Just no."

Duncan shrugged. "Why? I like it."

"Kehv's elbow, this traffic blows." Evan cut his eyes at him. "Sounds stupid, don't it?"

"I see your point." Duncan sighed. "Very well, I shall refrain from saying *booyah*, if you insist, though it pains me greatly. It is a most excellent expression."

"And *Kehv's elbow* isn't?"

"No. 'Tis absurd."

"Yeah? How 'bout *Kehv's big toe*? Bunghole? Nip? Navel lint? Butt cheek?"

Evan waxed on in this ludicrous fashion as they continued to motor through town, showing, to Duncan's way of thinking, a lamen-table lack of respect for the Dalvahni creator. He folded his arms on his chest and waited for Evan to wind down, but the profane litany continued as they crossed the river bridge and turned onto a heavily wooded two-lane road.

"I got it," Evan said, as they rounded a curve. "Kehv's nut sack."

"*Enough.*" Duncan brought his hand down on the seat. "By the sword, you try my patience with these inanities."

Evan grinned. "Booyah."

Duncan gave him a smoldering glare. "You were provoking me?"

"Yup, and it worked. Where to now?"

Following Duncan's directions, Evan turned the truck off the pavement and onto a narrow, bumpy dirt trail. "Damn, this road is a goat fuck." Evan swore as they hit another deep rut. "You sure you know where you're going?"

"I am a Dalvahni warrior. We seek the djegrali through space and time. We do not tire. We do not fail. We hunt. So it is written in the Great Hall."

"I'll take that as a no." Evan rapped the dashboard with his knuckles. "Good thing my girl comes with a navigation system."

"As do I." Duncan tapped his temple. "It is called the Provider."

"Har-de-har-har."

"I am glad you are amused. Stop here. We walk the rest of the way."

Evan pulled the truck under the pines on the side of the road. "Man, we're in the middle of nowhere." He pointed through the windshield at the thick layer of grime on the formerly shining hood. "And you owe me a truck wash. Alabama red clay dust all over my shiny new truck."

Duncan opened his mouth to remind Evan that 'twas he who'd insisted on bringing his truck, then shut it again. Some battles were not worth fighting.

He pointed to a series of rolling, wood-covered hills. "The cave lies roughly a league beyond those knolls. We will go on foot from here. Now would be an opportune time for you to shapeshift."

Duncan turned his head when Evan did not answer and found a muscular, spotted hound regarding him soulfully from behind the wheel. The dog panted and gave Duncan a look that clearly said *Well? What are you waiting for?*

Duncan opened the truck door and climbed out, and the hound scrabbled after him. "I would have opened your door, had you but waited," Duncan said.

The dog yawned and plopped down on his haunches, his tail rustling the leaves, as though expecting something. Belatedly, Duncan remembered the colorful handkerchief Cassandra had given him. A *bandana*, she had called the faded blue and black patch of fabric that had belonged to Toby. He fished the cloth from his back pocket and held it out. The dog sniffed the handkerchief and took off, his waving tail disappearing into the underbrush.

Duncan followed. Up ahead, the hound gave a husky, raucous bay and took off. Evan was on the scent, and his blood was up. Duncan blurred through the trees after him. He reached the limestone bridge and the cave in moments and came upon a chilling sight. The lightning-struck elm was gone, and several acres of the surrounding forest had been uprooted, trees tossed about like kindling. His skin prickled, and the hair on his arms stood up. Certain kinds of power left a residue. Something very powerful, more powerful than any werewolf or shifter, had been here. The very air pulsed with energy.

Cautiously, he edged closer. Whatever great force had swept through had left a devastation of upturned stones, gouged earth, and blasted trees in its wake. Bodies littered the blast area, a dozen or more corpses that had been turned inside out, as though torn asunder by some maniacal butcher. Blood and body parts spattered the leaves and upturned earth, and broken bones lay in shards on the ground. He bent over a mutilated male carcass. The man's hair was dark brown with rusty highlights. One of his arms had been torn off and tossed aside. Duncan examined the dismembered limb. The skin of the upper arm bore a tattoo, a wolf's paw with the letter *R* above it in swirling script. Someone or something had decimated more than a dozen members of the Randall pack.

Duncan made a swift but thorough examination of the gruesome scene, but found no sign of Zeb or Toby. He raced up the hill and entered the cave. Empty, but there were ominous smears of blood on the stones. Something or someone had suffered grievous injury. Toby? If so, the shifter was no longer here. His body had been removed, or he'd dragged himself into the woods to die.

Determined to track Toby down, Duncan left the cave. As he came down the slope, he heard a distant, roupy howl. The hound was on Toby's trail. Duncan took a last look around. Nothing to be done for these poor souls. They were beyond help. Turning his back on the grisly scene, he set out, drawn by the sound of hound's steady yawping. As he neared the woods on the far side of the clearing, Trey Peterson's dead wife appeared on a tangy scud of perfume. The ghost wore a clingy one-piece costume with a deep scoop neck, black buckle strap clips, and belt. The skintight garment and matching perky cap atop her blond tresses were fashioned from fabric randomly patterned with splotches of gray, green, and brown. Thigh-high lace-up brown boots completed her garb.

She struck a sassy pose. "My goodness, aren't you the cutest little thing? Have we met?"

Duncan regarded her uneasily. He'd met Meredith Peterson once and had not enjoyed the experience. She was, in truth, a most malicious shade. "Aye. At your husband's office some moons ago."

"Oh, yeah, I remember—the day Trey got himself killed, the loser." She made a face of disgust. "What a huge disappointment my hubby muffin has been—really gone to the dogs." She twittered nastily at her own humor. "What brings you here? Looking for the orb?"

"Nay, I am searching for someone. What do you know of the orb?"

"Plenty." Meredith studied her fingernails. They were long and sharp and painted a bilious green. "I overheard the werewolves and those Skinner skanks whining like little bitches about the run-in you had this morning. Sounds like you ripped them a new one." Her painted lips curved in a sneer. "I can't tell you how glad I am to hear it. I hate that white trash."

"If you were spying on them, perhaps you know something of Toby Littleton. He was their captive."

"The old gray-haired shifter? He's not so good. The werewolves did a number on him. It's bad."

"How bad?"

"They beat the crap out of him, and then the whole pack took turns chewing on him. Between you and me, I don't think he'll make it."

Duncan clenched his fists. "Where is he?"

"The swamp ape's got him. Traded the orb for the old dude, the dumbass."

"Sugar has Toby?" Duncan stared at the ghost. "And he gave Zeb the orb in exchange?"

"Uh uh uh. That's not what I said." Meredith shook a manicured finger at him. "Try and keep up. The hairball didn't give the orb to Zeb. He gave it to the other one."

"The other one? I fear I do not take your meaning."

"Sharp as a bag of marshmallows, aren't you?" Meredith propped her hands on her hips. "I'm talking about ghouly boy, of course."

"Who is—" Duncan halted, a feeling of dread clutching his vitals. "Surely you do not mean—"

Cocking her head to one side like some sort of exotic bird, Meredith regarded him. "I surely do. Dead eyes—tattooed out the yin yang. You creeps got a name for him, but I can't remember what it is."

"The rogue," Duncan ground out. "We call him the rogue."

"That's it." Meredith's eyes shone with malice. "The rogue has the orb."

Duncan swallowed the sudden taste of bile. "Did Gryff... I mean, is the rogue responsible for this slaughter?"

"Nah," Meredith said. "The one in the sparkly robe did that. He had a shine on him that reminded me of the Indera Strass bridal pumps I wore on my wedding day." She sighed at the memory. "Those shoes were to *die* for—peep toe and crystal encrusted with a shark tooth pattern. Twenty-eight hundred dollars, plus tax. People in this stupid one-horse town shit little baby kittens when they saw them."

"This shining presence you speak of, was he comely made? Dark of hair and eyes, with an aspect most quelling?"

Meredith's brows creased, and her glee faded. "If you mean did he make me want to pee my pants, then yeah. That's the one. I hid from him. He was pretty to look at, but he scared me, and I'm *dead*."

"Pratt," Duncan muttered.

Meredith stiffened. "What'd you call me?"

"I meant no offense. I refer to the being in the shimmering robe. He is a god."

"If *I* were a god—which I so should be because I'm freaking *awesome*—you can bet your ass I wouldn't have a stupid name like Pratt."

Duncan turned and thoughtfully surveyed the butchery behind them. "His ire must have been great for him to have wreaked such havoc."

"Ire schmire. He turned those assholes inside out 'cause he was *pissed*." Meredith's form rippled in a ghostly shiver. "He wanted the orb, and ghouly boy wouldn't give it to him."

"He would not?" Duncan said, staring at her in surprise.

"Nope, and I can't imagine why. I would have dropped that thing like a hot potato. Frankly, I don't see what all the fuss is about. I was expecting something different. A big diamond or a sapphire, or maybe even an opal, but it's an ugly old rock, and it *burned* him. I could see his hands smoking from way over there." She pointed to a distant tree.

"But Gryff would not give it to him," Duncan said slowly. "Then what happened?"

"Zeb wanted the orb, too. Got all huffy and was like finders-keepers-losers-weepers. Said the orb belonged to the pack. Ordered his mutts to take it from ghouly boy. They went for it and that's when Pratt"— she made a face—"that is *such* a lame name, put them through the blender. The Skinners took off like scalded cats, and so did Zeb. Some alpha, huh?"

She looked him up and down, like she was sizing him up for a meal. "Catch you on the flip side, Scrumpdillyicious. This job is a wash."

She evaporated on a lemony pong.

Chapter Twenty

Cassie paced the hallway, worry and dread gnawing inside her. Toby was out there, hurt or dying or dead, and Duncan and Evan had gone into harm's way to rescue him. She should have gone with them. The not knowing was driving her mad.

"How long do you think they'll be gone?" she asked her huge protector.

"In truth, I cannot say," said Grim. "We do not know for certain that your friend Toby is being held in the cave. The werewolves could have secreted him anywhere. If that is the case, the hunt may take longer."

"How much longer?"

Grim shrugged. "An hour . . . a day . . . a week. It matters not. Duncan will find him."

"A *week*? That settles it." Cassie grabbed her bag off the hall tree and yelled up the stairs. "Verbena? Shag your butt down here. We're leaving."

"Yessum," Verbena said, padding downstairs to join her.

Grim frowned. "This is unwise. I was instructed to be with you at all times."

"So be with us, but I can't—I *won't*—hang around here doing nothing." Cassie gave him a challenging look. "You coming or staying?"

"Very well," Grim grumbled. "I will accompany you, if you insist, though I feel certain Duncan would wish you to remain here. If it is your worry that the Skinners and the Randalls may return, I can protect you from that riffraff."

"This is about me keeping my sanity." Cassie yanked open the back door. "If I don't get out of this house, I am going to lose my mind."

Grim followed her and Verbena outside and across the yard to the Silverado, bringing a funnel cloud of disapproval with him. *He can get over it,* Cassie thought. She meant what she'd said—she either moved or dissolved into a weeping mass of anxiety.

The sickly-sweet odor of decomp hit her as she neared the truck. "Oh, dear," Cassie said. "I forgot about poor Mac. Hold on."

Grim raised his hand. "I can remedy the issue in a trice, if you will permit."

"No, thanks," Cassie said quickly. "My truck, my problem."

The Silverado was her baby, and no magical super being was going to monkey around with it. She hurried into the garden shed and pulled on rubber boots and a pair of thick gloves. Clomping back outside, she grabbed the garden hose and a deck brush and went to work. She power-washed the truck bed, applied Clorox Clean-Up to the liner, and rinsed. The truck bed still smelled faintly of eau de corpse, however, and so she emptied a gallon of white vinegar onto the bed, waited five minutes, and rinsed again.

She inhaled. Pickled cadaver. Fabulous.

"That's all I got," Cassie said, jumping down. "I see a new truck liner in my future."

She stripped off the gloves and boots, put them back in the gardening shed, and washed her hands with a bar of Fiona Fix-it odor-removing soap.

"Ready?" she said, slipping back into her cowboy boots.

The three of them climbed in the truck, and Cassie took the wheel. At the end of the drive, she turned onto the paved road that ran parallel to the river. Grim was silent, and Cassie gave her hulking passenger a nervous gander. She remembered reading somewhere that in monitoring active volcanoes, scientists observed a period of quiescence right before they erupted. Pathways became sealed. Pressure built up. The greater the blockage, the longer the quiet period, the more powerful the resulting explosion.

On the surface, Mount Grim appeared dormant, but little fissures of anger cracked his stoic demeanor, and rage and hurt seeped from him in a pyroclastic flow. His twin brother was the rogue. Grim had blamed himself for Gryff's death, ostracizing himself for centuries out of grief and guilt. To find out that it had been for nothing, a sham, and that Gryff was alive and the betrayer must have been a terrible blow.

Cassie felt bad for Grim, but she wished Conall had sent someone less volatile. She was riding around with two-hundred-plus pounds of rocket fuel in her truck. Grim was chlorine trifluoride, terrifyingly flammable and ready to explode.

Verbena felt it, too. She sat in the back of the extended cab, quiet as a mouse. Cassie glanced at the girl in the rearview mirror. The poor kid was chewing on her cuticles, her wide-eyed gaze fastened on the back of Grim's head like he was a bomb she expected to detonate any minute.

"So," Cassie said, breaking the tense silence, "how's Sassy?"

Grim's stern countenance measurably softened at his wife's name. "She is well, thank you. She is visiting her mother at present, planning our upcoming espousal."

"I thought you two were already married."

"We are," Grim rumbled, "but Sassy's mother is most insistent we repeat the process in church with a human priest. I do not mind. I would gladly marry Sassy a thousand times—nay, a thousand times a thousand—if she so desired."

"That would be a lot of cake," Cassie said. She kept her tone light, but she was more than a little envious. Grim Dalvahni loved him some Sassy Peterson. *Must be nice*, she thought with a twinge of wistfulness.

Once, she'd thought Duncan loved her like that, but he'd turned tail and run the first time they'd hit a rut. To be fair, it had been more of a ditch than a rut. She could still see his expression when he'd learned that she was a demonoid, revulsion and disgust etched upon his handsome face.

Looking back at it dispassionately and with the maturity of the intervening years, Cassie could see his side of things. It must have been a terrible shock to discover the woman you loved was the offspring of your age-old enemy. Scratch that. A different *species*.

Still, if he'd loved her, if he'd *really* loved her, it wouldn't have mattered.

You got it wrong, toots, said the squeam. *At the end of the day, you'll be judged by how well YOU loved, not the other way around.*

The thought made Cassie squirm. Duncan had told her that he'd returned to Hannah many times through the years in search of her. The Dalvahni were arrogant, implacable, autocratic, and supremely annoying, but they didn't lie. If Duncan said he'd come back for her, it was the truth.

Duncan didn't find her—*couldn't* find her—because she wasn't there.

Yep, you took off, the squeam said. *Soon as you buried the children, you were out of here like a shot and across the pond.*

Cassie had fled to Europe. She'd stayed there for decades, traveling here and there, apprenticing herself to various wizards to perfect her craft and licking her wounds. She'd returned sporadically to Hannah through the years on business matters, posing as this or that relative so the norms wouldn't glom on to her, but she'd never stayed long.

You told yourself it was so the norms wouldn't notice that you don't age, but that wasn't the real reason.

No, it wasn't. The Great Wall of Denial Cassie had built around herself was crumbling, and she could see things clearly now. The farm and Hannah represented loss and unspeakable pain. Home reminded her of Jimbo, Maggie, and Rose, and the fact that she'd failed them, failed her brother, and failed herself. Home reminded her of Duncan and the great aching void he'd left when he departed.

Staying away had allowed her to pretend that the children's deaths were his fault, not hers. If she kept moving, ran fast enough and far enough, the past and guilt wouldn't catch up with her.

When she did return, it wasn't to the old place. She'd bought the land and house on the river, miles from the farm, insulating herself from her failings and the bitter memories. Cassie swallowed and faced a difficult truth. She'd run because she was a coward, plain and simple, and that made her ashamed.

Maybe if she'd loved more, loved *better*, things would have been different. *Love is patient. Love is kind. Always hopes . . . always perseveres.*

Duncan's words shone in her mind, bright as neon. *I was a fool,* he'd said. *I returned within a fortnight to beg your pardon . . . to tell you that I love you. That I was wrong to leave.*

To tell you that I love you . . .

Duncan had used the present tense—"love," not "loved." With characteristic Dalvahni stubbornness and commitment to a quest, he'd never given up on her.

Two weeks. Two lousy, miserable weeks, that's how long he was gone.

If she'd stayed, if she'd had the fortitude to face her grief and Duncan's rejection, they might have been apart a few days instead of more than a century and a half. Oh, sure, they'd have had one humdinger of a fight. Cassie would have raged and cursed, and blamed him for the children's deaths. She might have even sent him packing.

But he would have come back, the squeam said. *Duncan will always come back. He would have besieged you, warrior that he is, returning again and again. Until he broke down the walls of your wounded pride and bitterness, until your grief and guilt were spent and you forgave him.*

And herself. Cassie swallowed the lump in her throat. The squeam was right. Eventually, she would have forgiven Duncan. She wouldn't have had a choice—love keeps no record of wrongs.

It made her sad, to think how things could have been had she been stronger, loved more deeply and had more faith, but it was too late. Time marched on. Things changed. She couldn't go back. But there was Here and Now, and that was something. Cassie had learned to find joy in the day by scooping up little bits of happiness when and where she found them. Otherwise, she'd have drowned in sorrow.

Great sex wasn't love, but it was something, right?

She waited for the squeam to argue with her. To tell her to go for broke and entrust her heart to Duncan one more time.

Nada. Radio silence. Superego out to lunch.

"What is our direction?" Grim asked suddenly, startling Cassie.

"I thought we'd run by Chez Beck's so Verbena can get her things," she said. "And I need to check on something while I'm there. The restaurant is a client."

"What sort of trade are you in?"

"Supernatural security, mostly. I do other things—love, healing, and money-luck spells, road openers for people seeking a new path or job, and banishing spells for the troubled—but security's my bread and butter. I offer plans for home and retail security. Anti-norm spells, disturbance alarms, and kith repellent are my biggest sellers."

"Kith repellent?" Grim gave her a curious look. "Are not most norms ignorant of the kith's existence?"

"The kith repellent is for the kith, not the norms." She grinned. "We are the things that go bump in the night, and we know it. The kith pay good money to keep the booger bears out. Beck and Toby have been my customers for years, starting with the bar."

"The watering hole formerly known as Beck's?" Grim asked.

"That's the one. The shifter bar was kith only. I installed anti-norm wards and spells to misdirect them so they couldn't find the joint."

"And your precautions worked?"

"Yep," Cassie said with undisguised pride. "Toby did the rest. He was the bouncer. Nobody got past the Great Snozzola."

"I do not understand this term."

"Toby can *smell* talent." Cassie guided the truck around a curve. "Or in the case of a norm, the lack of it."

"I can see how that would be beneficial when one runs an establishment for supernatural clientele. Have you placed similar wards around the restaurant?"

Cassie shook her head. "No, Chez Beck's caters to kith and norms."

"Is that wise?" Grim asked. "It seems to me a combustive combination."

"It is worrisome," Cassie admitted. "Most norms don't know about the kith, and we want to keep it that way. No shifting is allowed at the restaurant, and no magical shenanigans."

"Prudent, but easier said than done. Your solution?"

"I've created a sort of dead zone around the property where magic doesn't work."

"Ingenious."

"Thanks," Cassie said. "It was a challenging job. Kith talent comes in all shapes and sizes, and the spells require constant maintenance and upgrades."

"Your spells have no effect upon the Dalvahni," Grim pointed out. "We come and go as we please."

"All built into the program. Conall wanted it that way, and what the customer wants, the customer gets."

"I misdoubt you could have done it, at any rate," Grim said with casual arrogance. "The Dal are tricksome."

Cassie would have dearly loved to burst his balloon, but he was right, dammit. The Dal were a magical law unto themselves, more demigods than supers. Take Duncan, for example. In one morning, he'd conjured new clothes out of the ozone and bitch-slapped an angry troop of weres and shifters out of their forms without breaking so much as a sweat. Impressive and damn sexy.

Grim's stomach growled, and he shifted on the seat. "I am loath to trouble you, but would comestibles be out of order? I have not broken my fast."

Cassie glanced at the clock on the dashboard and was surprised to see that it was almost noon. "Sure." Executing a three-point turn, she headed toward town. "You hungry, Verbena?"

Verbena made a small noise from the back that Cassie took as assent, and in no time, they were crossing the river bridge and toodling down Main Street. Downtown Hannah was picturesque and neat. Oak trees lined the pristine sidewalks, the storefronts were freshly painted, and wrought-iron streetlamps dotted every corner.

She pulled into a parking place a few doors down from the Sweet Shop, and the three of them piled out. A bell jangled over the door as they entered. Viola Williams, the Junoesque owner, welcomed them with a smile. Miss Vi knew how to cook Southern, and she prided herself on serving the freshest locally grown vegetables. Her desserts were homemade: banana pudding, moist cakes with fluffy icing made from scratch, and pies piled high with toasted meringue. Her husband, Del, was a darn good cook, too, known three counties wide for his barbecue and the drunk sauce served on the side.

Pauline, their bony waitress, trotted over, her bun so unforgiving that she appeared to have given herself a face-lift. She showed them to a booth and plunked a huge glass of tea in front of each of them. "What'll it be?" she asked, giving them a skinny-eyed glare.

"Ribs. High on the hog, no herbs," Grim said without hesitation.

"Herbs? You mean you don't want no vegetables?"

"That is correct."

"Humph," said Pauline, jotting down his order. She spun on the toes of her orthopedic shoes, sharply addressing a man in overalls at another table. "Jim Bob Watson, you tump over another glass of tea, I'm gon' knock you into next week, and no lie." She turned back to glare at Cassie and Verbena. "Well? I ain't got all day. You two?"

Verbena squeaked out an order for fried chicken, dark meat.

"Just tea for me," Cassie said. Her stomach was roiling with unease, and the thought of food made her nauseous.

"Humph," Pauline grumped again, swelling in offense. "You one of them women don't eat?"

"I had a big breakfast," Cassie said, giving the waitress a placating smile.

Pauline, however, was not appeased. She gave Cassie a glare and stomped off, returning shortly with their food. Grim ate with the same deftness and attention to detail as Duncan, demolishing two slabs of ribs in short order. Verbena tucked away a surprising amount of food for one so elfin: two drumsticks and a thigh, field peas with snaps, macaroni and cheese, and a corn muffin.

Pauline returned to take their dessert orders, and Grim declined her suggestion that he sample the chocolate pie. "I thank you, good damsel, but I will have the butterscotch instead," he told her.

"Fine, don't listen to me. I just work here," Pauline said with a snarl, and flounced away.

Cassie ordered a piece of strawberry cake, mostly because she was afraid Pauline would thump her on the head if she declined dessert, too, but she couldn't eat it. She was too worried.

She was toying with a bit of icing when the door of the Sweet Shop banged open and a woman rushed inside. She was a vision in a fire-engine-red bandana top, black pleather leggings, and strappy red high-heel pumps with cheetah accents. She'd piled her mass of dark, curly hair up and away from her face with a banana clip. A gunmetal gray Chihuahua was clutched to her generous bosom. The dog was extremely ugly, with teeth like an alligator and malevolent black eyes. A puff of curly hair sat atop his tiny head, and nestled in the thatch of curls was a bow that matched the woman's bandana.

"Mothertrucker," the woman gasped, her blue eyes bulging. "They's after me."

Cassie recognized the woman at once. Her name was Nicole Eubanks, and she'd paid the "witch" of Devil River a call some weeks back, seeking help with a personal matter.

"You get that dog out of here, Nicole." Miss Vi hefted her zaftig body around the front desk to intercept her. "I done tole you a million times, you can't bring him in here. That animal's a menace. He should be put down."

Cassie wanted to shout hell-to-the-yes on that one. Frodo the hellhound had nearly taken her arm off during Nicole's recent visit. His mistress had driven out to Cassie's house and tracked her down on the porch, demanding her help. "Man troubles," she'd announced, gazing up at Cassie from the lawn with anxious blue eyes.

Nicole had been wearing stilettos that day, too, and the heels had sunk into the sod. She'd teetered drunkenly for a moment, then toppled to the ground like a demoed skyscraper. Cassie had hurried down the steps to help her up, but Frodo had objected. *Strenuously*. One look down Frodo's razor-lined gullet, and Cassie had backpedaled, leaving Nicole and her alligator Chihuahua to fend for themselves. Nicole had floundered to her feet, unaided, and after much coaxing, Cassie had reluctantly agreed to help her with her "problem."

And here she was again. What sort of pickle had Nicole gotten into now?

"Frodo wouldn't bite his own fleas," Nicole was saying to Miss Vi. "He's my precious baby."

"Then you got a sho-nuff ugly baby," said Miss Vi. "Now get him out of here. I mean it. I run a clean business, and I ain't getting no health code citation 'cause of that hid-juss mutt."

There was a shout from outside, and a small herd of men charged past the plate glass window at the front of the Sweet Shop.

"There they is," Nicole shrieked, glancing around wild-eyed for someplace to hide.

She spied Cassie sitting in the booth and froze, a look of incredulity and outrage on her chubby face.

"You," she said in a voice of deepest umbrage. "This is all your fault."

"What's my fault?" Cassie asked, stunned.

The other customers in the restaurant sat like mannequins, watching the tableau in horrified fascination. Cassie spotted Robyn James from the *Hannah Herald* at a nearby table. She groaned. Robyn was always looking for tidbits to liven up the paper. Local flavor, he called them. This little farce would make Wednesday's edition for sure.

"I come to you for help," Nicole said, trembling with ill usage, "and you done cursed me. The Bible says, 'Do not turn to mediums.' I done sinned, I reckon, and that's what I get for trucking with a maleficent being."

"Melody who?" a man whispered in a stage voice.

His companions shushed him.

Cassie rose from the booth. "Why don't we talk about this outside?" She handed Verbena two twenty-dollar bills. "Pay for our food, Verbena, please, while I have a word with Ms. Eubanks. I'm sure there's been a misunderstanding."

Nicole hesitated, and it hit Cassie that the woman was afraid. Of *her*. Nicole lived with a crazed velociraptor in a dog suit, and she was afraid of Cassie.

Cassie was appalled. "I won't hurt you," she told Nicole in a low voice. "If I've done something, I'll make it right, I promise. Please don't be afraid."

Nicole wavered, and Frodo decided the matter by wriggling free of his mistress's grasp. Snapping and snarling, he attacked the ankles of the diners. Customers scattered to the winds or scrambled on top of tables to escape the ravening canine. Dishes and glasses crashed to the floor, adding to the confusion.

Snatching up a broom, Miss Vi swung it at the dog, but the Chihuahua shredded it like a wood chipper. Miss Vi threw what was left of the broom handle at the dog and scrambled onto the checkout counter. "Out," she bellowed, pointing at Nicole in righteous wrath. "Out of my restaurant, before I call the police."

Nicole plucked the raging animal off the chair it was chewing to bits. "Come on, Frodo." She planted a kiss on the merkin crowning the dog's head. "We's leaving."

Cassie followed Nicole outside. She found her hovering on the sidewalk, her eyes twitching this way and that. "Now," Cassie said, staying well out of Frodo's reach, "what's this about a curse?"

Nicole sobbed, tears streaming down her face. The Chihuahua made a noise of distress that sounded like a miniature buzz saw and lapped at Nicole's wet cheeks. Nicole gave a watery chuckle. "Sweet boy," she said, stroking the malformed creature. She glared at Cassie. "I been dating Dan Curtis, one of Hannah's finest. His mama and sisters ain't been happy about us from the get-go, on account of I'm eight years older than him. A-and because they's skinny minnies and they say I'm fat." Her chin wobbled. "Dan likes my figure. H-he asked me to marry him. His mama started snooping around when he told her he'd proposed, and found out I'm divorced . . . a-and that I used to dance at the Booby Trap." Her voice broke. "They's Baptist, see? And Baptists don't even have sex standing up—too close to dancing." A tear dripped off her chin and into Frodo's waiting maw.

"I come to you for a charm. Something to make Dan fall out of love with me."

"I remember," Cassie said. "I told you not to let those spiteful women spoil your happiness, but you wouldn't listen, so I gave you what you asked for."

"Never did no such thing." Nicole's bosom heaved. "I asked you for a repelling charm. What you give me *attracts* 'em."

"What?"

Cassie stared at Nicole in horror. "Oh, dear. I've been a little out of sorts lately. Something must have gone wrong."

"You damn straight something went wrong." Nicole's plump face was flushed with righteous indignation. "You whammied me."

Chapter Twenty-one

Nicole gasped and spun around at the heavy tramp of feet. A dozen or more men of varying ages—several that Cassie knew for a fact were married—rounded the corner of the drugstore. When they saw Nicole, they charged, their eyes glazed with a strange fever. One of the men wore police blues—Dan Curtis of the grasping helicopter mom, Cassie presumed.

"Mothertrucker, here they come," Nicole shrieked. "You gotta fix this, Miss Cassie. I ain't cut out to be no love goddess."

The herd of men let out a collective bellow of distress and stampeded. Nicole shrieked and bolted, her hoochie heels chugging up and down on the sidewalk. The frenzied men swept past Cassie, knocking her aside, and thundered after Nicole.

"Think she'll make it?"

Cassie turned to find a silver-haired gentleman regarding her. Amasa Collier came from old money. He'd been a successful lawyer until he'd started seeing demons and his practice had dried up. The joke was on the norms. Amasa *did* see demons, though most folks thought he was a whack job. The norms didn't know half of what went on in this town, bless their hearts.

"I hope so," Cassie said. "You know Nicole?"

"Yep. She's quite the artist. Has a display in my gallery. Made a replica of *The Last Supper* out of cigarette butts that will make you weep. You should stop by." He gave her a sharp look. "Did you really whammy her?"

"Not on purpose." Cassie worried her bottom lip. "Apparently, the charm I gave her is defective." She sighed. "I take that back. Apparently, *I'm* defective. Something's up with my powers."

"Maybe I can help." Amasa unhooked a thin metal rod from his belt and held it up. "Know what this is?"

"A couple of coat hangers twisted together?"

"Contrabulator. M'own device." Amasa waggled the thing in the air. "Mind if I run a simple diagnostic test?"

"That depends." Cassie eyed the wire. "You planning on doing a probe?"

Amasa chuckled. "Nope. Nothing invasive. Simple scan. Won't hurt, I promise."

He waved the contrabulator in Cassie's direction, and to her surprise, the dang thing lit up and hummed.

"Hmm," Amasa said. "Lot of gray and murky brown in your aura."

"Meaning?"

"Blocked energy fields. Distrust. Reluctance to let go. Fear of sharing yourself with others."

Cassie felt her jaw unhinge. Amasa Collier had described her to a T.

"But whadda I know?" He gave her a sly smile. "I'm a crazy old coot. Ask anybody."

Amasa ambled off, whistling and swinging his contrabulator, and Grim and Verbena came out of the Sweet Shop. "All is well?" Grim asked. "You seem disquieted."

"No, I'm not okay. That woman who came into the Sweet Shop just now?"

"The buxom wench with the demon dog?"

Cassie nodded. "She bought a repelling charm from me a few weeks ago, and it backfired. I need to ride out to Chez Beck's and check my spell lines. Make sure they haven't been affected, too. If some kith were to get drunk and shift, all hell would break loose."

"Then let us go there forthwith," said Grim.

They got in the truck again and headed back across the bridge. Grim was silent. With nothing to distract her, Cassie's brain started to spin again. Where was Duncan? Was he in danger? Was Toby alive? Had Evan been able to sniff him out?

Chez Beck's was several miles outside of town on the banks of the Devil River, and by the time Cassie pulled into the parking lot and turned off the engine, she was frantic with anxiety and grateful for something to take her mind off her worries. The restaurant was closed until five, and the lot was empty, giving her a clear view of the premises. The front of the building faced the river, and a tree-lined veranda along the waterfront offered al fresco dining. For those who preferred the comfort of the indoors, the restaurant's full-length windows gave patrons a stunning view of the river. At night, Cassie knew, the place would be ablaze with lights. A huge floating dock with a bandstand was available for party rentals and weddings, and on evenings when things were hopping, music and laughter floated down the river.

"You go on ahead," she said, turning in the seat to address Verbena. "You know the code to get in?"

"Yessum," said Verbena. "My room's downstairs. I'll grab my things and be back in two shakes."

"Take your time. What I've got to do may take a while."

Verbena nodded and slipped out of the truck, skimming across the lot toward the building, her feet barely touching the ground. She punched in a code at the door and disappeared inside.

"She is swift, that one," Grim observed in an admiring tone. "Do the Skinners perchance have dryad blood?"

"The Skinners? I doubt it." Cassie exited the truck, pausing to grab a short ash staff from the gun rack. "At any rate, Verbena's not a Skinner. She says Old Charlie wasn't her dad. She goes by her mother's maiden name now, Van Pelt."

Grim climbed out of the truck, walking behind Cassie as she made a circuit around the building, checking her wards. He moved soundlessly and with agile grace for such a big man, but then, she'd yet to meet a Dalvahni klutz.

"Verbena Van Pelt has a musical ring to it," Grim said. "The Skinners have no claim on her, then?"

"Not a bit of it, but try and tell Joby Ray that. He won't take no for an answer."

"Conall says she strengthens the abilities of others. Is this true?"

"Oh, yeah," Cassie said. "Verbena's a walking, talking power booster. The Skinners are in a bad way, and they see Verbena as their out. Doesn't matter what *she* wants. Never did, according to Verbena."

"The desperate have nothing to lose, and that makes the Skinners twice as dangerous."

"Pretty much." Cassie flashed him a smile. "Which is why you're stuck babysitting us today."

She hesitated. Something had been eating at her all day, but in the face of Grim's raw grief and rage, she'd been reluctant to intrude. She hardly knew this big, forbidding warrior.

Tell him, her inner voice urged. *He needs to know.*

Cassie cleared her throat. "Um . . . Grim?"

"Yes?"

"I saw Gryff this morning before the demon attack."

Grim stiffened and his eyes went flat. "What of it?"

Why am I doing this? Cassie thought. This was none of her business. She should let it drop.

"I don't think he's with the demons by choice."

"He chose," Grim said in a cold, deadly voice. "He chose the enemy over his oath and his duty, over his brothers. He chose the djegrali over *me*." He slammed his fist into a pine tree, sending bark and splinters of wood into the air. "He allowed me to wallow in grief and exile and self-loathing for thousands of years. That is what rancors my soul."

"I saw him," Cassie persisted. "He's the walking dead. I know magic, and he's been bound."

"No chain devised can hold a Dalvahni warrior, and Gryff has been gone for millennia."

"I'm not talking about ropes and chains. I'm talking runes and dark spells. Wicked, bad mojo."

"You are mistaken. The djegrali do not have the power to bind the Dalvahni."

Okay, she'd tried. This was her cue to change the subject . . . but then her mouth opened of its own accord. "Maybe the djegrali didn't bind him. Maybe someone else did. Someone more powerful."

Grim glowered at her. "Such as?"

"I don't know. Another demon hunter, maybe?"

"You would accuse a Dalvahni warrior of dabbling in the dark arts?"

"That's what you suspect Gryff of, isn't it?"

"Gryff is an anomaly."

"I'm not accusing anyone," Cassie said, choosing her words with care. "I'm thinking out loud. What about one of the Kirvahni? Could one of them be responsible?"

"Nay, I think not. And to what purpose, I ask you?"

"Greed? Power? Same reason you thought Gryff had gone to the dark side, I guess." Cassie shrugged. "I don't pretend to have the answers, but I know what I saw, and I'm telling you, Gryff is under some kind of compulsion."

Grim's rigid expression did not relax, but his golden eyes were shadowed with uncertainty. Good. She'd given him something to think about.

Cassie left him to mull it over and walked away from the building to check the spells along the property line. Opening her senses, she started at the northwest corner and continued down to the river, examining the shimmering strands. She hadn't gone far when Grim joined her, keeping pace with her but maintaining a respectful distance to allow her to work. There were lines of strain around his mouth and eyes, but he made no reference to Gryff, and Cassie did not bring it up again. Sometimes, in her experience, you planted a seed and let it grow.

"All is as it should be?" Grim asked when she'd finished and they were walking back to the building.

"Yeah." Cassie heaved a sigh of relief. "Everything seems okay."

"And your magical malady? Know you the cause?"

"Nope, but I'm sure it will pass."

"I certainly hope so," said Junior Peterson, the restaurant's spectral piano player, as he appeared in front of them. Or part of him did. The ghost's form was snowy and grainy, like an old-timey, vacuum-tube television with bad reception. He nodded at Grim in greeting. "Good to see you again, Grimford. How's my baby girl?"

"Sassy is well, I thank you, sir."

"Bring her to the restaurant for dinner one night," Junior said. "She can hear me play." He made a face and looked down at his missing bottom half. "That is, if Cassie can fix this . . . this whatever it is."

"Oh, my goodness." Cassie gaped at him in shock. "How long has this been going on?"

"Can't say for sure," Junior said in his plummy drawl. "I've been working other gigs for the past three months and haven't been here. I show up this morning to practice my piano, and this happens." He indicated his staticky body. "And that's not all." He whistled, and a Dalmatian dog head—and nothing else—came bobbing out of the woods like a friar's lantern. "Trey's got it, too."

"I'm so sorry," Cassie said, horrified. "Does it hurt?"

"No, but the noise is driving me crazy. Crickets in my ears. Can't hear myself think, much less play the piano."

"There must be a glitch in the wards that I missed. I'll be right back."

Frazzled and worried, she snatched up her bag and hurried off to run another spell check, then noticed her Dalvahni shadow. "You don't have to follow me around, you know," she told Grim. "This will take some time."

He crossed his arms and gave her a look that was pure Dalvahni. "I will not leave you. I gave Duncan my word."

"Okay. Knock yourself out."

"I fail to see how that would be beneficial."

"I didn't mean literally. I meant suit yourself."

"Another inexact expression. Were I to suit myself, I would be with my wife or in pursuit of my knave of a brother."

Cassie sighed. Grim wasn't a bad sort, but he lacked Duncan's sense of humor.

It took her the better part of an hour to find the problem—a banishing charm deeply embedded in the nullifying wards like a computer virus. Cassie was horrified. This was not the way she did things. Something must have distracted her the last time she was here. She pulled her yearly planner, an old-school spiral-bound notebook containing the months of the year, out of her bag. Hannah was hell on electronics, and paper worked best. With a feeling of foreboding, she flipped the pages to the last diagnostic she'd run at Chez Beck's.

May—the same month she and Sassy had been captured by the witch and very nearly killed.

May—when she'd fled the cabin and the nightmare confrontation with her mother and run smack into Duncan, standing under the oak where Jamie and Maggie, and baby Rose were buried.

Leave me alone, Duncan, she'd shouted at him. *Just leave me the hell alone.*

Her finger moved through the days of the month to the square marked *Chez Beck's.* She'd made her quarterly service call to the restaurant the next day. Good grief, she must have accidentally installed the banishing charm while running the diagnostic. She'd been reeling and upset, and her emotions and her desire to push Duncan away had spilled over, infusing the spell. Junior and Trey were lucky they hadn't vanished altogether.

She slipped the planner back in her bag. "I think I know what's wrong."

"Felicitations. That is half the battle."

"Amasa Collier used his contrabulator on me. He says my aura is out of balance. Too much gray and brown."

"And the implication?"

"Magical constipation, misgivings, control issues, and fear of intimacy." Cassie ticked the list off with her fingers. "In other words, I'm a complete mess."

Grim looked like a man who'd just glimpsed his grandmother naked. "I see. Know you the cause of this dread infirmity?"

"Oh, yeah. I've got a pretty good idea."

She located the banishing charm and removed it, and she and Grim walked back to the restaurant, where they found Junior chatting up Verbena. The ghost was fully formed and looked remarkably solid, probably because he was standing next to the Enhancer.

"Crickets gone?" Cassie asked Junior.

"Not so much as a chirp. I am much improved, thank you, and so is Trey."

The Dalmatian pranced up, head, tail, and everything in between visible, confirming Junior's pronouncement.

"Excellent," Cassie said, relieved. "We'll be going now."

Junior waved and faded from view. A moment later, the sound of piano music drifted from the restaurant.

"Got everything you need?" Cassie asked Verbena.

"Yessum." She hefted a duffel bag. "I'm set."

Grim took the bag from Verbena, and the three of them walked back to the Silverado. As Cassie wheeled out of the parking lot, the Dalmatian chased them, barking joyfully, until they turned onto the road. Glancing in the rearview mirror, Cassie saw the dog turn and trot into the woods.

"Where to now?" asked Verbena.

"Home," Cassie said.

At some point, when things quieted down—if they ever did—she needed to sit down and go through her planner. Compile a list of the homes and businesses she'd visited since May, and call her clients and schedule rechecks. She'd botched a repelling charm and scrambled a couple of ghosts. Lord only knew what else she'd done.

Take poor Nicole, for instance. She was freaking Helen of Troy, the face that launched a thousand rednecks, and it was Cassie's fault. She was determined to make it right, for Nicole and each and every one of her customers, if it took her a month of Sundays.

She'd told Grim she'd figured out her problem, and that was the truth. In a word, her problem was Duncan. The image of his hard, muscled body rose in her mind. He'd kept her in a stew for months, and that had made her careless and distracted, but that was in the past. No more denial. No more holding back. Her magical woes were at an end.

Duncan was the cause, but he was also the cure.

Cassie wanted him. There. She'd admitted it, but he wanted her, too, with a force he could barely contain. Big, strong, beautiful Duncan had trembled—*trembled*—when he'd kissed her this morning. The knowledge was heady.

Soon and very soon, her hedonistic demon sang with an anticipatory shiver of pleasure. *Soon you'll be with Duncan.*

But only if he returned to her, safe and sound.

Anxiety squeezed Cassie's lungs, and her lusty thoughts were drowned in a new tide of dread. What was happening out there? Toby was in trouble because of her, and Duncan and Evan had gone into harm's way to save him. Because of her. All because of her.

She drove faster, suddenly frantic to reach the house. Why the hell hadn't she stayed put? She'd done it again. She'd run. What if something had happened to Duncan? The thought sent a shaft of white-hot pain through her.

Still think you're not emotionally involved? the squeam snickered.

"Shut up," said Cassie.

Grim turned his head and gave her a reproachful look. "I said nothing."

"Not you." Cassie gripped the steering wheel. "I was talking to myself."

Grim gave her a hard look and returned his gaze to the passing scenery.

The river road was a snarl of pavement winding through thick trees, but the Silverado hugged the familiar curves. Cassie's nerves wound tighter, the need to reach the house a steady tick in her head like a metronome.

Three more miles to go.

Two.

Her driveway was around the next bend. She spotted her mailbox in the distance and slowed, turning onto her graveled road. The truck bumped down the drive, through the woods, and into the clearing.

Home. Cassie parked in her usual spot and slung her bag over her shoulder. She reached for the door handle and froze. A large, furry face stared back at her through the driver's side window. Snow white and fluffy as a bunny, the enormous creature regarded her with guileless, pink-rimmed eyes the color of an October sky.

The bigfoot pressed its broad, pink nose to the window. "Dunk?" The deep voice that emanated from the massive chest was the chirping trill of a Siberian cat. "Where Dunk?" The bigfoot's black lips quivered. "Doggie hurt."

Raising a shaggy arm, he pointed to a mangled lump of gray fur on the back porch.

"*Toby*," Cassie cried.

"Cassie, wait." Grim made a grab for her as she flung open the door. "The creature could be dangerous."

Cassie ignored him. Leaping from the truck, she ran for the house.

Chapter Twenty-two

The bluetick bayed in the distance, and Duncan set off through the woods, his eyes scanning the broken ground for hidden pitfalls. Fallen branches thrust bony arms from the thick carpet of leaves on the forest floor, and lichen-spotted boulders were scattered about like a game of knucklebones abandoned by giants. Skirting a downed beech, Duncan churned up a hummock, his ears attuned to the hound's excited barking. Abruptly, the dog fell silent.

Duncan paused, listening. From the southeast, there came a faint, distressed woofing. He followed the sound and found Evan, fully dressed once more in jeans, boots, and the blue shirt, seated on a shelf of rock in a mossy gorge. Dogwood trees, lacy ferns, and a tangle of frothy vines grew along the embankments. Though it was fall, the leaves had yet to turn and the ravine was a cool, green hollow.

Nearby, a rill chuckled noisily over tumbled rocks, but judging from Evan's morose countenance, he did not enjoy the song. He sat hunched, arms resting on his thighs, his gaze on his feet.

He lifted his head when Duncan came trotting up. "I lost the raft," he said, his expression surly and out of sorts.

"Raft?"

"Toby's scent, man," Evan snapped. "It was in the cave—my nose was full of it. I followed it through that bone yard—what the hell happened back there, anyway? I've seen some messed-up shit in my time, but that was majorly janked. Thought I was going to horf. Anyway, I followed it into the woods, but I kept losing it. It was there, faint, but smothered by another scent. Something floral and sweet." He shook his head. "I'd catch a whiff of Toby and lose it. Then *pfft*, it was gone."

"Do not castigate yourself," Duncan said. "Sugar has Toby.

Though he seldom bestirs himself, he can move quite briskly when motivated, and the bloodbath we have witnessed would have overset him mightily. He is a gentle soul."

"Sugar?"

"The boggy boon. Big hairy man, chuchunya, grass ape. There are sundry names for his kind, too many to recount." Evan gave him a blank look and Duncan said, "We discussed this with Mac earlier. There is a troop of the creatures hereabout. Sugar was left to die because of his unusual coloring. He is stark white, you see, and obtrusive."

"You're telling me a pigment-challenged, lavender-scented bigfoot has Toby?"

"So the shade Meredith Peterson informs me." Duncan paused, adding with scrupulous honesty, "Though she did not comment on his odor."

"Meredith's here?" Evan jerked like he'd been shot with a steel-tipped bolt. "Oh, hell, no."

"Calm yourself. She has departed," Duncan said. "And now that we know Sugar has Toby, we can be gone as well."

Evan got to his feet. "You know I have to ask. How'd you get to be pals with a bigfoot?"

"I happened upon Sugar in the woods some moons past. He was caught in a trap and sorely hurt. I healed his injuries, and we became friends."

"A demon hunter and his woolly booger. How sweet." Evan took a step and winced. "Lead the way, but not too fast. I'm tired, and my feet are killing me."

"Tired? For shame. Modern convenience has made you indolent."

Evan found this remark so offensive that he vociferated most of the way back to the truck. Duncan let him spew, his mind on Meredith's revelations. Gryff had the orb and Pratt wanted it. The implications of what he'd learned were enormous. Conall must be informed, and Kehvahn, as well.

They climbed in the truck and Evan cranked the engine. "We need tunes," he announced, pushing a button as they headed back in the direction they'd come.

A tortured wailing poured into the truck through the output device called "a sound system."

"Sweet merciful Kehv," said Duncan.

Evan jabbed the button a second time, and the yowling diminished. "What, you don't like music?"

"That is not music. That is someone strangling a cat."

"Very funny. What's eating you, bro?"

Duncan sighed. "I confess I am in turmoil. You know of the rogue?"

"Grim's twin? Yeah. What about him?"

"I saw him this morning, and he is much changed. More scarecrow than warrior, a wraith clad in a hollow skin. My mind was filled with misdoubt when I beheld him, and now I wonder . . . could it be that we were wrong, and Gryff is more wretch than villain?"

"I dunno, but if I had a brother, I'd want to find out," Evan said. "Take it from me, sometimes people don't have a choice, although Captain Asshat will tell you different."

"My counsel to you, as a friend? Do not address Conall as Captain Asshat, if e'er you hope to reconcile with your sister."

"That street runs both ways. Conall should treat *me* with a little respect."

"Agreed."

"Yeah? Well, don't hold your breath. Conall Dalvahni will cut me some slack when Jesus comes back in a pink dress."

Duncan mulled over this peculiar remark and finally decided 'twas a reflection of Evan's sincere doubt that relations with his sister and the captain of the Dalvahni were likely to improve. As he entertained serious misgivings on that score as well, he decided to change the subject. "Know you the direction of the Randall enclave? I should like to ascertain that Mac's mother and sister are safe."

"No idea," Evan said. "Told you, I don't hang with weres. Ask Cassie. She dated that Zeb fellow."

"Do not remind me."

Evan gave him a sideways glance. "You two working things out? You were going at it mighty hot and heavy this morning."

"In a manner of speaking. Cassandra has consented to be my thrall, and I hers."

"Say *what?*"

"We have fixed upon a physical relationship. Sexual congress without the emotional component or lasting commitment."

"Bed buddies, huh? You okay with that?"

"Not in the slightest, but I shall strive to be content with carnal pleasure." Duncan's jaw tightened. "For the present."

He would find a way to make Cassandra trust him again. He would lay siege to her heart and break down her defenses, no matter how long it took. A Dalvahni warrior was stalwart. A Dalvahni warrior was tireless. A Dalvahni warrior knew not defeat.

For this Dalvahni warrior, there was no choice. Cassandra was his heart's blood.

Evan shook his head. "Straight-up boning. No demands or complications. Sounds like a mangasm to me. Why mess with a good thing?"

"Is that the sort of arrangement you desire with Taryn?" Turning in the seat, Duncan regarded him. "Coupling and nothing more?"

"Yeah, sure." Evan lifted his shoulders in a dismissive gesture. "What else is there?"

"A great deal, as it happens. Having indulged in . . . er . . . boning for thousands of years ere I came to Hannah, I prefer Cassandra and complications."

"Why?" Evan sounded genuinely puzzled.

"I do not know that I can explain," Duncan said. "Suffice it to say that I was not alive until I met Cassandra, and I have been dead lo these many years without her."

"That is some seriously nauseating shit, my friend."

"'Tis but the truth."

Evan guided the truck off the narrow trail and onto the paved road that led back to Cassandra's. "So what exactly is a thrall?"

"Sexual creatures designed to sate a warrior's physical needs. We have congress with them to maintain our detachment and dedication to the hunt, unhampered in battle by emotion."

"Sex as one of the perks of the job, huh? Nice company benefit."

"Lest you think we take advantage, the thralls are succubi that feed on emotion. The relationship is beneficial to both species."

"Oh, yeah? How often do you go in for a lube job?"

Duncan chuckled. "Lube job—a term denoting a common service wherein certain parts of a motorized carriage are lubricated to facilitate the machine's operation. Your quip, however, refers to the coital act. Amusing."

"Can't put anything over on you," Evan said. "How often?"

"The Great Directive does not prescribe a strict schedule, only that a Dalvahni warrior avail himself of a thrall at regular intervals."

Evan drove on in silence for several miles, his expression brooding. Something was bothering him, though Duncan could not guess the direction of his thoughts.

"Are there male and female thralls?" Evan asked at length in the tone of one whose curiosity was beyond bearing.

"Naturally."

"And do the Kir have the same deal? With the thralls, I mean."

"Of course, though the establishments are kept separate for privacy and due to the somewhat fractious nature of the relationship between the Kir and the Dal." Duncan stared through the glass at the lush forest of the river basin they were passing through. Hard to believe horror and death had stalked these quiet woods but a few hours past. "Depletion is beneficial to all demon hunters, be they male or female."

"Shit." Evan's hands clenched and unclenched on the wheel. "Shit, shit, *shit*."

Duncan turned his gaze from the green blur outside his window. "Something is amiss?"

"Yeah. It makes me crazy to think about—" Evan's expression closed. "Nothing. Forget it."

"Complications, my friend?"

"I don't want to talk about it." Scowling, Evan turned the motorized carriage onto the road leading to Cassandra's abode, and the truck crunched down the long, wooded drive. The house came into view, and Evan slammed on the brakes.

"Holy shit," he said, gaping. "It's the Bumble."

Sugar stood near the back steps that led to Cassandra's house. In the sunlight, the boggy boon's shaggy pelt glistened bright as snow. His eyes, wide with terror, were fixed on Grim as the warrior advanced on him, sword drawn. Cassandra knelt on the porch beside a bloodstained gray heap, her face pale and set. Her lips were moving. She was saying something to Grim, but the warrior paid no heed. He was in battle mode, and bent on the kill.

Duncan was out of the truck and across the lawn in a blur of movement. "Hold, Grim," he said, stepping in front of the quaking bigfoot. "Sugar is harmless, on my oath as a warrior."

"Sugar?" Grim lowered the sword. "By the gods, Duncan, I am in no mood for your jests."

"'Tis no jest, I assure you. Sugar is quite tame. More to the point, he is under my protection. Sheath your weapon, I pray you, for I will suffer him no harm."

Grim snarled a word, and his sword disappeared.

"Dunk?" Sugar warbled from behind Duncan.

Duncan turned to reassure the boggy boon. "Be at ease, my friend. My brother is a trifle grumpish, but Dunk will not let him hurt you."

"Grumpy?" Sugar's anxious gaze darted to Grim and back to Duncan. "Owie? Paw?"

Duncan rubbed his jaw to hide his smile. "How perceptive of you. Pain would certainly account for his choler." He turned to Grim. "Sugar would know an, perchance, you have suffered some injury that has caused your distemper?"

Grim glowered. "Now see here, Duncan—"

Sugar's baritone trill drowned him out. "Sugar like Dunk," the boggy boon declared, seizing Duncan in his bearlike arms. "Dunk heal Sugar owie."

"Yes, yes," Duncan said, his ribs creaking from this exuberance of affection. "Put Dunk down. There's a good fellow."

Sugar dropped him at once. Raising a long, hairy arm, he pointed to the porch, his expressive face wrinkled in consternation. "Sugar bring doggie. Dunk heal doggie's owie?"

"Dunk shall do his best."

Sugar's blue eyes brightened. "Sugar good boy?"

"A very good boy," Duncan said. "Your mother will be proud."

"Mama . . . treat?"

"Of a certainty. Hie thee home at once and tell Miss Lucy that Dunk says give Sugar a treat."

"Dunk says treat." The boggie boon nodded and grinned, showing large, square teeth. "Sugar good boy." With that, Sugar loped away.

"By the sword," said Grim, watching Sugar disappear into the woods. "In truth, the creature is not hostile?"

"Quite gentle," Duncan assured him. "I misdoubt Sugar would bite his own fleas, an he had them. He was adopted as a cub by a childless human woman. Miss Lucy dotes upon him to excess, and she is most scrupulous about cleanliness."

Evan sauntered up. "Bathes him regular, huh? Baby shampoo would be my guess, and a shit ton of it. That's why he smells like a giant lavender fart."

Grim looked thoughtful. "Now that you mention it, the creature is redolent."

"Duncan, I need you." Cassandra's voice was strained. "It's Toby. Can you help me get him in the house?"

Duncan, I need you. Ah, sweet merciful Kehv.

Every fiber of Duncan's being responded to her sweet words, and he was at her side at once.

She looked up at him, her beautiful, expressive eyes filled with anguish. "It's bad." Her mouth trembled. "Oh, Duncan, look what they've done to him."

Duncan felt as though a knife had been slipped between his ribs. Her concern and affection for the old shifter were plain, and the knowledge made him burn with jealousy. A fine warrior he was, to be sure, envious of her feelings for a friend.

But I desire her love, too, he thought with a wistful pang. *More than anything.*

He would not get it. Still, he would accept what she offered and rejoice. To be near her, to be with her, to have her in his arms once more, these were riches he had despaired of obtaining.

Swallowing his bitterness, he knelt beside Cassandra on the porch. Toby was in dog form, a great gray wolfhound, and he was moribund, his rough coat torn in dozens of places by savage bites. He'd lost a great deal of blood, and his deep chest rose and fell in shallow breaths. At Duncan's gentle touch, he moaned and shuddered in pain.

"Duncan?" Cassandra's voice shook with unspoken questions.

Duncan finished his examination and settled back on his heels. "In truth, he has suffered grievous hurt."

Evan edged closer to the porch. "Will he be a werewolf? I mean, now he's been bitten?"

"I know not," Duncan said. "Cassandra?"

She shook her head. "No. Randalls are born weres, not cursed. That kind of lycanthropy isn't contagious any more than the kith are infectious to norms." Her breath caught on a sob. "But werewolf bites can turn septic, a-and Toby has s-so many."

She covered her face with her hands and burst into tears. The sound shattered Duncan and his jealousy and heartache were swept aside by the urgent need to comfort her. He pulled her into his arms. She was trembling violently, and he willed his strength into her shaking form. "Easy, my sweet," he murmured. "You must be strong for Toby."

"You're right." Cassandra swiped her eyes. "Verbena's upstairs getting a room ready for him. Let's take him inside."

Shaking off her distress, she slipped from his grasp and into the house. Duncan let his empty arms drop and watched her go.

Behind him, Evan whistled. "You poor, dumb son of a bitch. You got it bad."

"This, I already know." Duncan turned to Grim. "My thanks for safeguarding Cassandra in my absence. Howe'er, I would ask another boon."

"You know you have but to ask."

Duncan inclined his head. "Be so good as to inform Conall that I have tidings of the orb. Ask him to inform Arta as well. Tell the captain I will report to him anon, but first, I must do what I can for Toby."

Grim turned to leave. "It will be done."

"And Grim, you will wish to be at the meeting. I have news of Gryff."

Grim's big body went rigid. "I will deliver the message and return for your tidings." Without another word, he disappeared.

"Guess I'll head home," said Evan. "Got a business to run. Let me know if I can do anything."

"My thanks for your good offices today," Duncan said. "Give my regards to the Vikings in your larder."

"What?" Evan made a face. "Never mind. I don't wanna know." Strolling to his truck, he climbed in and drove away.

Duncan lifted his hands, and the dog rose into the air. He guided the mortally injured shifter into the house and up the stairs to the landing, where Cassandra waited, her face pale and tense with worry.

"This way," she said, hastening down the hall ahead of him.

Duncan floated the dog into the bedchamber and looked around. Cassandra and Verbena stood near a big four-poster bed that had been stripped and covered in a clean white sheet. The room was neat and simply furnished. A small table with a lamp sat next to the bed, and a comfortable chair and footstool had been placed by the window for reading. A squat chest the locals called a "dresser" sat near the door, with an oval mirror above it.

Duncan carefully lowered the dog onto the bed. "Have you goldenseal, calendula, and St. John's wort among your stores?" he asked Cassandra.

"I think so, but aren't we going to use magic to heal him?" Her voice was thick with tears, and her face was pinched with the effort not to cry. "T-the three of us, I mean."

"Of a certainty," Duncan assured her, "but I have no experience with werewolf bites, and Toby's are many and putrid. I would be prepared in the event our combined magics are not enough."

In truth, Duncan doubted the shifter could be saved, but he kept this thought to himself. He had no wish to add to Cassandra's distress.

"Of course." Her stricken gaze was on Toby's battered and bloody form. "I'll get whatever you need."

"Bring hot water also, and clean bandages," said Duncan. "And yarrow, if you have any, to fight the fever."

Cassandra's lips moved as though she were committing the list to memory. She hurried from the room. Verbena gave the bloody form on the bed a wide-eyed glance and darted after her, leaving Duncan alone with the suffering animal.

Much troubled, Duncan moved to the bed and began a second, more thorough examination of his patient. He had failed Cassandra once, when the children had died. He would not fail her again, an he could help it.

He was making mental notes of the sundry lacerations on the wolfhound's body when the dog began to convulse, back legs pattering against the sheet as violent spasms racked his body. "No," Duncan said with a muttered curse. "You must not die. You cannot."

Raising his hands over the dying animal, he opened his senses. His palms glowed, and green light coursed from him, engulfing the convulsing dog. To Duncan's relief, the dog's spasms immediately eased, then ceased altogether.

A good beginning, Duncan thought, *but not enough.*

Concentrating on the dog's terrible wounds, he bathed the stricken animal with wave after wave of healing light. The radiance grew and spread. Slowly, painfully, the torn flesh stopped oozing and began to mend. Fur sprouted and grew. Ragged gashes closed, grew red and then pink, and faded. But the dog's breathing was still rough and labored. The poor creature had suffered severe trauma, blood loss, and shock, and his strength was spent.

Desperate to spare Cassandra further pain, Duncan focused all his will on restoring Toby to full and complete health.

Heal, he commanded, sweat running down his face and back at the effort. *Better, stronger. Hale and hearty.* Gritting his teeth, he added another push. *You will be whole, a new man. For Cassandra.*

He bore down, pouring everything he had into the effort. Suddenly, there was a blinding flash of light, and Duncan was thrown across the room and slammed against the wall.

Footsteps thundered on the stairs, and Cassandra rushed back into the room. "Duncan?" she cried, spying him sprawled on the floor. She dropped the basket in her hands with a crash, and jars and bandages rolled across the floor. "Are you all right?"

She was bending over him when Verbena came hurtling into the chamber, breathless. "Mr. D? You done fell out, too?"

"Nay, I am unhurt." Duncan got to his feet. "Naught but my dignity has suffered."

"What happened?" a deep, masculine voice demanded from the other side of the room. "I feel like I been stepped on and squished."

The three of them turned to look at the bed, and Duncan's jaw dropped. Toby lay on the bed, clad in jeans and nothing else. His body was unmarred by injury or hurt, and he was . . .

No, it could not be. Astounded, Duncan stared at the shifter. This went beyond mere healing. This entered the realm of blatant, unadulterated meddling.

"*Toby?*" Cassandra and Verbena squeaked in unison, echoing Duncan's astonishment.

"It's my name, don't break it." Pushing himself to a sitting position against the headboard, Toby glowered at them. "What's gotten into you people?"

"It's . . . um . . . it's just that—" Cassandra gulped and faltered, speechless.

Toby scowled. "Dagnabbit, somebody answer me. Why's everybody looking at me like I got three heads?"

"You were grievously wounded," Duncan said, collecting himself. "Steps had to be taken, else you would have died."

"Steps? What kind of steps?" Toby narrowed his eyes at Cassandra. "Out with it. What's going on?"

"Don't ask me, ask Duncan," Cassandra said with a helpless gesture. "He did this."

Duncan gave her a look of reproach. "Your loyalty unmans me, my sweet."

"Well, you *did*," said Cassandra, flushing.

"Did what?" Toby's voice rose in frustration. "What in the Sam Hill's going on?"

Duncan cleared his throat and indicated the mirror on the wall. "Methinks 'twould be better an you see for yourself."

"Oh, you do, do you?" Toby gave him a black look. Rolling off the bed, he reeled like a drunken sailor to the mirror on the wall. For a long moment, he stared at his reflection, his throat working. He held out his hands, examining the smooth, unblemished skin. Jerking his stunned gaze back to the mirror, he regarded the dark-haired, firmly muscled young man in the glass.

"Lord love a duck," Toby said, finding his voice at last. "What in tarnation have you done?"

Chapter Twenty-three

The severity of Toby's injuries, coupled with Duncan's intervention, had wiped the shifter's memory.

"Everything's hazy," Toby said, returning to bed at Cassandra's insistence. He allowed her to tuck several pillows behind him, then reclined. "I remember going out to Zeb's. Then I woke up, and I was like this." His piercing gaze met Duncan's. "Does Cassie have the right of it? Is this your doing?"

"Yes, but, in all honesty, 'twas not mine intent to reverse your age." Duncan was bewildered by Toby's transformation. "My thoughts were bent on healing you, and naught else."

"So . . . you've never youth-a-nized anyone?" asked Cassandra. "Before Toby, I mean."

"Nay."

"Oh, dear." She looked conscience-stricken. "I think Verbena and I may be to blame."

"Me?" Verbena squeaked. "I ain't done nothing to Mr. Toby."

"No, but I think we did something to Duncan," Cassandra said. "Remember when we helped heal him? There was a sort of surge."

"Oh," Verbena said. "*Oh*."

"What is this?" Duncan asked, startled.

"I think Verbena and I whammied you. Not on purpose, of course," Cassandra added hastily. "My magic's been hinky lately, and Verbena was there, and—" She lifted her shoulders in a helpless gesture. "You got enhanced."

"By the sword," Duncan said. "Is such a thing possible?"

"I don't know." Cassandra turned to the shifter. "Toby? This is your area of expertise. What do you think?"

The shifter sat up in bed and inhaled deeply. "Yep. He stinks out loud. He's been supersized." He tapped the side of his nose. "The schnoz knows."

"Indeed?" Duncan raised his brows. "Then might I suggest you examine your own scent."

"Whatchoo talking about?"

"Given the . . . er . . . magical outburst that propelled me across the room, in all probability you have been 'whammied,' too."

Cassandra's eyes danced. "Toby, you're a Dalvahni-oid."

"Great Jumping Jehoshaphat," said Toby.

Cassandra perched on the edge of the bed and smiled fondly at the shifter. "I'm just glad you're well. But I cannot get over the change in you."

Duncan was forced to acknowledge that Toby's alteration was nothing short of a miracle. The aging shifter was no more. The man before him was young and in his prime, with shining brown locks, a noble nose, and a face and body unmarred by the passage of time. Only the mismatched eyes remained the same, one purple, the other topaz.

"I'm on the Council, and they're bound to put up a squawk." Toby rubbed the taut line of his jaw. "Don't like it when we draw attention to ourselves, and this ain't the kind of thing to go unnoticed."

"Could you pose as a relative?" Cassandra asked. "I've done it before, to keep the norms from getting suspicious."

"Reckon I could, if I had any. You and Beck are the closest thing I got to family." Toby's expression was glum. "Lord, this is going to be a major pain in the ass. I'm going to need a new driver's license, and I don't know what all."

Cassandra twinkled at him. "The Skinners could probably help you. Something tells me they know how to fake an ID."

Toby made a noise of disgust. "Skinners. Like I'd truck with them no-counts."

"I could alter your license in a trice, if you so desire," Duncan offered. "'Tis easily done."

"No, thanks. You've done enough."

Cassandra worried her bottom lip. "I feel terrible. You wouldn't be in this mess if it weren't for me. I swear to you, I had no idea Zeb is a lunatic."

"Don't get your drawers in a knot." Toby reached out and took her hand. "How was you to know the sumbitch has a screw loose?"

"A whole bucket of them." Cassandra entwined her fingers with the shifter's. "I didn't know. Of course I didn't. If I'd had the slightest idea he was cuckoo for Cocoa Puffs, I never would have asked you to go out there. You know that, right?"

" 'Course I do," Toby said, squeezing her hand. "You and me, we go way back."

"Yes, we do," Cassandra acknowledged with a rueful laugh. "Way, way back."

Gazing at their clasped hands, Duncan suddenly wished he'd been less assiduous in his attention to Toby's recovery. The thought instantly shamed him. Gods, he was better than this. He loved Cassandra. He wanted her happiness, did he not?

Yes, but he wanted her to be happy with *him*. The green-eyed monster wanted to tie a heavy weight around Tobias Littleton and throw him in the river. Noble intentions be damned.

He felt Cassandra's curious gaze upon him.

"Duncan, are you all right? You look odd." She dropped the shifter's hand and jumped to her feet. "Oh, my goodness, of course you're not all right. That kind of magic takes it out of you. You must be exhausted." She came to him and laid a concerned hand on his arm. "Are you light-headed? Do you need something to eat?"

At her solicitous touch, the hot ball of misery in Duncan's chest swelled until he feared he would choke on it. She loved Toby, not him. Her concern sprang from gratitude that he'd intervened on the shifter's behalf.

"Duncan?" Her eyes were shadowed with worry.

"I have not eaten since we broke our fast," Duncan said, "but I have not the time for it now. There are matters of import I must attend to."

"You're leaving?" Disappointment shadowed Cassandra's lovely face. "But I thought . . . what I mean to say is—" She flushed and gave him a ferocious scowl. "Forget it."

"Worried I might renege?" Her dismay was heartening. At least she desired him. There was that.

Conscious of Toby and Verbena's curious gazes, he drew her out of the bedroom and gave her a hard kiss. "I will return anon," he promised in a low voice.

She sighed and traced a circle on his T-shirt with the tip of one finger, a simple touch Duncan felt to the bottoms of his feet and everywhere in between.

"Frankly, I wouldn't blame you if you didn't. Most men would say I'm too much sugar for a dime."

Duncan assimilated the odd expression. "Ah, but I am not a man." Tilting her chin, he smiled down at her. "I am Dalvahni. Fear not. I will not tarry long." Unable to resist the lure of her luscious mouth, Duncan kissed her again. "Be ready, sweet hornet. When I return, I mean to hold you to our bargain."

Delicious color climbed up her cheeks, but she looked him square in the eye. "Likewise." Sliding out of his arms, she stepped back. "What about you, Tobes? You hungry?"

"Nope," the shifter said as she and Duncan reentered the room. "Still feel washed out."

"You should try to eat something. There's camp stew in the freezer. I'll fix cornbread to go with it."

"I'll help," Verbena said, slinking out of the corner.

She skittered from the room at Cassandra's heels, and Duncan turned to find Toby watching him. "You and Cassie mend your fences?" Toby asked, narrowing his mismatched eyes at Duncan.

"After a fashion. We have agreed to have . . . relations."

"Relations?" Toby grunted. "That a twenty-dollar word for fucking?"

"I do not care for that term, particularly where Cassandra is involved."

"Don't give a shit if you care or not. My concern's Cassie. Don't want to see her hurt." Toby gave him a hard look. "*Again.*"

"Cassandra has told you of us?"

"Nah. She told Beck, and Beck told me, but here's the thing. I know you been pestering Cassie for months, and I know how mule-headed the Dalvahni can be. So I need to know, this agreement your idea or hers? 'Cause I won't have her bullied."

"I would never bully Cassandra into coupling with me. 'Twas she who suggested our . . . er . . . pact, and she who set the boundaries."

"Sounds like her. She's a big one for keeping folks at arm's length. That one's on you, I reckon. You hurt her."

"I am fully conscious of my transgressions where Cassandra is concerned." Duncan's chest burned with the old, familiar ache. "I will not hurt her again. You have my word."

"See that you don't. How long you plan on hanging around this time?"

"For so long as Cassandra allows."

"And afterward?"

"Afterward?" Cassandra would tire of him, eventually, and he would be forced to leave. Duncan's mind shied away from the dreadful thought. Taking a deep breath, he forced himself to consider it. "Afterward, I will step aside and let her go."

Though without her, there would be nothing left for him but to wander the darkness in search of the djegrali until luck favored the demons and he was slain. Gods, he was a wretched creature.

Toby slipped on the shirt Cassandra had unearthed from a closet somewhere in the house. This was not the shifter's first sojourn in Cassandra's abode. The discovery came as a nasty shock to Duncan.

I like men and I like sex, Cassandra had said. Had she and Toby coupled? The green monster roared to life.

"What of you?" Duncan demanded. "What are your intentions toward Cassandra?"

"Same as they ever was, I reckon."

"Meaning?"

"Meaning that's my business." Toby raked his dark hair out of his face. "Tell you what. I'll take Verbena home with me. Give you two some privacy."

"Is that wise? The Skinners—"

"I can handle the Skinners. 'Sides, they won't know she's with me."

"You have my thanks."

"Ain't doing it for you. Doing it for Cassie. See I don't regret it."

Toby turned and left the room. In a seething temper, Duncan dematerialized at the edge of the woods. He reinforced the wards around Cassandra's property, and then, after a brief struggle with his temper and unreasoning jealousy, he added a recognition spell to allow Toby and Verbena to pass through the spell wall unmolested. He would dearly have loved to bar the shifter from the place, but he would not do that to Verbena.

Satisfied that Cassandra would be safe in his absence, he reappeared outside Chez Beck's. Welcoming light poured out of the main building's windows, and the gazebo on the river was bright with lanterns. Music drifted over the water from the pavilion. Someone had booked a private party, and people were dancing. The restaurant had, by virtue of Conall's presence, become a combination watering hole and meeting place for the Dalvahni.

Duncan watched the twirling figures on the floating dock. He imagined a smiling Cassandra in his arms as he spun her around the floor. Such a thing would never be. She trusted him with her body and her pleasure, but not her laughter or her tears. The thought made him want to rend something.

Turning, he made his way down the smooth path leading to the back of the eatery. He approached an unmarked door and placed his palm against the metal surface. Tendrils of smoke curled from the lock and dispersed, and the door swung open. Duncan stepped inside, and the portal closed soundlessly behind him. This was Conall's war room, the space where Duncan and his brothers conferred with the captain on matters of moment.

The room was large, consisting of the entire bottom floor of the restaurant, and shielded by powerful wards. No careless norm or snooping supernatural creature would encroach here undetected. The design was simple and without ornamentation, a warrior's digs, comfortable and utilitarian. Large chairs and tables built to accommodate the Dalvahni frame were scattered around the room. On one wall was a handsome bar and larder kept stocked with food and drink. The Dalvahni had prodigious appetites.

And not just for victuals, Duncan thought, his body tightening. He was keen to settle this business and return to Cassandra. His hunger for her was a restless, seething thing inside him. She would not be his in truth, but a sip was better than a dry cup.

On another wall sat Conall's desk. Behind the desk, floor-to-ceiling bookshelves were heaped with scrolls. The stone fire pit in the center of the room lay empty and cold, a concession to the blistering Alabama heat that leached into fall.

Duncan filled a tankard with ale, loaded a plate with cold meat and cheese, and sat down to eat. He was finishing his repast when the door opened and Conall and Grim strode in.

"Duncan," Conall said.

Duncan set down his tankard and rose. "Captain," he said, and added a nod to Grim. "Brother."

The air hummed, and Arta materialized. The High Huntress was a tall, cool blonde with eyes the color of spring leaves. She was dressed in silvery gray doeskin hunting garb and carried a bow and a quiver of arrows on one shoulder. No knives were visible on her person, but Duncan did not doubt for a moment that she was armed to the teeth. A Kirvahni huntress could take the eye from a sparrow on the wing, and Arta was their leader. Her skills would be unrivaled.

To Duncan's surprise, the air rippled and warped, and Kehvahn appeared. The god wore a brown robe that was badly in need of pressing. A pair of bent glasses sat on the bridge of his rather pointed nose, and his brown, feathery hair stood on end. He wore the abstracted expression of a monk or scholar, but his eyes were kind, and his mouth curved in a humorous smile. A large white bird with jeweled eyes sat atop one of the god's shoulders, its extravagant tail feathers brushing the back of Kehvahn's knees.

Duncan felt a sudden swell of affection. "Master," he murmured with a bow of respect. "You have a bird."

Kehvahn reached up to stroke the fowl's sleek head. "Her name is Shirra. Grim made her and gave her into my keeping. Is she not lovely?"

"Made?" Duncan glanced at Grim, but the big warrior appeared to be fascinated with the wall.

"Much as he brought Dell into existence." Kehvahn gave Duncan a measuring look. "My children are a constant delight."

It was Duncan's turn to squirm. "I take it you know of Toby?"

"A change that remarkable makes a great deal of noise, and I am not deaf."

"What is this?" Conall turned his cold, black stare on Duncan. "Has something befallen Toby? My wife has a great deal of fondness for the shifter."

"Toby was savaged by the Randall pack unto death, and I healed him." Duncan rubbed the back of his neck. "Unbeknownst to me, my . . . er . . . talents have been altered, thanks to Cassandra's magic and Verbena's talent as an enhancer."

"And Toby?" Conall demanded.

"Toby has been restored to youth and vigor," Kehvahn said. "What is more, he is now part Dalvahni."

Conall regarded Duncan askance. "Brother, you never cease to surprise me."

"I surprised myself," Duncan admitted. "The change in Toby was an accident."

"Then I would advise you to be more careful in the future. You bring tidings?"

"Aye, of the rogue and a strange stone called the orb." Quickly, Duncan relayed what he had learned, describing Gryff's condition, the slaughter in the woods, the alpha's madness, and Pratt's consuming interest in the orb. "'Tis plain and unremarkable, by all accounts," he said of the orb. "Brown in color with a yellow streak and devoid of beauty. Yet for some reason, Pratt desires it."

"Why?" asked Arta. "It is powerful, this orb?"

"Beyond measure," Kehvahn said. "The Heart, it is named, and 'twas fashioned by He-Who-Made-All-Things, ere Pratt and I came into existence. To possess it is forbidden." His expression saddened. "Which is, doubtless, the reason my brother covets it. He has never been one to brook opposition, and he delights in mischief. No sooner is he forbidden something than he must have it at any cost. Pratt stole the Heart eons ago and used it to tear the veil, releasing the djegrali to wreak havoc."

"Then why did he not keep it?" asked Arta.

"Oh, I think he has ... until recently," Kehvahn said with a wave of one thin hand. "Only one who is pure of heart can touch the orb, and the Heart rejected Pratt when he misused its power, wounding him sorely. He dared not touch it again, lest it destroy him utterly. Yet he could not part with it, either, and so he devised a plan." He turned his gentle smile on Grim. "Can you guess how he resolved his difficulty?"

"Nay, Master," said Grim.

"Our best and our brightest," Duncan blurted. He turned to Conall. "That is how you described Gryffin. Methinks Pratt has been using Gryff to carry the orb."

"Exactly." Kehvahn looked pleased. "Nicely done, Duncan."

"What is this?" Grim demanded.

"I fear we have misjudged our brother," Duncan said. "Gryff is no true rogue. He is a pawn."

"The markings." Grim's voice was strained. "What Cassie said is true, then? Gryff is a prisoner?"

"Aye," said Duncan. "'Tis my belief that Pratt faked Gryff's death and enslaved him with some loathsome magic. He is a tool used by the god to keep the orb within his grasp." He met Conall's gaze. "Just as Evan was bound and used by the demons that gained mastery over him. Gryff had no choice, and neither did Evan."

Conall had the grace to look uncomfortable. "If this is so, then how came the werewolves to have the orb?"

Arta spoke up. "Pratt healed in time, and his arrogance and desire to wield the orb returned." She turned to Kehvahn. "Have I the right of it, Master?"

"You were ever perceptive," said Kehvahn with a nod of approval. "'Tis my thought that as Pratt's wounds knitted, his yearning for the orb grew until he could bear it no longer. He took the orb from Gryffin. The orb, sensing his ill intent, burned him again, and he dropped it. Thus was it lost."

"The shooting star," Duncan said. "Pratt sent Gryffin to retrieve it, but Zeb found it first. He took it home and declared it the Randall talisman. The Heart drove him mad and sickened the pack."

"And the young were stole it to save his family," said Kehvahn. "Recognizing the orb's power, even in your inebriety, you led Sild-hjort to the orb. He gave it to Sugar, knowing it would not harm an innocent. Sugar exchanged the Heart for the shifter and returned it to Gryffin, completing the circle."

"Sugar?" Conall asked, frowning.

"One of the elder beasts," Duncan said. "The folk of this province call them bigfoot. Sugar is stark white, as the eponym implies. We became friends when I mended his hurt paw."

"Brother," Conall said, "you have been busy."

"My captain, you know not the half of it."

"But what of Gryffin?" Grim was pale beneath his tan. Approaching the god, he knelt on one knee. "Grant me this task, I beg of you, my master. I would be the one to free my brother from dread bondage."

Kehvahn rested his hand on Grim's head. "Your love for your brother does you credit. Look for Gryffin an you will, though the task of freeing him falls to your sister." He turned to Arta. "Inform Taryn at once that the nature of her mission has changed from apprehension to deliverance."

Arta bowed. "It shall be done, Master."

"And what of Pratt?" Conall asked. "Is his perfidy to remain unchecked?"

"Do not concern yourselves with Pratt. My brother will be dealt with . . . in time." Kehvahn gave them a misty smile. "And now, farewell, beloved. I have tarried too long."

The god vanished.

Chapter Twenty-four

Cassie hurried into the kitchen and set the oven to 450 degrees, then placed the camp stew in the microwave for a few minutes while the oven preheated. "To knock the chill off," she told Verbena, selecting the thaw option. When the microwaved dinged, she dumped the slushy stew into a heavy saucepan and turned it on low. Taking her favorite crockery bowl from the shelf, she mixed cornmeal, flour, eggs, oil, and rising ingredients together with buttermilk to form a batter.

Standing at Cassie's elbow, Verbena watched this process. "Reckon you could learn me how to cook?"

"I'm not a gourmet, like Hank, but I'll be glad to teach you what I know."

"Don't wanna be like Hank. Wanna be like you." Verbena hesitated. "Reckon you could learn me to talk good, while you's at it?" She looked down at her feet. "If'n you don't think I'm too stupid."

"You're not stupid." Cassie scraped the sides of the bowl with a spatula. "Proper speech is mostly a matter of habit and reading. The more you read, the more you'll know. Dr. Seuss said that."

"Who?"

"A very wise man, and a philosopher."

"You got any of this Seuss feller's books?"

"No, but I'm sure they have them at the Hannah Library."

Verbena's shoulders slumped. "Ain't got a car."

"Never mind. I'll take you. While we're there, you can get a library card. That way, you can check out any book you like."

"Really?" Verbena's eyes glowed.

"You betcha."

"That 'ud be wonderful."

Under the girl's interested gaze, Cassie added more oil to a cast-iron frying pan and put it in the oven to heat. "When the oil's hot, we'll add the batter," she explained. "The hot oil is what makes the crust nice and crunchy."

Ten minutes later, Cassie removed the hot pan from the oven, using a thick mitt. Carefully, she placed the pan on a cold eye of the stove and emptied the contents of the bowl into the frying pan.

"Lordy," Verbena exclaimed, jumping a little as the thick mixture hit the hot oil with a satisfying sizzle.

"And now we wait," Cassie said, placing the cornbread in the oven.

Half an hour later, Toby strolled into the kitchen. "Cornbread smells good."

"You get your appetite back?" Cassie asked.

"And then some. I could eat the ass out of a leather duck."

Cassie laughed. "I see you found one of your old shirts." She nodded at the table. "Take a load off. It's almost done."

"Cassie's gon' learn me to cook," Verbena announced as Toby pulled out a chair and sat down.

"Teach you to cook," Cassie murmured.

"Huh?"

"I'm going to *teach* you how to cook."

"That, too. And she's gon' take me to the library so's I can get me one of them books by that gopher feller."

"Dr. Seuss," Cassie said. "And I said he was a *philosopher*, not a gopher."

"That right?" Toby rubbed his jaw to hide his smile. "Tell you what, you come home with me tonight—I'm still feeling puny, and I'd appreciate the company. First thing in the morning, I'll take you to the library, then bring you back here."

"Sure, Mr. Toby." Verbena slid Cassie a knowing look. "Got me a notion, too. Reckon Mr. D and Cassie would like to be private."

To Cassie's annoyance, she blushed. Good grief, what was she, sixteen? But the girl was right. She wanted to be alone with Duncan.

Toby noticed her heightened color and chuckled. "Mind if I borrow the Dodge? My truck's at the house."

He was referring to the 1960s Dodge D100 pickup the former owners of her property had left as a lawn ornament. The truck had been sun-faded and sat on rotted tires. A scurry of squirrels had nested under the hood, gnawing holes in every belt and hose, but Cassie had fallen in love with the old blue and white beater on sight. Over the course of several years, she'd had it restored, installing a new engine and transmission, tires, and a refurbished interior and exterior.

"Of course, but there's no rush," Cassie said. "Eat something first."

"Oh, I ain't leaving until I eat," Toby assured her. "Nobody ever called me to dinner twiced."

While Toby ate, Verbena excused herself and went upstairs to pack her things for the night. "May take me a while," she said. "I kind of throwed things in a bag when we was at the restaurant, and I need to sort 'em out."

"Take your time," said Toby. "I'm in no hurry."

When Toby finished eating, he insisted on helping Cassie tidy up the kitchen. Afterward, they carried their tea glasses out onto the porch. It was late afternoon, maybe an hour before full dark, and the rich, musky scent of the river hung in the air. In the trees, birds sang a twilight aria before conceding the stage to the symphony of bugs and frogs waiting in the wings. A spring peeper near the water grew impatient and launched into a high-pitched chirp. A leopard frog, not to be outdone, answered with a chuckling croak.

"Choir practice," Toby said with a grunt, taking a seat in one of the rockers. "I love to hear the critters sing."

"Me, too," Cassie said, plopping into the rocker beside him.

Something was different, but what? Then it dawned on her. The hammering had stopped. Either Duncan's carpenters had grown tired of working overtime or his house was finished. What sort of house did a Dalvahni warrior build? she wondered. She tried to guess and gave up. There was no telling, but she was looking forward to finding out.

"You learn that technique in a master gardening class?"

"What?"

"The lawn." Toby raised his glass, indicating Cassie's once-green grass. "What the hell happened?"

Cassie looked out upon her formerly pristine landscape and sighed. The slope leading down to the river was scorched and pitted in dozens of places, the flower beds had been demolished, and Jeb had trampled her herb garden. Thinking of the work ahead of her made her tired. "Demon fight. Happened first thing this morning."

"Must've been a doozy." Toby pointed to the abandoned plinth near the river. "What's that?"

"The base to Jeb Hannah's statue."

"You stole Jeb Hannah's statue? Why in tarnation did you do that?"

"I didn't steal it. It was there when I got up this morning."

"Huh," Toby said. "Demons put it there, did they?"

"I don't think so. I'm pretty sure Duncan got pounded on chocolate and left it for me."

"Most fellers bring flowers."

"Duncan's not 'most fellers.' "

"I've noticed," Toby said. "Where's the rest of it? Or did the cheapskate just bring the base?"

Cassie chuckled. "Oh, he brought the whole thing." She coughed a few words into her hand.

Toby sat up straight in the rocker. "Come again? I could swear you just said you brought Jeb to life."

"I did," Cassie said. "It seemed like a good idea at the time. Jeb's crackerjack at fighting demons."

"He is?"

"Yep." Cassie made a swinging motion with her hands. "Whacks them with his giant peanut."

"His giant peanut," Toby repeated, staring at her in disbelief. Rising from his chair, he eased to the edge of the porch and looked around as if he expected to see Jeb peeking from behind a bush. "Where is he now?"

"No idea. Wandering around somewhere. Last time I saw him, the sheriff was chasing him in his Jeep."

"Good God almighty."

Toby's stunned expression and tone of utter astonishment sent Cassie into a fit of the giggles, and once she'd started laughing, she couldn't stop. She laughed until her sides hurt and tears ran down her cheeks. Just when she'd catch her breath, she'd glance at Toby's incredulous face, and that would set her off again. At length, however, the whoops subsided, and she collapsed against the back of the rocker to catch her breath, her sides aching.

"Good to hear you laugh," Toby said. "You been wound tight since I don't know when."

"Oh, Toby." On impulse, Cassie jumped up and threw her arms around him. "I do love you."

"Love you, too, baby doll." He gave her an awkward pat and pushed her gently away. "You need to calm down, boy," he said, addressing someone behind her. "It ain't what you think."

Cassie whirled to find Duncan standing in the doorway.

"I am not a boy." Duncan's tawny eyes blazed. "I am older than you by millennia."

"Yeah? Reckon being immortal don't keep you from being an idjit." Ignoring the signs of Duncan's simmering temper, Toby turned back to Cassie. "If you'll give me the keys to the Dodge, Verbena and I will shove off."

"Sure," Cassie said, hurrying inside to find her purse.

A quarter of an hour later, she waved good-bye to Verbena and Toby from the back porch as the Dodge puttered down the drive and disappeared into the trees. Her skin tingled with awareness, and the hair on her neck and arms stood on end. If she'd been standing in the open, she'd have hit the ground, certain she was about to be struck by lightning, but the sky was blue and cloudless.

A subtle, woodsy scent tickled her nose. *Oh, there's a storm brewing, all right*, she thought. *A storm of the Dalvahni kind.*

The air thrummed with suppressed energy, and so did she. *Let it come*, she thought, vibrating with exhilaration. *I'm ready. Been ready.*

She turned. Duncan stood near the porch door, his expression stony and unyielding as marble. He radiated displeasure, and the nimbus surrounding him crackled and sparked with dark energy. He wasn't merely angry. He was livid.

Cassie braced her legs and glared back at him. "Stop it. I know you're ticked, and I know why."

"Indeed?" His tone was flat, emotionless. "Pray, enlighten me."

"You're jealous."

"You are mistaken. I am disappointed." He folded his arms across his broad chest. "I thought we had an agreement—an exclusive relationship for so long as it lasts. I depart but briefly and return to find you in the arms of another."

"I wasn't 'in his arms.' I was giving him a hug. Friends do that, you know. Toby's like family. We've known one another for more than a hundred years."

"You declared your love for him. I heard you." He took a deep breath, as though struggling with something, and let his arms drop. "So be it," he said, his voice dull with weariness. "I release you. Be with him, an it pleases you."

"Well, I don't release you," Cassie said as he started to shimmer around the edges. "So don't even think about leaving."

Duncan's wavering form solidified, and he stared at her in surprise. "I do not understand."

"Obviously." Cassie tapped one sandaled foot. "Listen and listen good, Duncan Dalvahni, because I'm only going to say this once. I've got thirty years on Toby, but he's always been like a father to me, maybe because he's always looked much older. At any rate—"

"That is no longer the case," Duncan said, interrupting. "Tobias's mien is now that of a young and virile man. What is more, his appearance is not displeasing."

"Yeah, he's a real heartbreaker, but that doesn't change the way I feel about him."

"Which is?" Duncan asked, watching her with an intensity that was unnerving.

"I love Toby, but I'm not *in love* with him. I don't want to marry him. I've never had sex with him and I don't want to. I want to have sex with *you*. Is that plain enough, or do I have to spell it out?"

"I believe I possess sufficient intelligence to grasp your meaning."

"And another thing," Cassie said, the words welling from a place of deep frustration. "I didn't have sex with Zeb. We had dinner a few times, and that was it. He kissed me. Once. Our ... relationship, if you can call it that, ended the night I saw you in the parking lot of Beck's Bar. So you can stop being jealous of him, too."

"So noted."

"Excellent." Cassie marched across the porch and shoved past him. "Now, if you'll excuse me, it's been a long day, and I'm tired."

"Hold."

Such was his tone of command that Cassie froze with her hand on the doorknob.

"Our arrangement still stands, then?"

His deep, rich baritone sent a quiver of awareness through her. Merciful heavens, he was going to be the death of her.

214 • *Lexi George*

Closing her eyes briefly, she faced him. "Yeah, but not if you're going to be a dick, and not if—"

He jerked her into his arms and kissed her, a bruising caress of possession and desire. Cassie's head swam as the world dissolved around them and they fell into nothingness. She clung to Duncan and cried out, but in the space of a moment, they were back on solid ground. She opened her eyes and gasped. The porch and house were gone, and they stood in a large clearing deep in the woods. Silhouetted against the purpling sky was an enormous tree with thick, spreading limbs, a trunk the size of a small house, spreading roots like steel girders, and a dome-shaped crown. The tree shone in the gloom like a burst of fireworks, aglow with the light from myriad lanterns that twinkled among the leafy branches like lightning bugs.

Nestled high among the massive limbs was an elaborate tree house, three circular pods with pitched, shingled roofs and railed porches connected by walkways. The cottage in the tree shone with welcoming light, and a soft breeze coaxed a winsome tune from the wind chimes dangling from the eaves. A spiral staircase with burled and twisted railings wound around the huge trunk. It was altogether lovely and magical, like something out of a fairy tale.

"It's beautiful," Cassie said, enchanted. "I half expect a troop of elves to greet us over the railings."

"The elves went home."

Startled, Cassie opened her mouth to ask for an explanation, but her question was forgotten when Duncan swept her into his arms. "I can walk," she protested as he started up the curving staircase.

"A thrall will be silent."

Oho. So that's how we're playing this.

Cassie's insides fluttered, and she was jittery and shaky with excitement. She was going to be his thrall, his to command.

And then he would be hers, his gorgeous body subject to her every whim.

Her every whim—Cassie resisted the urge to wriggle with excitement. In the years of their separation—one hundred and eighty-two in all—no one had compared to Duncan. No one had even come close. He was the gold standard.

One-hundred eighty-two years, sixty-five days, and nine hours, her inner voice said. *But who's counting?*

Cassie ignored the pesky whisper. She needed this, and she refused to overanalyze it. She and Duncan were going to have sex. No baggage. No pretensions. No false protestations of devotion. No emotional scenes. She would be his plaything, and he would be hers, satisfaction guaranteed. Was she brilliant or what?

Clueless, more like, the crafty voice said.

Cassie stifled the squeam. You just couldn't make some folks happy.

She settled back to enjoy the ride as Duncan climbed the stairs that wound around the tree and among the lighted branches. The lanterns swayed at the slightest whiffet of air, setting shadows dancing along the limbs and the rough trunk. She studied Duncan, memorizing his features. Looking at him was no chore. He was extraordinarily beautiful—unreal, even, like something rendered by an artist's brush. Strong, stubborn jaw, cleft chin, and prominent cheekbones. And his mouth . . . firm and kissable. Designed to make a woman sigh.

It was perfect, really, that mouth, the bottom lip slightly fuller than the upper. When he was in a teasing mood, the corners tilted just so, expressing amusement and tenderness, but when he was angered or displeased, that gorgeous mouth firmed to a hard, intractable line.

Right now, his jaw was set, and his oh-so-tempting mouth was tightly under control. Toby thought she was wound too tight? Duncan was a coiled spring.

Excellent, she thought, itching to trace the stern line of his jaw with her fingers. *I'll make you relax, Mr. Dalvahni, and in the loveliest way.*

They neared the top of the huge tree, and Duncan stepped onto a deck inlaid in a complex pattern of alternating planks of dark and light wood. Cassie expected him to set her down then, but he kept going. He showed not the slightest strain from carrying her, but then he *was* Dalvahni and supernaturally strong.

The railed porch encircled the tree, and Duncan strode along the soaring walkway until he came to a heavily carved white oak door. He muttered something in a language Cassie did not recognize, and the door swung silently open.

He carried her inside and lowered her to the floor. Cassie looked around, wide-eyed, at a bedroom unlike any she'd ever seen. The walls were curved and finished in gleaming woods of varying hues. White oak pillars supported the high, conical roof and beamed ceiling. Centered beneath a large skylight was an oversized bed with carved posts that resembled the antlers of some fantastic beast. A large tub was sunk in the floor in front of three arched windows with a spectacular view of the night sky.

Cassie was enchanted. She wandered around the room, taking in details she'd missed: a bookshelf cleverly tucked behind a soaring pillar, the spiral design of the beamed tower ceiling, a comfy divan situated in front of a large window that invited a cozy session with a good book.

She paused in front of a large, arched window with her back to Duncan and gazed out at the velvet sky studded with stars. This place was so beautiful it made her throat ache, a hidden aerie apart from the world, sheltered and safe. Inexplicably, she was filled with sadness and an unnamable longing.

"When you said that you were building a house, I didn't expect this." Her throat tightened with sudden tears. "This . . . Duncan, this is beyond lovely, like something from another world."

"A thrall was instructed to wear her hair down."

Cassie stilled, confused and disconcerted by his harsh, peremptory tone and his abrupt dismissal of her.

"Excuse me?"

"A thrall would do well to plead with a warrior. A thrall swore to abide by a warrior's wishes. A thrall has not done so."

"I said I would wear my hair down, but it was hot," Cassie said. "I was cooking, and—"

"A thrall will take it down, and now."

Chapter Twenty-five

A wild eagerness seized Cassie and swept aside her melancholy. With a trembling hand, she reached up to remove the stretchy tie that held her hair in a loose knot.

"Hold," Duncan commanded in a voice like iron. "I would do it."

Cassie lowered her arm and heard him cross the room. He moved with surprising grace and lightness for a big man. He came up behind her and pressed his lean, hard body close to hers. Heat poured off him, and she was enveloped by his crisp scent: woods and snow and fresh air.

His fingers stroked the sensitive skin at the nape of her neck before moving to the band that bound her hair. He pulled the pliable loop free, and her locks tumbled down.

"Whenever I found myself in a dark place, I had but to think on the color of your hair to be warmed by sunshine." Leaning closer, he buried his face in her locks. "Like fragrant silk. You smell good enough to eat."

The images his rough words evoked made Cassie's knees grow weak. "It's my shampoo." Her voice was a breathless scritch. "Evie Douglass makes it special for me in exchange for herbs from my garden. It's scented with grapefruit, camellias, and lilies."

"Evie Dalvahni now," he corrected. "My brother Ansgar's wife."

Yes, that was right. Evie was married now. She'd found her happily-ever-after. So had her friend Beck.

Cassie frowned, disconcerted by a pang of wistfulness. Why was she mooning like a young girl? There was no such thing as happily-ever-after.

Duncan brushed her hair aside to trace an intricate design on her bare neck, and Cassie's pensiveness was forgotten. She felt the soft huff of his breath against her skin, then the scorching heat of his mouth as he sealed the mark with a kiss. She jumped in surprise as he nipped her shoulder. He was claiming her, an alpha male staking his territory.

Duncan's hands slid around her rib cage and cupped the heavy weight of her breasts. His thumbs tightened, pinching her sensitive nipples through her T-shirt and bra. "I do not care for this binding you wear." His deep voice executed an exquisite dance along her nerve endings. "I would have it gone."

It's called a bra, and it fastens in the back. Take it off, please, Cassie wanted to beg, but desire had her in its grip, and the words died in her throat.

Her unspoken plea was answered when Duncan reached under her shirt and unhooked the bra. He slid the straps from her shoulders, letting them dangle loosely on her upper arms.

"Put your hands against the window," he ordered.

Cassie complied and felt the cold kiss of metal against her skin as he cut the straps with a knife. The bra fell to her waist and was gone, tossed aside by Duncan's impatient hands. He stepped back, and Cassie almost wept with loss. God, she wanted him. She was weak with wanting him.

She closed her eyes and pressed her forehead against the cool glass. Her demon blood was awake and roaring for satisfaction. The demon wanted consummation, and *now*. It wanted his hands on her and the hard thrust of him inside her. Her breasts were so tight they ached, and the place between her legs was hot and wet. It was all she could do not to turn and throw him onto the bed, taking what she wanted.

What they *both* wanted. It would be easy. She was a demonoid, after all, and very, *very* strong.

You promised, the voice teased. *You said you would be his thrall. This is what you wanted. What you bargained for. Time to pay the piper.*

"Turn around, thrall," Duncan said. "I would see you."

Cassie's leg muscles quivered. Taking a steadying breath, she faced him. On the surface, he seemed contained and in control, but for the telltale tightness of his jaw and the tension around his eyes. This magnificent male desired her, and he was on the brink, at the breaking point.

Good. They would shatter together.

"Shoulders back," Duncan ordered.

Cassie obeyed, keenly aware of the rub of soft cotton against her nipples. Her senses seemed heightened. The clean scent of Duncan was in her nostrils, she could hear the thunder of her heart, and she tingled from head to toe.

Duncan looked her over, taking his time, his gaze lingering on the high, rounded curves of her breasts and the shadow of her areolas against the thin cotton of her shirt. Reaching out, he lightly caressed a sensitive peak, his golden eyes darkening at her sudden intake of breath. His fingers moved to the other peak, flicking, teasing, until her breasts were tight and full, the peaks hard and straining for attention against the garment that confined them. The scalding heat in the pit of her belly spread to her core, until Cassie feared she would melt.

Much more of this, and she *would* melt.

"Undress."

His sexy baritone vibrated through Cassie. Her skin flushed, and the thrumming pulse in her veins heightened to the point of pain. God, she was on the verge of an orgasm, and he'd barely touched her.

"As a warrior commands," she murmured.

Aware of Duncan's unyielding gaze upon her, Cassie stepped out of her sandals and kicked them aside. She reached for the button at the top of her shorts and paused, gripped by a sudden, unheeding recklessness. Unfastening the button, she slowly undid the zipper, each gesture measured, teasing. She was playing with fire, but she didn't care. She wanted to be burned, consumed by Duncan. She wanted him to burn, too.

She wanted . . .

Her mind shied away from the almost-thought. This. She wanted this. Nothing more, nothing less. This would be enough. It had to be.

She inhaled, her lungs filling, expanding. It felt like the first deep breath she'd taken in years, freed of the crushing sorrow and guilt she had carried for so long. Tears burned her eyes, and she was flooded with a sense of blooming wonder. Something sprang to life inside her, something fragile and infinitely precious. Something she'd thought dead forever: hope and the tender blossoming of joy. Duncan's return had released her from her self-imposed prison. Why that should be, she did not pause to consider. It was simply enough that she could breathe and look forward to tomorrow unburdened by self-loathing and regret.

The shorts slid down her hips and went the way of her sandals, leaving her clad in her T-shirt and panties. She stood there, returning his stare, but made no move to further disrobe.

Duncan frowned in disapproval. "Why do you stop?"

"You told me to undress. You did not say completely."

"You are impertinent, thrall. You know well what I meant."

A knife appeared in Duncan's hand—the same one, Cassie assumed, he'd used to cut away her bra. It was a beautiful weapon, small and finely crafted, with a bone handle etched with runes. White fire danced along the shimmering blade. This, Cassie knew instinctively, was no manmade weapon.

Her heart thundered with anticipation. Duncan sliced the offending garment away from her body in two quick motions and stepped back. His gaze drank in her form, taking in her naked breasts and the strip of cloth at the juncture of her thighs.

His stoic demeanor had vanished altogether, and his features were taut with strain. "I am well pleased with you, thrall."

Cassie lowered her eyes in feigned shyness. "A thrall rejoices in your approval. A thrall would know your pleasure."

"A warrior will school a thrall, and gladly."

Cassie lifted her gaze at the soft swish of cloth and nearly groaned aloud. Duncan had removed his T-shirt, revealing muscled arms and a torso that made her want to weep with longing. His body was strong and ripped and toned, with no fat, strength and grace embodied in the perfect male form. A tantalizing dusting of golden-brown hair ran from his navel and disappeared into the waistband of his jeans.

She'd seen him before, of course, rising from the river like a pagan god, but every time was a visceral shock.

It wasn't fair. How was she supposed to resist him when he was so goddamn *perfect*?

He opened his jeans, and his heavy erection pushed against the thin cloth of his briefs. "The bed," he said through gritted teeth. "And now."

Cassie complied. Moving across the room, she was acutely aware of the gentle sway of her unbound breasts, the urgent ache that ran from her belly to the place between her legs, the cool sensation of the floor against the soles of her bare feet.

"Slow," he said, coming up behind her. "Too slow."

He placed his hand between her shoulder blades and pushed. She bent at the waist, and he wrapped her hands around one of the heavy bedposts.

"A thrall will hold on," he said, tugging at her panties. "A warrior will have his pleasure now."

Yes, Cassie thought, swallowing a moan. *Yes, yes, yes.*

The flimsy scrap of cloth slithered down her hips and pooled around her ankles. Gently, almost reverently, Duncan caressed her rounded rump before sliding his hand between her legs. He made a sound of satisfaction when his fingers found the pearly liquid at her sheath. "Merciful gods," he said. "I can wait no longer."

She heard the soft shush of cloth as he shoved his clothes aside, and then the head of his cock was nudging her from behind, seeking entry into her wet channel. She opened her thighs and arched her lower back to give him greater access, and was rewarded by a delicious pressure. He found her slick entrance and entered her in one swift stroke.

His cock was big and hard, like the rest of him, and Cassie was already on edge. She came at his first thrust with a force that made her cry out.

"Sweet blessed Kehv," he groaned as she pulsed around him.

He began to move in eager, punishing thrusts. Was he punishing her or himself? Cassie did not care. She took him in gladly. He was inside her, they were connected, flesh to flesh after an eternity apart, and she felt *alive*.

She held on to the bedpost for dear life and offered herself to him, whimpering with need now. He grabbed her by the hips and lunged harder, faster, as though in response to her unspoken entreaty. The exquisite tightness bloomed in Cassie's belly and breasts and spread until her whole body was on fire, every cell of her being attuned to Duncan, to his flesh in her flesh. The sheer, unadulterated rightness of it made her sob. The lovely tension inside her coiled and heightened as her body reached for bliss.

Her second orgasm hit her with the force of a hammer blow, and she screamed.

"*Cassandra.*" Duncan came, his powerful body shuddering with the force of his release.

His legs gave way, and so did Cassie's, and they crumpled to the floor at the foot of the bed.

He wrapped his arms around her and pulled her close. She was intensely aware of the throbbing place between her legs and the unaccustomed wetness between her thighs. Sex was messy and glorious, and never more so than with Duncan. She would miss this when it was over.

To her horror, tears trickled down her cheeks. She'd had an awesome, mind-blowing orgasm, and she was crying. No biggie. Postcoital tears weren't uncommon. Something about the body countering the release of dopamine, if she remembered correctly. Her sadness had *nothing* to do with Duncan or the thought that this would not last. Her emotional overload was the result of going without for too long. Abstinence didn't make the heart grow fonder. It made a bitch hormonal and cranky.

Duncan released her and got to his feet. Without ceremony, he picked her up and tossed her onto the bed.

Cassie glared up at him, his sweet, adorable hornet. "Hey, what's the big idea?"

Duncan bent and removed his boots, then stripped out of his jeans and briefs. He was hard again. It had been a long time since he'd allowed himself physical release, a very long time, and his randy body wanted more.

He wanted more. He wanted everything. He wanted Cassandra, every part of her, though the gods knew he relished her body. Being with her again should have been enough, but it was not. He would never be sated. To have but the smallest part of her was a misery, like being invited to a sumptuous banquet, then forced to sup on unsweetened gruel.

Consequently, Duncan was in a black mood.

He told himself to be satisfied with the scraps she offered, but he ached to tell her how he felt, to caress and kiss her, to explore her from head to toe, rediscovering every inch of her lovely body. He hungered for her, longed to worship her with his hands and mouth, to confess his ardor, to pour out his love for her, but their accursed agreement fettered his tongue.

She wanted his cock, not his adoration. She wanted the pleasure he could give her, but nothing of his soul. Nothing of tenderness. Nothing of love.

Duncan had love enough to fill the valleys of the moon to over-flowing, but Cassandra kept her heart tucked safely away behind walls of distance and distrust.

There was a certain irony in that, he supposed. He was the architect of his own destruction. He'd hurt and betrayed her, abandoned her in her time of need, and she'd closed herself off. Cassandra was now more Dalvahni than he, reserved and wary, contemptuous and afraid of emotion.

She'd cracked him open and left him vulnerable, but she cared not that his heart beat and bled for her and her alone. It was enough for her to couple and move on, detached. Dispassionate. Disconnected.

It made him want to beat his head against a stone wall and rage with grief.

"Duncan?"

She knelt on the bed facing him, her lovely face flushed and her delectable, tempting body on display. She was unself-conscious in her nudity, and all woman, his sweet delight, with full, round breasts, a slender waist and flat belly, firm, strong legs and calves, and a smoothly curved rump. Silken blond curls covered her mons, and he wanted to bury his face between her legs and feast on her until she came in shuddering delight.

"A thrall will kneel on all fours on the bed," he ordered.

"Yeah? Why would a thrall do that?"

"A thrall was warned that a warrior has appetites. A thrall will assume the position, and now."

She tilted her head, regarding him. Her pale hair was tousled and fell to her creamy shoulders in soft waves. Her lips were red and swollen from his kisses, and her beautiful violet-starred eyes were sultry and gleamed with mischief.

Gods give him strength, she had her hand around his heart. She was his salvation and his undoing.

"No. I don't think so."

"No?" Duncan's eyes narrowed. "What of our agreement?"

"Our agreement was mutual. I'll be your thrall, and you'll be mine." She swept one hand over the bed. "My turn. On your back, thrall."

Duncan took an instinctive step away from the bed. "I presumed . . . that is, I thought that you—"

"You thought I'd let you call the shots forever? You know me better than that." She gave a little bounce on the bed that make her spectacular breasts jiggle in a most alluring way. "Not happening, mister."

Duncan was Dalvahni, and scoffed at danger. He'd once confronted a raging minotaur in single combat, battling the monster alone and deep within the earth. He had done so without flinching, slaying the dread beast and moving on. He'd bearded rock trolls in their dens and faced a horde of fire demons in the jungles of Athaal. He'd fought the djegrali in their many forms—giant, dragon, basilisk, hydra, ogre, gorgon—without dismay, but this?

This he could not do.

He could not submit to Cassandra's caresses and pretend he did not care. At her merest touch, his hard-won control would turn to ash, and he would disintegrate into a babbling, pitiful creature, professing his adoration like some lovesick, mewling swain.

A consummation devoutly to be wished, but his wishes did not matter. Cassandra did not want his love. She wanted to use him as her plaything.

He took refuge in cruelty. "Later, perhaps, when I grow bored with you, as I assuredly will." He crossed his arms and regarded her, his lip curled in contempt. "Please me, and perhaps I will allow you to satisfy your whims, but not yet."

She laughed. "Stop being a dick. We had a deal. What's the matter, afraid you can't handle it?"

Yes, he wanted to shout. *I know I cannot.*

Aloud, he said in a hateful drawl, "Handle what? Your feminine wiles? You overestimate your charms."

"Ooh, a challenge. I like it. Are you going to come here or not?"

Duncan did not move, rooted to the spot.

"Bad thrall. I am not happy with you." She slipped off the bed and padded over to him. Hands on hips, she circled him, slowly. She was playing with him, Duncan realized, his heart thudding at her nearness. He had taunted her, and she was exacting her revenge.

She stopped in front of him, naked and glorious. "You are a pretty thing."

"Pretty?" Duncan was stung. "That is not a word one uses to describe a Dalvahni warrior."

"Excuse me—a handsome specimen." She reached over without warning and wrapped her hand around his rigid cock, stroking him. "Impressive here, too. Yes, you will do nicely."

The air hissed from Duncan's lungs. What had she said to him when he'd toyed with her thus? It was hard to think with her hand on him and his blood pounding.

"A thrall rejoices in your approval," he grated as her hand slid to his balls, then returned to her stroking. "A thrall would know your pleasure. Where do you want me?"

"The bed, for starters," Cassandra said. "I mean to ride you hard and often."

She was throwing his own words in his teeth, the minx, repaying him in kind. Short of fleeing, he was done for. He gave it serious consideration and rejected it. A Dalvahni warrior did not quit the field.

Moving like one in a trance, Duncan walked over and lay down on the bed.

"Much better," Cassandra purred in a husky voice.

She glided across the room and put one knee on the bed, the mattress dipping slightly at her weight. She crawled toward him on all fours, slowly, purposefully, a lioness stalking her prey.

Duncan braced himself, a condemned man, and awaited his doom.

Chapter Twenty-six

His torment began with the lightest of touches, feathery strokes along his calves that made him shiver.

"So strong and flawless," she said, stroking his hard thighs. "The picture of masculine beauty, but why so tense? A thrall does not enjoy my touch?"

"A thrall will bear it," Duncan said through his teeth. "Though it is like to kill him."

"Kill him?" Her hands moved past his straining cock to explore the ridges of his belly. "Am I abhorrent to you, then?"

Abhorrent? She was the sweetest thing in life. Duncan's blood was on fire, and he was shaking with need. How could she ask that? She must know what she did to him. The evidence of his desire was undeniable.

I cannot do this, he thought in desperation. He'd been delusional to think that he could bear it.

Her hands moved to his chest, her fingers caressing his nipples, and he fisted the bed linens to keep from yanking her into his arms. She took one of his nipples in her mouth, her right hand sliding down his belly.

Her hand closed around him once more. "My, you're tense here, too, and very strong," she murmured, stroking the rigid length of him.

She pressed hot kisses down his belly. Duncan, realizing her goal with a surge of panic, raised his head from the pillow. Cassandra's pale hair was spread across his belly in a silken fan. The sight was so beautiful, so intimate that Duncan's heart clenched.

"Nay, Cassandra." His voice was hoarse with strain. "Do not."

She paused, her mouth but scant inches from his cock. "What is this?" Her tongue flicked out, tasting him. "A thrall would say me nay?"

"A thrall would beg you—"

She took him in her mouth, and Duncan was lost. The heat of her mouth, the delicious, seductive pull of her lips, the stroke of her tongue were his undoing. Pride be damned, and their "bargain" with it. He resolved to end this farce, and now. And if she made a fool of him? So be it. That dog was out of the cage, in any event. He was a fool for Cassandra, always had been, always would be.

Reaching down, he grabbed her by the arms and dragged her up his body. He wrapped his hands in her hair and tugged her face close to his. "I warn you, Cassandra. There is but so much a warrior can take."

She raised her brows, haughty as any queen. "A thrall does not warn. A thrall obeys."

He rolled over, pinning her beneath him. "Behold me defiant."

She gazed up at him, a wrinkle of displeasure etched between her brows. "We had an agreement. It was my turn."

"No more turns. And to the Pit with our agreement."

Her lush mouth parted in surprise, then she stiffened and pulled away. "But you said—"

"I know what I said—believe me—but 'tis a vow I cannot keep."

"I don't understand."

He sighed and rested his forehead on hers. "I know you do not, and more's the pity." He raised his head and caressed her cheek with his thumb. " 'Twould be better an I show you."

She gazed up at him, an expression of wary curiosity in her indigo eyes. "Okay."

"I would hear you say it."

"Yes, Duncan, I want you to show me. Pretty please with cherries on top."

He sat back on his haunches and flipped her over.

"Duncan? What are you doing?"

"Demonstrating," he said, sheathing himself inside her feminine channel. "This is what you want, is it not?"

"Oh, yes," she said, wriggling her hips to take him deeper. "And clearly, you want it, too."

She was right, the gods help him. She was snug and warm and wet, and he wanted her. His greedy body took over, and he pounded inside her, stroke upon hard stroke. She responded, clenching around him as she neared her completion.

Gritting his teeth, he pulled free of her sweet flesh and sat back on his thighs.

"Duncan?" She reclined on one hip and regarded him from beneath sultry lids. "Is something wrong?"

"Yes, something is wrong. You want to boink, and I do not."

Her lips parted in shock. She went very pale, and then flushed. "Well, excuse me," she said, scrambling for the edge of the bed. "Obviously, I've made a mistake."

He lunged, catching her by the waist, and pulled her into his lap. "I do not want to boink. I want to make love to you."

"I suppose you think there's a difference?"

"Of a certainty there is a difference, a vast distance." Duncan gave her a little shake. "I am in love with you, you impossible woman. I have *always* been in love with you. I misdoubt I will ever stop."

She shrank from him then, his wary love. He could see the old shadow of distrust in her eyes.

"You do not believe me," Duncan sighed. "For that, I have myself to blame. But I tell you this, here and now, and I bid you listen for once, my stubborn hornet. *I love you.* That is who I am. I do not know how to be anything else, save the warrior who loves his Cassandra."

She lowered her eyes, one finger tracing the line of his collarbone. "I see. And if I can't or won't return your feelings?"

He took a deep breath. "Then I will remain your thrall, but know this. When we engage in coitus, you will be boinking, but *I* will be making love. Do I make myself plain?"

"Crystal clear."

"I wanted you to know. I wish there to be no dissemblance between us." Duncan studied her face, trying to guess her reaction, but 'twas impossible. She sat very still, her eyes lowered. "Cassandra?"

She looked up at him, then, her lips trembling. "Wherever did you learn that ridiculous word?"

"What word?"

"Boink."

Duncan frowned. He'd poured out his heart to her, laid his soul bare, and she wished to discuss his vocabulary? "Evan."

"Why am I not surprised?" Cassandra straightened. "Very well, thrall. You have permission to make love to me."

Demon Hunting with a Sexy Ex • 229

"I do?" Duncan's blood sang. "I feared you would be displeased and send me away."

"If I had, would you have gone?"

"Nay. I will not leave you again." He wrestled with himself a moment, and added, "Though I will not stand in your way, an you wish to be with another."

"Liar." She sighed. "I suppose I'll have to make do, then. A hard thrall is good to find."

"Do you not mean—" He grasped her meaning and chuckled. "Brazen wench."

Taking her face in his hands, he kissed her the way he'd longed to kiss her for years past counting, worshipping her with his mouth and tongue. With a little moan, she parted her lips and took him in, brushing her tongue against his. "Cassandra," he groaned against her mouth.

Catching her hair in his hands, he tilted her head, exposing the smooth column of her throat, and trailed kisses down to her collarbone. Moving his mouth lower, he licked her rosy nipples until she was shivering and moaning. Taking a wet peak in his mouth, he sucked until the pebbled tip was hard against his tongue.

"Duncan." Cassandra's eyes were closed, and her pulse was visible in her throat. "That feels so . . ."

"Good? Right? Perfect? I think so, too."

He pushed her onto her back and spread her thighs until she was open and vulnerable to him. She watched him, unabashed. She was his fierce, untamed sorceress, and he loved her to distraction.

His breath caught in his throat. "Ah, Cassandra, you are so lovely."

The flesh between her legs was a delicate pink that deepened to red, and she was wet with arousal. He caressed her there, stroking the damp, golden curls and her glistening opening until she was writhing and gasping. Later, he would kiss and lick her there, tasting her as she shuddered around him, but first . . .

Lowering his body over hers, he thrust inside her. His skin was on fire, and his heart was pounding fit to burst. She was warm and slick, and tight.

Ah, he thought, wanting to weep from the sheer perfection of it. After a lifetime of darkness and despair, he was where he belonged.

She wrapped her legs around his waist and held on, tilting her pelvis to take him deeper. He groaned, thrusting his hips faster, the slow, exquisite pressure building at the base of his spine. Little lightning streaks danced behind his eyes. She was close, oh so close. He could feel the ripples of ecstasy along his shaft.

And then she was over the edge, taking him with her. Duncan called her name and let go, giving himself to her, heart and soul.

Cassie awoke in Duncan's arms. Morning light poured through the skylight in pale, buttery beams that warmed the gleaming wood floor. Duncan had been insatiable, and the memory of his amorous attentions gave her a shiver of delight. Her breasts and the place between her legs were tender, but it was a pleasant ache, and Cassie found that she was eager for more. It had been a long time since she'd been with anyone, and she couldn't seem to get enough.

Can't get enough of Duncan, you mean, her inner voice smirked. *Might as well admit it. You're not fooling anyone.*

The squeam was right. Cassie couldn't get enough of Duncan. She didn't want anyone else. And in keeping with her determination to be honest with herself, she admitted that she never had. Her affairs had been brief and unsatisfying, junk food without any substance. It had always been Duncan, right down the line.

She waited for the old panic to set in, but her serenity remained undisturbed. He said he loved her, and she believed him. The open, bleeding wound his departure had left had healed, and she'd forgiven him. She forgiven herself.

And? the squeam prodded.

And she trusted him, which was a huge, big whoop-de-do deal, given their history.

And?

Cassie's introspection ended as Duncan stirred and pulled her close, giving her a long, lingering kiss that made her blood heat to a slow boil. They were facing one another, and he hiked her left hip over his right thigh and entered her slowly, taking his time. They fit together perfectly, pieces of a mysterious puzzle that had been lost and found.

"Sore?" he murmured against her mouth as he slowly withdrew and entered her again.

"A little, but—" Cassie moaned as her body responded to his, the tingling ache building and building. "I don't care. Don't stop."

"As milady commands," he said, increasing the sensuous rhythm.

He really is amazing, Cassie thought as she spiraled into pleasure. Quite, quite amazing, and he was hers.

Afterward, she lay sprawled on top of him, her knees on either side of his waist, her breasts crushed against his hard, muscular chest, her left cheek resting on his shoulder. She reached out with one hand and played with his hair. "Gorgeous, like the rest of you," she said.

"What is?"

"Your hair. Don't ever cut it."

"An it pleases you, I will not."

"It pleases me. You please me." She rose on her knees and, taking his face in her hands, bent to kiss him. "Duncan, I—"

A bell chimed somewhere below them in the tree, and Duncan sat up, taking her with him. "Ah," he said. "Breakfast."

"Breakfast?" Cassie said, startled. "How . . . I mean, who . . . ?"

"You will see." Giving her a quick kiss, he slid from the bed and padded across the room to a heavily carved walnut armoire that sat against one wall. He opened the wardrobe, took out a long black robe, and donned it, tying the sash around his lean waist. The garment snugged his broad shoulders and opened in a deep vee at the throat, exposing the hard planes of his chest.

Reaching inside the armoire, he took out a second robe. "You should dress, else Nettle will catch you abed," he said, handing her the robe. "He is nothing if not efficient. The food will be here anon."

"Nettle?"

"A piskie. I freed him from the mage who'd most cruelly bound him, and now he serves me." Duncan shrugged. "Of his own accord, and not at my behest. Piskies cannot bear to be in another's debt."

"How long has he served you?"

"I forget. Some eight centuries, I believe."

Eight centuries. Shaking her head at this, Cassie slipped into the robe, a white silk garment that brushed the tops of her feet. She was cinching the luxurious robe at her waist when the door opened and the strangest little man she'd ever seen bustled into the room with an empty tray. He was short and old in appearance, with a brown, wrinkled face like a withered plum, a long, hooked nose, and bright red hair. His unshod feet were disproportionately large and wide for his frame, with long, hairy toes, and he was dressed in moss and lichen.

He stomped over to Duncan and said something in a coarse little voice that reminded Cassie of a squirrel's chucking.

"Thank you, Nettle," Duncan said with a nod. "We will come at once."

The piskie barked something sharp at Duncan and disappeared.

"Nettle informs me that our repast awaits on the terrace," Duncan said, his lips twitching. "He says the scones grow cold."

"Scones?" Cassie perked up. "What are we waiting for?"

It was a beautiful morning, warm and clear, and the blue sky above was dotted with fleecy white clouds. A small table on the porch had been set with snowy linen and china. They were at the top of the enormous tree with a view of the lea and the surrounding woods. The meadow was thick with oxeye sunflowers and asters, and the river gleamed in the distance.

Standing at the rail, gazing down at the silvery-green canopy, it struck Cassie that she'd never seen a tree like this one before. "This is a very unusual tree. What kind is it?"

"I do not think it has a name. The seed from whence it sprang was a gift from Conlaoch, one of the Tuath Dè Danan. I rescued him from a rather sticky business, for which he was grateful."

"First Nettle, and now this Conn fellow? You've been a busy boy."

"I have lived a very long time, Cassandra, and been bestowed great power. I would not be much of a warrior should I refuse to lend succor to those in need."

"It's a very big tree. You must have planted it a long time ago."

"Nay. I planted the seed when I purchased the land from Lucy Hall."

"But that's not—" Cassie stared at him. "Magic?"

Duncan inclined his head. "But of course. 'Twas a very special seed."

Stranger things had happened, and this *was* Hannah.

"It's beautiful," she said. "The most beautiful tree in the world."

The branches beneath them shivered, though the day was windless.

"The tree is delighted by your praise. What of the house? Does it please you as well?"

"Oh, yes," Cassie said. "I love it. I've always wanted a tree house."

"Then it is yours."

She turned from the rail in surprise. "Oh, no. I couldn't. This is your home."

"You are my home, Cassandra. All that I have is yours—my life, my heart, my body."

"But I have a house."

He shrugged. "Now you have two. Come." He held out his hand. "We must eat lest we provoke Nettle's wrath." They breakfasted on poached eggs, warm scones with fresh butter, berries, and a variety of delicate cheeses, washing the whole down with cups of fragrant hot tea sweetened with honey.

"Nettle does not eat meat," Duncan said in a voice heavy with regret. "The mage who bound him forced him to subsist on rabbit ears. Like many of his kind, Nettle is surpassing fond of cream and sweets, you see, and the mage withheld his favorites to force his compliance and bend him to his will."

"Rabbit ears?" Cassie shuddered. "That's horrible."

"Aye. To this day, the very sight of a rabbit makes Nettle weep."

"What happened to the wizard when you freed Nettle?"

"Nettle turned him into a hare and loosed the hounds on him. They caught him and ate him."

Cassie blinked. "Goodness. Remind me not to make him angry."

"Only a fool earns the enmity of the piskie folk."

As if summoned by their conversation, Nettle appeared and began to clear the table.

"Thank you, Nettle," Cassie said. "Breakfast was delicious."

The piskie chittered something at her and scurried away. Cassie was wondering whether she'd insulted the funny little man, when a gruff, familiar bark drew her to the rail. A large, shaggy wolfhound mix trotted out of the woods and across the flowering meadow.

"It's Toby," Cassie said. "I wonder what he wants?"

The dog shook a spray of water from his coat and sniffed the bole of the tree. The wolfhound's form blurred and Toby stood looking up at them. He was wearing jeans and a Lynyrd Skynyrd T-shirt, and his dark hair was wet.

"There you are," he said. "Been looking for you. What in tarnation you doing up a tree?"

"This is Duncan's new house. Isn't it wonderful?"

"It's a pip. Sorry to horn in, but you got company. They were waiting in the woods near the top of the driveway when I brought

234 • *Lexi George*

Verbena home. For some reason, that was as far as they could go. Me and Verbena drove right on through."

Duncan grunted. "I placed wards about the property to keep out strangers in my absence."

"Huh," Toby said. "That explains it."

"Who is it, Toby?" Cassie asked.

"Werewolves—a woman and a little girl. The kid's in bad shape." Toby's mismatched gaze found Duncan. "The woman's asking for you. Says Mac sent her."

"Mac's dead," said Cassie. "Where's Verbena?"

"At the house. Don't fret, she's all right. Your visitors can't get past the wards, remember?"

Cassie turned to Duncan. "What do you think?"

"I think Mac's mother and sister have come to me for help, and I shall give it. I gave Mac my word."

"Hey, Cass," Toby yelled. "If you mean to take up here, you need to build a bridge, or at least have a dock and a boat. I ain't swimming across the river every time I get a hankering to say howdy."

"He's got a point," Cassie said to Duncan. "We *are* rather isolated here."

"My fiendish design exactly," Duncan said, jerking her into his arms and kissing her.

Cassie wrapped her arms around Duncan and returned his embrace, her tongue stroking his. He tasted of honey and scones and the berries they had eaten. The world called and their idyll was over, but they still had this moment.

"Ha-loo?" Toby called from the bottom of the tree. "Anybody up there?"

Or maybe not.

Chapter Twenty-seven

Cassie leaned over the rail to speak to Toby. "Give us a few minutes to bathe and dress. We'll meet you back at the house."

"Gotcha," Shifting back into dog form, Toby took off into the woods, his long legs eating up the distance.

The tub in the bedroom was filled and waiting when Cassie and Duncan went back inside. Nettle chittered, indicating a stack of warm towels, and scuttled from the room.

The hot, scented water felt incredible, and Cassie could have lingered there until she shriveled, especially since Duncan was in the tub with her. He insisted on washing her hair and her body, and Cassie returned the favor. Things got rather heated and quickly, and it was only the thought of the sick child waiting across the river that kept Cassie from jumping Duncan's bones and screwing him stupid.

As they dried off with the fluffy towels Nettle had provided, Cassie gave the tub a wistful look. "Later," Duncan said, sliding his hands under the clinging cloth to caress her damp skin. "There will be time and plenty for a lingering bath."

"Promise?"

He kissed her. "A Dalvahni warrior does not lie."

Cassie looked around for her clothes, then remembered that her bra was in shreds and Duncan had sliced her shirt in two. To top it off, her panties were nowhere to be found. Consequently, she had to be satisfied with wearing her shorts, sandals, and a shirt borrowed from Duncan. The shirt was miles too big, so she knotted it at the waist.

"I like your bosom unbound," Duncan said, testing the weight of her breasts with his hands.

"Yeah? Then you would have loved the sixties. I burned my bras."

He frowned. "Allow me to clarify. I like your bosom free of constriction when we are alone."

Cassie dimpled at him. "I thought you might feel that way."

Duncan took her in his arms, and they returned to the cottage across the river the same way they had come, materializing on her porch.

"Give me a minute to throw on some clean clothes," Cassie said, starting down the hall for her bedroom.

Duncan put his hand on her arm, stopping her. "No. It could be a trick of the alpha to gain entry. Stay inside until I ascertain the situation."

"No," Cassie said. "I'll go with you—"

But he was already gone.

Fuming, she dashed into her room and dressed in clean clothes in record time, then rushed into the hall.

"Everythin' all right?" Verbena stood at the top of the stairs, a book in her hands. The expression on her engaging face was dreamy and befuddled, and Cassie was seized with the sudden, fanciful notion that Verbena was Sleeping Beauty, awakened from a hundred-year nap.

"I'm not sure," Cassie said. "Toby says there's a woman and a sick child in the woods. Duncan's gone to check. Would you mind sprucing up the other room, in case they wind up staying here? Change the sheets, that sort of thing."

"Sure," Verbena said. "I'd be happier'n a dead pig in—I mean, I'd be delighted to help."

Cassie nodded absently, her mind on Duncan and their visitors. She was halfway down the hall when it struck her that Verbena's speech patterns had changed. She backed up and put her hand on the stair rail.

"Verbena?" she called up the stairs.

"Yessum?"

"Did Toby take you to the library?"

"Sure did, last evening afore—*shoot*—before we drove out to his place. They're open until seven. Got me one of them—I mean, I *obtained* a library card, and checked out some books. Finished them last night, so Toby took me by there again this mornin'." Verbena peered over the bannister at the top of the stairs. "Did you know there's a seven-book limit? Don't that rile—I mean, doesn't that make you mad? I can read that many like 'at." She grimaced and corrected herself. "Like that."

"That is annoying," Cassie said. "Clean sheets are in the hall closet."

She dashed onto the back porch and saw that Duncan was coming down the driveway carrying a limp bundle in his arms. A woman hurried beside him, her expression creased with sorrow and worry. It was the Randall woman Cassie had seen during the fight on the lawn, the one Zeb had smashed in the mouth and booted out of the pack.

"Orb sickness," Duncan said, striding up to the porch. "I will need milk thistle, licorice root, and wild ginseng. Belladonna, too, for the fever."

Cassie stared at him in dismay. "Milk thistle I have, but not the rest."

"Lucy Hall is something of an herbalist. Mayhap she will have what we need."

"I'll call her right away. Verbena is getting the room upstairs ready. But what about the wards?" Cassie asked, remembering. "Will Lucy be able to get through?"

"Lucy is no stranger, and my friend," Duncan said. "The recognition spell I wove distinguishes friend from foe. The spell is akin to that which you placed around the bar to keep out the norms, but in reverse."

Ah, Cassie thought in understanding. She made a mental note to talk shop with Duncan later. Compare spells, that sort of thing. But not now.

Duncan carried the child inside, and Cassie hurried down the steps to speak to the distraught mother. Upon closer inspection, she saw that the woman bore signs of orb sickness as well.

"You're ill," Cassie said, going to the ailing woman. "Come inside."

The woman swayed and clutched Cassie's arm. "Just help my baby. Please. I know you got no cause to like the Randalls, but Blaze didn't do nothing."

"Hush, now," she said, putting her arm around the woman's shoulders. "We're going to do everything we can for you."

She half carried the swooning woman into the house and upstairs to the bedroom Verbena had prepared. Duncan was already there, tucking the whimpering child into bed. The girl was no more than eight years of age, frail and wasted. Most of her hair had fallen out, and ugly sores covered her thin arms and legs.

"Blaze," the mother sobbed, lurching for the bed.

"Shh," Cassie said, helping her to a chair by the bed. "Duncan is a healer. Let him do his work." She tucked a lap blanket around the shivering woman and went to him. "The mother is sick, too," she said in a low voice. "And the child?"

His jaw worked. "Gravely ill." He considered the gray-faced mother. "The mother's condition seems less severe."

"She's an adult. Maybe her immune system is stronger?"

"Mayhap. Or the child came in closer contact with the orb."

"I'll call Lucy," Cassie said.

She slipped out of the sickroom and went downstairs, her limbs heavy with sorrow and dread. Death was hard, but the death of a child...

Cassie thought of Jimbo and Maggie and little Rose, and felt a stab of pain. Her normal reaction would be to push the pain away and ignore it, but she was done being a coward. Taking a deep breath, she let the memories flood through her, the good and the bad. Jimbo's and Maggie's sweet smiles and laughter, their faces flushed and soft with sleep in the firelight as they slumbered on the feather tick. The satin feel of baby Rose's skin, the child's breath, sweet as an angel's kiss on Cassie's cheek as she slept in Cassie's arms.

The anguish of losing them, baby Rose to the fever and Jimbo and Maggie to the Hag. The dull knowledge that she had failed them and her brother; the almost unbearable pain as she buried them beneath the tree.

You were young. Your heart was broken, and you were grieving. The squeam's voice, for once, was kind, rather than snarky. *You didn't know about the Hag. You told Jimbo and Maggie to play on the porch because you were terrified they'd come down with the baby's fever. You had your hands full nursing Rose. You had no idea the children had disobeyed you and gone into the woods. The Hag tricked them, lured them away from the house with her magic. She was a powerful witch, and you were just a girl. You couldn't have stopped her, no matter what.*

"I loved them." Tears ran down Cassie's face. "I still do."

Of course you love them, and they love you. Love doesn't have an expiration date. It endures. They want you to remember them, and they want you to do it without sadness. They want you to forgive yourself and them.

"Them?" Cassie was shocked. "But they didn't do anything. *I* did."

They left you, just like Duncan did. Forgive them for dying, and be happy. That's what they want. Oh, and help Blaze and her mother. They want that, too.

Cassie wiped her eyes. She felt lighter, somehow, whole. Going to the phone in the hall, she dialed Lucy Hall's number.

"Hello?" A woman's voice spoke at the other end of the line.

"Miss Lucy? This is Cassie Ferguson. Sorry to bother you, but Duncan Dalvahni needs your help. It's an emergency." Quickly, Cassie relayed the details of the child's illness.

"Don't have any wild ginseng on hand," Lucy said, calm as you please when Cassie had finished. "I'll send Sugar into the woods to find some. He's a good boy, and he's got a nose like a pig. I'll rustle up the rest while he's gone. We'll be along directly."

She hung up without saying good-bye, leaving Cassie to stare at the humming receiver in her hand.

Toby peered through the front door. "Got a towel? My hair's wet. Don't want to drip on your wood floors."

"One sec. I'll grab one."

Cassie hurried into the master bath, returning with the towel. Toby took it from her and gave his head a vigorous rub.

"Thanks," he said, stepping in off the porch. "Everything all right?"

"The child is upstairs, and Lucy Hall's on her way with some herbs." Cassie twisted the hem of her shirt. "I didn't have what Duncan needed, so I asked Lucy to help."

Toby squeezed her shoulder. "Don't fret. Duncan saved me, and I was three parts gone. And we got the enhancer."

"About that," Cassie said, remembering the change in the spritely girl. "Verbena seems . . . different."

Toby chuckled. "Noticed, did yah? You should have been there, Cassie. It was something to see."

"What was?"

"You got something to eat? Swimming always makes me hungry."

Cassie was delighted to have something constructive to do. Hungry, she could fix. "There's cornbread left over from last night," she said.

"That'll do."

Cassie followed Toby into the kitchen and watched him slice a hunk of cold cornbread. "Sorry," he said, taking a big bite. "No time for breakfast. Verbena had a bee in her bonnet. Bound and determined to be at the library this morning first thing when they opened."

"I have a microwave, you know. You don't have to eat it cold."

"Lord, gal. I've eaten a whole lot worse'n cold cornbread in my time. Remember Reconstruction?"

"I was in Europe."

Running from grief and memories, Cassie thought.

"Forgot about that. What about the Depression? Know you were around for that."

"Yes, I remember the Depression." Cassie opened a cabinet and removed a bottle of Alaga. "Cane syrup?"

"Is a pig's butt pork?"

Taking that as a yes, Cassie fetched a plate and fork, then watched as Toby doused the cornbread in the thick liquid and wolfed it down.

"There," he said, wiping his hands and fingers with a napkin. "Reckon I'll live."

"You were saying about Verbena?"

"Oh, yeah. So I take her to the library last night, like I promised, and we stayed until closing time. About an hour and a half, I reckon." Toby went to the sink and rinsed his plate. "Never seen anything to beat it."

"What do you mean?"

"I mean, that gal started in the children's section. Read everything quicker'n you can say Johnnie ate a tater."

"She was browsing? Looking at the pictures?"

"Nope. She read 'em, and then she moved on to the adult books. Made it to the letter *C* before the librarian shooed us out. Took her back this morning so she could finish the rest. Pestered me to death until I did. Never seen such a one for reading."

Cassie stared at him, open-mouthed. "Are you telling me Verbena has read everything in the Hannah Library since last night?"

"Yup. Took her home, and she went through everything on my shelves. Read the World Book, front to back, all twenty-two volumes. Read all my biographies—Jefferson, Hamilton, Lee, Alexander the Great, the Bear. Then, nothing doing but she had to read my *Popular Mechanics*. I got every issue, so that took a while, but she finished them, too."

"Holy cow."

"Yup," Toby said again. "Reckon enhancing's not her only talent. Going to be hard to keep her supplied with books. On the plus side, she can fix your car, make a table, and can vegetables." He rubbed his jaw. "As I remember, there was an article in one of them issues about how to make beer. Hope she read that one."

There was a rap on the back door. "That must be Lucy," Cassie said, relieved.

The old woman and the sasquatch waited on the back porch. Lucy Hall was in her eighties. Her gray hair was fashioned in a bun, and her face was lined and careworn, but there was an air of vitality about her, and she carried herself like a much younger woman.

"Miss Lucy," Cassie said, opening the door and ushering them in.

Sugar had to stoop to enter the house. The bigfoot carried a large, rectangular tote bag made of canvas in one paw. In the other, he clutched a handful of wilted purple flowers. He shuffled on his back paws and looked around, his blue eyes rolling nervously in his huge head.

"Show Miss Cassie what we've brought, son," Lucy said.

Sugar started and held out the bouquet. "Pretty?" he said in his warbling voice.

Cassie took the flowers. Bringing them to her nose, she sniffed. The blossoms had a pungent, floral scent that reminded her of lavender. A feeling of well-being washed over her, and she found herself grinning like a fool. "They're beautiful, Sugar."

"Pretty," he repeated. "For Dunk."

"You brought Duncan flowers?" Cassie said, confused.

"They're for the child," Lucy said. "Sugar brought some home a while back." She gave the large creature a fond pat. "You're forever bringing me pretties, aren't you, sweet boy?"

"Mama," Sugar said with a nod. "Pretty."

"Pretty strange," Lucy said. "I've lived in these parts all my life and consider myself something of a green thumb, but I've never seen this plant before." She gave a decisive nod. "But I can tell you this. No sooner did I bring those flowers inside than my rheumatism flat disappeared. Haven't had a twinge since. What's more, I've got a heart murmur. Congenital defect in the aorta. I was born with it, and Doc Dunn's been after me this age to have it replaced. Says it's calcified and not working like it's supposed to. Puts me at risk for a stroke."

She gave Cassie a challenging look, as if she expected her to argue.

Cassie had no intention of arguing with Lucy Hall. She'd sooner argue with an irritated badger. The old woman was ferocious.

"Doc Dunn's a good doctor," Cassie said, groping for the appropriate response. She'd never been sick a day in her life. "Or so I hear."

"He's a meddlesome old fool," Lucy said. "Replace my valve, would he? What am I, a carburetor?" She sniffed. "You should've seen his face when I went in for my last checkup. My valve has regenerated. No more stiffness or calcification. He actually accused me of going to Mobile to have it fixed. Like it's any of his never mind if I did." Her mouth tightened. "But I didn't do any such thing. It was the flowers."

"Miss Lucy?" Duncan's deep voice sounded from the top of the stairs. "Is that you?"

"Dunk," Sugar chortled, hopping up and down in excitement. "Sugar bring Dunk pretty."

"Give Miss Cassie the basket, Sugar Britches." Lucy gave the bigfoot an indulgent smile. "He gets so excited."

"Basket." Sugar handed the tote to Cassie. "Sugar good boy?"

"Yes," Cassie said, unable to resist the entreaty in the bigfoot's blue eyes. "I'm sure we can find you something. What would you like?"

"Treat," Sugar said, as though Cassie was a little slow.

"He loves baby gherkins," Lucy said. "And apples and carrots. Sweets aren't good for him. He's got a beautiful smile, and I don't want him to ruin his teeth."

Sugar beamed at this, showing a mouthful of large Chiclet teeth.

"I'm sure we can find him something." Cassie turned to find Toby loitering in the hall near the kitchen door. "Would you mind checking the pantry?" she asked him. "I think there's a jar of pickles in there."

Lucy noticed Toby and gave Cassie an accusatory glare. "You

didn't tell me you had company. I never would have come. Don't trust strangers where my boy's concerned. He's too precious."

"Toby won't say anything," Cassie said. "Will you, Tobes?"

"Toby?" Lucy scowled. "You related to Tobias Littleton?"

"Yes, ma'am," Toby drawled. "Real close kin."

"You his son?"

"Grandson, actually." Undeterred, Toby gave her a lazy smile. "No need to worry. Sugar's safe with me. We're friends, aren't we, boy?"

The bigfoot sidled closer to Toby, his black nose quivering. "Doggie?"

"That's right."

Sugar beamed. "Dunk fix owie?"

"Yup, and then some. You want that treat?"

"Treat," Sugar said with a happy nod. "Sugar good boy."

"So I hear," Toby said.

Cassie left Toby to handle Lucy and the bigfoot, and hurried upstairs with the basket of medicinals. She rapped on Verbena's door and stuck her head in the room. The girl was curled up on the bed, surrounded by dozens of books from Cassie's library. It took Cassie three tries to get her attention.

"Can you come next door?" Cassie said when Verbena looked up at last. "Duncan may need you."

"Sure thing," Verbena said, tenderly setting aside her book.

Cassie and Verbena went down the hall and slipped quietly into the bedroom. The mother was much improved. Pink color flooded her once-waxen complexion, and she seemed strong and whole. She hovered near the bed, her anxious gaze on her child.

Duncan bent over the shivering girl. Green light poured from him, bathing her pitiful form, but the hideous lesions did not heal.

"Duncan?" Cassie set the hamper down by the door. "I've brought Verbena, and I have the supplies you asked for."

"I cannot help her." He lifted his head, and Cassie saw that he was crying. "I healed the mother, but this is beyond me. The damage from the orb is too great."

The girl's mother cried out in anguish and slumped to the floor.

"Oh, you poor thang." Verbena darted to the woman's side and knelt beside her.

"This is not your fault, Duncan," Cassie said, starting toward him. "You must not blame yourself."

"And what of Mac?" Duncan slammed his fist into the wall, knocking a gaping hole in the beadboard. "What of my promise to him?"

Blood dripped from his smashed knuckles onto the floor.

"Duncan, your *hand*." Tossing Sugar's flowers onto the bed, Cassie rushed to his side to examine his injuries.

"It is nothing. See? Already I mend."

He was right. As Cassie watched, the bones and flesh healed before her eyes.

"Would that I could do the same for this poor child." Duncan raised a shaking hand to his forehead and froze, staring at the drooping flowers scattered across the coverlet. "These blooms," he rasped. "Whence came they?"

"Sugar brought them," Cassie said. "Lucy Hall says they work wonders."

"But this is marvelous." Snatching up the flowers, Duncan removed the bone-handled knife from his pocket and began to cut up them up. "A mortar and pestle, quick, Cassandra. And hot water, honey, and a spoon. Hurry."

Cassie gave him a startled look and ran downstairs to find the things he needed. She headed for the kitchen to heat the water, and Verbena scurried to the workroom for the mortar and pestle.

In the kitchen, Cassie found Toby and Lucy at the farm table enjoying a glass of iced tea. Sugar loomed near the sink, slurping the brine from an empty jar of sweet pickles.

"What's going on?" Toby asked when he saw her face.

"No time," Cassie said. "I'll explain later."

She tucked a spoon and a small jar of honey into her pocket, snatched up the whistling kettle, and pounded upstairs to the sickroom. Verbena had beaten her there, and Duncan was mashing up some of the flowers with the pestle. The child's mother hovered nearby, her expression a heartrending mixture of grief and hope.

Duncan motioned impatiently for the kettle and added some of the hot water to the plant mash in the bowl.

"Honey," he said, holding out one hand. Cassie dug the jar out of her pocket and gave it to him. He added a generous dollop of honey to the mixture and stirred. "We must get this mixture down the child."

"What about the mother?" Cassie asked.

"She is distraught. You will assist me?"

"Of course," she said, going to the bed.

Duncan strode up to the moaning child. "Lift her so she does not choke."

Cassie climbed into the bed and took the child in her lap. "Hello, sweetheart," she murmured, summoning the voice she'd used with Jamie's children so long ago. "Time to take your medicine."

The girl turned her head. "No. Don't want it."

"You want to get well, don't you?" Cassie stroked the child's dull, patchy hair.

The little girl blinked up at her. "You're pretty. Like a fairy princess."

Cassie smiled. "Thank you. I'm Cassie, and you're Blaze, right?"

"Samantha Blaze," the child whispered. "I don't feel good. Hurts. Make it stop."

"Samantha Blaze is a lovely name." Duncan eased his weight onto the edge of the mattress. "Will you take your medicine now?"

His deep, hypnotic soothed the suffering child like a balm. Keeping up a stream of gentle nothings, he coaxed the liquid in the bowl down the little girl, spoon by spoon, until the mortar was empty. Blaze sighed and drifted to sleep in Cassie's arms.

She touched the child's cheek. "Her fever is cooling. What now?"

Duncan set the bowl aside with a sigh. "Now, we wait."

Chapter Twenty-eight

"I can't believe it," Cassie exclaimed an hour later. "Blaze's fever is gone, and the sores on her body are healing."

She was seated at the kitchen table with Duncan, Toby, and Lucy. Sugar stood next to the counter, munching on a basket of apples. The bigfoot tossed one into the air. His long tongue shot out, snagged the fruit, and *snap*, the apple was gone.

"Sugar, don't play with your food," Lucy said, giving him a mom look. "It's impolite."

Sugar ducked his head. "'Kay, Mama."

"What *are* those flowers?" Cassie asked Duncan. "You recognized them, didn't you?"

"Yes, and I confess, I am all astonishment. They are Tandaran windflowers, exceedingly rare. Their healing properties are without equal. Wherever did Sugar come by them, Miss Lucy?"

"In the hills growing along the crater," Lucy said. "Shug brought some home, and I gandered pretty quick what they could do, so I got him to show me where he'd found them. Dug up every one I could get my hands on and toted them back to my greenhouse. Temperamental little suckers. Took me a while to figure out how to make them thrive."

"Tan what?" Toby wrinkled his nose. "Where's that, Georgia?"

"Nay, Tandara is—" Duncan shook his head. "It matters not. The crisis is past and the child lives, thanks to you, Miss Lucy."

"No thanks needed." Lucy's voice was gruff. "I know what it is to love a child." Her doting gaze went to the bigfoot. "Some would say what I feel for Sugar ain't the same, but I say love is love."

"Where's Verbena?" Toby asked, looking around. "Haven't seen her for hours."

"In the sickroom," Duncan said. "I asked her to linger there awhile. The mother is still distressed and in need of reassurance. I asked Verbena to abide there so that her peculiar gift may speed the healing process."

"She's reading, ain't she?" Toby grunted as Duncan nodded in assent. "That' girl's gon' explode from learning."

"Let her alone," Lucy said. "She's obviously bright and hungry to better herself, and *I* say that's a fine thing." She pushed to her feet. "I'd best be going. Keep me posted on the little ones."

"Thank you again," Cassie said, walking the old woman to the back door. "You and Sugar saved the day."

"Duncan saved the day," she replied. "I brought the flowers, but he knew what to do with them." She gave Cassie a sharp look. "You're a mighty lucky gal, Cassandra Ferguson. Duncan's a good man. Got a heart big as all outdoors and made for loving. He's been kind to my Sugar. Rescued him from a trap. When I think of my baby lying in the woods, hurt and scared, and no one to help him . . ." Her voice faded off, and her chin quivered. "Well, all I can say is, I'm grateful to Duncan and thankful he was there to help my Sugar." Removing a linen handkerchief from her pocket, she blew her nose defiantly. "Duncan taught Sugar to talk. Did you know that?"

"No," Cassie said, surprised. "I had no idea."

"That's right." Lucy nodded. "Sugar couldn't say a word until Duncan came along. You got any idea what it means to a lonely old woman, to hear her boy call her 'Mama' and tell her he loves her?" She looked fierce. "He's promised to look after Sugar when I'm gone. What have you got to say about that?"

"That's between you and Duncan."

"Your business, too, unless I'm mistaken. Anybody with eyes in their head can see he's crazy about you."

Cassie shifted, uncomfortable with the turn the conversation had taken. Her relationship with Duncan was supposed to have been simple and uncomplicated, a physical affair to the mutual satisfaction of both. But things had shifted, and nothing was turning out the way she'd planned. She hadn't had time to absorb the changes—changes in her perception of Duncan, and changes in herself. She had a lot to figure out, and there'd been very little time. Until she did, she didn't want to share her feelings.

Lucy was watching her. "Cold feet?" she said, cackling. "You're a fool, Cassie Ferguson. You think a man like Duncan comes along every day? He's the best thing walking on two legs. You let that one get away, you'll regret it." She slipped the handle of her pocketbook over one bony arm. "But there's no accounting for stupid. You'll find it everywhere." Turning, she bellowed down the hall, "*Sugar.*"

The bigfoot stuck his head out of the kitchen. "Mama?"

"Shag your fuzzy butt down here, son. Time to go home. We don't want to miss *Days of Our Lives.*"

"Sands," Sugar chirped, galumphing down the hall.

"He loves his stories," Lucy said. "And *Thomas and Friends.* Crazy about that dadburn choo-choo."

Cassie saw them out, then carried a tray with ginger ale, sandwiches, and fruit upstairs to the sickroom. Verbena was sitting in a chair, her head bent over a book. She looked up when Cassie entered. Putting a finger to her lips, she pointed to the bed where the mother and child were asleep and whispered, "Wore slap out, both of them."

Cassie set the tray down on the dresser and spread a quilt over the exhausted woman. "Are you hungry?" she asked, turning to Verbena. "Would you like something to drink?"

"No, thank you."

Curious, Cassie moved closer. "What are you reading?"

"It's called *A Little Princess.*" Verbena placed her finger against the inner spine to mark her place. "It's about this girl, Sara, who goes to this fancy school. Her pappy's a fine gentleman, and Sara's treated like gold until her pappy is reported dead. Then the fly's in the soup, and no lie. Miss Minchin—that's the old bat what runs the school—hears tell that Sara's money is gone, and turns rattlesnake mean. Starves Sara, and works her, and makes her sleep in the cold."

"I remember that book," Cassie said. "I hated Miss Minchin, and I felt sorry for poor Sara."

"Me, too," Verbena said. "But it ain't—isn't—altogether sad. There's a monkey in the story, and a nice man in a turban. Things work out in the end. The man in the turban works for the rich man next door. Turns out, this rich feller was friends with Sara's pappy. He adopts Sara and takes her out of that terrible place."

"You already know the story?"

"Yup." Verbena tucked her legs under her. "Read it last night at the library. Liked it so much, I checked it out this morning. I done—

I mean, I've read it four times so far." She stroked the hard cover with wistful fingers. "Sara and I got a lot in common. Folks think she's a dud and no-count just 'cause she was poor. And Sara knows what it is to be hungry. Starving in an attic—starving with the dogs . . ." She lifted her slender shoulders. "Reckon there ain't a whole heap of difference."

Verbena went back to her reading, and Cassie left the room to return to the kitchen. She'd left Duncan and Toby eating lunch, and as she stepped into the hall, she could hear the low murmur of their masculine voices in conversation. Toby said something she couldn't quite make out, and Duncan laughed.

The sound sent a pleasant shock through Cassie's body. Duncan's laugh was rich and deep, hot cocoa and brandy, and it never failed to warm her to her toes. It was one of the many things that made him attractive. It was one of the reasons she—

Grim materialized unexpectedly in front of Cassie, and she staggered back, clutching her chest. "*Grim*. You scared me into next week."

"Where is Duncan?" Grim's expression was haunted. "I must speak with him."

Cassie took one look at his stark face and led him down the hall without another word.

Toby glanced up from his plate when Cassie and Grim came in. "Head up, boy," he told Duncan. "Here's trouble, unless I'm mistook."

Duncan shoved to his feet. "Brother, what is toward?"

"It is Gryffin." Grim's voice shook. "I saw him in the woods. You were right, brother, though I did not credit it until I saw him with mine own eyes. He is a dupe, and he suffers most dreadfully." A tremor racked his big body. "The orb consumes him, brother. His palms smoke and burn from its touch. The pain . . . ah, gods, the pain. I cannot bear to think on it."

Grim dropped his face into his hands, and Cassie felt a surge of sympathy for the huge, fierce warrior.

"Do not despair, Grimford." Duncan strode over and clapped the big warrior on the shoulders. "We will find a way to save Gryff."

Grim lifted his head, his expression eager. "You will help me free our brother, then?" He clasped Duncan's forearms. "I knew I could count on you, Duncan."

"Of a certainty," Duncan said. "We will set out at first light on the morrow."

"Nay, we cannot wait. The matter must be dealt with at once. Taryn has gone stekaath."

Duncan swore. "Stekaath? Then she is unaware that things have changed?"

"You have the right of it." Grim released Duncan and stepped back, his face very white.

"What is 'stekaath'?" Cassie asked.

"It means 'shadow,' " Duncan said. "Taryn has gone to ground. She was ordered to find and slay the rogue, and she is very, very good at what she does. That is why she was chosen for the task. Unfortunately for Gryff, Taryn is unaware that the situation has altered."

"Aye," said Grim. "My fear is that she will find and slay Gryff ere we can stop her."

"I'm thinking she'll find that hard to do," Toby drawled. "You Dalvahni boys are hard to kill."

"True," Duncan said, "but Taryn has been given a sheaf of special arrows fashioned by Kehvahn himself." He shrugged. "What our master has wrought, he can undo."

"Oh, my God," said Cassie, horrified.

"What of Conall?" Duncan asked Grim. "Does he know of this?"

" 'Twas he who sent me," Grim said. "Rebekah nears her time, and he will not leave her. He bade me ask that you accompany me in his stead." He glanced at Cassie and cleared his throat. "The captain informs me that you have long haunted these woods and hills, and know them exceedingly well. 'Tis his thought that your many sojourns here in pursuit of a certain . . . quarry . . . may be of use."

"The captain is nothing if not astute," Duncan said, giving Cassie a look rife with sensual promise. "Very well, brother. Let us be about it. I am eager to see the thing done and hie me home."

Toby pushed back from the table. "I'll come with you. If this rogue's anywhere about, I'll smell him."

"I thank you," Duncan said to him, "but I would have you remain here, an you would."

Cassie put her hands on her hips. "To keep an eye on me, you mean."

"To keep you safe, my hornet. You are the dearest thing in life to me."

Duncan pulled her close and kissed her right there, in front of the others. A few days ago, Cassie would have slapped him silly for manhandling her in such a fashion, but today, she didn't mind at all.

"That's sweet, Duncan, and I appreciate it, but I'm a big sorceress and can take care of myself." Pressing her palms against his hard chest, she smiled up at him. "Toby's right. He has a nose for supers. The faster you find Taryn and Gryff, the faster you come home to me."

Duncan's eyes flared. "Cassandra? Are you saying . . . ? Dare I hope that you—"

"Yes." Cassie blushed. "I tried to tell you this morning, but we were interrupted."

"*Cassandra*. My heart." *Blip.* Duncan whisked her out of the kitchen and into the hall, away from the others. He pressed her against the wall. "Say it, my love. I would hear you say it ere I leave."

This was it. Time to step off the ledge and fly . . . or go splat.

"I . . ." Cassie's throat tightened, and her heart jerked against her ribs. She tried again. "Duncan, I . . ."

But try as she might, the words wouldn't come. Cheeks burning, she exhaled in frustration. What was the matter with her? Why couldn't she say it? This was ridiculous. She gave it another try. "I care about you, Duncan," she managed at last after a titanic struggle, "and I don't want anything to happen to you."

Lame, but better than nothing, right?

The squeam made a gagging noise. *Not even close. Miss Lucy was right. There's no accounting for stupid.*

Duncan stood motionless, silent. The awkward hush stretched and stretched. Unable to bear the tension, Cassie lifted her gaze to his face. Disappointment, she expected. Fury would not have surprised her. Instead, she found him gazing at her with such an expression of tender amusement that Cassie's breath caught.

"'Twas not what I hoped for," he said, pressing a hard kiss upon her lips, "but 'tis a vast improvement upon 'Go away, Duncan, ere I shoot you with my gun.'"

Releasing her, he stuck his head through the open kitchen door. "Let us away, my boon companions."

Grim strode into the hall with Toby behind him in dog form. The back door opened, and they were gone. Cassie ran after them, watching through the glass as they crossed the lawn and melted into the trees.

Cassie swallowed, her throat thick with tears. She should have told him. Why the hell was she still so afraid?

She stood looking out the door a long time, then turned back toward the kitchen. As she went down the hall, the telephone rang.

She picked up the receiver. "Hello?"

"Miss Ferguson?" a woman whispered in a frantic tone. "You got to unwhammy me. I can't take being a love goddess no more. Me and Frodo's run out of places to hide. I ain't et or slept in days."

Oh, good Lord, she'd forgotten about Nicole.

"Where are you?" Cassie asked.

"In the back of Webb's Hardware. Me and Frodo snuck in to use the construction phone in the storeroom. We's hiding behind a bin of nails. Went back to Miss Evie's, and them crazy men was waiting for us. Squatting on the roof like a bunch of birds. Mr. Ansgar runned 'em off, but we couldn't stay." Nicole began to cry. "Yesterday, a bunch of them fools chased me up a sycamore tree. I'm a retired pole dancer, Miss Ferguson. I ain't no Zacchaeus. I'd be up there still, sitting on a limb like a dang squirrel, if my Precious hadn't runned them off." She gasped. "Somebody's coming. If they got a penis, I'm done for. Take this spell off'n me, Miss Ferguson. *Please.* I can't take it no more."

The phone went dead.

Cassie returned the receiver to its cradle. Going to the hall tree, she selected an ash staff from the stand and went out onto the front porch. She stood there quietly for a moment, listening to the steady slosh of the river, calming her thoughts and gathering her will.

Carefully, methodically, she recreated the repelling spell she'd cast on Nicole. It shimmered to life before her, a network of sparkling lines. She could see right away where she'd botched it. Several of the lines at the center of the spell formed a pulsing heart, throbbing with power. This was extremely potent magic. Thank goodness for Frodo. If not for the nasty little dog, Nicole might have been torn apart by her "admirers."

Cassie was appalled. This was sloppy work, the mistake of a neophyte, not a seasoned wizard. She hadn't made a mistake like this since . . . well, since ever. She examined the beating heart at the center of the spell. Projecting, no doubt about it. She'd been moping over Duncan when she'd cast the spell, and her unresolved, unacknowledged feelings had gotten woven into the incantation.

Rifling through her mistakes over the past few months, she had an epiphany. She hadn't lost her touch. She'd been in denial, stuffing her feelings for Duncan, refusing to recognize them, and it had screwed with her magic, big-time. But that was in the past. She'd faced her feelings for Duncan and accepted them.

Oh, yeah? Guess that's why you told the guy you love him.

Okay, she had a little more work to do in the own-your-feelings department, but she was making progress.

Now to make things right for poor Nicole.

Focusing on Nicole and her happiness and well-being, she carefully deconstructed the spell in her mind. The force filled her until she thought she might fly apart.

Pointing the staff at the shining spell, she muttered, "Erasus."

The spell unraveled and disappeared with a pop.

"There," Cassie said, pleased. "That should do nicely." She left the porch and returned the staff to the stand in the hall, then climbed the stairs to the sickroom.

Verbena looked up from her reading and greeted her with a smile. "They're feeling much better," she said, waving the book in the direction of the patients.

Cassie had witnessed the windflowers' magic with her own eyes. Nonetheless, she was amazed at the difference in mother and daughter. It was extraordinary. With her color returned and her vitality restored, the mother was a handsome woman, with thick brown locks and large brown eyes. The little girl was sitting up in bed eating grapes, and she, too, was vastly improved. Her eyes were no longer clouded with pain and fever, and the terrible sores that had riddled her body had almost faded away. Even her molting hair looked healthier, though the bald patches remained.

She looked up when Cassie came in. "Thank you for the grapes, Miss Cassie," she said, offering her a shy smile. "I feel lots better."

"I'm so glad, Blaze." Cassie turned to the mother. "I'm happy to see that you're both feeling better."

The mother rose. "I don't know how to thank you for your kindness, miss. Blaze and I had no place else to go."

"Cassie," she reminded her. "I'm sorry. I forgot to ask your name."

"Laura." The woman blushed. "I should have introduced myself before. Too upset to remember my manners."

"Of course you were upset," Cassie said. "Perfectly understandable, given the circumstances."

Laura looked away, shamefaced. "We've been shunned. The pack wouldn't even let us back in our house to get our things."

"I heard," Cassie said with a rush of sympathy for the woman. "What Zeb did was cruel and heartless."

Not to mention abusive, she thought, angrily remembering the vicious blow the alpha had given Laura.

"Zeb," Laura spat. "He got what he deserved."

"What do you mean?" Cassie asked. "Is he dead?"

"No. Shunned by the pack, same as me and Blaze. The Randalls got a new alpha now."

"Shunned? Why?"

"Zeb's crazy as a loon, and the pack got tired of his mess, I reckon," Laura said. "My cousin Gina slipped into the woods to speak to me. Our mothers were sisters, and we grew up close." A spasm of grief crossed her face. Pressing her lips together, she continued, "Gina says Zeb got a bunch of the pack killed going after that stupid stone, and it was the last straw. The pack chased him off. Too little, too late, as far as I'm concerned. My Mac's dead and it's Zeb's fault, may he rot in hell."

"I want Mac," Blaze said, and began to cry.

"Shh," Laura said, comforting the child.

"Shunned," Cassie repeated, unnerved.

Zeb was out there, unmoored and unhinged, a powerful werewolf with nothing to lose, and Duncan was unaware. A terrifying premonition seized Cassie that she'd never see him again. Dread seeped into her bones, stealing her breath and robbing her of strength.

She should have told Duncan when she'd had the chance. She should've—

"What's that?" Verbena looked up from her reading. "Sounds like a dog in pain."

"Toby?" Cassie's heart pounded. "He went into the woods with Duncan and Grim to look for the rogue."

"That ain't Toby." Verbena dropped her book and jumped to her feet. "That's Bo-Bo, and he's in trouble." She darted out of the room, quick as a hummingbird.

"Verbena, wait," Cassie cried, running after her.

But Verbena was too fast. Cassie caught a flash of movement and heard the back door slam. Cassie dashed downstairs and flung open the door in time to see Joby Ray step out of the trees at the edge of the lawn, looking as shabby and disreputable as ever.

Verbena streaked across the lawn, her feet skimming the ground. "Don't you hurt him, Joby Ray. You turn Bo-Bo loose, or so help me, you'll be sorry."

He held up a nondescript orange mutt by the scruff. "Come and get him, Beenie, if'n you want him so bad."

He thrust out his arm, and the dog jerked and howled as though it had been pressed against an electric fence.

No, not electric—a magical fence. The spell line Cassie had erected shimmered in the sun. Superimposed on her wards was a network of glistening threads. Duncan had strengthened the wards, and the repelling spell he'd cast was unable to differentiate between man and animal. To the shield, a Skinner was a Skinner. The poor dog was being tortured.

"Stop it," Verbena shrieked, running closer. "You's hurting him."

Joby Ray grinned and waited but made no move to step out on the lawn.

With horrifying clarity, Cassandra realized his game.

"Verbena, *stop*." Cassie jumped off the porch and sprinted after the girl. "Don't go near the wards. It's what he wants."

The girl paid no heed, sobbing as she ran.

"That's right," Joby Ray crooned, holding the yowling dog against the wards. "You gon' have to come right up to me if'n you wants him."

"Verbena, stop," Cassie shouted again. "Don't go any closer."

Verbena ignored her. Running to the edge of the lawn, she reached through the shield and snatched the dog from Joby Ray. Sparks sizzled at the contact. Verbena's hands closed around the dog, and she jerked him through. The animal went limp in her arms, head lolling and tongue hanging out.

"Bo-Bo?" Verbena sank to the grass with the dog in her lap. "Please don't be dead."

Shooting Joby Ray a glare of dislike, Cassie ran up. "You'd better leave, Skinner, before Duncan catches you."

"Oh, he ain't gon' catch me." Joby Ray smirked, his fingers flicking deftly over the wards. "Saw him take off into the woods with a dog and another big son of a bitch. I'll be long gone afore he gets back."

Cassie tugged on Verbena's arm. "Come away from the spell line, Verbena. It's a trick."

"Got it," Joby Ray said with a crow of delight. "Thankee, Beenie, for the boost. Good to know I ain't lost my touch."

Cassie stepped in front of Verbena. "Go away, Joby Ray. This is your last warning."

"Shut your yap, bitch." Joby Ray stepped through the shield. "I've had about enough of your sass."

His arm jerked up. Too late, Cassie saw the billy club. The club came down and the world went black.

Chapter Twenty-nine

Toby sniffed and bounded into the trees with a deep, throaty huff. "He has caught a scent," Grim said. "Perhaps 'tis Gryff."

Duncan nodded and stilled, looking back in the direction of the cottage on the river. Unease shivered through him, and he had the sudden, deep misgiving that Cassandra needed him.

"What troubles you, brother?" asked Grim.

"I do not know," Duncan said. "A presentiment of danger." He gave Grim a rueful smile. "Or mayhap 'tis merely my longing for Cassandra. 'Tis ever thus with me."

"You love her." It was a statement, not a question.

"Aye," Duncan said. "With all my heart."

"Enough to bind yourself to her?"

"Brother, I have been bound lo these many years and have no wish to be free. If, howe'er, you ask whether I would make her my life mate an I could, the answer is yes. 'Tis my most earnest and heartfelt desire to join my life with Cassandra's one day."

"The lady has doubts?"

"Aye, so I fear." Duncan grimaced. "And I have no one to blame save myself. I hurt her deeply many years ago, and she trusts me not."

"Conall has told me of this," Grim said. "You and your Cassie met some hundred years past?"

"Longer than that. Closer to two centuries than one."

"Then you, and not Brand, are the first of our kind to fall in love."

Duncan stared at his brother. "By the sword, you are right."

"And with a demonoid," Grim said. "It explains much. I would that you had told me. Perhaps I would have viewed your fondness for levity with more tolerance."

"I misdoubt it. You ever saw me as a sad scapegrace."

"True enough." Grim sighed. "And then I met Sassy, and everything changed." He spread his arms wide. "You see before you the happiest of warriors." He dropped his arms, his smile fading. "But for my brother's grief, my joy would be complete. I have so much, Duncan, and Gryff has lost everything. His honor, his brothers, his health. Even his mind has flown. When I saw him in the woods, he knew me not, mine own *twin*. How can I be happy when he is in abject misery?"

"We will find him, Grimford," Duncan promised. "We are Dalvahni, and we do not falter from our purpose."

Toby woofed again, and this time the message was clear. The dog had found something—or someone.

Duncan and Grim blurred through the woods, zipping past trees, streams, and hillocks, and came upon the wolfhound at last in a narrow defile between two hills. The hound sat on his haunches before a fallen log, having his ears rubbed by Taryn. It struck Duncan that the huntress looked wan and tired, an unusual circumstance, given the robust and unflagging nature of the Kirvahni constitution.

She rose when she saw them, inclining her head in acknowledgment. "Brothers," she said in her fluid voice. "I am even now hot on the rogue's trail, but tarried to rest, and was greeted by this noble hound. What brings you here?"

"The very same," said Grim. "We seek Gryff."

"Your loyalty to the brotherhood does you credit, Grimford, but as I have told you before, I cannot allow you to interfere with my duty," Taryn said with unshaken calm. "My most sacred duty, imposed by Kehvahn himself. I have been tasked with bringing in the rogue, and that I will do."

"Bring him in, by all means," said Duncan, "but rescue him instead. A startling revelation has been made. Gryffin is no rogue but a victim of Pratt's wickedness. Kehvahn desires you to free Gryff, not slay him."

Taryn raised her brows. "I know nothing of this. What is more, you cannot release me from my vow."

"Arta was to have informed you, but you have been stekaath." Grim clenched his fists, and Duncan could sense his roiling tension. "Consult with her, I beg you, ere you do something you will regret. A warrior's life is at stake."

Taryn frowned. "Forgive me, but I cannot help but be skeptical, given the timing of your interference and the proximity of my quarry."

"You would accuse us of dissemblance?" Grim growled, stepping forward.

Duncan grabbed him by the arm. "Your wariness is natural, but I swear to you by the sacred three that we speak the truth."

Taryn hesitated. "I desire but to do my duty. Yet I would not err, especially when the matter is so momentous." She looked off into the distance, her gray eyes grave. "Very well. I will consult with Arta."

Duncan relaxed. "It is well, sister. In the meantime, we will continue the search, for Grim is heartsick at his brother's plight and cannot rest until he is freed."

Toby sprang to his feet, barking sharply in warning. The atmosphere changed, and Gryff appeared on a rush of air. In an instant, Taryn's bow was in her hands, an arrow fitted upon the string.

"Nay," Grim shouted, springing between Gryff and Taryn. "Can you not see his affliction?"

Taryn lowered the bow, staring at Gryff, white-faced with shock. The rogue was as Duncan remembered: gaunt, barefoot, and in rags, his skin scored with writhing markings, his eyes vacant, his expression slack and uncomprehending. He held the orb cupped in the palms of his hands. His flesh burned and smoked, regenerated because of his Dalvahni blood, and scorched again. The pain was surely excruciating, but if he felt it, he showed no reaction.

He opened his mouth, his lips working, as though he'd forgotten how to speak.

"Girl." The word was a guttural rasp. "Help. Girl."

Gryff vanished, leaving them stunned and bewildered.

Taryn was the first to find her voice. "I saw him. He is most grievously tormented, but he is not evil."

Grim glared at her in affront. "We told you as much. A Dalvahni warrior does not lie."

"I do not expect you to understand," she said, "but 'twas necessary I see the thing for myself." She shivered. "He is filled with rage. Such bleak, unspeakable rage."

"'Tis plain he came to deliver a warning," Grim said, looking troubled. "What think you he meant by it?"

"Cassandra." Fear squeezed Duncan's lungs, and his apprehension returned full force. "I sensed she was in danger earlier and paid no heed."

"Nay, Duncan," Grim said. "Cassandra is most beauteous, but she is a woman full grown, not a girl."

"I must go to her, nonetheless," Duncan said. "You would do the same, were it Sassy."

"Of a certainty," said Grim.

"Abide here but a moment. I will return forthwith. If my fear is realized, I may need your help."

"We will both abide," said Taryn.

An instant later, Duncan materialized on Cassie's lawn. He sped across the grass and into the house. Stilling, he opened his senses and sought her, and knew at once that she was gone. Her presence was a living, breathing thing, and 'twas absent. "Cassandra?" he said, knowing she would not answer.

Unreasoning panic twisted his vitals. Ah, gods, he could not lose her again.

He whirled at a soft noise and spied a woman down the hall. She stood unmoving, staring at him. He looked at her for a moment, blinded by terror, before it struck him that it was the Randall woman, Blaze's mother. She held the speaking device called a telephone clutched in one hand.

She set the device down. "Thank God you're here. I was about to call the sheriff. Cassie and Verbena have been kidnapped."

Duncan strode up to her, and the woman recoiled at what she saw in his face.

"Who took her?" he demanded. "Tell me."

"That polecat Joby Ray," she said, her eyes wide. "I came downstairs to get Blaze some more grapes and heard a noise. I looked outside and saw Joby Ray."

"He got through my wards." Duncan swore. "How can this be?"

"Joby Ray's talent is burgling," she said. "He's got a string of arrests for B&E long as your arm, but he keeps slipping past the law."

"Verbena," Duncan said, thinking quickly. "He lured her close to the shield, and she unwittingly enhanced his ability."

The Randall woman shrugged. "Don't know anything about that. All I know is he got in." Her mouth twisted in distaste. "Oh yeah, and Zeb was with him."

"The alpha was here with the pack?"

"Nope. Zeb's on his own now. Been shunned. I'm thinking the Skinners are his new pack."

Duncan had heard enough. He disappeared.

Cassie woke up to utter blackness and a splitting headache. The taste of bile burned the back of her throat, and her stomach heaved. She moaned and concentrated on not throwing up.

A match flared in the darkness, illuminating Verbena's pale face. "You okay, Cassie?"

"Been better. You?"

She saw Verbena's face crumple as the match flickered and died. "We's in trouble now, for sure," the girl whispered. "Them Skinners done grabbed us."

"*We're* in trouble." Cassie fumbled and found Verbena's hand. "And the Skinners *have* grabbed us."

"Don't make no difference how I talk." Verbena's voice was dull with hopelessness. "I ain't gon' see the light of day again. Joby Ray'll make sure of 'at. Said he's gon' keep me locked up so's I won't run away again."

"Don't worry about Joby Ray. Duncan will find us."

Duncan. Cassie's chest tightened. She loved him, and she was a pluperfect idiot for not telling him so.

Praise Jesus. Glad you finally figured that out, the squeam said. *Somebody should have knocked you in the head ages ago.*

"Joby Ray says won't nobody ever find us 'cause the Skinners don't stay in one place no more." Verbena struck another match. "We's in a camper, see, and we can't get out. They got the windows boarded up and the door barred on the outside. I done tried." The match went out. "The Skinners lost everything after Old Charlie died. They's on the move now. Don't stay in one place too long."

"I don't care," Cassie said. "Duncan will still find us."

"How? He don't even know Joby Ray's got us."

Cassie felt a flare of panic. Dear God. She hadn't thought of that. It was hard to think with her head pounding, but she had to try. "Then we'll rescue ourselves," she said with a confidence she was far from feeling. "We handled that old demon, didn't we?"

"You ain't got your staff."

"Maybe there's something here I can use. We'll look around, but give me a minute. My head is killing me."

"Don't go to sleep," Verbena said, slipping back into proper speech. "You probably have a concussion. Read about it in a book on first aid."

Cassie smiled despite her headache. Verbena had read the entire library in a day.

"Joby Ray won't let me read." Verbena's voice broke. "That's the hard part, knowing I won't be allowed to read no more."

"Tell me more about Bo-Bo," Cassie suggested, sensing the girl's grief and terror. "You must've known a lot of dogs. What makes him so special?"

"One of Old Charlie's prize bitches went into heat, and a neighbor's dawg . . . I mean, *dog* . . . got into the pen," Verbena said. "Charlie didn't realize what had happened until the pups was born—four of the prettiest spaniels you ever seed, and an orange mutt."

"And?"

"Old Charlie throwed Bo-Bo in a bucket to drown. I fished him out. He's been my dog ever since." Verbena sniffled. "That is, until . . ."

Her voice trailed off, and Cassie supplied the rest. "Until Beck saved you from the demons and you went to live with her and Conall. You and Bo-Bo got separated."

"Yep." Verbena's voice was thick with misery. "I couldn't go back for him. The Skinners wouldn't have let me have him, anyway, out of pure-in-tee meanness. 'Sides, I was scared if they got their mitts on me, they'd never turn me loose." She lapsed into silence for a moment, and then added, "Looks like I was right about that."

"We're going to get out of here," Cassie said. "Let's look around for a piece of wood I can use. Have you got another match?"

"Two more." There was a soft scratch as Verbena lit another match. "We'd best hurry."

Cassie took a quick look around at the inside of the camper and was revolted. The place was filthy, full of beer cans, trash, empty plastic bags, and rat droppings. At least, she hoped it was rat droppings. The furniture was made of hard plastic and vinyl, and bolted down; there was no trace of wood of any use to a wizard.

Verbena struck the last match.

"There," Cassie said, pointing to a skinny object on the floor in the far corner. "What's that?"

Verbena crawled through the rubbish. "Broken pool cue."

Cassie did a fist pump. "Hand it to me."

Verbena put the pool cue in Cassie's hand as the last match flickered and died. Cassie didn't need the light now.

She ran her hand down the cool shaft and grinned in the dark. "Maple. Balance, promise, and practical magic. We can use all three."

There was the screech of a metal bar being lifted, and the camper door swung open. Joby Ray stood in the doorway. To Cassie's surprise, it was still light outside. She'd lost track of the time in this glorified tin can.

"Ladies," he said, showing his pointy teeth. "Come to check on you. Make sure you're enjoying your 'commodations."

He reeked of beer and cigarettes, and he was looking extremely pleased with himself. He reminded Cassie of a banty rooster she'd once had, small, mean, and aggressive. She'd hated that rooster. She'd done a happy dance when a fox had eaten it. Too bad there wasn't a fox handy right now, a giant fox, big enough to swallow Joby Ray and the rest of the Skinners whole or squash them like roaches.

A giant? Cassie gave a small gasp. Of *course*. She would've done a facepalm if her head didn't hurt like the dickens.

Joby Ray climbed into the camper, a battery-operated lantern swinging from one hand. "Lock it behind me and then beat it," he barked to someone over his shoulder. "Don't want our little chickens to fly the coop."

The door slammed shut, the metal bar dropped back into place, and the sound of footsteps faded away.

"There." Joby Ray set the lantern down on the kitchen bar, and soft light flooded the interior of the camper. "Now we can have us a chat."

Crunching through a clutter of aluminum cans, he sprawled onto a window seat covered in torn Naugahyde and looked at Cassie, his beady eyes glittering. "You mean to hit old Joby with that pool cue?"

"No," Cassie said. "I'll leave that pleasure to someone else."

Joby Ray chuckled. "You know, I could've slit your throat and let you bleed out, but I been hankering to get to know you better since the first time I clapped eyes on you. And then there's Zeb. He means to use you as leverage."

"That right? Leverage for what?"

"The orb. He's obsessed with that damn rock. Me, I'm just horny, and you are the finest thing I've seen in many a day." He leaned closer. "I like a woman with gumption. Like to beat it out of her. You and me, we's gon' have fun."

"I think you and I have a different definition of that word."

Gripping the broken pool cue, Cassie formed the image in her mind and pushed the thought outward, though the effort made her queasy and sent shooting pains through her head. "Alacritas," she said in a clear voice.

Joby Ray straightened on the bench. "What's that?"

"Alacritas," Cassie repeated. "Alacritas, alacritas, alacritas."

"What's that mean?"

"It's Latin for piece of shit," Cassie lied.

"You got a smart mouth." Half rising from the bench, Joby Ray grabbed Cassie by the hair. He dragged her through the rubble and between his spread legs, jerking her to her knees. "I'm gon' learn you some manners."

With a surge of panicked revulsion, Cassie guessed his intention and began to struggle. "Duncan will kill you," she said, panting. "If he doesn't, I will."

He tightened his cruel grip on her hair and yanked her closer. "Duncan ain't here, and I think it's about time you put that sweet little mouth of yours to good use."

He reached for the zipper of his jeans with his free hand.

"No," Verbena shouted, scrambling through the litter on the floor. "You leave her alone."

With the sound of screeching metal, the camper door was wrenched off its hinges. The rogue stood in the doorway, the orb clutched in his smoking hands.

"Girl." He stared at Verbena. "Help girl."

"Get him," Verbena cried, pointing to Joby Ray. "He's hurting my friend."

Moving like an automaton, the rogue shifted the orb to one hand and reached through the door. He grabbed Joby Ray by the shirt and plucked him out of the camper.

Verbena helped Cassie to her feet and they staggered outside. Cassie was shaking with reaction and adrenaline, her head was throbbing, and her scalp was on fire. They were in a clearing in the woods in the center of a circle of trucks, RVs, and campers in varying degrees of decay, a jumble of rusting, fading vehicles that Cassie had no doubt were stolen. She heard music, voices, and raucous laughter from the far side of the little camp. Smoke drifted between the vehicles, and the fatty smell of cooking meat hung in the air. The Skinners were having a party.

Remembering Verbena's comment about the Skinners' diet, she shuddered.

The rogue looked at Verbena in unspoken question, still holding the struggling Joby Ray by one arm. "Girl?"

"I don't care what you do with him," Verbena told the rogue. "You can throw him in the river for all I care."

The rogue nodded and turned, dragging Joby Ray with him.

"Help," Joby Ray hollered. "Somebody better drag their ass over here and help me."

An RV door slammed open, and Zeb Randall stepped out. He was banged up and bruised, his hair was a graying tangle, and he looked like he'd slept in his clothes, but at least he no longer had the crazy eyes. Cassie felt a spasm of hope. Maybe she could reason with him, smooth this thing over without anyone getting hurt. She was tired, her head hurt, and she wanted to go home. To Duncan.

Zeb saw the orb, and his eyes blazed.

Whoops. Cassie's hopes sank. *Crazy eyes.*

"Give it to me," Zeb said, lunging at the rogue. "The orb is mine."

Suddenly, the air grew thick and oppressive. Cassie groaned and sank to her knees, her temples pounding at the unexpected change of pressure. A robed man appeared, handsome as any Dalvahni, with striking, well-formed features, strong shoulders, and flowing dark hair.

Not a man, Cassie amended upon further consideration. No mortal being emanated that kind of raw power. There was a god among them, and he was angry. The atmosphere crackled with his rage.

"Ah, Gryffin, there you are." The god's voice was a low rumble like distant thunder. "I am not happy with you."

The rogue shot a startled look at the god and dropped Joby Ray to the ground.

"No, no, my chary fellow," the god said as Gryffin began to dematerialize. "Unlike your oafish brothers, I weary of the chase. You will be still."

He lifted a finger, and the rogue froze, unable to move. The god flowed over the ground like water running downstream, his feet not touching the ground, and reached for the orb.

"No," Zeb shouted. "It's mine. I found it."

The werewolf threw himself at the god and bounced off as though he'd encountered an invisible wall.

"You would interfere with me again?" the god said. "I find you tiresome."

He motioned, and Zeb sailed through the air. The werewolf smacked into a tree and slid to the ground in a bloody heap.

"And now to deal with you," the god said, lifting both hands to destroy the rogue.

Something crashed in the woods and the trees at the edge of the camp shuddered and swayed as something impossibly large and strong passed among them.

Just around the corner of the street I reside, a booming voice sang.

> *There lives the cutest little girl I have ever spied,*
> *Her name is Rose O'Grady, and I don't mind telling you*
> *That she's the sweetest little Rose the garden ever grew.*

The trees parted, and the Savior of Hannah stepped out. With a startled exclamation, the god whirled around. His hold on the rogue slipped. In an instant, Gryff was gone.

"*No,*" the god roared, and vanished after him in a shattering crack of thunder.

I never shall forget the day she promised to be mine, Jeb sang.
As we sat telling love tales in the golden summertime.

Swinging his giant peanut, the avenging colossus stomped through the camp. *Whack,* a camper went flying. *Whack, whack,* a truck was flattened. Skinners scattered like roaches out of a burning outhouse.

'Twas on her finger that I placed a small engagement ring
While in the trees, the little birds this song seemed to sing.

"It's that peanut feller." Verbena clapped her hands and jumped up and down in excitement. "Look at him go."

Joby Ray scrambled to his feet, his eyes starting from his head, and took off.

"He's getting away," Verbena cried.

Cassie cupped her hands to her mouth. "Jeb!"

The behemoth turned, a truck raised high overhead.

Cassie pointed at Joby Ray. "Fetch."

Jeb smashed the truck into the ground and obediently did an about-face.

Sweet Rosie O'Grady, he belted, barreling after the terrified Joby Ray.

> *My dear little Rose,*
> *She's my steady lady,*
> *Most everyone knows,*
> *And when we are married,*
> *How happy we'll be;*
> *I love sweet Rose O'Grady,*
> *And Rosie O'Grady loves me.*

Cassie almost felt sorry for Joby Ray. Almost.

He didn't stand a chance.

Chapter Thirty

Duncan materialized amid utter destruction. He looked around the trash-strewn glade with a feeling of paralyzing dread. The campsite was a ruin of twisted metal, smoking hulks, and upturned vehicles. Whate'er unspeakable calamity had befallen this place, Cassandra could not have escaped unscathed.

He went to his knees and threw back his head, roaring in raw, animal pain.

A sound pierced the blackness of his agony, the sweetest sound Duncan had ever heard, sweeter by far than the soul-soothing sound of birdsong after a killing winter.

"Duncan?" Cassandra said. "Duncan, it's all right. I'm alive."

And then she was there, kneeling on the ground beside him, her arms around him as she shook, and laughed, and cried.

She pressed glad kisses all over his face. "I thought I'd never see you again. Oh, Duncan, I love you. I was an idiot not to tell you before. I was afraid. I think I've been afraid since you left, all those years ago. Please forgive me."

Duncan held her away from him. "What did you say?"

"I said I love you." Cassandra smiled at him through her tears. "I love you, you big galoot. I've never loved anyone else."

Duncan felt shaky and unbalanced, as jittery as a maid on her wedding night. "You are certain? Think on what you are saying, Cassandra. Do not play with me, I beg of you."

Cassandra sat back on her thighs, a frown in her eyes. He was making her angry, his sweet hornet, but he had to be sure.

"I love you," she said. "I love you with all my heart. I've always loved you, but if you don't believe me, then fine."

She tossed her head and winced.

"You are hurt." Duncan pulled her into his lap. "Why did you not say so?"

"I was so glad to see you, I forgot."

Duncan liked that. He liked that very much.

"Where?" he demanded. "Show me at once."

"Here." She touched the area above her forehead and winced again.

With gentle fingers, he probed and found a sizeable knot. "You have a lump the size of a goose egg."

"I should. Joby Ray hit me with a billy club."

"He *what*?"

"He hit me with a cudgel. Knocked me out. I have a terrible headache."

Carefully, Duncan set her aside and got to his feet.

Cassandra looked up at him. "Where are you going?"

"To kill Joby Ray."

She jumped up and threw her arms around him again. "That's sweet, but you'll have to wait your turn. Verbena is having a few words with him right now."

"Is that wise, to leave her alone with the miscreant? You can be certain he means her ill."

"Oh, she's not alone. Jeb is with her. She's perfectly safe, I promise you."

The air shivered, and Grim and Taryn arrived. "What ho," Taryn said, looking around. "Someone had a merry fight."

"It was Jeb," Cassandra said. "The Skinners kidnapped me and Verbena, and Jeb ran them off."

"My brother . . . Gryff . . . the rogue," Grim said. "Have you seen him?"

Cassandra nodded. "Joby Ray had me and Verbena locked in a camper and wouldn't let us go. Gryff rescued us."

"He did?" Grim seemed surprised. "Whyever would he do that?"

"He likes Verbena," Cassandra said. "She asked him to grab Joby Ray, and he did."

"Where is Gryffin?" Grim said, looking around. "I would speak to him. Try to convince him to abide with us."

"Gone, I'm afraid. This . . . *being* arrived. He was a god, I think, and he tried to take the orb from Gryff."

Duncan and Grim exchanged glances. "Pratt," Duncan said.

"Is that his name?" Cassandra shivered. "He was a real piece of work. I think he meant to kill Gryff. Would have, too, if Jeb hadn't arrived like the cavalry. The peanut feller saved the day."

"The peanut feller?" Taryn said, opening her eyes wide.

Cassandra twinkled at her. "That's what Verbena calls him."

"I confess my curiosity," Grim said. "I should like to meet this peanut feller."

"I'll introduce you," Cassandra said. "He's over here."

Cassandra turned and walked away, and Grim and Taryn followed her. Duncan came behind more slowly. He was stunned, bemused, his world turned on end. Cassandra loved him. She *loved* him.

Ah, gods, he desperately wanted to believe her, but after so many years of longing, hoping, dreaming, and praying, it seemed too good to be true. She had been under extreme duress. What if, upon reflection, she changed her mind? That would kill him.

But what choice did he have? He could not leave her. She was everything to him.

He quickened his pace and caught up with her. She looked up at him and smiled, and he was lost. He loved her. He loved enough for both of them.

The four of them picked their way through the debris. Rounding a pile of smoking metal, they came upon Verbena, the Skinner weasel, and the animate statue.

"By the sword," Grim said.

"Quite splendid, is he not?" said Taryn. "I caught but a brief glance at him during the demon fight, but he is quite the intrepid fighter, and surprisingly good with a club."

Jeb—the peanut feller—held Joby Ray by the nape of the neck, pinched between two of his enormous bronze fingers. Joby Ray's narrow, sallow face was tight with anger and fright. Verbena stood before the varlet, her hands on her hips.

"Get this through your thick skull," she was saying. "I'm no relation to you, and I don't owe you a thing. To the contrary, your family has treated me abominably, and that's not including the stunt you pulled today. Cassie and I should press charges against you for kidnapping, unlawful imprisonment, and assault, but Cassie has agreed that we won't, provided you leave me alone."

"Listen at you, talking all fancy and getting above your raising," Joby Ray sneered. "You ain't fooling nobody, Beenie. You can put a dress and garters on a pig, but it's still a pig. You can't change what you are."

"That may be true, Joby Ray, but here's what I'm not. I'm *not* a Skinner. Never have been, never will be, thank the good Lord. Are we clear?"

"Yeah, yeah," Joby Ray said. "Whatever. Just tell this tin asshole to let me go."

Verbena motioned. "Turn him loose, Jeb."

Jeb dropped Joby Ray to the ground

Mr. Johnson had troubles of his own, Jeb sang with a sad shake of his head.

> *Had him a yellow cat that wouldn't leave home,*
> *He tried and tried to give that cat away,*
> *He gave it to a man goin' far away,*
> *But the cat came back the very next day,*
> *The cat came back, couldn't stay away.*

"I understand what you're saying, Jeb," Verbena said, "but what else can I do?"

Joby Ray adjusted his twisted clothes. "I tell you what you can do, Beenie. You can kiss my ass. And you'd better sleep with one eye open, 'cause I'm coming for you."

"One more thing, Joby Ray," Verbena called after him as he sauntered away. "I want Bo-Bo. I raised him and he's mine."

Joby Ray turned with a cruel laugh. "Bo-Bo? The mutt's dead. Killed him myself."

Cassandra gasped. Rushing to Verbena's side, she tried to put her arms around the girl, but Verbena shrugged her off.

"Leave me be." The girl stepped forward. Her face was very white. "You shouldn't 'uv done that, Joby Ray."

Joby Ray laughed again. "I see you forget your fancy words when you's riled. Knowed it was fer show."

"You shouldn't 'uv killed Bo-Bo," Verbena said again. "Now you done gone and made me mad."

"Whatchoo gon' do about it, Beenie?" Joby Ray taunted. "Enhance me to death?"

"Do you know what an antonym is, Joby Ray?" Verbena asked in an eerily flat voice. "'Course you don't. It means opposite. Know what the opposite of the word *enhance* is, Joby Ray? It's *diminish*."

She raised her hands, palms outward and facing Joby Ray, and Duncan felt the tug of gathered power. He glanced at Cassandra, assuming it was she, but she shook her head and looked at Verbena. Her message was clear: Verbena was the wielder.

Duncan was surprised and unsettled. Gathered power was a thrumming in the veins, the zing of energy along the nerves. This sensation was different. It was enervating, draining.

The sensation deepened, and he heard Cassandra murmur in alarm. Beside her, Taryn and Grim shifted nervously. They felt it, too, then, this singular magic.

"What?" Joby Ray said, sneering at their unease. "Little Beenie's giving me the hands. Big deal." He shivered in mock dread. "I'm shaking in my boots."

Suddenly, he grunted and clutched his belly. "What's happening?" The shifter went to his knees, a look of horror on his face. "Whatchoo doing? Stop it, Verbena."

"I'm draining you," Verbena said without an ounce of emotion. "I'm sapping every last drop of talent from you, you weasel-dick, dog-killing bastard. You'll never shift again or break another lock. You're done."

When it was finished, Verbena walked over and looked down at him. "Welcome to Normville, Joby Ray," she said. "Tell the rest of the family they mess with me again, I'll un-kith them, too."

She stepped over the prostrate man and ran, sobbing, for the woods. Jeb Hannah turned and lumbered after her.

"Verbena," Cassandra cried, starting to follow the girl.

Duncan pulled her into his arms. "Let her go, my love. The peanut feller will keep her safe, and she'll come home when she's ready."

"Home." Cassandra buried her face in his neck. "Take me home, Duncan. Please."

"As milady commands," he said.

Nodding in farewell to Taryn and Grim, he stepped into the void. The world melted around them, and they were standing in Cassandra's drive.

"I meant the tree house," Cassandra said, with a little huff when she realized where they were.

"I beg your pardon," Duncan said, much chastened. "'Twas my thought you would wish to ascertain the well-being of Blaze and her mother."

"I suppose you're right," she admitted with a sigh. "Very well. Let's go inside."

Toby bounded out of the house, his expression anxious. "You okay, doll? Those dadburn demon hunters beamed themselves up and left me behind. I been worried sick." He looked around. "Where's Verbena?"

"In the woods," Cassandra said. "She's okay. Just needed a little time." She made a face. "Family drama."

"That's too bad." Toby held the door for them to enter, then followed them into the hall. "Those Skinners won't take no for an answer." He nudged Duncan with his elbow. "I'm thinking you and I ought to pay them a little visit. Set 'em straight, if you know what I mean."

"I do not think the Skinners will trouble Verbena further," Duncan said. "She's made her feelings quite plain."

Blaze's mother came down the steps. "You all right, Cassie?"

"I'm fine," Cassandra assured the woman. "A headache, but nothing a good night's sleep won't cure. How are you and Blaze?"

The woman gave Cassandra a grateful smile. "I'm right as rain, and Blaze is feeling much better. In fact, I'm having trouble keeping the little rascal in bed." Her joyous expression dimmed. "She should be well enough to travel in a few days, and then we'll be out of your hair."

"Where will you go?" Toby asked.

"I don't rightly know." The woman's delight faded. "Don't have a place in mind."

"Then you and Blaze will stay here until you get on your feet," Cassandra said. "There's plenty of room."

"Oh, no. We couldn't impose."

"I insist. You'd be doing me a favor, actually."

The woman looked puzzled. "I don't understand."

"W-e-l-l." Leaning closer, Cassandra said in a confiding manner, "You see, Duncan and I are getting married soon, and—"

"We are?" Duncan said, the world tilting under his feet.

"You are?" Toby echoed.

"Yes, we are." Arching her brows, his love looked at him in a way that made Duncan's heart hammer. "Aren't we?"

"*Cassandra, my love.*" Tugging her into his arms, Duncan kissed her.

"It's all very well for you to say *Cassandra* in that dramatic way," his sweet hornet said, "but that isn't an answer." She thumped him on the chest. "Are we getting married, or not?"

"Of a certainty," Duncan said, kissing her again. "'Tis my heart's desire to call you mine own."

"Good," Cassandra said with a happy sigh. "Then it's settled. Laura and Blaze will stay here—"

"Laura?" Duncan said.

"Blaze's mother." Cassandra motioned to the woman. "As I was saying, they'll stay here with Verbena so Verbena won't be alone. It's the perfect solution."

Laura looked dumbfounded. "I don't know what to say."

"Say yes," Cassandra said. "Duncan has a place across the river, and we'll be staying there."

Duncan cleared his throat. "Strictly speaking, my love, *you* have a place across the river. 'Twas a gift, an you recall."

"Yes, it was." Cassandra gave him a smile that made him dizzy. "You see?" she said to Laura. "I can't possibly live in two houses at once. That settles it. You and Blaze *must* stay here."

Laura threw her arms around Cassandra and hugged her. "Thank you. You won't be sorry, I promise." She wiped her eyes and sniffed. "Oh, my goodness, I almost forgot. A woman named Nicole called this afternoon and left you a message. I wrote it down." She pulled a piece of paper from her pocket. "She said to tell you that somebody named Irene is dead." She looked up from the note. "I'm so sorry. Was Irene a friend or a relative?"

"No," said Cassandra. "I don't know anybody named—" The answer dawned and she laughed. "Si-reen. The si-reen is dead. That's wonderful news."

Laura excused herself and went back upstairs to attend to her daughter, and Toby congratulated them on their happy news and headed home.

Duncan took Cassandra in his arms. "Now, I would hear you say you love me again."

She smiled up at him, and his heart stuttered. "How about this? How about I tell you *and* show you? Would you like that?"

"Yes, milady," Duncan said. "A thousand times, yes."

And he whisked her across the river, where she did just that, and most satisfactorily. A Dalvahni warrior does not lie.

Evan slumped on his cushy leather man couch and stared, unseeing, at his expensive big-screen television. He was miserable in his own home, filled with a gnawing restlessness he could not explain, and that pissed him off.

What the hell? This house was the brass ring, the thing that had kept him going through the shit storm nightmare that had been his life with the demonic 'rents. A home of his own, his dream come true. A cozy crib, a clean, safe place to lay his head, not a vermin-ridden roach motel or a flophouse littered with drugged-out norms wallowing in their own piss and puke.

So why did he feel like he was coming out of his own skin? Why was he so *angry*?

The scented candle on the coffee table climbed up his nose. Violets. The candle smelled like frigging *violets*. He'd stood in the grocery aisle smelling candles until he'd gotten dizzy, searching for one that reminded him of *her*. Pathetic.

Lashing out, he kicked the table with his foot, knocking it over. The candle jar shattered on the floor, and glass and bits of wax went everywhere.

Cursing, he trudged into the utility room to fetch the broom and dustpan. He was sweeping up the last of the mess when the doorbell rang.

He wouldn't answer it. Whoever it was, he was in no mood for company. He would stay here, prowling his once-comfy sanctuary like a trapped animal, longing for something he couldn't have.

Red, the Kirvahni itch he could never scratch.

Shit, he'd been better off with the 'rents. Physical pain he could stand, but this . . . this feeling, like an amputee reaching for a missing limb. This was goddamn awful.

The bell chimed again, high and insistent. Someone was going to get the ass-chewing of their life.

Evan threw the broom down and stomped through the house. He

yanked the front door open, the blistering rebuke dying on his lips. Taryn stood on his porch, salvation and every good thing that ever was dressed in jeans and a flowy top, her glorious hair braided over one shoulder, and an almost shy smile on her lips.

He drank in the sight of her, storing the image of her away for the lonely future.

"What do you want?" he demanded in the surliest tone he could muster.

The shy smile faded, her familiar mask of reserve dropping into place. She held up a crockery jug. "I brought mead for the Vikings, and I . . . I thought we could talk."

"Mead for the—" He frowned. "Oh, for Christ's sake, don't you know better than to listen to Duncan? There aren't any damn Vikings."

"No?" She lowered the jug and straightened her shoulders. "Nevertheless, I still think we should talk about what happened in the woods."

"That?" Evan let his lip curl in an expression of contempt. "That was nothing. It's forgotten already."

"I see."

"Good. Now go away. I'm busy."

"You do not comprehend me. I *see* you, Evan. I see your feelings, and you are lying. What happened in the woods was *not* nothing. It has shaken you to the core, as it has me. It has changed everything."

Evan's chest was on fire. He wanted to grab her, to hold on to her and never let her go, but that would be a mistake, and he knew it.

"Okay, you got me," he said. "That kiss was fucking fantastic, but it'll never work. Oh, sure, it'll be great . . . for a while, and then we'll tear each other apart. We're too different."

A storm gathered in her gray eyes. "What are you afraid of?"

Everything, he wanted to shout. *You, god dammit. I'm terrified of you.*

"I'm not afraid of shit," he said, taking refuge in defiance. "I'm just not interested in your scrawny ginger ass. You got that?"

Taryn's face paled and she set her lips in the tight little line that drove him nuts.

Carefully, she set the jug on the bench by the door. "I see. Forgive me for disturbing you. 'Twill not happen again, on my word as a Kirvahni."

Shoulders stiff, she turned to go. It was the right thing to do, and Evan knew it. They would be a disaster together.

She would end him.

She was walking away from him. She was leaving. He should let her go. He should—

"Aw, hell," Evan said, leaping after her.

"Red, I didn't mean it. You're right. I was lying. Red? *Red.*"

He caught her at the top of the steps. Pulling her close, he buried his face in her hair. She smelled like spring violets and rain and redemption.

"Don't leave. God, Red, I—"

Words failed him, so he kissed her, pouring all his hunger and yearning and need into the kiss. Need for her. Only for Red.

A strangled sound made him look up. Old Lady Copeland was standing at her mailbox watching them, her eyes bulging.

Evan pulled Taryn into the house and closed the door.

Love Lexi George? Look for Lexi writing as Alexandra Rushe in her upcoming fantasy, *A Meddle of Wizards*, available from Kensington in January 2018.

LEXI GEORGE writes laugh-out-loud paranormal romance and fantasy. She lives in Alabama with her Balinese cat, Sabrina Lynn, and a muscular thug of a Siberian called Samson. Readers can visit her at www.LexiGeorge.com.